Secret Seekers Society

SOLOMON'S SEAL

J.L. Hickey

Black Rose Writing | Texas

ISBN: 978-1-68433-068-3
PUBLISHED BY BLACK ROSE WRITING
www.blackrosewriting.com

Printed in the United States of America
Suggested Retail Price (SRP) $20.95

The Secret Seekers Society: Solomon's Seal is printed in Palatino Linotype

Dedicated to my loving boys,
Wyatt, Cass, and Finn.
Stay mischievous forever.

Secret Seekers Society

SOLOMON'S SEAL

Preface:
Aten Island
Sixteen Years Ago

Professor Aten was surrounded by a group of well-dressed men, all of which were outfitted in fine, tailor-made suits. The group stood out like a sore thumb, as most people who visit a bright and sunny beach would dress accordingly in flip-flops and board shorts. However, these men were not on vacation to enjoy the tropical weather, or to take a dip in the ocean's cool waters. No, these men were strictly there for business.

"Beautiful, isn't it?" Aten kneeled down on the beach and ran his fingers through the fine grains of brown sand. He smiled slyly as he felt the tiny pebbles slip between his fingers. He took a deep breath of the fresh crisp air and held it in his lungs.

"A beach is a beach. You've seen one, you've seen them all. Am I right?" one of the cockier businessmen joked. The group chuckled in response. Aten, however, did not find the man's musings funny in the least.

"How sad you are; simple and small minded." Aten stood back up with the aid of his smooth black cane. He dusted the sand off his hands as he stared out at the ocean.

"Excuse me, sir?" The man was a bit off put by his comment.

"You stand on the beach on an island untouched by modern man. The amount of people who have walked these sandy beaches can be counted on two hands, and we make up half of them." Aten turned in disgust to face his men. "This is unhindered perfection; a creation solely touched by the hands of Mother Nature herself, untainted by our greedy human needs. No roads, no houses, no pollution... just pure and raw perfection. This is no beach like *any one* of you has ever had the pleasure to set foot on—you would do well to remember that."

"Okay…" the man replied, a bit confused.

"What's his deal today?" the fattest of the men whispered.

"I surround myself with such tasteless and unrefined people…" Aten shook his head in disbelief. "You would salivate over materialistic things; find beauty in a sports car, perfection in a two-thousand-dollar bottle of imported wine and a paycheck could buy you all of the above. But you feel nothing right now."

"Sir, I apologize if I offended you."

"The earth has been altering and changing for billions of years: tectonic plates shifting, oceans rising, and temperature drastically changing over millennia carving out this world we now inhabit into what we know it as today," Aten went on to explain. "Lands carved and cut up with imaginary borders so governments can own and systematically destroy, pillage and take from the Earth's natural resources… Most people will live a life never seeing any part of this ancient world that has not been altered by our dirty filthy hands."

"Now, here we stand on this very day, on this magical shore where an expansive ocean meets the perfect beach… with the privilege to see the Earth as it was intended—raw and undisturbed. Man did not create this beach, our hands did not build these rocks, nor did artists paint that perfect blue sky. Our science and our technology had nothing to do with any of it! If we never existed, this beach would still be here; if we die tomorrow, it remains. A million different worldly events took place to create this over four billion years ago and you feel nothing of its beauty."

"I mean, it is a beautiful view," the man said, trying to backpedal and maintain peace on his words.

"Bah!" Aten scoffed at the remark. "Your suits took mere months to create; people plundered the Earth for its cotton to weave, using the machines your ancestors invented to stitch them together. You all salivate over their price tag and how it makes you feel because society views your social standings on your three-thousand-dollar bespoke suit. And yet, here, amongst the beauty that can only be created by God himself, you make jokes about luxury beach resorts…."

"But sir… I don't follow. Are we not here to decide if we want to build on this land?"

"Of course," Aten couldn't help but hide his grin, "I am not saying

I want to protect this secretive island from the hand of man. I am just saying that there is more to life than sport coats and Ferraris. And because it's remote with no true governing laws, it is perfect for our cause. It is just sad that one of the last few uninhabited areas of the world must disappear."

"But sir, it's a tropical climate..." one of the suits spoke up with a concerned tone.

"Your point?" Aten said plainly as he turned back towards the beautiful ocean waves crashing gently onto the beach a few feet from where the men stood. "Barnaby, transfer the funds to the Costa Rican government tomorrow morning. I want this island prepped and ready for construction by next month. We must move forward with the next few steps as hastily as possible. I want complete control over the island with no interference from outside governments."

"Sir, I do not know if that time frame is—"

"I did not ask you for your opinion on the matter," Aten interrupted, his eyes now wild with anger. "I told you to get it done!" Aten took a deep breath to calm himself before he continued on, "Gentlemen, have I ever led any of you astray?" Aten didn't wait for the group to respond. "No, never. I promise, you all, that this island is the blueprint to our dreams."

Another man attempted to speak. "But I'm looking over some of these habitats for the creatures on our list; this climate is only suitable for maybe twenty percent—"

"Silence!" Aten turned forcefully towards the youngest of the well-dressed men. Aten felt the anger swirling inside of him and he slapped the young man squarely across his face. The force of the blow sent the man's wire-framed glasses completely off his face. He fell to the beach from the blow, his glasses broken in half and blood poured from his nose.

"I said this is the place!" Aten coolly readjusted his silk tie. "Now, come." He extended his hand to help the man back to his feet. He then brushed the sand off the man's suit, and pulled a small red handkerchief from his breast pocket. "Look at yourself, you stepped out of line and got blood all over that oh-so-important bespoke suit." He tossed his handkerchief at the man's face. "Clean yourself up. You disgust me."

"Y-yes, sir. Sorry, sir." The man winced in pain.

"I tire quickly when people doubt me. You all realize I am the face of Aten Corp? I am the man that has lined each and every one of your pockets with gold. If I had not recruited you all as my advisors, you would be nothing. You owe those suits, your luxury resort vacations, and those thousand-dollar bottles of imported wine to me, right?"

"Yes, sir, we do," another man replied, a little hesitant to speak up.

"Good, then I suggest not forgetting who the boss is." Aten responded. "As I was saying, this island is perfect in so many ways. We can replicate ecosystems with biospheres so the tropical climate will not hinder our ultimate goal. Just like my dear old friend Claudio Calenstine. You all remember him, right?"

"Yes, of course, him and his estate," Another man replied.

"Yes, and the *Belmonte* Estate," Aten corrected. "He has ecosystems created for every type of habitat you can think of. Hell, the old fool even has a frozen tundra deep underground where I hear he houses a Yeti—rumors of course." Aten couldn't help but smirk as he spoke of Calenstine. "No, this beautiful, remote island is perfect for many reasons."

"This will be very costly, sir." The accountant was punching numbers on his calculator. "The tropical storms around the area will create difficulties transporting equipment and goods. The thick jungle will be costly to build around—"

"I will own this island," Aten interrupted. "Do you simple fools understand what that means? It will be the property of Aten Corp. I will build a state-of-the-art facility and house the very best technology money can buy. In turn, I will allow our scientists freedom to research anything I can dream up, unrestricted by any government laws. No more moral restrictions or pesky ethical interferences. This island will become our sandbox, to build and destroy as we see fit. My friends, here in our little secret island, we can become gods. No man will pollute this beach, a God in the making will...."

Chapter 1
The Enlightenment 101

Hunter sat, eagerly, waiting for the first day of class to start. He counted down every second that ticked away on the wall clock. To make matters worse, as if any first day of school wasn't bad enough, today was not just any normal class. It was the first course in the Belmonte Estate's Enlightenment studies, which was something he and his little sister Elly didn't know very much about, except that they were top-secret courses to train them in the art of monster hunting.

No big deal, at least that's what Hunter kept trying to tell himself.

The classroom was not what most children would consider typical by any means, and nor should it be, considering the purpose of the Enlightenment. Gone were the elementary charts that were often displayed proudly on most classroom walls, and missing were the funny posters with kittens or puppies proclaiming that reading is indeed "fundamental." There were no maps of the world, art projects from years past... or anything of the sort. The classroom was in fact something that would probably give most children nightmares. Terrible, wicked nightmares.

There were a *few* normal things. A large oak desk sat at the front of the class for the teacher to sit at. There were a few rows of tables and chairs for students, and of course a dusty chalkboard at the head of the class. Beyond that, it seemed more like a mad scientist's laboratory than any sort of learning facility.

Hunter felt a bit at odds with his surroundings. There were numerous shelves in the back of the class containing jars filled with murky green liquid and random grotesque oddities—small reptiles, strange creatures, and random animal parts. The walls were decorated with numerous photographs and drawings of strange creatures and cruel-looking plant life. There was even a human skeleton, which Hunter hoped was a fake, sitting at the back of the classroom on a chair with a dunce cap on it. On the opposite side of the class was another skeleton; some sort of large bear-like creature with a horn coming from the middle of its skull.

This was definitely not your typical classroom experience.

Everything made Hunter feel uneasy: the first day of school, the mysteriousness of what the Enlightenment was all about, and the fact that he and his sister were still trying to get used to their new lives at the Belmonte Estate, without their loving parents.

Hunter was thirteen years old and a bit small for his age in both height and weight. What he lacked in size, he easily made up for in heart. He had proven this when he and his friends had stared down the snarling and vile creature known as the Beast of Bladenboro just a few months before, successfully capturing it and returning the Belmonte Estate to order. Hunter ran his fingers through his unkempt and messy brown hair and sighed. He peered over at his sister Elly with a worried look.

Elly ignored him. They had never been in the same class before— back in their old school they were two grades apart. They only saw each other during lunch break, where Hunter usually ignored her in favor of his older friends. Elly was only eleven, two years her brother's junior. Unlike Hunter, who was nervous about their first day of Enlightenment, she was excited, having stayed up all night reading her textbooks in anticipation of class. Elly was a beautiful young girl with dark auburn hair and a few freckles spread across her nose and cheeks.

Elly knew Hunter had a history of being bad in school. He always got in trouble for being a class clown, spending many hours in detention hall. She was determined for him not to get her in trouble in their new school.

Hunter fought back a yawn—as nervous he was, he was still exhausted. He had had a sleepless night, tossing and turning until early in the morning. When he did finally fall asleep, it wasn't long before he was startled awake from a nightmare.

He had had the same dream he suffered through every night.

He and Elly were sitting at their dinner table, eating breakfast with their parents. Everything was amazing for a while; everyone was laughing and chatting about nonsense. Somehow, in the dream, he suddenly remembered that his parents had died in a plane crash. He realized that this happiness wasn't real—it was all fake. Then his parents began to slowly fade away from him. Elly started screaming to save them, but all Hunter could do was cry. Then he was trapped in a taxicab being driven towards the estate with no way to escape. He woke up every night soaked in sweat, his pillow wet from tears.

He hated that dream.

Even now, Hunter couldn't help but think about his parents as he waited for the bell to ring. He thought of last year when he had started fifth grade. His mother had made him a special breakfast, chocolate chip and banana pancakes with thick-cut bacon and freshly squeezed orange juice. She had spent the morning talking about how wonderful his first day of class would be and about all the new friends he would meet. Even though he was nervous, his mother had always known how to put his mind at ease.

That was then though, and now Hunter and Elly had no parents. They were orphaned. No one to tell them everything was going to be okay. No special breakfast, no loving hugs or kisses.

Hunter had grown to despise the word "orphan." Whenever he heard it spoken, he felt his stomach tighten into painful knots. He had already heard it whispered around the halls of the estate in as they made their way from the rec rooms to their quarters. People pointed and stared, "Those are the Jakobs kids. Their parents just died..." or "Poor little orphans, no family... how hard it must be..." were just a few of the things they had heard.

His teacher, Professor Linda Jean Pike, stood in front of the class quietly waiting for the school bell to sound and signal the first day of the Enlightenment. Professor Pike was an older lady, nearing her sixties. She was a small-framed woman with dark grey hair pulled neatly back in a bun that was held in place with her trusty number-two pencil. Hunter couldn't tell if she looked nice or not. She looked so stern, all business and no fun. .

As Hunter sat in his stiff and uncomfortable chair, he had to fight back the welling of tears that rose up. He couldn't help but find it funny; no matter how much he tried to forget about his parents, it was always at the most inopportune times that memories flooded his head. He felt lonely and scared and wished for anything that was familiar to put him at ease. He never thought he would ever miss his old middle school, but there he was, staring back at Professor Pike, who hadn't muttered a single word since entering the classroom, wishing more than anything in the world that he and his little sister were back at their old middle school.

The one good thing about the class was that behind him sat his good friend, Alistair Jenson. Alistair was a charming young boy with short blonde hair and a devilish grin. Hunter and Elly hadn't met too many people during their short stay at the estate, but Alistair and Hunter had bonded very quickly. Alistair would joke and say it was destiny because Alistair's father, Benjamin Jenson, and Hunter's uncle, Joe, had been best friends when they were their age as well. They were a perfect fit.

Alistair raised his hand to ask a question but received an angry look in response from Professor Pike.

"No speaking until the bell chimes, child," she said bluntly.

"Seesh…" Alistair sighed in disbelief. "This is going to be a fun class," he whispered to Hunter.

"Quiet, please!" Ms. Pike slammed a wooden yardstick onto the desk, causing Alistair to almost fall out of his chair in shock.

The clock finally struck seven, and a loud bell rang throughout the classroom. Ms. Pike turned promptly to the large dusty chalkboard behind her and pointed with her yardstick towards the words:

Introduction to Enlightenment:
Course 101
Professor Pike
NO TALKING!

"Welcome to the Introduction to the Enlightenment, course number 101," Professor Pike said quickly with a proud smile. "If you have not read your welcoming packet with your parents already, let me explain how the Belmonte Institute operates. Those of you in this classroom range in age and grade levels; we do not concern ourselves with such trivial matters. All that matters is you are all a part of the sacred bloodline. You are all potential future members of the Seekers Society due to your heritage and are therefore enrolled in two separate schools: your regular scholastic courses, in which you will follow your normal grade level requirements, and the Enlightenment courses, which will educate and train you in all things regarding our society. Anything and everything taught and discussed in the Enlightenment studies cannot be discussed outside of this establishment. You were sworn to secrecy when you accepted your enrollment, and you will be expected to honor said agreement." Professor Pike walked around from behind her desk and stood before the class, her hands behind her back. She stood promptly as she spoke.

"There are two groups of people who serve the Belmonte Estate: Seekers and Commoners. People like us, who study, educate, discover, and explore the unknown, are called 'Seekers.' Those who keep the estate functional are the caretakers, the grounds men, and the cooks. We *DO NOT* speak of Seekers' affairs in front of any Commoner. We have our own building here where all Enlightenment courses will be taken, and a second school building where your scholastic courses will be taken. Keep these two aspects of your lives completely separate from one another. Is that understood?"

"Yes," the class mumbled together, a bit fearful of the serious tone.

"With that being said, welcome to the Enlightenment! You will learn many of the world's deepest and darkest secrets in the forthcoming years. You will quickly learn what *really* is *real*, and what *fiction is*. You will find out soon enough that the Enlightenment is not so much a school, but more of a training program."

Professor Pike walked to the other side of the classroom towards a large metal door. It looked more like a large safe than any door

Hunter had ever seen; it was even equipped with a combination lock as well.

"Now, let the fun begin!" Professor Pike smiled as she carefully input a combination. "Ah, there we go," Professor Pike said as she swung the heavy door open.

The children couldn't see anything, as the room was pitch-black. They heard Professor Pike mumbling for a few minutes, seemingly speaking to herself.

"This is crazy, right?" Hunter looked back at Alistair, who watched on with anticipation.

"My dad said he had Professor Pike when he was in the Enlightenment. He said she's a no-nonsense stickler, but the best teacher he'd ever had. He told me to expect something crazy on the first day!"

"Really?" Elly interjected with excitement in her voice.

"Quiet, Alistair! Don't get us in trouble," Liv added.

Liv Lee-Kay Winters was Alistair's cousin, and another new friend of Hunter and Elly. Hunter had almost forgotten Liv had sat one row over and three seats behind him. He was waiting impatiently for the class to begin when he saw Liv enter. She smiled and waved to him. Hunter could feel his cheeks blushing when he waved back. Liv was a thin and stylish girl, whose beautiful long blonde hair fell softly to her shoulders. Hunter thought she had the prettiest blue eyes he'd ever seen. She was the daughter of one of the most, well-respected Seekers in the estate—a no-nonsense muscular man named Abram Winters. Liv was only twelve, but she looked much older than her age, something she hated. She exchanged brief words with Elly and laughed before taking a seat behind her cousin Alistair.

"Okay, jeez," Alistair replied.

Professor Pike finally came out from the darkened room pushing a large flatbed cart with rickety wheels. Atop of the cart was a large metal crate with a thick white sheet laid over it, hiding its contents. The children thought they could hear breathing from beneath the cloth, and whatever it was, they could definitely smell it. It was a bitter gruesome stench that burned Elly's nose.

"Now, it is prudent we make no sudden moves or noises. Understood?" Professor Pike pushed the cart in front of the class. She walked over to the main light switch. "We must create a darkened habitat, for daylight is harmful to this creature." She flipped the switch, sending the classroom into complete darkness.

"What's going on?" Elly whispered to Alistair.

"Beats me." Alistair's eyes were glued to the sheet. He thought he saw it move a little.

"Something alive is in there," Hunter added.

"What I am about to reveal to you is our first lesson in the Enlightenment. Truth always lies somewhere in the middle. The reality of the unknown often gets misinterpreted and tangled. Believe in the unbelievable. However, you must also not believe in everything you hear. Understand?"

Hunter didn't understand. It seemed to him that Professor Pike was speaking in riddles.

"Without further ado," Mrs. Pike quickly ripped away the sheet, exposing the contents of the cage to the class.

Hunter's mouth dropped in awe, and the class let out a collective gasp at the horrific sight.

"Quiet! No loud noises!" Mrs. Pike scolded in a very serious whisper.

"We do not want to alarm her," She added with a smile.

There in the confines of the metal cage was a small creature with dark grey skin. The thing hung upside down by its clawed feet. The creature was skinny; Hunter could see its rib cage as it breathed. It was fairly small, about three feet in height. Its arms were folded high across its chest with its face hidden beneath them. It was mostly hairless, with only sporadic white ones popping out across its entire body.

"What is it?" Liv whispered, looking away from the beast with disgust.

"Looks like some humanoid bat-type creature," Alistair replied, never once taking his eyes off the creature. "Awesome...."

"Smells so bad," said the closest student to the crate as he turned away with a disgusted look.

"Well, children?" Professor Pike said, waiting for a response.

The class fell silent. Hunter looked around to see if anyone was brave enough to respond. Everyone looked pretty shocked, with the exception of Alistair, who smiled brightly.

"It's a cryptid?" Alistair spoke after raising his hand.

"Correct, Mr. Jenson, but what type of cryptid is it? There are many different cryptids out there, you know."

The class fell silent again.

"Who knows about vampyres?" Mrs. Pike questioned.

"I do!" Liv raised her hand.

"Ms. Winters, please do tell," Professor Pike said, smiling.

"Well, I read a lot of books about them. They are just like people, but they have fangs and suck blood. If you're bitten, you become one. There are a lot of different versions out there. Some burn if light touches them, and some sparkle. Some are violent killers, but my favorite ones are the romantic ones."

"All twisted truths from reality," Mrs. Pike chimed in. "We all know vampyres do not exist, right?" She shook her head in frustration. "We are led to believe they are merely fictional stories told for entertainment—fairy tales read at dusk to scare children from wandering about at night," Professor Pike mocked.

"Professor Pike?" Alistair raised his hand.

"Mr. Jenson?" she replied.

"I read about vampyres being traced back to Vlad the Impaler," Alistair answered.

"Yes, the story of Dracula," Professor Pike answered back bluntly. "Also, fiction. No truth behind it at all."

"Oh…" Alistair sank a little bit in his chair.

"This is my point," Professor Pike noted. "Believe in the unbelievable. Our society views vampyres as myths or fictional beings written about over thousands of years ago in numerous texts. Yet, here before you, I show you that they are real."

"That thing is a vampyre?" Elly frowned.

"I think I still like the romantic ones better," Liv added.

"Do not believe everything you hear." Mrs. Pike shot the kids a dirty look for talking. "You read vampyres sparkle, that they have the power of flight, or that they can turn into bats on a whim, they sleep in caskets, and that stakes through the heart are the only way to kill them." Professor Pike walked up to Liv with fiery eyes. "All false and twisted forms of the truth that could get you killed out in the field."

"Sorry..." Liv muttered quietly as she sunk back into her chair.

"Do we understand now?" Professor Pike walked back to the dusty chalkboard and began writing as she spoke. "Believe the unbelievable because vampyres are real. Do not believe all you hear and read because most of what comes from outside these walls is rubbish."

"Does it just hang upside down all day?" a freckle-faced kid in the third row asked.

"Excuse me?" Professor Pike shot another dirty look toward the kid. She quickly opened a drawer from her desk and pulled out a flashlight.

"The next lesson is an important one. Understanding how fiction sometimes stems from truth. If you dig deep enough into the popular myths, you may find some roots of truth. For instance, vampyres *do* suck blood. They *do* hunt in the night." Professor Pike suddenly flashed the light into the face of the slumbering vampyre. It shrieked violently, and the creature's mad eyes glowed bright green in the reflection of the light. It fell to its feet and violently jumped to the other side of the cage, trying to escape. It snarled, exposing its sharp teeth and fully exposing two large fangs for the class to gasp at. The creature had a sharp jaw line with two pointy ears atop its head.

"They also hate the light," Professor Pike went on. "Now, as you see through this demonstration, they do not burn or sparkle. However, they are nocturnal creatures, and lights of any kind burn their eyes. As you can tell, they hate it."

"It's freaking out!" another kid yelled, a bit frightened.

"Of course, it is," Professor Pike answered. "I just told you they hate the light."

"Did you see its fangs?" Hunter whispered to Alistair.

17

"Very cool, huh?" he answered back.

"I am sorry, Natalia, my dear." Mrs. Pike switched the light out. She then quickly walked over to the back of the classroom where a large glass cage held a dozen or so rats. She grabbed one of the larger, fatter rodents and made her way back. It squealed trying to escape her grip.

"Natalia?" Elly asked.

"Yes, this vampyre's name is Natalia. I have had her in my possession for over a decade."

"She's your pet?" The freckle-faced kid's eyes widened in disbelief.

"Not a pet, a companion." Professor Pike held the rat by its tail and dangled it between the bars of the cage. The creature blinked its eyes slowly, attempting to adjust its eyesight. Once it saw the rodent, it snatched it quickly from her hands. It fiercely bit into the rodent's neck and began sucking its blood. The rodent squealed in pain until the silence of death overtook it.

"Gross!" Liv muttered once again. She clearly wasn't enjoying their first lesson.

"It is not gross. It's the natural order of life," Professor Pike added as she began writing down a list of information about vampyres for the class to copy "Vampyres are not humans, but they do, however, share some similar characteristics. They average about three feet tall when standing upright. Yet, they rarely walk that way. Instead, they spend most of their time climbing, jumping from tree to tree, and crawling. When you see them in the wild, they are much like chimpanzees—fast and ferocious and extremely agile. They nest in dark wet places and sleep upside down, much like bats. This is probably where the concept of vamypres that can shape-shift into bats comes from." Professor Pike stopped suddenly. "Heavens, I almost forgot! Clyde, do me a favor?"

"Yes, ma'am?" the freckled faced boy replied.

"Toss that blanket back over Natalia for me before I turn the lights back on. No worries now, as she is occupied with lunch, and she won't even notice you."

"Um… okay" Clyde slowly and carefully draped the blanket over the cage. Natalia snarled once, causing Clyde to jump back in fear.

"I forgot to pass out one of the most important items a Seeker must have!" Professor Pike pulled out a large dusty crate from underneath her desk. "I always get so excited to show off Natalia that it completely slips my mind." She blew on the box, sending a thick cloud of dust towards the front row of children. "Oh, sorry! I took the box out of storage last night and didn't have time to properly clean it. Ten years in storage will collect a decent amount of dust."

Professor Pike opened up the large wooden crate and pulled forth a collection of thick leather-bound books. She went from row to row passing them out. When Hunter finally received his, the first thing he noticed was the emblem on the front of the book. He had seen it before, and he knew immediately that it was the emblem of the Secret Seekers Society. It was a large oval with a two-headed snake shaped like a large "S" in the middle of it. The emblem was then divided into four sections. There was a mighty sword stuck in a stone, a large creature Hunter knew as Bigfoot, a ring with a six-pointed star, and finally, a water creature that resembled the Loch Ness monster.

"These are your Seeker Journals. All great Seekers have one. It is where you will keep your notes both in the field and out. Keep it close always and never lose it! This book has saved many of the Seekers' lives—that much I promise you. Start your entries today, and at the end of the semester, fifty percent of your grade will be based on your journal, so start writing!"

"I hate taking notes," Hunter muttered under his breath.

"Cheer up! They're vampyre notes!" Alistair smiled.

"Vampyre's," Professor Pike went back to jotting down notes on the chalkboard, "have vile bites. Please note, children, and write this down. Unlike popular belief, a bite does not turn one into vampyre. However, it does have a very good chance of spreading a life-threatening disease known as porphyria. Prophyria is a disease modern scientists have wrongly 'disproved' as being connected with ancient vampyres. How very wrong they are because it's real and it's deadly."

Hunter scrambled to keep up with Professor Pike's notes. She was rattling off so much information on vampyres that his hand was quickly cramping up. Hunter would never have thought in his wildest dreams that on his first day of Enlightenment he would come face to face with a real vampyre.

The class was exciting, and before Hunter knew it, the bell signaled the end of the class.

"Children, it looks like I lost track of time! Make sure to read chapter one in your Introduction to Cryptids book before class this Wednesday!"

"Homework, already?" Hunter frowned. "It's the first day of class."

"I've already read the first chapter; it's all about different types of creatures," Elly stated with a smile as she packed up her notes.

"Can I borrow your notes?" Alistair swung his backpack across his shoulder.

"I guess so, but couldn't you keep up?" Elly asked.

"I just want to compare. She talked so much about vampyres that I don't want to miss anything."

"That's true, maybe we can all compare together," Liv added.

"We have time before our traditional studies start. Want to do that now?" Elly suggested.

"No, we're supposed to meet with Margot after class, remember?" Hunter answered, annoyed that his sister had forgotten.

"Oh yeah…"

"What for?" Liv asked as the group made their way out of the building.

"We're going to meet up with our uncle in the infirmary to tell him about our first day," Elly answered as they made their way out of the room.

"So," a tall boy who had sat in the back of the class interrupted, "these are the famous Jakobs kids, aye?" His name Corbin Alvin Krueger, and he was son of Gerald Krueger. Tall and muscular for his age, Corbin stood about two feet taller than Hunter. He had bright orange curly hair and a thin scraggly mustache that was probably long overdue for its first shave. At fifteen, he was two years older than

Hunter, and stood out from the rest of the class due to his age.

"Can you believe this, sis?" Corbin said, turning to his sister.

"Hunter and Eliza. You two made quite a scene during the Orientation. Ruined it for the lot of us," Lunette Krueger added. Lunette was Corbin's twin sister, despite the fact that the two didn't seem to look all that much alike. She had dark brown curly hair and was a little bit on the hefty side. She snorted as she laughed at Hunter and Elly.

"What are you guys talking about? They didn't do anything," Liv interrupted.

"You're right, but their stupid uncle did. Almost got himself killed, too," Corbin added with a grin.

"That's a terrible thing to say!" Alistair grew red in the face with anger. "He saved a lot of people when that beast attacked the auditorium."

"Who are you guys anyway?" Elly shot back.

"Our dad is Gerald Krueger—the best Seeker in the world. He's not a traitor like your parents," Lunette spit.

"Traitor?" Hunter frowned. "You better take that back!"

"Shut up! You two don't know what you're talking about," Liv shouted as she wedged herself between Hunter and Corbin.

"Don't act like you haven't heard the rumors," Corbin added.

"We should beat the snot out of you two for what your parents did." Lunette cracked her knuckles and grinned.

"Children!" Margot's voice broke the tension. "What's going on here?"

"We'll talk later," snarled Corbin, who quickly retreated in the opposite direction from Margot.

"This conversation is far from over," Lunette added, following behind her brother.

Margot was a beautiful young woman in her mid-twenties. The children especially enjoyed her company due to her vibrant energy and youthful charm. Margot was more than just a friend to the children. In fact, after Hunter and Elly's Uncle Joe had gotten injured during the Beast of Bladenboro's attack, she swore to help Joe watch over the children and act as a second guardian.

Alongside her, on a long chain-link leash, was a beast of a dog named Trayer, who looked more like a giant dark-green bear than a pet. Trayer had been given to the children during their first few days at Belmonte Estate in hopes his companionship would help the children integrate into their new home.

When the kids had received Trayer as a puppy, he had easily stood three feet high, and his head sat at eye level with Elly's. Three months later, Trayer had grown exponentially. He wasn't quite done growing yet, but he was close. When he reached maturity, Trayer would be roughly the size of a full-grown steer.

Trayer was a Cusith, a mysterious breed that originated in Scotland. Margot taught the children that Cusiths were thought to be demonic creatures. Village reports described them as a dog-like version of the grim reaper that would drag souls into the afterlife. In reality, their size and strange-colored hair simply looked frightening when combined with them being extremely rare in the wild, causing many false myths about them to be formed. In truth, there had never been a more loving and loyal dog than Trayer.

Trayer's excitement upon seeing the children was too much for Margot to handle, and she lost her grip on the leash. Trayer ran full speed at the children with his tail wagging uncontrollably, sprinting so hard the earth beneath his paws flew out behind him in great big clumps.

"Big boy!" Hunter outstretched his arms with excitement, and Trayer jumped playfully into them. The two fell onto the grass with the mighty dog licking Hunter's face.

"Gross!" Hunter laughed.

"Trayer, down!" Margot snapped her fingers.

Trayer whined for a second before sitting down.

"Children, that conversation didn't look very nice," Margot said while handing the leash over to Elly.

"Just some jerks," Alistair answered.

"They said our parents were traitors," said Elly.

"Forget about it," Hunter added.

"No, I will not forget about it! They said what?" Margot's face turned red with anger.

"It's nothing." Hunter picked up his backpack, which Trayer had knocked out of his hands.

"Were those the Krueger children?" Margot asked, a bit more demanding in tone.

"The one and only," Alistair told her. "I hear their dad's the best Seeker in the world too."

"Pay them no mind." Margot dusted the dirt and dry leaves off Hunter's back. "I'm sorry you had to hear such ridiculous nonsense. Let's not bring this up to your uncle. I don't want him getting upset while he's in recovery."

Chapter 2
A Broken Man

Joe had lost track of how many days it had been since the attack. He sat all day and all night in the stark white hospital room. Most of his time was spent staring out his one small bedside window, lost in his own thoughts. He didn't realize it had been three entire months since the Beast of Bladenboro had attacked him during the Orientation. He hadn't walked since that fateful night.

A young, attractive doctor knocked on his door and poked her head in. "Joe, how are we feeling today?"

"Same as always," Joe answered plainly, staring off at nothing through the window.

"I see you didn't take your pills. Is there a reason?" The doctor jotted down some notes on her chart.

The doctor's name was Julie Wong, and many considered her to be a surgical prodigy. She had gotten a reputation as a miracle worker after numerous successful operations that most doctors in her field deemed impossible. Bright and determined, she had dedicated her life to putting people back together—physically and emotionally.

Dr. Wong was a thin woman with a bright smile. She almost always had heavy bags under her eyes due to the demands of her job. Her work didn't leave much time for sleep; she was always on call and loved every minute of it. She was the surgeon who had saved Joe's life when his mangled body had been rushed to the hospital after the disastrous Orientation. The nursing staff told Joe, almost on a daily basis, that he shouldn't be alive today. It was a miracle; thank God for Dr. Wong.

Joe couldn't help but laugh whenever he heard that. It was ironic to him, as he didn't feel very much alive, and he definitely didn't look like a miracle.

"I'm not depressed, so they're not needed," Joe answered.

"I see..." Dr. Wong pulled up a chair next to his bed. "Your niece and nephew are on their way up," she added.

"It's their first day of Enlightenment," he answered back.

"Those kids love you, and you're all they've got. They don't want to see their uncle a broken man. They want to see you smile and laugh. You can't fake it forever."

"Doc," Joe finally turned to look at Dr. Wong face to face, "I *am* a broken man. I can't walk."

"The only thing broken in *you*, Joe," Dr. Wong said forcefully, "is your *will*."

"It's been months..."

"So, you just quit?"

Joe didn't answer. What could he say? He had already quit and knew it deep in his heart.

"All right then, either you start taking these pills," Dr. Wong handed Joe three small oval pills and a glass of water, "or I will start crushing them up in your apple sauce."

"Okay, I get it," Joe swallowed down the pills.

"You may have given up on yourself, but we have not!" Dr. Wong smiled.

Joe didn't respond.

"How's the physical therapy going with Margot?"

"Painful and discouraging," he said.

"It's a big mountain we're going to climb. The first step is in believing there is an end to this, and that we're going to get there in time."

"Right," said Joe simply.

"Uncle Joe?" Hunter poked his head into the room.

"Hunter!" Joe forced a smile. He was, in truth, happy to see his niece and nephew, but it was hard to show it.

"Is this a bad time?" Margot asked as she entered with the kids.

Elly didn't say anything instead she ran to her uncle's bed and gave him a hug.

"Uncle Joe," Elly frowned as she poked her uncle's foot, "can you feel it yet?"

"No honey, I'm sorry," he answered.

"Please come in," Dr. Wong answered Margot. "He could use some company to lift his spirits."

"Children, keep your uncle company while I walk the doctor out," Margot smiled.

Out in the hallway, Dr. Wong gestured with her hand.

Margot closed the door behind her. "Is everything okay?" she asked.

"No improvement yet," Dr. Wong answered.

"I see."

"I need to speak to you about his physical therapy," Dr. Wong said with a sigh.

"It's hard because he doesn't try much anymore. I spend more time trying to motivate him than actually doing the exercises."

"He's lost his spirit. He spends all day and night staring out the window. Hardly eats and won't take his meds."

"What can we do?" Margot frowned.

"I know we hoped he'd regain feeling, but we could always operate," Dr. Wong suggested.

"It's too risky... You said it yourself. Plus, the last time I mentioned it to Joe, he flipped out. I don't think it's an option."

"It may be our only option," Dr. Wong added.

"Thank you, Doctor. We'll think about it." Margot smiled and turned back into Joe's room.

"Margot, can we order some lunch to eat with Uncle Joe?" Elly asked.

"Are you hungry, Joe?" Margot forced a smile.

"I suppose I could eat a little," Joe agreed.

"Well, why don't you play host to the kids while I run down to the cafeteria and bring up some food?" Margot replied.

"Easily done," Joe high-fived Hunter. "Bring extra dessert!" he said, forcing another smile.

Margot nodded and made her way out of the room.

"You guys all right? You seem bothered. How was your first day of Enlightenment?"

"We got to see a vampyre," Elly answered.

"Professor Pike is still showing off Natalia?" Joe laughed.

"It's gross-looking," said Hunter.

"One time, Ben and I were out in the field and we set out to North Carolina to hunt down a suspected nest of vampyres. Turned out there were some Romanians smuggling oddities to some traveling carnival. Anyway, the little bastards got out and nested in some old barn. We captured three of them. They're scary, nasty little things."

"You actually hunted them in the wild!" Hunter eyes grew wide.

"The smugglers didn't even know what they had. Idiots were selling them as Chupacabras," Joe explained.

"We weren't supposed to say anything..." Elly added with a bit more of seriousness. She couldn't forget the words Corbin and his sister had said.

"About what?"

"These dumb kids," Hunter interrupted. "Don't worry, it was nothing."

"They called Mom and Dad traitors!" argued Elly.

"Eliza, shut up! Margot said not to say anything!"

"Who called your parents traitors?" Joe's lips tightened in anger.

"Some jerk named Corbin and his sister Lunette," Elly answered.

"Corbin..." Joe thought for a second. "That's Gerald's kid."

"Do you know their dad?" Elly asked.

"Gerald's something else... you could say I know him. Your mother, Ben, and I went through the Enlightenment with him. I see the apple doesn't fall too far from the tree. He always was a jerk to your mother and I, even back when we were kids."

"What did they mean though?" Elly asked.

"I honestly don't know. I left the Seekers, remember? Not sure what's been going on in these walls the last ten years. I promise you though, your parents were no traitors."

"Elly," Hunter said angrily, "I told you Mom and Dad were not traitors."

"I know, it's just…"

"It's nothing, Elly." Uncle Joe stretched out his arm to his young niece, who now had swollen eyes filled with tears. "You'll learn as you get older that people will say terrible things for reasons you may never understand. It will hurt, it may confuse you, but you just need to remember how it feels so you won't ever do the same to anyone else, understand?"

Elly nodded with a small smile.

"Look," Joe pointed to Margot, who had brought up a few helping hands that carried a wide variety of food.

"I wasn't sure what everyone wanted, so my friends here helped me bring up a little bit of everything. Leftovers from yesterday." Margot set a giant tray down on the table next to Joe's bed that was filled with an assortment of fruits and vegetables, pasta salad, broiled potatoes, and lunchmeats.

"After your afternoon classes, Ms. Ellingbee would like to meet you both to discuss the rest of your Enlightenment courses," she added.

"I forgot we had regular classes after lunch." Hunter frowned.

"I have English next hour; I'm excited!" Elly added in between mouthfuls of fresh strawberries.

"I got math." Hunter frowned again.

With that being said and lunch winding down, the children swept up their backpacks and made their way out of the infirmary, back to the other school building. Unlike their Enlightenment classes that were held in the Francis Drake Building, on the east side of the estate, the scholastic classes were held in the Friedrich Building of Higher Intelligence on the opposite side.

Chapter 3
An Old Mystery

Hunter and Elly waited to meet up with their friends, Alistair and Liv, after their scholastic courses finished up. The group decided that every day after school they would meet in the estate's botanical garden, which sat at the rear of the plaza. Filled with exotic, rare plants and beautiful flowers, the botanical garden was by far one of the most elegant areas of the estate. It sat directly behind the mansion and was hard to miss due to its sheer size and color.

Elly thought it was the prettiest place in the entire estate. The children were used to seeing strange paintings and weird macabre assortments of mounted animal heads inside the mansion. The mansion had been creepy to them at first, but they had both grown accustomed to seeing such oddities fairly quickly. The garden, however, was the polar opposite of the mansion's inner décor. It was enormous and showcased a brilliant array of colors with a wide assortment of some of the most exotic flora in existence. Elly had a soft spot in her heart for gardens. Sitting outside waiting for their friends, she could smell the wonderful sweet scent of some of the flowers. The flowery aroma flooded her with memories of her and her mother sitting out in their backyard tending to their garden. Like most things about the children's past, these good memories always brought with them a sense of dull pain as well.

Earlier that day, Elly had found herself half-listening to her Social Studies teacher explain the class syllabus, while she peered out the window where she counted six different attendants hard at work on the garden. This was a daily routine during the spring and fall seasons. The Belmonte Estate's founder, Professor Claudio Calenstine, only hired the very best people to tend the garden. Elly was normally very attentive in class, but she found herself more interested in the group of people constructing a large dome over the garden. She couldn't tell until now, as they waited outside the large plaza for their friends, that the dome was made of a very thick, clear plastic and completely covered the garden.

"Hey, guys, waiting for us before going in?" Liv smiled brightly as her and Alistair finally caught up.

"What's this dome thing?" asked Elly, looking at it, still in awe of its enormity.

"Can we go in?" Hunter asked.

"Of course, we can! It's pretty cool actually. Elly, they do this every year." Liv led the group through a small opening in the thick and surprisingly heavy plastic cover. "My dad took me here on my eighth birthday. That's before I even knew what the estate was, and he always told me he worked at a museum for the fanciest and prettiest flowers in the world. Come to think of it now..." Liv paused with a look of bewilderment on her face, "I always wondered when I was little why we never went inside the estate."

"It's weird finding out our parents kept this secret from us for so long, huh?" Alistair added. "My dad never took me here as a kid, but when he'd leave me at my moms for weeks at a time, I never really knew why. My mom just told me he traveled for a living."

Liv continued to lead the group towards the first collection of exotic flora, where she stopped in front of a collection of beautiful bright yellow blooms.

"These are what I was smelling while we were waiting outside the garden." Elly kneeled down and deeply inhaled the wonderfully extravagant smell.

"These are called 'Raskovnik' and were always my favorite too. These are the only ones left in the entire world," Liv explained, pointing towards a wooden sign sticking out from the earth next to the exhibit.

"They smell so beautiful," Elly added.

"It's just a flower, and all flowers smell good." Hunter wasn't nearly as impressed.

"Well, these are said to be magical and not *every* flower smells good," said Liv, a bit displeased with Hunter's lack of interest.

"Magical flowers?" Alistair snickered at the thought.

"Yes, *magical!*" Liv gave her cousin a dirty look. "They are said to be able to open any lock in the world."

"A flower that opens a lock?" Hunter shook his head in doubt.

"Sounds like rubbish to me," Alistair added, giving Hunter a look of disbelief.

"Well, that's what the legends says." Liv sounded defeated.

"Don't listen to those dumb boys." Elly stood up from the Raskovnik flowers with a bright smile on her face. "I believe you. Look... their leaves are even shaped like tiny keys."

"Thank you anyway, Elly," Liv went on to explain, "My dad explained to me how they keep the garden alive year-round. They construct this giant bio dome, and see here," she pointed to a series of metal wires running through the dome's plastic material, "I always thought those were just a foundation to keep the dome up, but my dad says they're actually heaters to monitor the temperature. They have sprinklers all over the grounds, too. He said they construct this plastic dome during certain times of the year, and it can simulate any type of season or weather needed to keep the plants alive."

"All this for flowers?" Alistair shrugged. "I don't see the point."

"Yeah, they're just plants," Hunter added.

"Shut up, Hunter! It's beautiful," Elly snapped back, growing tired of the boy's snarky remarks.

"These aren't just flowers," Liv frowned at Hunter. "I told you that we have some of the rarest plants in the world in here. My dad says Professor Calenstine spends a lot of money keeping the habitat just right."

"Look at this one!" Hunter darted ahead of the group towards an enormous plant that was roughly his size in height but double his width. The plant had multiple large green leaves sprouting from its base with prickly thorns protruding from them. The plant itself was shaped like a large bulb that was dark green at its base and slowly turned to a dark blood-red towards the top of the bulb.

"Hey, guys, you gotta see this!" Hunter turned his back to the monstrous-looking plant in order to wave his friends over.

"Hunter!" Elly screamed.

"Look out, kid!" One of the garden attendants jumped forward and knocked Hunter down on the ground.

"Jeez!" Hunter gasped as he hit the ground hard with the man on top of him. "Why did you do that?"

"Can't you bloody read?" The man wore an all-white jumpsuit that covered his entire body, including his head and a thin light blue hospital mask across his mouth and nose. He stood up and dusted off his suit before pointing to a sign next to the plant.

DANGER!
Carnivorous Plant
Stay Away!

"Hunter, that thing took a bite at you!" Alistair's mouth dropped in amazement. "He saved your life!"

Hunter peered back at the once-calm plant to see it now fully blossomed, exposing multiple rows of sharp thorn-like teeth. It repeatedly snapped at him.

"Violent things," the man said. He pulled the mask from around his head and pulled down the white body suit. He was an older man with dark grey hair and a full, well-trimmed beard.

"It tried to kill me?" Hunter couldn't stop his voice from trembling.

"Well, it wouldn't have killed you. I don't think it could have eaten such a large meal. They usually snack on squirrels, birds, chipmunks... it'll bite anything though. Maybe take a chunk out of that leg of yours," the man replied half-jokingly.

"Are you okay?" Liv ran over to Hunter, her face flushed from the commotion.

"Yeah, I guess." Hunter's heart still pounded wildly. "Thank you! I didn't know plants could attack."

"Well, you gotta be careful in this garden." The man frowned at his now stained jumpsuit. "Great, this is never going to wash out. Look," he went on with a bit more of a serious tone to his voice, "I know it's pretty in here with all the flowers, but it's also pretty dangerous."

"I come here all the time and never noticed that one before." Liv started jotting down notes in her Seekers Journal Professor Pike had given them earlier.

"Well, we just planted it a week ago. Brought it up from the Demeter Station," the man added.

"The *what* station?" Alistair asked.

"Demeter," the man said slowly. He walked Hunter over to a small bench near a display of tulips and roses. "Have a seat, relax, and catch your breath. They haven't told you about the Demeter Station yet?"

"We've only had one class so far," Liv added.

"Oh, I see! I suppose I should have known that. It's the eastern observatory, which is a truly massive version of this botanical garden. If you think there are rare plants up here, you'd be amazed with what we've got over there. Literally, the most rare and dangerous plants you never knew existed."

"Wow! Cool!" Alistair smiled. "Let's meet up over there every day instead."

"Well, that would be hard to do." The man took a seat next to Hunter. "The majority of that place is deep underground and is locked down with super-tight security checks."

"It's bigger than this place?" Hunter asked. "because this place is bigger than the football field at my old school! It's huge."

"Well, it's about a hundred times this size with multiple levels. Each level recreates a specific climate zone. Professor Calenstine definitely fancies his plants. You know, there are a lot of medicinal purpose plants in his collection." The man lifted up Hunter's T-shirt sleeve to expose a small wound. "You're hurt! Let me get my medical aid bag and clean you up. By the way, my name is Luther Burbank, and I've been working here for the last twenty years."

"Must have hit my elbow on a rock or something." Hunter watched as the kind man cleaned his cut with a cotton ball and applied antibacterial spray. Hunter tried not to show the pain on his face as the man sprayed his wound with the stinging liquid.

"There you go; good as new." Mr. Burbank firmly placed a bandage around the wound. "Sorry, I didn't mean to push you down so forcefully."

"Better that than losing an arm to that thing," Hunter laughed.

"What's that?" Alistair pointed towards a large stone statue in the middle of the garden.

"Oh, that's Monte," Luther answered as he walked the kids towards it.

"Monte, Professor Calenstine's dog?" Hunter remembered meeting the small lap dog when he spoke with the professor in his office for the first time.

"Correct," Luther smiled. "The great professor named the estate after his best friend; Monte is short for Belmonte. I always thought it was funny his best friend was a dog," Luther noted with a faint smile on his face.

The statue was over twenty feet high and made from beautiful, aged marble. It was of Monte sitting and staring skyward as if he was looking into the heavens. The version of Monte depicted in the statue was much younger than the frail and scruffy dog Hunter remembered sitting eagerly on the old man's lap. The statue was definitely old; years of weather had chipped away at it.

"How old is this statue, it looks way too old to have been made in honor of Monte. Dog's don't live that long," Alistair noted.

"True," Luther laughed. "Monte is by far the oldest dog alive in the world today, and his master is the oldest man."

"So, wait a minute," Elly edged her way into the conversation, "no one has ever given us a real answer, but how old is the professor?"

"Yeah, we've seen him in some really old photos," Hunter added. "Remember, Elly, when we saw that old photo with him in that book about the Beast of Bladenboro? It was like sixty years old, and he was still an old man back then."

"I dare say that I hope I haven't said too much. That question is not for me to answer," Luther added. "Even if I were to try, it would be a guess. I think only the professor himself knows that answer."

"C'mon, just tell us," Elly pleaded.

"Well, I *can* tell you some public information. That way you can deduct your own opinions on his age," Luther answered slyly.

"What do you mean?" Liv answered back, a bit confused over what sort of general information he was getting at.

"Well you're all members of the Belmonte Estate now, and its historical records are intact at the library. Do some research, as that's what this estate is founded on anyway—all sorts of research. Everyone knows Calenstine opened the estate, right? Find out the background of the mansion, and you will have some sort of idea."

"Why didn't we think of that?" Elly frowned.

"I'm sure you were all too busy trying to keep the estate safe from that monster that escaped," Luther winked.

"Oh, you knew about that?" Hunter asked a bit embarrassed.

"Of course, I live here. Pretty brave of you kids. We all know what you did, and we are thankful." Luther looked at his wristwatch. "Well, look at the time; I need to wrap it up for the day. You kids mind these signs we have posted, there are some nasty poisonous plants in here that will give you a wicked rash."

"He's right, it's getting late, and we need to meet with Ms. Ellingbee in the library about the rest of our Enlightenment courses," Elly said.

"Thanks again." Hunter waved to their new friend as they walked off in a rush.

"Maybe we can dig up some info on the estate too," Alistair noted.

The kids gathered up their things and made their way back into Belmonte Manor, heading through the main foyer, where all the mounted heads of the mysterious creatures were proudly on display. From there, they entered the main elevator and went down to SB-1, where the grandiose library was housed.

"You're late, children," Patricia scolded. The elevator door chimed and the children stepped out in a rush. Patricia Ellingbee sat alone at one of the large library tables with four folders laid out in front of her. Each of which had one of the children's names highlighted on them. Ms. Ellingbee held a prestigious position at the Belmonte Estate. She was Professor Calenstine's personal caregiver as well as being in charge of running everything operational in the mansion, everything from running the scholastic programs to the daily upkeep for the entire estate, leading hundreds of people from maintenance to Seekers. Her job was never ending. Patricia Ellingbee was in her late fifties with short red hair and a round face. She was stern when needed but a loving person who wanted only the best for the children.

"Sorry, Ms. Ellingbee, but Hunter almost got eaten by a plant in the gardens," Alistair took a seat at the table next to Patricia as he explained the incident.

"W-what? Hunter, is that true?" Patricia's jaw dropped in disbelief.

"Er… well sorta…" Hunter was caught a bit off guard, elbowing Alistair to get him to shut up. "You weren't supposed to say anything," he whispered to him.

"Sorry!" Alistair whispered back.

"You children need to respect the estate, inside and outside of the mansion. There are too many things you don't know about, dangerous things." She shook her head. "You lot are going to be the death of me if you don't start behaving."

"We're sorry, Ms. Ellingbee, but it was my idea," Liv added. "Elly and I love the flowers. It's so pretty in the botanical gardens."

"I understand that," Patricia passed out the folders to each of the children, "just *be* careful."

"We promise." Elly thumbed through her folder, excited to see all her future courses lined up for her to read about.

"Before I begin and explain the rest of your first-year courses, how was the Intro to Enlightenment?"

"It was all right," Hunter replied.

"Just all right?" Patricia was shocked at the lack of enthusiasm.

"It was awesome! We got to see real a vampyre!" Elly added.

"Yes, Professor Pike and her Natalia." Ms. Ellingbee frowned. "I fought tooth and nail with the professor about not letting her keep that disgusting, disease-ridden beast as a pet, but he insisted it was okay. It smells wickedly awful."

"Sure is a lot of paperwork here," said Liv.

"Yes, well, let me explain to you all how the extracurricular activities outside of your regular scholastic courses work. As you know, a very select group of students in the estate qualify for the Enlightenment." Patricia took a long sip from her hot tea. "This is based solely on your bloodline. The Seekers are a very small, select group who get trained in a vast field of studies. Your regular studies are from noon to six p.m., Monday through Friday. Your Enlightenment courses are nine in the morning to eleven Monday through Saturday. There are six courses you will take a year. It takes six years to graduate before you can take your trials to become an actual member of the Secret Seekers Society. Are we following so far?"

"Yes," the group said, nodding.

"There are six programs. Your first year, they all start out as introductory courses. Upon passing the intro classes, each year you will move forward into higher-level courses. The six classes are as follows. Enlightenment General Studies is with Professor Pike every Monday, where you will be learning about our history and what it means to be a Seeker, including, but not limited to, our philosophies and creed. Tuesdays you'll be attending Survival Fitness courses with Jonathon Gates—"

"Jonathon Gates!" Alistair eyes widened with delight. "*The* Jonathon Gates? From the television show *Myth Hunters*?"

"Yes, dear," Patricia sighed. "Mr. Gates has a television show on that Fantasy Channel. To this day, I have no idea how he talked the professor into letting him have a television show. Cable television is not quite secretive, is it?"

"I can't believe Jonathon Gates is going to be our teacher!" Alistair was shaking with happiness.

"Who is this guy?" Elly asked, clearly unimpressed.

"Jonathan Gates is the coolest guy on television. I'm pretty sure

I've told you about him," Alistair went on, speaking incredibly fast. "He has a team of scientists and cryptozoologists, and they go off into the wilderness for weeks, all over the world, searching for monsters. He's done episodes on Bigfoot, Yetis, Skunk Apes, Mongolian wyrm monsters, mermaids... all sorts of cryptids. He became world famous when he found an almost perfect Bigfoot print in the Alps three years ago. One time, they went to this island and..."

"Yes, he is quite famous in the field. A bit too famous for my liking," Patricia added. "Now, let's get back to the business at hand. There is much to discuss still." She continued, "Wednesdays you're with Morty Latimer for Botany classes. Quite a handsome fellow he is." She hid a faint smile.

"What? Mr. Burbank doesn't teach it?" asked Hunter.

"Luther? Oh, heavens no. He's just a botanist who helps maintain the gardens. I mean he did graduate from Yale, but no, Professor Latimer is the most brilliant botanist alive today. Moving forward, Thursday you're with Dr. James Lannin for Legendary Creatures, and Friday is Ancient Relics and Scrolls with Camille Badgero, our newest professor. Finally, Saturdays you will be with Thomas Hobbes learning about Spirits and Demonology, and personally my favorite subject. I am a bit of a medium after all."

"Spirits," Hunter asked. "Like ghosts?"

"Exactly that, my boy," she added.

"What's a medium?" asked Liv.

"Well, you will learn that in your classes." Patricia smiled.

"Seems like a lot of work..." said Hunter. "School is hard enough, but now we have double the classes."

"No one ever said learning to become a Seeker was easy. When you graduate the six-year program and complete your trial, you'll be asked to go around the world, exploring some of the most remote areas on the planet, investigating some very scary places. You may have to live off the land and look for creatures that may be *very* dangerous. You all remember the Beast of Bladenboro?"

The children nodded.

"Well, I asked to meet you kids here in the library because I am sure you all have homework. We have one of the grandest libraries in the world, so I figured I could leave you here to your studies. Now, don't stay up too late because you all have Enlightenment courses tomorrow." Patricia smiled and couldn't help but feel a sense of pride as she readied the children for the next chapter in their lives.

"I shall see you children soon." She nodded before walking off and entering the elevator.

"Wow, Jonathan Gates!" Alistair said again.

"Don't ask for his autograph the first day of school. That's embarrassing!" Liv laughed.

"Says you!" Alistair replied. "I'm gonna see if he'll sign my backpack! No, better yet, I'll bring a canteen, as that would be really cool!"

"Stupid homework! Fifty math problems on the first day." Hunter frowned as he opened up his large math book.

"Forget homework," Alistair said. "We should look into the estate like Luther said."

"Yeah, good idea!" Hunter slapped his book shut with a thud. "Math can wait."

"I dunno, guys," Elly said. "We need to make sure our grades stay up."

"I agree," said Liv. "We have time later for looking into all that stuff."

"Well, while you two actually do homework, Alistair and I will go look around the library a bit."

Hunter and Alistair stood up from the desk and made their way towards the back of the library, leaving the two girls alone with their studies.

"Dumb boys," Elly said as she flipped through her notebook.

"It's okay, I'm sure they will catch up before class tomorrow," Liv replied, flipping through her Social Economics book. "To be honest, I'm really interested in what they find out. So, let them do all the dirty work while we keep our grades up," she stated with a laugh.

"So, how's your uncle doing?"

"Uncle Joe...." Elly thought for a second about how to answer the question. "He seems okay, but I think when we leave, he's really sad."

"He's not getting better, is he?"

"No... still can't feel his legs. Dr. Wong said he should feel lucky, and she was surprised he had movement below his shoulders."

"That's so sad." Liv tried to hide her frown.

"I don't understand how that creature ever escaped. We're always told how the mansion is state of the art," said Elly.

"Yeah, doesn't seem like that thing could have just snuck out of its cage."

"Someone had to have let it out, but why?" Elly put her book down, finding it harder than ever to study.

"Who on Earth would want that thing running around here putting so many people at risk?" Liv asked.

"It hurt a bunch of people. Not just my uncle, but Sebastian too..."

"And that agent, Mr. Roberts..." Liv added. "They never found him... just his stuff."

"We need to look into this more and figure out who would've wanted it out. I don't think anyone else is looking into it."

"It seems like they may be afraid to find out the answer. Has to be someone inside the estate, right?" questioned Liv.

The girls spent the next hour attempting to focus on their homework but found their minds wandering off. They couldn't seem to shake the topic of who let out the Beast of Bladenboro from its state-of-the-art cage. It was a scary thought that someone in the estate may have a hidden agenda, and it didn't sit well with either of them.

After about an hour, Hunter and Alistair reappeared alongside a giant, ancient robot named Plato, whose sheer size and girth meant he towered over the boys.

"Look who we ran into!" Hunter smiled.

"Plato!" Elly jumped up from her seat and ran to give the colossal automaton a mighty hug. She was only tall enough to wrap her arms around one thick metallic leg. Her fingers couldn't even touch as she embraced him.

"Greetings, children. I am elated to receive your presence here in my tidy library." Plato had no mouth, but when he spoke, his bright blue eyes illuminated with every word. He had a peculiar voice that sounded very electronic.

"Plato, we haven't seen you in a few weeks," Liv added. "Have you been hiding?"

"My duties have been exponentially increased with this year's lineage courses being underway. The library must be efficient and orderly to encourage young scholars to peruse intellectual interests. If my digital humanoid emotional translator application is accurate, I would like to share with you that I am feeling very 'delighted' to speak with you all."

"I think your humanoid digital emotional translator thing is working perfectly, Plato," Liv laughed.

"I am continuously reprogramming its efficiency. I believe I have altered it to work at a ninety-seven point six and one-sixth percent of achieving the correct human emotion when exchanging discourse. I am currently reworking the program to begin each statement with a brief emoticon to ensure participants within my vocal confines understand my feelings," Plato explained.

"Um, what?" Hunter asked.

"Explanation: I am currently unable to express emotion through body language, pitch of voice, or facial expressions like humans. After centuries of studying the human condition, it is noted that body language and physical responses are a key indicator in understanding one's feelings. To replicate, I will substitute physical emoticons with verbal cues. The application should be running within the next few days as I continue to work out its bugs."

"You're amazing, Plato!" said Elly.

"Hunter and Alistair have requested information on the origins of the Belmonte Estate," Plato added.

"You guys have to hear this!" Hunter sat next to Liv with a wide smile. "You'll never believe it."

"Go ahead, Plato. Tell them what you told us," said Alistair.

"There are multiple files in the estate's directory that are encrypted, and although I am privy to such intelligence, I am not permitted to release any data outside of the user profiles with granted access."

"C'mon, get to the good stuff. Tell them about when the estate was founded," Hunter interrupted.

"Belmonte Manor, and its subsequent land, was founded by one Professor Claudio Calenstine during the year 1802 when he returned from a near fatal expedition to the area that is now commonly known as 'Florida.'"

"Wait... what?" Liv frowned, a bit confused over what she had just heard.

"That makes the professor over two hundred years old!" Elly shook her head.

"That's impossible," Liv protested. "The records must not be right."

"Correction," Plato interjected, "the files are precise. Belmonte Manor and its estate started construction in 1802 and finished in 1807. It has seen numerous additions and construction over the course of its existence, including subterranean development."

"Maybe it wasn't *the* professor, but maybe it was his great, great, great, great grandpa," Liv suggested.

"I don't know. We found those old photos of him," Hunter replied with eyes filled with excitement.

"Yes, but maybe they just look a lot alike. People say I look a lot like my mom when she was my age," Liv explained.

"Professor Claudio Calenstine's age is unconfirmed, as is any information going back further than 1802," Plato answered.

"Let's face it, guys," Alistair laughed. "If anyone in this world is over two hundred years old, it has to be the professor."

"Plato," Elly flipped her Seekers Journal open to a fresh page, "what about the Beast of Bladenboro. Can you tell us anything about that?"

"The Beast of Bladenboro is a winged feline cryptid that—"

"No, we mean about how it escaped," Liv added.

"A security breach occurred manipulating the Ocelot Room's inner cellblocks. It is unconfirmed where or how the breach occurred. It is known that only one cell had been disrupted—cell number 0012987. It housed subject number 1228. Codename: the Beast of Bladenboro," Plato answered.

"So, like, someone physically broke in?" Hunter asked.

"Likeliness of a physical break-in within the Ocelot Room and farther into the cellblocks is below a probability rate of .0001 percent," Plato replied.

"So, then it was a hacker?" Alistair asked.

"A hacker?" Liv repeated with a confused look.

"Yeah, someone must have broken in to the estate's computer servers and manipulated them."

"After the incident occurred," Plato interjected, "diagnostic reports were run through the entirety of the Belmonte central intelligence mainframe to counterattack any potential erroneous connection ports from outside sources of the safeguarded central nodes," replied Plato.

"And?" Alistair waited for the robot's response. Alistair loved computers; he was a bit of a genius when it came to them. When he was younger, his father, Benjamin Jenson, would bring old computers home from work for Alistair to break down and rebuild. Alistair even knew a bit about hacking as well.

"There was record of one potential threat during the time frame."

"I knew it!" replied Alistair. "Could you trace it?"

"Negative," Plato replied.

"So that's a dead end," Hunter sighed.

"Well, at least we know it was someone who knows a lot about computers." Elly jotted something down in her notebook.

"Or someone who knows someone who knows a lot about computers." Liv shook her head. "It could be anyone."

"Why are you making so many inquiries today?" Plato asked.

"We were just curious about how old the professor really was," Hunter replied.

"Liv and I were talking about Uncle Joe, and we wanted to figure out who could have released that thing, and why."

"I have been following Master Joseph's condition," Plato responded. "He is doing well; vital signs have been adequate for over a month. He has recovered."

"Well, sort of," Hunter added.

"I do not compute," Plato replied. "Vital signs are strong. Records indicate weight loss and a lack of appetite."

"He can't walk, and he tries to hide it around us, but he's really sad," Elly explained.

"Processing..." Plato paused for a second as if he was thinking or perhaps running complex algorithms—whatever a robot would do. "May I be excused, children?"

"Um... sure." Elly jumped up from the table to give Plato a hug goodbye. "Thanks for your help!"

The large automaton slowly turned away from the children and headed back towards the far end of the library.

"That was a little abrupt, don't you think?" Alistair added.

"Plato seemed shocked that Uncle Joe was upset" said Hunter.

"Well, it's getting late," Liv said, changing the subject. "I think I'm going back to my room to get ready for tomorrow."

"Yeah, we should all be getting ready," Elly added.

The children packed up their bags, once again, and headed back up to their rooms on the second floor. It had been a long day, and the children were growing much more tired than they ever could have imagined. A lot weighed on their young minds, most notably their uncle's condition. It was hard to see him in such low spirits. They wanted to help him get better, but neither Hunter nor Elly had the faintest idea what they could do. Elly found it easier not to think about it and instead decided she would focus her attention on trying to figure out who could have let the Beast of Bladenboro out to begin with. She wanted justice for all the people who were hurt because of it. Tomorrow was just around the corner, and this time it was Alistair who couldn't sleep. Tomorrow, he would meet his idol, the famous cyrptozoologist and reality television star, Jonathon Gates.

Chapter 4
Celebrity Status

Fifteen minutes had passed since the bell to signal the children's first day of Survival Fitness, and the teacher, Mr. Jonathon Gates, still hadn't shown up. The children sat uneasily in the room, anxiously awaiting their teacher, and a bit lost for words.

"Where is he?" Alistair shook his head, fighting off an ever-growing yawn. He was so excited to meet Mr. Gates that he hadn't slept a wink the night before.

"Shut up," Corbin sneered from behind him. He threw a piece of wadded-up paper at the back of Alistair's head. "If the teacher doesn't show we get a free day with no class, you idiot."

"Don't talk to Alistair like that." Elly shot the dirtiest of looks at the tall and muscular Corbin.

"Or what?" Corbin mocked. "You're going to send your older brother, Hunter, after me? That little twerp? I'm shaking in fear over here." Corbin and his sister snickered.

"Maybe I will!" Elly shot back.

"It's okay, Elly," Alistair whispered. "Just drop it."

"Oh really?" Corbin stood up. "The family of traitors is going to stand up to the son of the most famous Seeker in the world?"

"Traitor?" one of the other kids in the class whispered.

"What? You guys haven't heard?" Lunette now chimed in with a wicked laugh. "The Jakobs family were traitors. Their parents were double agents, selling our secrets to the Aten Corporation for extra money."

"That's not true! You're lying!" Liv shouted. "You have no idea what you're talking about!"

"Our parents would never do that!" Hunter stood up, clenching his fists tightly. He had never felt anger like this. His blood boiled, and his jaw tensed in downright hatred of the twins.

"It's true because our father figured it out. He told that old professor of ours, and he didn't believe him, despite the proof." Lunette now stood beside her brother.

"He didn't believe him because it's nonsense!" Elly felt the warmth of tears well up in her eyes.

"Traitors, selling our secrets to the one group who wants to see us fail. Your parents were dirty double agents. You both should be expelled from the enlightenment; your lineage should be banned from ever being a part of our society."

The class went into an uproar of whispers and questions.

"Children!" A large, muscular man barged into the classroom, and Jonathon Gates stood before the class wearing his journeymen clothes of thick black boots with khaki-colored pants tucked into them. His button up, off-white shirt was topped by a large scarf around his neck. Gates had dark red hair that was thinning on top, making him look a bit older than he truly was. "What on *earth* is going on?"

"Corbin is being a jerk!" Elly replied.

"Act your age and take your seats, the lot of you! First day of class and already there's a fight breaking out?" Gates shook his head with embarrassment. "We're a team here! If we were out in the wild and got into a fight with the people who are supposed to help keep us alive, we're as good as dead."

"He called our parents—" Elly's attempted explanation was interrupted.

"I don't care what childish antics were at play; all of you need to grow up. This class is serious; you will learn information that will save your lives on numerous occasions; what plants you can eat, how to dress a wound, and how to stay alive if you're lost in freezing climates. We will be out in the field, learning in the wild, and if you can't pay attention in here, you may find yourselves lost out there."

"Great, he hates us," Alistair sighed, sinking deep into his seat.

"Now, let's get this class started. We begin with the basics, learning the different terrains and their characteristics. We will end with watching a video of my hit television series, *Myth Hunters*, so you can get a view of what it looks like out in the field."

Alistair spent the rest of the class a bit bummed out. Meeting Jonathon Gates hadn't gone as planned, thanks to the Krueger twins. Gates spent most of the class peering at the clock as if he couldn't wait for the course to be over. He was a busy man after all and probably needed to catch a flight out to film somewhere, at least that's what Alistair told himself. Overall, Alistair enjoyed the class, especially watching old episodes of Gates' *Myth Hunters*, which he had already seen numerous times. The specific episode that he had shown was the one where Gates and his crew were in Northern Africa looking for a mysterious creature named Aswang, a shape-shifting vampyre type creature that terrorized the natives, feasting off their livestock.

Alistair decided that after class was not the best time to ask Jonathon Gates for an autograph. He opted instead to just wait on his friends, who followed shortly with backpacks in hand.

"To the botanical gardens?" Elly asked.

"Sure," Hunter said with a nod.

Before they were able to take one step farther, Hunter was forcefully pushed down to the ground by Corbin, who had snuck up behind him, grabbed a fistful of hair and thrust him down as hard as possible.

Hunter hit the ground face first; the force was so hard it knocked the wind from his chest.

"Hey!" Alistair yelled.

"Stupid jerk!" Corbin kicked Hunter in the ribs as hard as he possibly could. "Traitors getting us in trouble with the teacher, so we'll teach you!"

"Stop it!" Alistair dropped his backpack and lunged towards Corbin, who easily moved out of the way.

"You're going to keep defending these traitors?" Corbin sneered.

"Leave him alone!" Alistair huffed in anger. "You're nothing but an oversized bully with a jerk-face."

"Fair enough." Corbin cracked his knuckles and grabbed Alistair by his shirt, tossing him up against the building. Alistair was surprised how strong Corbin really was.

"Let him go!" Liv yelled.

"You're a traitor in my book too then!" Corbin grinned as if he was truly enjoying the scene he was causing. He held Alistair up against the wall with his left hand and drew back his right. He struck Alistair square in the nose. The force of the blow sent Alistair straight to his knees, his nose bleeding profusely.

"Get help!" Elly yelled to Liv as they both turned to run away.

"Not so fast, ladies." Lunette grabbed both the girls by their hair. "Since you're all friends, you should probably watch what the Kruegers do to traitors."

"Stop it!" Liv yelled. "I'll tell my dad!"

"Shut up!" Lunette spun the girls around by their hair.

Hunter rose to his feet, holding his side where Corbin had kicked him. He breathed heavy, but he didn't feel any pain. Anger coursed through his veins, and he was surprised that he felt nothing but the will to attack Corbin with every ounce of his being.

"You want seconds?" Corbin made his way back over towards Hunter.

"Hey!" a large boy about Corbin's age shouted from afar. "Leave those kids alone!" the boy shouted as he made his way over. The kid wasn't tall like Corbin, but he was thick, with large arms. Hunter could see his face as he approached; his cheeks were red with anger, and his lips were pursed tightly together in a frown.

"Who are you? You're not in the Enlightenment classes," Lunette mocked from afar. "You're not even supposed to be near this building, so get out of here before my brother hurts you too."

"You're right, I'm not in those classes," the kid yelled back. "And if kids like you are in those classes, I'm glad I am not." The boy helped Alistair to his feet.

"Get out of here before you get hurt." Corbin went to push the kid, but even with all his force, he couldn't move him. It was like trying to push a tree trunk out of the way, and Corbin realized quickly that he may have bitten off more than he could chew.

"Wanna try that again?" The boy smiled.

"Lunette, let's get out of here." Corbin spit at the boy's feet. "I suggest you stay out of our business."

The twins quickly retreated and stormed off towards the estate, cursing under their breath.

"Err... thanks." Alistair stood up holding his hand to his bloody nose. He hid his tears the best he could, and thankfully, no one made any mention of them.

"Name's Remington Montgomery, but all my friends call me Remy. Least all my old friends did." The boy had a friendly smile about him. "That kid sure is a jerk."

"His name is Corbin, and he has it out for us." Hunter winced, trying to breathe through the pain that surfaced once his adrenaline rush was wearing off.

"Don't like him much," Remy stated. "Had lots of kids like him at my old school before I moved here with my dad"

"I'm sorry to hear that." Elly frowned. "It would be awful with a school full of the Krueger twins!"

"I don't know what we would have done if you didn't show up," Liv said, hugging their new friend.

"Um... err... no problem." Remy blushed. "Just finished up with my tutor. I was walkin' back to the estate when I heard you girls screamin'..."

"That was brave of you," Elly said with a smile.

"So, what do you do here?" asked Hunter, who had finally caught his breath.

"Nothin' really. Help my pops with his work 'round here when I'm not in school or gettin' tutored. I was good at football at my old school and played goalie for the soccer team. I played a lot of sports when we lived in the city. Then my dad took up a job here... we don't do sports or nothin' like it here. I'm not that good at studyin', so...."

"Well, you're good at protecting people from bullies." Alistair smiled through the pain. His nose was swelling up causing his voice to have a nasal quality.

"Yeah I s'pose so." Remy couldn't hide his smile. "Thanks."

"What's your dad do here?" Liv asked.

"Oh, he's one of the foremen for all the construction that's been goin' on. He likes it here; I miss my old school though."

"Yeah, I think a lot of the kids miss their old schools," Hunter answered. "I know I do."

"Well… lots of the kids from down at the regular school already lived here for years. Their families have, at least that's what my pops tells me."

"Well, if you like, Remy, Liv and I can help you study. We both get all A's," Elly offered with a smile.

"Oh…" Remy frowned.

"What's wrong?" Liv asked.

"My pops told me I wasn't s'posed to make friends with kids from the Drake school building."

"What? Why not? We go to your regular school too," Alistair added.

"I dunno, but he said not to. He told me it was the rules. Said, 'this year's different from last, 'cause a new group of kids will be coming, and they'll be expecting more from them, so don't bug 'em,' he said."

"Well, that's just dumb," said Elly. "We can be friends with anyone we want."

"Children?" Jonathon Gates had just exited the classroom with a large backpack slung across his broad shoulders.

"What is going on?" He saw Alistair holding his nose, the blood now drying on his hand.

"Err…" Alistair frowned, not quite knowing what to say.

"What happened?" Gates dropped his bag and kneeled down to check on Alistair's nose. "Just what I need, a fight on my first day back."

"Those kids who were picking on us in class beat us up," Hunter replied. "Punched Alistair in the nose, threw me down and kicked me."

"And who are you?" Gates looked at Remy with anger. "You're not from my class."

50

"I'm Remington Montgomery. I live here with my pop. He's a foreman."

"I see." Gates stood up. "Follow me back to the classroom—all of you."

Mr. Gates' classroom was much different from Professor Pike's. There was nothing cryptic about it; it was filled with maps of the world and had outdoor gear hanging from the walls. There were some common plants on a shelf that the children learned during class were safe to eat and common in most parts of North America. Gates also had many framed pictures of himself and his television team out on their journeys around the world, including a huge award he had received for finding one of the best Bigfoot handprints in the wild.

"Take a seat up on the table." Gates nodded to Alistair. He went over to the sink and wetted down a washcloth. "Clean up your face, you have blood all over it."

"Yes, sir," Alistair answered.

"Why did the Krueger twins want to pick a fight with you guys?" asked Gates.

"They think our parents were traitors," Elly answered softly.

"You're the Jakobs kids, correct?" Gates stopped for a second and looked at Hunter and Elly as if he was thinking something he was afraid to say aloud. "Kids will be cruel sometimes," he finally stated. "Now, let me get a good look at your nose. Hmmm... well, good news, it's not broken."

"Feels like it is," Alistair said with a frown.

"Well, it's swollen a bit. We'll get some ice for it. How about you? How's your side?"

"Oh... I'm fine. Hurt to breathe for a minute is all," Hunter answered.

"Don't listen to those kids about your parents. You know, I went on an expedition with your mom once. That was before she got married to Geoff." Gates took a seat next to the kids.

"You did?" Elly replied.

"We were close for awhile; wonderful girl your mom was. She had the biggest heart of anyone I ever met. No way was your mom a traitor, this place was her life. She lived and breathed the Belmonte Estate."

"That's weird." Hunter was a bit shocked to find out his mother and his Professor were friends.

"What, that your mother and I were close?" Gates replied with a smile. "It was a long time ago. We had both just finished up the Enlightenment ourselves. Couldn't have been older than eighteen… Wow, that makes me feel old," Gates chuckled.

"I remember it like it was yesterday. We were planning a trip together to Eastern Africa to search for the fearful Agogwe. Next thing I know, Professor Calenstine asks her to accompany some anthropologist named Geoff Jakobs for a multi-year expedition to seek out thunderbirds in South America. He wanted to find a living specimen and learn more of their cultural influence. Of course, your mother had to take it. It was a chance to lead up to her first Seekers expedition. That's when I was spending most of my time out in Africa doing studies. I came back and they'd married."

"Oh… that's how our parents met?" Elly asked.

"She was a wonderful person, and she found a wonderful husband as well. Your father cared a lot for her, not that I need to tell you kids that." Gates paused for a moment. "I left for a while after that, opted to do most of my Seeker duties overseas. After that, I spent little time here in the estate. I didn't really come back until the professor asked me to teach in between filming my show. I didn't see your mother much after that, and when I heard the new…." Gates couldn't help but to frown as he spoke. "—Listen, I'm so very sorry about what you children are going through. A lot of people here really loved your parents, and it's been hard on the estate to deal with their loss. Please let me know if there is anything I can ever do for you guys."

"Okay, thank you," said Elly.

"Mr. Gates?" Alistair jumped down from the table, "Umm… I was wondering. I mean, I know you're our teacher and…."

"I am not a teacher; I'm your trainer. There's a difference." Gates winked.

"Oh, well, can I get you to sign my canteen?" Alistair dug deep into his backpack and pulled out a stainless-steel canteen.

"You're a fan?" Gates took the canteen and signed his name with a permanent marker he kept handy.

"He wouldn't stop talking about you all last night," Liv laughed.

"That's great! Tell you what, if you can get an okay from your parents, next time we go out into the field and it's not too far, maybe we can have you guys come out with us."

"Really?" Alistair eyes lit up. He had already forgotten about the swelling of his nose.

"Just make sure your parents okay it," Gates laughed. "Maybe it'll be good for some extra credit."

"Wow!" Alistair stared at the signature.

"So, why are you hanging around the Francis Drake Building?" Gates asked Remy.

"Oh, sorry! I know I'm not supposed to be around here," Remy answered nervously.

"He heard us screaming and came to help," answered Elly.

"Is that true?" Gates seemed impressed at the young man's courage.

"Yeah. I was comin' back from my study session... I'm sorry."

"Sorry? Don't be sorry. A big guy like you probably scared them away pretty easily."

"Oh...." Remy wasn't sure how to respond.

"Don't get all bent out of shape over these so-called rules about the kids in the Enlightenment. You're all just kids, right? Some of the parents are a bit crazy over the whole ordeal—afraid of secrets getting out. Truth be told, when the Beast of Bladenboro escaped, there were more than just the Enlightenment kids running around this place. Not too many secrets are all that secret anymore."

"Really?" Remy smiled.

"You seem like a good kid, and that's all that matters." Gates looked at his watch. "Wow, I'm late. I gotta catch a flight. I'll be back next week for our second session. You kids stay out of trouble."

Mr. Gates ran out of the classroom in a hurry, leaving the children behind with their new friend Remy.

"Mr. Gates is right." Elly walked over to Remy with a big smile.

"What?"

"We could use a friend like you to protect us from those jerks."

"I don't like fightin'," Remy said, frowning. "It's all I did at my old school."

"No need to fight, they won't bother us as long as you're around," Alistair explained.

"Oh... all right then." Remy shrugged.

"C'mon," Elly took Remy's hand, "we're going to go to the botanical gardens in between classes; you can hang out with us."

The children didn't let the actions of the Krueger twins affect them too much. They were happy to make a new friend at school, especially someone as kind as Remy. Remy spent the rest of the early afternoon with the kids getting to know them better. He had no clue that he had just befriended the kids who had single-handedly caught the Beast of Bladenboro. He had also just learned of Hunter and Elly's loss of their parents. He couldn't believe all the two young kids had been through in such a short time. Remy enjoyed their company because he never felt like he fit in with any of the kids in his grade. He always felt like an outcast in the estate; everyone seemed so much smarter than he was. All the other kids' parents where scientists, lab technicians, or doctors that worked in the estate's many laboratories, but he came from a family of carpenters and was constantly teased about it. Hunter and his friends were the first group of kids who had made him feel normal.

Chapter 5
A Secret Meeting

"You wished to speak with me." Professor Calenstine sat behind his large oak desk with a small scruffy dog sprawled out on his lap. "Monte here used to be so full of energy and excitement when he was a pup. Now look at him, tuckered out from all the commotion of your arrival. I dare say that he is just like his old master."

"He looks as happy as ever though." Margot offered her hand for the dog to sniff, and the dog obliged but quickly lost interest, returning to its lazy slumber. "Thank you for taking the time out of your busy schedule to meet with me." Margot took a seat, and it became clear to the professor that she was troubled about something. The stress showed on her face.

"Some tea, my dear?" Calenstine poured her a cup of the steaming hot beverage. "Two sugars if I remember correctly." He gave her a warm smile as he dropped each one in, making small splashes.

Professor Calenstine was a brilliant man and was about as old as could be. His many decades of living had turned his body frail and boney, and he was now confined to a wheelchair. But nobody knew better than Margot that as old as the professor may look, his mind and spirit were as sharp as ever.

"Yes, thank you." She took a long sip of the hot brew. She found the tea to be surprisingly strong, almost choking on its tartness.

"Valerian root tea is a bit bitter, but it does wonders to calm your inner spirit." Calenstine nodded as he also took a sip himself. "A cup of this and my worries seem to float away."

"I could use that right about now," she replied, her face heavy with sorrow.

"It shows, my dear," Calenstine said, nodding.

Margot was normally a lively young lady, but the recent months had taken its toll on her both mentally and physically. She tried to hide it, but the restless nights had left deep, dark bags under her eyes, her skin was pale, and her hands were constantly shaking for no reason. No matter how hard she tried to stop them, she would constantly find them twitching.

"A lot has been going on," she replied, holding the hot cup of tea in her hands. The steam from the cup felt calming on her face. She breathed it in deeply, finding a bit of peace in the fresh aroma.

"Yes, I am aware." Calenstine let out a sigh as he sat back in his wheelchair. "How is your fiancé? He should be arriving soon from his latest trip."

"Sebastian..." Margot fought for the right words, but deep down, she knew there were no '"right" words. "To be honest, ever since he stormed out of the mansion that night and got attacked by that monster, things have been different."

"I see." Calenstine tapped his boney finger rhythmically on his desk. "It's true what they say about love; it can be a tricky thing at times. If the love is true, then time will heal all. I would not worry too much about it."

"It's very confusing, sir. So much has happened... with him, with the kids... with Joe." Margot felt her lips purse tightly together as she spoke.

"You are still young, my dear. Growing and learning. If you did not find it confusing, that's when I would be worried. But, please, go on."

"Well... when I agreed to take the oath to help Joe be Hunter and Elly's guardian, I had no idea how upset and angry Sebastian would get. I did it for the children—they need us. He's just so jealous."

"Yes, I see." Calenstine frowned. "Second-guessing your choice over the guardianship?"

"No, never." Margot fiddled with her fingers uncomfortably. "Those children need me. They have lost so much."

"I am a wise old man, Margot, but if you came to me for advice about love, I must tell you that is the one thing I was never very good at."

"No, I understand that. I just, when you asked about Sebastian... I'm sorry."

"Please, no apologies needed, my dear. If I had any advice to give, I would be honored to share it."

"I really came to ask about the children. There have been a few issues that... well... I just don't know what to say to them."

"About their uncle's condition, I assume?"

"Yes, well partly at least. As much as we push and regardless of how many hours I spend with him in recovery, there have been no improvements. He's just so hurt and confused. He has fits of anger where he just curses and yells."

"Yes, I know. I have been following his condition closely. I fear he will spend the remainder of his days confined in that wheelchair—much like myself."

"I think it's slowly killing him. He's so depressed and so lonely. He can barely even hide it around the kids anymore. They see it every day when they visit. It hasn't even been four months since they lost their parents. He won't eat, and he won't take his meds... it's all such a mess. I just don't know how much more I can handle."

"He is broken in more ways than one." Calenstine let out a heavyhearted sigh. "I was so excited to see Joseph return to our home. It saddened me when he left our family for his own dreams, but I respected it. When he lost his sister, he was there for the children despite his own demons. I saw a fire in him when he came back here. When he looked into those children's eyes, it was obvious he was going to stay here and see them through the Enlightenment. I think he found happiness again. Then that whole disaster with the Beast of Bladenboro happened."

"We will be moving him back home soon; hopefully getting him out of the infirmary will lift his spirits," said Margot. "Hopefully it helps him heal inside and out."

"I see." Calenstine opened his desk drawer and pulled out a long cob pipe and a small bag of tobacco, which he stuffed it with. "A habit I can't seem to beat." He lit the match and inhaled the smoke deep into his lungs. "Dr. Wong approached me a few days ago with the option to do surgery. Selective peripheral neurotomy, at which she is the very best! 'Brilliant' is the only word worthy to describe her talents. He would be in the best of hands."

"Joe won't do it. He is violently opposed to any sort of spinal surgery."

"I see."

"It's just such a mess. Every time the kids visit, I see the change in them, and it's not a good one. They're hurting so bad, so confused over all the bad things that have happened to the ones they love. They need their uncle back... and now. There are kids out there spreading rumors, saying their parents were traitors selling secrets to Aten Corp."

"Children can be so cruel." Calenstine shook his head with disapproval at Margot's comments.

"I told them it wasn't true..." Margot paused hoping for an answer, but Calenstine was eerily silent. "It's *not* true, right? I knew Kim and Geoff, and they were great people—so loving and caring."

"Kim and Geoff got in over their heads." Calenstine took another sip of tea. There was an uneasy sense of calmness in his voice as he spoke. "I dare say I think I may need another cup to calm these nerves."

"Wait, what do you mean?"

"It is bothersome that these rumors are being spread. We are discussing extremely confidential issues here, and I must beg of you to keep this between us. Do you understand?"

"Of course, I do." Margot's mind was running a mile a minute. What was Professor Calenstine hinting at?

"It appears as if things were much more complicated than I ever knew."

"No... it's not possible. They wouldn't."

"I am sorry; I can't answer your question. Instead, I must ask you to not think on the matter. Bury the entire notion and reinforce to the children that their parents were kind, good people."

"You can't be serious. Just tell me they weren't traitors."

"I cannot be forthcoming with this information. As much as I would like to share an answer with you, I cannot. Tell me what do you know of Aten Corp?"

"I know they're a shady corporation that wants to see us fail. I know that Professor Aten barged in here two months ago and threatened you. I know Dominick told him our location, and that Aten is trying to get our people to work for him."

"Yes, it is true; Declan Aten is an evil and vile man. He has done some of the wickedest things one can imagine. Six years ago, we got word that his corporation had been constructing some sort of offshore facility where he was planning on doing some very dangerous research. I offered to meet him in hopes of talking some sense into the man," Calenstine explained.

"His name is 'Declan'? You knew him way back then?"

"We have had a long, troubled past. Old business partners... Good old, Deckie."

"So, you invited him to the estate?"

"Heaven's no! He was never to learn of our location. Unfortunately, Dominick led him here. I sent Patricia Ellingbee and five of our best Seekers to meet him at a very secure location. Patricia was to offer Aten a place here within our estate to conduct research. He could save his money and work alongside the best of the best in every field imaginable."

"But if he's so evil, why would you open your doors to him?" Margot asked.

"I was afraid of what he would do if he went unchecked—keep your friends close, and your enemies closer sort of thing," Calenstine explained, taking another long drag from his pipe. "I suppose it was silly to think a man who once *literally* stabbed me in the back for his own fortune would accept such an invitation. He didn't even show up, sent one of his suits to laugh in Patricia's face and said some day he would find our estate and burn it to the ground with me in it."

"Why does he hate you so much? What did you ever do to him?"

"To say it's complicated does not do it justice. Let me explain a bit. When we were much younger, we discovered something that could change the world for better or for worse. It was an accident that we met. When we stumbled upon each other by pure happenstance, we were both leading separate expeditions to this mysterious place. It was a dangerous journey, and both of our teams met severe losses. Many of my men turned back, and more died as they tried to push forward. I nearly died from the journey due to little food, little water, and being lost in a strange land. I was the last of my group alive. That's when I found him, sitting at a small camp alone, skinny and malnourished. When I approached and looked at him face to face, I was at a loss for words. He was alive and stricken with fever. I was lucky enough to have a few doses of antibiotics left. It seemed as if fate had brought us together. I stayed with him for the next few nights, nursing him back to health. He had a bit of food he was able to share. If we had not found each other, we would have surely died— him from the fever and me from starvation. Once we regained our bearings, we traded notes. We knew we were close to the find. We pushed each other on farther and farther. People said it was a legend and wasn't real. The moment we found it, we knew."

"What was it? Where *were* you?"

"I cannot tell you much so forgive my generalities, but once we found this magical thing, his true self showed. We found something so powerful, so magical that it could rebuild or destroy a world, and we, literally, had the power of the gods in our hands."

Margot could not believe what she was hearing. Calenstine was deep in thought as he told the story, almost as if he were in a trance. Every word he spoke was filled with emotion, embedded with sorrow.

"I... I told him that we had to destroy it. We had to unearth it and let it slip away back into nothingness." Calenstine frowned. "You couldn't understand. Aten was not just a stranger I met on some afternoon stroll in a mysterious uncharted land. We knew we were connected, and it was fate that had brought us together. We were one and the same."

"Okay…" Margot listened, not quite sure what he meant by the two being connected.

"He argued against its destruction. He wanted to take it with us, to become partners, and to make a fortune off its powers. We decided to sleep on it. That night, there was a struggle."

"What happened?" Margot hung on every word the professor spoke with anticipation.

"That night, I died." He whispered staring off into space.

"What?" Margot's mouth dropped open.

"I've said too much." Calenstine wiped the final tear away from his wrinkled cheek.

"What do you mean you *died*?"

"About the children's parents," Calenstine said, dodging the question. "Aten is an evil man with a notorious secret agenda. Whatever happened is whatever it may be, and I am sure Kim and Geoff would never align with such evil."

Margot was at a loss for words. She couldn't believe everything she was hearing.

"Please," Calenstine leaned forward and spoke carefully, "I ask you to assure the children that their parents were great people. Kim was one of the best Seekers I have ever known. Geoff was a devoted and loving father who followed his wife's footsteps into the society. Do not let them listen to rumors, the truth is being twisted. The less the children know, the safer they are."

"Was the plane crash an accident?" Margot asked.

"I do not know, but I have my suspicions."

"Oh my god…" Margot's eyes began to tear up.

Chapter 6
Solomon's Seal

The week was going by faster than Hunter could have ever imagined. He wasn't too keen on the regular studies, math and social economics were never his favorites, but every Enlightenment course the kids had taken thus far was fascinating. Wednesday had come and gone, and the day was spent learning about botany with Professor Latimer. Hunter was surprised to learn of all the legendary and mythical plant life that existed and would be the primary focus of the class. They also learned they would get to spend quite some time in the Demeter Station learning firsthand about some of the rarest flora in the world, including a giant tree called Yggrasild that was supposed to have magical qualities. Professor Latimer even admitted that there was much to learn about the tree still. He even promised to show the class the magical tree in all its magnificent glory if they all passed their final exams.

Elly and Liv were in heaven during the botany lecture, whereas Alistair and Hunter fancied Dr. Lannin's Thursday class, Introduction to Legendary Creatures, quite a bit more. Lannin's class was all about the famous and "not-quite-so-famous" legendary creatures labeled as cryptids. The professor wrote out a long list of creatures they would be studying. Much to Hunter's excitement, the list noted but was not limited to: the sasquatch, wendigos, griffins, harpies, elves, goblins, and faeries, to name a few. Dr. Lannin told the children that there were hundreds of legendary creatures that had gone into hiding from modern man.

"Now, children, not all of the cryptids we have discussed have been found or proven to be real." Dr. Lannin grinned as he stood before the group, flipping a large chart with numerous artists' renditions of each creature. "For instance, there are numerous books and much research has been done on faeries; thousands of people have claimed to have seen them and been affected by their magic all over the world. Yet, there is zero proof in the field that they are anything more than fantasy. However, take the most popular of all legendary creatures, the infamous Bigfoot, as another example. Modern culture has no proof of their existence. Despite countless photos and videos, there is nothing concrete out there to prove their existence. Outside our wonderful estate, Bigfoot is merely a fictional character. However, anyone who knows anything about them knows for a fact that they exist in all parts of the world and on every continent. Living proof resides right here on our very own grounds."

"You mean they have a Bigfoot captured on the premises?" Alistair eyes grew wide in excitement.

"No, no, heavens no," Dr. Lannin replied.

"Oh." Alistair sank back into his chair, defeated.

"Not captive, as that would be cruel. Living in the woods and protected from the outside world. They are free and wild, as it should be." Dr. Lannin winked at the class with a proud smile.

Dr. Lannin was a younger man in his mid-thirties with jet-black hair that he kept buzzed short. He came from Asian descent, was a very skinny man, and usually wore khaki pants and a black polo shirt. You always knew when Dr. Lannin was in a room because he had one of the deepest voices the children had ever heard. He was a passionate man, and when he was in front of the class teaching about legendary creatures, it was easy to tell that there was nowhere else he'd rather be.

"I want to be like him when I'm a seeker," Alistair said, picking up his class notes and shuffling them around before tossing them into his folder. "He knows everything!"

The kids had been lucky enough to not get bothered by the Kruegers that day; this was mostly due to the fact that Hunter and Alistair had devised ways to get around them. They left for class early in the mornings to ensure they would get to the room with plenty of time to spare. They all stayed long enough after class so even if Corbin and his sister, Lunette, were waiting around to cause any problems, their new friend Remy would have had enough time to be outside waiting.

All the strategic planning didn't stop the twins from their constant snarky remarks in class though. It seemed like whenever they had a chance to say something rude or whisper a comment to a classmate about Hunter and Elly's parents being traitors, they took advantage of it. Remy truly became the group's savoir during the few times they did run into the twins. Remy's appearance prevented any sort of confrontation. Remy would smile and nod to Corbin, who would usually reply by spitting at the ground in his direction and cursing his name.

"That Corbin kid really hates you guys," Remy noted as they watched the twins storm off.

"I'm just thankful the estate is so huge; we never seem to run into them inside. They make classes hard enough," Hunter explained.

The rest of the day was uneventful, and the children found themselves swamped with homework and little free time to do much else. Hunter had never spent so much time in a library. There was a bright side to it all because the group got to spend quite a bit of time with Plato. Not to mention, Hunter was almost always with Liv. Not that he had mustered up the courage to speak to her alone. He hadn't quite mastered the art of talking to girls, but he did enjoy being around her even if she spent most of the time with his little sister.

Their first week of Enlightenment was coming to an end with only two classes left. Hunter and Elly woke early as usual and readied themselves to spend the morning with the young and exuberant Professor Camille Badgero. She headed the Intro to Ancient Relics course. Camille was the youngest of the children's professors. She had wavy blonde hair that fell to her shoulders and bright green eyes. She was fresh out of college, and as the children quickly found out during her brief course introduction, she had spent the majority of her life living in the estate with her parents, who were archeologists studying ancient ruins. She wasn't a member of the Seekers per se, but after she had graduated from an Ivy League college, and with her work studying the myths and legends of ancient relics, Professor Calenstine had basically begged her to return and teach.

"The world is filled with so many secrets," Camille lectured. "Not just with legendary creatures, mysterious plants, or eerie spirits, which you will learn about tomorrow morning with Professor Hobbes. But also with ancient and powerful relics, items that contain magical qualities, or worse, deadly curses. Who can share with me an example of a relic that would fall under this category?"

The class fell silent at first. Eyes darted around the class looking for somebody to take charge with an answer. Elly raised her hand.

"I read about something called Solomon's ring; it's supposed to be magical."

"Solomon's ring!" Camille's bright green eyes widened with excitement. "Also known as Solomon's Seal. Very interesting, Ms. Jakobs, and right you are! It is a relic that I am quite fond of myself. When I was finishing up my college years, I centered my thesis around this mysterious object, which in turn is why Professor Calenstine asked me to be here today."

"What is it?" Hunter asked, a bit skeptical.

"Solomon's ring was said to be worn by King Solomon himself and was supposed to house magical qualities. Some say the ring can control spirits and grant the ability, for the wearer, to communicate with the dead. Others proclaim it allows the wearer the ability to speak to animals and plant life. Its origin was from Medieval Jewish, Christian, and Islamic legends. It even appears on your sweaters as a part of the Seekers' sigil."

"Really, it can control spirits?" Alistair asked. "More importantly, ghosts are real?"

"Well, let's not get to ahead of ourselves," Camille laughed. "As you will learn tomorrow with Professor Hobbes, spirits and other paranormal activities that fall under that category are definitely considered 'fringe' sciences. I am not saying the legends are true—"

"Fringe?" Liv interrupted.

"Sure. 'Fringe science' is a label for studies that fall outside what modern science considers 'normal.' Much of what you do as Seekers would be considered under the realm of fringe science. Shape shifting wendigos, man-eating plants, ancient rings that can grant you powers to speak to the dead, and hunting for spirits based on mere speculation rather than proof are all considered fringe sciences."

"So, is there any proof the ring exists?" another kid asked.

"Well, I am proud to say that, during my thesis in grad school, with the help of the professor, who funded my research, we found what we believe to be the *very* ring we speak of. It is here in the estate in the very safe hands of Professor Calenstine."

"We have it here?" Hunter blurted out in excitement.

"Why yes. It is hidden away in a safe place," she explained.

"Does it work?" Alistair asked.

"Well, I cannot comment on that. I was forbidden to wear the ring once we unearthed it. I quickly handed it over to the professor. He knows best when it comes to such things. In the end, I had an amazing thesis and graduated top of my class."

The class ended and the group rounded up their notes and supplies. As usual, they waited a bit before exiting Camille's classroom in hopes of not running into the twins. When they made their way out, Remy greeted the group with his usual crooked smile, waiting patiently to walk down to the botanical gardens. Unfortunately, as they made their way there, they ran into Corbin and Lunette getting scolded by Patricia Ellingbee, who was waving her index finger at the two siblings. She was red-faced and yelling quite loudly.

"How dare you think it's acceptable to treat anyone with such violence and rudeness! Punching and kicking a child while he is down! Spreading rumors—god-forsaken, mean, and evil rumors!" Patricia went on, barely able to catch her breath as she yelled.

"Oh no," Alistair frowned. "This is not good."

"They're really going to hate us now," Elly added.

"I spoke with your father about the amount of trouble you two are in! One more mess up like this," Patricia's hands were shaking with anger, "and you will not be able to continue on with the Enlightenment! Do you understand?"

The twins shook their heads. Corbin was red with anger as Patricia yelled with fury. His sister wept quietly, tears running down her face. She wasn't nearly as scary looking as she had been before. The whole time Patricia was reprimanding the twins, Corbin glared over her shoulder, staring at Hunter and Alistair with cold eyes.

"Now, get out of here and report to Professor Latimer in the botanical gardens; he will have you in detention for the rest of the week. Spreading manure! That's what the two of you will have to look forward to for the rest of the week!"

With that said, the children knew they had to find a new place to hang out, because no way were they going to share the botanical gardens with the twins, especially after the punishment and tongue-lashing Ms. Ellingbee had dished out.

"Children," Patricia said as she turned to see the look of horror on their faces. "I am sorry you had to see that. Please understand, I made sure to tell them that the lot of you had nothing to do with us learning of their treacherous behavior. Not that it matters, but if they even lift a finger in your direction, Professor Calenstine will have them removed from the Enlightenment. You kids focus on your studies and don't listen to a word of what those rotten kids say."

Hunter nodded, not having much to say. He knew Patricia meant well, but he knew what this little week-long, fiasco of punishment meant for him.

"Great!" Alistair frowned once Patricia left. "They're going to want to kill us."

Chapter 7
Ghosts, Spirits, Ghouls, and a Dinner Date!

Hunter awoke the next morning to his alarm ringing loudly. He promptly shot out of bed and quickly dressed before the alarm even went off. Normally, he would spend the first fifteen minutes hitting the snooze repeatedly, and his sister would run around the bedroom yelling at him to wake up before he made them late for class. Today was different though. Hunter was up and eager for the day to begin before Elly had even crawled out of bed. "Hurry up, Elly. We gotta get ready!" Hunter darted around the room grabbing his school sweater and his backpack

"Who *are* you?" Elly yawned, surprised by the difference in her big brother's morning routine.

It was the last day of their first week of Enlightenment courses. Unlike the regular students in the estate, where the classes were held Monday through Friday, Hunter and Elly had to go to Enlightenment courses six days a week. Today was Saturday, and that meant they had Spirits and Demonology with Professor Thomas Hobbes. Hunter had always found ghosts and spirits interesting, and he had been eager for this class ever since Patricia told them about it back at the library. He'd even read the first two chapters of the textbook already!

Hunter had his parents to thank for his interest in the spectral world. As a young boy, his mother would take him down to their local library and allow him to check out any book he liked from the children's section. Hunter always went directly to the ghost stories and would pick out the scariest looking book he could find. He and his mother would spend every night reading a scary story to each other before bed. When he got older, he and his father would spend every Tuesday night, after all his homework was done of course, watching their favorite reality television show, *Spirit Stalkers*, on the paranormal channel.

As much as Hunter tried to push the death of his parents into the back of his mind, it had only been a few months since the disaster had taken their lives. It was often late at night when the thoughts and depression crept into his mind. He was thankful for his busy schedule at the estate, even with his regular classes, which he didn't care too much for. Because of his hectic schedule, his brain was always crammed with his studies. He didn't have much time to think about anything else.

When Hunter first arrived at the estate, he had searched the small library the estate's caretakers had adorned the children's bedroom with, and found some books that discussed the theory of life after death. Ever since their parents' plane crash, Hunter had become very interested in the notion of the human soul, spirits, and ghosts. He wasn't sure what had become of his parents when they died, but he always wondered if they were watching over him like some sort of guardian angels.

Despite the enthusiasm to spend the morning with his new professor, Thomas Hobbes, learning about spirits, ghosts, and ghouls, he was equally excited for after class. Hunter and Elly had a lunch date with their uncle and Margot. It was the first day since Uncle Joe's attack that he was getting up and out of the infirmary.

On the way to the Francis Drake Building of Enlightenment, Elly wouldn't stop going on about last night's botany homework, which Hunter had failed to finish.

"You didn't finish chapter three?" Elly scolded.

"No, I fell asleep after the first paragraph," Hunter lied, knowing full well he'd opted to read up on his fascinating Spirits and Demonology book in favor of boring plants.

"It was so interesting. We learned about..." Elly went on about photosynthesis, carbon dioxide, and a whole slew of other technical terms that Hunter didn't understand or care about.

"Sounds like regular boring school stuff," Hunter replied.

"Well, we also learned about the Lunar Blood Orchid, which is really cool. It only blooms during full moons and only once every fifteen years. It has long tentacle-like vines with little suction cups that drain the blood of anything it can attach to," Elly explained matter-of-factly, as if proving Hunter wrong that it was a 'boring' assignment.

"All that really matters—" Hunter stopped walking, grabbed his sister's arm, and turned her to face him, looking very serious. "Was it yesterday that we learned about Solomon's Seal?"

"Yeah? So what?" Elly shrugged, not making the connection and pulling her arm away from him.

"And today we're learning about ghosts," Hunter hinted at his point, but Elly still couldn't make the connection.

"Okay..." she replied.

"The ring is supposed to grant people the power to speak with spirits," Hunter explained.

"Well, they said it's supposed to do that, or grant the wearer the ability to speak to animals. They don't know what it really does... if it does anything at all," said Elly, making her way back towards class.

"But we have it here in the estate! Professor Camille said so herself."

"So, what?" Elly was growing tired of her older brother's schemes.

"So, what..." Hunter frowned. "Our parents are dead! Did you forget that already?"

"No!" Elly turned back around to face her brother, her face red with anger. Her brother's words had cut her deeply. How could he say something so cruel? "I know they're dead," she shot back. "What's the ring got to do with them?"

"Because if we have it, we can speak to them." Hunter spoke softer now; the anger had left his voice. All that was left was the bitter sound of desperation. "Don't you want to at least try? Just to hear their voices one last time?"

Elly turned around without saying a word and promptly wiped

away the tear from her cheek. The Francis Drake Building was up ahead. She didn't want to be embarrassed by walking into her first day of the class crying.

"Hunter," Elly stopped after a few steps, "ghosts aren't real. We won't ever hear their voices again."

"Fine," Hunter gave up for the time being. "Let's just go to class."

෨

Professor Hobbes was a brilliant man when it came to the knowledge and understanding of the paranormal world, and even during the first day, the kids learned more than they could have ever dreamed about the spiritual world. Who knew how complex and complicated ghosts could be? Hunter was in awe with the amount of vocabulary words he had to jot down throughout the lecture.

Professor Hobbes reminded Elly of the photo of the old man on the popcorn boxes her mother used to buy at the grocery store. He was an older man, in his late sixties, with a wrinkly forehead and white hair that was perfectly parted down the middle. He wore thick, black-framed glasses that sat at the tip of his nose as he read aloud to the class. One couldn't forget about his signature red bowtie, which he wore on a daily basis—it had blue polka dots as well. Despite his age, he was known as a lively old man amongst his peers at the estate.

Hunter felt terrible about yelling at his sister earlier in the morning, but he did his best to focus on Spirits and Demonology. He painstakingly took notes. He was enjoying the simple fact that the Krueger twins wouldn't even dare look in his direction. He had decided that maybe they were wrong about Patricia getting involved because it was the first peaceful class since they had started the Enlightenment.

"There is so much we still do not know about this field of paranormal activity. There are spirits, demons, ghouls, ghosts, and poltergeists, and that's just the tip of the iceberg. There is so much more for us to learn about, and we continue to develop and learn new techniques every day. But before we begin, we must note in all seriousness that of all the dangerous fields you as Seekers may go into, this branch is by far the most hazardous. Sure, you may get mauled out in the wilderness by a Yeti, or you may get a limb bitten off by an Awahool beast in the Serengeti, but..." Hobbes paused for a second, "when you play around with the spirit world, physical damage is not the only thing you must worry about. You also put your very soul at risk. I am talking about possessions and soul sucking. There could be evil entities that attach to you and drain you of your life presence."

Alistair gasped at the thought of a demon sucking his soul from him.

"But then again," Professor Hobbes' voice suddenly changed to a bit more jovial, "this is all hypothetical; there is no hard evidence that any of this is indeed *real*." Hobbes laughed, as it was apparently very real to him after seeing the things he'd witnessed in the field. "So, if everyone will please take one of these EMF detectors and pass them around, we will begin our lesson in magnetic fields and their correlation to searching out spiritual activity."

ᔆᔆ

"You guys still going out with Margot and your uncle?" Liv asked as the group made their way out of the classroom.

"Yeah, we're supposed to meet upstairs in the dining quarters. Margot said she asked the estate's head chef to do something special for us," Elly answered, unable to hide her excitement.

"Sounds like a lot of fun," Liv smiled. "What's the occasion anyway?"

"We dunno," Hunter added.

Elly gave him a dirty look.

Alistair pulled Hunter aside as the girls made their way forward. "What's up with your sister?"

"She's mad at me. I yelled at her before class about our parents."

"What do you mean?" Alistair frowned, not quite sure how to respond. He never really knew what to say or how to act when

72

Hunter brought up his parents.

"Well, remember Solomon's ring we were told about?"

"Yeah, of course. I have three entire pages dedicated to it in my Seekers Journal."

"Well, I told Elly we needed to get that ring. Professor Camille said it was here in the estate, hidden for protection. With that ring…" Hunter frowned.

"You think you can speak with your parents," Alistair finished for him.

"Well… maybe. Even if there's a small chance for me to speak to them again, how could I not try?" Hunter sighed. "Elly got mad at me and said ghosts aren't real."

"If I can be honest with you," Alistair spoke softly, "if we believe in ghosts and spirits, I would hope your parents weren't one of them. Professor Hobbes said ghosts and spirits are lost souls stuck on Earth. Wouldn't it be better for them to be in heaven or wherever they need to be?"

"I guess." Hunter felt the tears begin to well up in his eyes.

"Look," Alistair paused, "if you want to try this out, and you need a friend to help you, you know I'll be there."

"Really?" Hunter smiled. "We could get into a lot of trouble."

"Ha!" Alistair chuckled. "My dad said he expects us to get into trouble. Personally, I think he likes it when we get into these situations."

"C'mon, guys!" Liv yelled from quite a way up the path. "Hunter, you're going to make you and Elly late for lunch!"

ᴄ⋅ᴐ

Elly and Hunter made their way up to the cafeteria where Margot had decorated a large table with streamers and balloons that read, "Welcome Back!" Hunter thought the table looked really nice, despite the fact that the cafeteria was huge and there was only a small section decorated.

"Children, does it look nice?" Margot smiled brightly. "I spent all afternoon getting it ready."

"Looks really great, Margot." Elly took a seat at the table and tossed her backpack onto the floor. "Where's Uncle Joe?"

"Dr. Wong is bringing him down." Margot placed the flower centerpiece on the table.

"What's the big celebration?" Hunter added as he grabbed a handful of crackers and cheese spread.

"Hunter!" Margot snapped. "Wait for your uncle before you go eating all the appetizers!"

"Yeah, Hunter, stop thinking about yourself all the time," said Elly.

"Elly," Margot frowned, "that was rude."

"Sorry." Elly's lip curled in frustration.

"Children, I asked you and your uncle here because we are celebrating his release from the infirmary! He will be able to go back to his own room tonight!"

"Really? Is he walking now? You fixed him?" Hunter's eyes lit up with hope.

"Well, not exactly," Margot responded, but before she could explain, Dr. Wong came through the large swinging cafeteria doors pushing Uncle Joe in his wheelchair.

"Hello, everyone!" Dr. Wong said with a smile. "I brought a friend along with me."

"Uncle Joe!" Both Hunter and Elly jumped down from their chairs and ran over to their uncle, who for the first time since the attack was dressed in jeans and a sports coat.

"Hey, guys, hope you weren't waiting long." Joe reached out for a hug from both kids.

"Please, come and have a seat, and I'll go check on the food." Margot waved the group over to the table.

"Wow, all this for me?" Uncle Joe actually smiled without having to force it.

"Yes, everyone is very excited to have you back at the estate and not locked up with me every day." Dr. Wong laughed as she pushed Joe's wheelchair up to the table.

"So, I have to ask, how the heck am I supposed to get around my place being stuck in this blasted wheelchair?" Joe took a handful of crackers and cheese and devoured them. "My God," he said through a mouthful of food, "it's so good. I won't miss the hospital food—no offense, Doc."

"None taken. Enjoy the food Margot has made for us," Dr. Wong said as she dished up her own serving.

"I'm glad you like it. I was up all night making the crackers by hand." Margot dished up a second helping for Joe. "Well, about your wheelchair problems, Professor Calenstine has had a team of carpenters rework your apartment. They have spent the last week making your living quarters wheelchair friendly, even putting in handrails for you to get around when needed."

"I see," Joe replied, unable to hide the frustration in his eyes. "Suppose I have to learn to live like this now—a life full of handrails."

"Well…" Dr. Wong swallowed a mouthful of food, "one of the reasons we invited everyone here was to talk about some options."

"Options?" Uncle Joe repeated, but before anyone could respond, another guest made their way through the large swinging doors to the cafeteria.

Much to Joe's delight, there in the threshold stood the enormous automaton Plato, entering awkwardly through the doorframe.

"Master Joseph," Plato said with his robotic hum of a voice, sounding delighted, "I came over as hastily as I could. The infirmary records indicated your release, and through my interlinking of the security systems, I noticed the luncheon Margot was constructing to celebrate. I hope I am not intruding on the festivities."

"Plato, you old rusted bucket of bolts!" Joe wheeled himself away from the table to meet Plato halfway. "I owe you my life. You'll never intrude on anything as far as I'm concerned."

"Gratitude: it is a pleasure to hear your voice. I am making a record of your statement as proof on my behalf that I may intrude upon you at any moment of the day," Plato responded as he kneeled down onto one knee and extended his large hand to shake Joe's.

"Was that an attempt at a joke?" Joe smirked.

"Indeed. I have programmed multiple complex human algorithms with the intended purpose of monitoring and running artificial intelligent applications constructing and deconstructing the human condition specifically known as humor. Your laugh and facial expression confirms that you understood said joke. I am pleased."

"Well, yes, I suppose I did. However, you could create all the computer programs in the world to try and explain how to tell a joke, but everyone has a different sense of humor, and not everyone will find the same thing funny. Perhaps you should write a separate program that identifies and saves personality traits of all the individuals you meet. So, you can keep track of what certain people find funny."

"Interesting notion." Plato paused as if he was processing the information Joe had given him. "It is so very pleasing to see you outside of the infirmary," Plato finally replied.

"Please, come have a seat with us at the table, Plato. You're always welcome." Margot smiled.

"Yeah, we're starved!" Elly said, smiling from ear to ear. The children hadn't had many "happy" events in their recent history. Through all the sadness and suffering the children had endured over the last few months, this moment seemed to define the closest they had felt to feeling happiness once again.

"It's not very often all of us are together like this," Margot added as she waved in a few of the chefs from the kitchens. From the large double swinging doors that separated the dining hall from the kitchen came three men dressed in chefs' apparel. Each of them carted in big metal dining carts filled with food.

Immediately, Hunter's stomach let out a loud growl. The savory aroma from the main courses hit his nose, and he couldn't keep his mouth from watering. The chefs began setting serving plate after serving plate of the food in front of the group.

"Oh man, barbequed brisket!" Hunter's eyes widened. There was a wide assortment of food for the group to pick from such as honey-glazed carrots, biscuits and beef stew, and bacon wrapped shrimp, just to name a few of the delicacies presented before them.

"Wow, I feel like there's more food here than there was at the Orientation for the entire estate."

"Oh!" Margot felt a bit embarrassed. "I wasn't sure what your favorite food was, so I sort of helped make a little bit of everything."

"No complaints." Joe dished up a heaping pile of mashed, redskin, garlic potatoes. "Right, Hunter?"

"Definitely not," Hunter said with a mouthful of food, some of which fell from his mouth onto his lap.

"Manners, young man," Margot scolded. "Eat with your mouth closed."

"Sorry." Hunter took a deep swallow of food.

"You're gross," Elly said in disgust as she cut off the smallest piece of brisket possible before eating it.

"So, what are these options, Doc?"

"I am glad you asked," Dr. Wong replied, wiping her mouth with her napkin before continuing. "Despite our efforts with physical therapy, we are not seeing an improvement with your condition."

"By condition, you mean my legs being paralyzed," Joe corrected.

"Well, yes," she agreed. "I know we put this decision off, but now we need to really sit down and think about surgery."

"No, thanks," Joe replied as he popped a giant piece of pork roast into his mouth as if there was simply nothing to discuss.

"Joe," Margot interjected, "we need to at least discuss this openly."

"No, we don't." Joe attempted to keep his cool. The topic of having the surgery instilled bitterness and anger in him. Surgery was simply not an option, and he didn't understand why people wouldn't leave it at that.

"We have a decent chance of helping you walk again," Dr. Wong replied.

"Correction," Plato said, "a realistic percentage of full recovery of Master Joseph's current condition through selective peripheral neurotomy is only at a twenty-five percent."

"Plato," Margot scowled, "you're not making this any easier."

"Plato is correct. For the average surgeon, the probability of walking away from the surgery is twenty-five percent." Dr. Wong said bluntly. "But I am not an average surgeon. I can fix you, Joe. I saved your life once. Any other hospital in the world, and you wouldn't be sitting here enjoying this fine meal with your loving niece and nephew. I can do this. You can walk again."

"Let me tell you a story," Joe dropped his knife and fork, and pushed his plate away in disgust. "My sister died not even four months ago. I am now the guardian of these two beautiful children."

Hunter and Elly both stopped eating; the seriousness of the conversation had suddenly ruined both their appetites.

"She died in a horrific plane crash. Our father was only fifty-nine when he went into a routine surgery, a surgery he'd had done multiple times in his life, and it wasn't even an intensive surgery. He was a wonderful father.... would've been a wonderful grandfather too, but Hunter and Elly never got to a chance to know him. Do you want to know why? It was because something happened in this 'routine' surgery. We were never told what or how it happened. They said he just couldn't recover. Too many surgeries and too many years of medicines trying to fight his illness; it all wore him down."

"I am sorry for your loss, but any surgery has its risks." Dr. Wong spoke her words softly.

"I barely defied death once," Joe went on, ignoring Dr. Wong. "Now you want me to put my legs first? Put them ahead of these children's last remaining family? Are my legs more important than seeing and watching them grow up? No, thank you. I would rather roll around in this god-forsaken wheelchair and be here for them than risk my life for a twenty-five percent chance of walking. Say what you want, but you know any number of given things could happen. I may never wake up. I could die. "

"Okay... we just thought..." Margot was at a loss for words.

"Margot," Joe picked up his knife and fork and cut himself another piece of pork roast, "you have been so amazing through this. Spending every day with me, pushing me to get better, even when I moped around whining about how unfair life is. I owe you so much. Same for you, Plato and Dr. Wong. But right now, here at this table and at this very moment of our lives, I want to share my happiness and gratitude for you all. I do not want to discuss this surgery. You have worked so hard on this meal, let's enjoy it." Joe felt the warm flow of tears down his cheeks, and he quickly brushed them off.

"Uncle Joe..." Elly had never seen her uncle cry before. Even when he stared the wicked Beast of Bladenboro in the eyes, terrified for the life of those he loved, he didn't flinch. She thought her uncle was a super hero and the bravest man in the world, yet here he sat, broken in a wheelchair with tears of pain rolling down his cheeks.

"I'm sorry." Dr. Wong stood up from the table. "I will let you be with your family."

"Please stay," Margot replied.

"It's okay," Dr. Wong said. "If you ever change your mind, please know that I *will* fix you." Dr. Wong walked over to Joe and shook his hand softly. She leaned in and whispered into his ear before she turned away and exited from dining hall, "You're an amazing person."

There were a few moments of awkwardness as Joe wiped the tears from his face before he finally broke the silence. "Hunter, you're not eating your food!"

"Umm... sorry. I just...."

"I bet you want some more of those honey-butter biscuits." Joe grabbed one of the rolls and tossed it across the table to Hunter. Not expecting his uncle to send any sort of food airborne over the table, the roll hit Hunter square in the head.

"Ow!" Hunter laughed as the biscuit fell onto his plate, landing safely on his mashed potatoes and gravy.

"Good throw, Uncle Joe!" Elly chuckled.

"Listen, let's enjoy this meal. Margot, after months of hospital food, this is more than a treat. I cannot thank you enough."

"Master Joseph," Plato stood up from kneeling on the floor, "if you will excuse me, I would like to begin encoding the individual human humor condition application you suggested. I would like to retire back to the Ocelot Room now."

"Plato, please come visit me soon. Thank you for all you've done."

"Gratitude: you have always been kind," Plato stated. "I will see you soon."

The group continued to eat the wonderful spread of food Margot had made. The mood lightened quickly with Joe focusing the group away from the grim reality of his condition with constant jokes.

"I don't know if I could muster another bite," Joe finally boasted.

"You had four plates!" Elly counted out the plates Joe had stacked up at his side.

"I'm very glad you enjoyed it. The chefs helped so much; I can hardly take the credit for it," said Margot.

"You're too modest," Joe told her.

"Aha! Here you are!" Suddenly a young, strapping man with meticulous blonde hair and mysterious grey eyes dashed into the dining hall. He wore a fine, dark, navy blue suit that was tailor-made with a dark royal red vest underneath it. He stood out from the rest of the room with his lively energy. His name was Sebastian Bell, and he had just returned from an overseas expedition.

"My lovely fiancée, what is this?" Sebastian eyes squinted in confusion. "A little early for my welcome home dinner, is it not?"

"Wonderful..." Joe said with a sigh.

"Um... Sebastian?" Margot stood up nervously from the table. "I wasn't expecting you to return for a few more days."

"I was able to finish my project for Professor Calenstine early. I wanted to surprise you." He stood with his arms outstretched, waiting for Margot to dash over into his embrace.

"Well, please come have a seat. I'm sure Joe and the kids don't mind if you join us."

"Oh?" Sebastian tipped his head to the side with frustration, his arms now at his side. "It's been forever since I left the infirmary for my trip. You can't meet me with a hug at the very least?"

"Yes... of course. I'm sorry." Margot made her way over to her fiancé.

"Sebastian is so handsome." Elly stared at his grey eyes from afar.

"He's not that great," Joe mumbled, focusing his attention away from the scene.

"Yeah, I agree," said Hunter.

"Please, Sebastian, come join us," Joe yelled from the table, purposely not making eye contact with the man.

"Such a feast!" Sebastian twirled Margot and leaned her back to kiss her deeply right in front of the group.

"Sebastian!" Margot whispered angrily. "There are children here."

"I do apologize, my love. I haven't seen you in over a month, so, please forgive me! I let my emotions get the best of me," he said as he lifted her back upright.

"How romantic," Elly smiled as she watched Sebastian spin Margot around like a princess.

"Please listen," Sebastian said, pulling Margot closer to him so he could whisper softly into her ear. "I felt so terrible about our fight and storming out on you that night only to get mauled by that hideous creature."

"You also stormed out once you were out of the infirmary. You've hardly returned any of my calls either," Margot whispered back hotly.

"I know I behaved poorly. I lost sight of the truth, my love. I'm not used to feeling so… what's the word? Jealous! It's such an ugly emotion. I apologize, and I know that you have no feelings for this man who you sit and dine with."

"We'll talk about this later." Margot pulled away from his grip. "Joe asked you to join us, so it's up to you if you want to stay," she replied as she took her seat.

"But of course." Sebastian strutted towards the table. "Is this the lovely Elly I met before? I hardly recognize you. You've grown so much since our last dance. Your beauty escapes all words, my darling. I do say that I feel very bad for the young masters here with us at the estate. Surely there are many hearts you will inevitably break."

Elly was too shy to reply to Sebastian's charming antics, so instead she turned completely red and looked down at her plate.

"May I take this seat next you, my dear?" Sebastian pulled a chair out next to Elly.

"Um… sure." Elly looked over at Margot for approval. Margot couldn't help but smile and nod.

"Be careful, Elly. Sebastian here has a way with words." Margot dished up a plate of food and handed it over to Hunter. "Could you pass this over to Sebastian, please?"

"Do girls really like this crap?" Hunter whispered into his uncle's ear as he passed the dish along.

"I suppose so," Joe replied bitterly.

"You like her, huh?" Hunter whispered again.

"Excuse me?" Joe shot an awkward look at his young nephew.

"What's the occasion?" Sebastian winked at Elly as she handed the plate of food over to him.

"We're celebrating Joe's return home. He was released from the infirmary today."

"Only now? You mean to say that you have only now just been released? I dare say how sad that is," Sebastian replied.

"Yes, sad," Joe replied, watching as Sebastian seemed to care more about his plate of food than the fact he had been laid up in the hospital for months.

"You know, we have a few things in common." Sebastian didn't look at Joe as he spoke, instead carefully eating his food. "Hmm... the food is a bit cold," Sebastian frowned. "Chef!" he yelled across the dining hall. A chef quickly hurried over to him. "This will not do. I just endured a twelve-hour flight. Please bring me something fresh and hot."

"Sorry, dear," Margot replied, a bit embarrassed. "We ate over an hour ago."

"No need for an apology, my love, I simply wish for it to be heated up. I'm sure it's delicious."

"You were saying?" Joe interrupted.

"Pardon me?" Sebastian smiled in return as if he had no idea what Joe was referring to.

"You said we had a few things in common. I'm interested in what you think they may be," Joe explained.

"Oh well, simply put. For starters, we both share affections for my lovely fiancée, Margot," Sebastian said bluntly.

"Excuse me?" Joe quickly turned angry.

"Sebastian, how rude of you to suggest—" Margot dropped her fork from the shock of his blunt statement. It made a loud clank as it struck her plate.

"Forgive me," Sebastian interrupted her. "Is it not true that you took up guardianship over these two charming children with him? You also nursed him back to health if I remember correctly with physical therapy and the like. I only meant that your kindness alone must bring some sort of affection. If you are shocked at my statement, I do think you misinterpreted." Sebastian was enjoying himself, and it showed with his cocky smile as he spoke. "You have a large and warm heart, my love, and through your kindness, I do feel that Joe and I both share equal feelings when it comes to your loving charm. Not to say he harbors personal feelings for you. Heavens, Joe knows you are spoken for and madly in love with me. He is too much of a gentleman to try to court you. After all, we're getting married."

"Margot is a wonderful person," Joe said, clenching his fists in anger beneath the table. "So I suppose you're right. I care deeply for her and all she has done for my family. She has become a good friend."

"Friendship..." Sebastian mused aloud to himself. "Such a fickle thing it can be."

"I don't follow," Joe replied.

"Beyond our feelings, so to speak, for the lovely Margot, we also have in common the battle scars from that vile Beast of Bladenboro. We were both attacked and lived to tell tales of its ferocity."

"I see," Joe said.

"The wicked creature left me with two large scars on my back that I fear will never heal."

"Sebastian—" Margot was growing uncomfortable with the conversation.

"Yes, my dear?" he replied, cutting her off again. "I also lost a very important state-of-the-art cell phone in the woods. It was a satellite phone that could get a signal anywhere in the world. A very special friend gave it to me."

"Awesome," Joe mocked. "You lost a phone and got a few scars. I lost the use of my legs."

"Oh heavens!" Sebastian frowned. "So sorry to hear of your loss, how sad that is. Whatever would I do without my legs? To think, to not be able to dance on our wedding night." Sebastian looked over to Margot with affection before turning his cold grey eyes back towards Joe. "I am very sad for you, my friend."

"Don't be." Joe shook his head in disbelief.

"Did you say you lost your phone in the woods?" Hunter added.

"Yes, it was priceless."

"We found a phone ringing in the woods. It must have been yours," said Hunter.

"You did? Did you keep it? Where is it now?"

"No, it was ringing, and when we grabbed it, it suddenly died. So we left it."

"Damn it!" Sebastian cursed.

"Sebastian, watch your language!" Margot snapped. "You are talking to children."

"Yes, love, sorry," he replied bitterly.

"Someone named 'Declan' was calling you."

"Excuse me? Who?" Sebastian's cocky grin turned suddenly to a frown.

"Declan," Hunter said again.

"Did you say 'Declan'?" Margot remembered the name from her conversation with Professor Calenstine.

"Children, you must be mistaken. I know no, Declan. Perhaps it wasn't my phone you found. Or perhaps your memory of that night is foggy."

"'Declan' was the name; I remember it," Hunter replied, angry that Sebastian had claimed they were wrong.

"Well then, perhaps it was someone trying to offer me a job. I get plenty of business calls from strangers looking for my services. I am a hot commodity after all."

"Do you know who Declan is? Honestly," Margot asked, her eyes serious.

"Heavens, my love. What's wrong? I honestly know no one named

Declan. Funny name, isn't it? Declan." Sebastian laughed it off. "So, children, it is nearing the middle of November, you must have already started the... what is it you all call it?" Sebastian tapped his finger on his chin as he thought. "Yes, the Enlightenment."

"We did, we started this week," Elly answered.

"Must be learning a lot?"

One of the chefs finally came out of the back kitchen with a hot plate of food for Sebastian.

"Well, it's about time," Sebastian said under his breath.

"We have been learning a lot," said Elly. "But we've been spending a lot of time trying to learn more about the Beast of Bladenboro and how someone could have let it out."

"I see," Sebastian said. "I wouldn't worry so much about that. I am sure it was some sort of random mishap. Accidents happen. Everyone is safe now, yes?"

"In all the years of the estate, there has never been a random mishap," Joe stated.

"Well, sounds like we were due for one, am I right?" Sebastian joked as he gently cut a small sliver of pork loin before plopping it into his mouth.

"But that accident hurt Uncle Joe and you too. Don't you want to know?" replied Elly.

"What's done is done," Sebastian added bluntly. "So, what's your favorite class?"

"I love Botany with Professor Latimer," Elly answered quickly.

"Uncle Joe, we learned in Spirits and Demonology that there's a ring called Solomon's Seal that grants the owner the ability to speak to spirits."

"Is that so?" Uncle Joe replied. "Be careful with some of the stuff you learn about in the Enlightenment. Not everything they teach you is true. A lot of it is purely skeptical."

"They said they found it, and it's hidden here in the estate. We could talk to mom and dad if we had it."

"Shut up, Hunter!" Elly yelled.

"Solomon's Seal, you say?" Sebastian interrupted. "Interesting,

Hunter, do you believe in ghosts and spirits?"

"I dunno…" Hunter thought for a second. He had never believed in them before. He also didn't believe in vampyres, and yet he had met one for the first time a few days ago. "Maybe…."

"Such a power for one to have, to speak to the dead! Yes, I can see why Professor Calenstine would hide such a gift if it truly existed," said Sebastian.

"We don't want anything to do with that ring," Elly added, angry with her brother for bringing the subject up.

"Well," Sebastian stood up and patted his mouth with his napkin, "I have had my fill for the day. Delicious meal, my love. Please, would you be so kind as to escort me to our room?"

"I suppose." Margot stood from the table and looked over at Joe. She gave him a look as if she were trying to say she was sorry with her eyes.

"It's fine," Joe said, smiling back in understanding.

"What do you mean, 'It's fine'?" Sebastian glared. "My fiancée does not need permission to escort me to our room!"

Joe shot Sebastian a glare, unable to find the words.

"Sebastian," Margot snapped, "tonight was for us to move Joe into his new room, which Professor Calenstine has modified to suit his wheelchair needs. He needs someone to show him."

"Bah!" Sebastian huffed. "Call Patricia to do it. We have not seen each other for ages!"

"Joe," Margot reached in for a gentle hug and whispered into his ear, "I will have Patricia show you. I am sorry."

"Thanks," Joe whispered back. "C'mon, kids, wheel your uncle up to his room. Elly, jump on for the ride of your life." Joe wheeled over to his young niece and tossed her on his lap. "Hunter, you're driving!"

Hunter smiled and began to push Uncle Joe and his sister out of the room.

"Bye, Margot and Sebastian!" Elly waved happily to the couple as they left.

Margot stood staring at Sebastian now that they were alone in the room. Her mind was racing a mile a minute. She was enraged by his attitude, but deep down, she was happy to see him. She couldn't seem to make head or tail of her mixed feelings.

"Dear, it's been such a long flight. I am tired, and I have missed you so. You look a bit angry with me. I am sorry if I offended you or your friend. I truly didn't mean it."

"It's fine." Margot couldn't help but grind her teeth as she spoke.

"I just remembered," Sebastian said. "I am very sorry, dear. I must make an important phone call. Can you be a doll and wait here for a minute?"

She nodded.

Sebastian quickly made his way out of the room through the large dining hall doors.

"I guess I don't have a choice." Margot fell onto her chair, letting out a stressed sigh. "What a mess."

Chapter 8
Strange Friends

Sebastian left the dining hall and slipped through the wide double doors into one of the mansion's many long, winding hallways. He took a small lightweight cell phone from his breast pocket and flipped it open. He dialed and then held it to his ear for a minute before speaking.

"Dominick, is that you?" Sebastian whispered into the phone, eyeing his surroundings to make sure he was alone. "Yes, good. You need to listen, and no, I can't speak up … Just bloody write this down. I have a plan for you to get back at your dear old cousin Abram and release a wonderfully terrifying monster on the estate! The best part is, it all focuses on the Jakobs kids … Yes, *he* will love it! You must ask the boss if he's willing to hand over to us the cursed Daupnir Ring … Yes, I know it's cursed, as I just said that, you fool … Well, don't act like one, and I won't call you one."

"Sebastian?" Margot made her way out into the hallway. "What's all the commotion? Who are you speaking to?"

"Blast it, I have to go! I'll call you later with the plans." Sebastian quickly hung up.

"Darling, I said I had to take an important business call," Sebastian replied.

"Did you call that person a fool? That's not very professional. What were you talking about?"

"I told you my, love," Sebastian moved swiftly over to his fiancée, wrapping his arm around her waist and pulling her close, "just business. You always tell me how my work bores you, so I will forgo the tedious details."

"You sounded angry." Margot couldn't help but frown as she stared into Sebastian's cool grey eyes.

"What's wrong, my dear?"

"You seem so different, so far away," said Margot, pulling away from his embrace.

"I… apologize, my dear," Sebastian said, turning away from her. "I have not been myself in recent months. This job… it takes me away from you so much. Professor Calenstine sends me around the world, and sometimes I feel like I have no home. I called my partner to check up on the status of our last assignment, and he lost some crucial field evidence."

"Oh, I am sorry."

"Please don't be." Sebastian swung back around and grabbed Margot's hand holding it tightly within his own. "The professor will be delighted with my findings of a new cryptid in South America. A sea serpent that the locals fear is dining on their youth that bathe in the rivers."

"Oh, how horrible!" said Margot with a gasp.

"Well, there is no proof it ever actually ate any children, or if it truly even exists…" said Sebastian, "but I am home now."

"I hate it when you leave," she replied.

"I know my last visit ended poorly." Sebastian held his head low in shame. "I acted…" he paused for a second, "…I *have* been acting like a jealous fool. There is so much going on in my life that sometimes I worry about losing you. Half of our relationship, we've been a world apart."

"I know it's been hard, but it's not like this is new to us," Margot pointed out.

"Do you trust me?" Sebastian looked deeply into her eyes.

"Well… yes of course," she replied, hiding her slight hesitation.

"Things may get a little confusing, but everything I do is for us and our future life together. Please remember that. If there is one true thing in this world of shadows and mysteries, know that it is my love for you."

They held each other in that hallway for quite some time. Not much else was said, but Margot found comfort in his embrace. She felt secure and safe in his arms. She had forgotten how caring and wonderful he had been to her in light of recent events. She wanted the Sebastian that had kissed her that night to be the same man she had fallen in love with years ago when he first made his entrance into the estate as a guest of Professor Calenstine. She remembered his excitement and youthfulness as he made his way through his first tour. Yet, deep down, she knew in her heart of hearts that the man holding her now was changed, different, and darker in some strange way.

Chapter 9
A Secret Seekers Meeting

Somewhere deep beneath the Belmonte Estate is hidden a large and very ancient stone chamber; its whereabouts is known only to the living members of the Secret Seekers Society. At the center of this cave-like structure sat a few dozen hooded figures huddled around an oval table. This table was enormous and had been constructed from the cave itself, carved from the cave's cool, stone flooring. At the center point of the stone table was a magnificent altar, set ablaze with a dancing flame.

The chamber was enormous in all aspects. Its walls were circular, coming together smoothly into a perfect dome at the top. The room was decorated with ancient markings from people long lost to the pages of history. This catacomb sat untouched by modern times; its beauty only gazed upon by very few select eyes, since its origin. It was a magical place, and sitting before the altar, one could feel the raw, pure energy of something greater within it. The catacomb was so far underground that no natural sunlight was able to penetrate its depth. Instead, twelve large torches were evenly spaced out around the perimeter to light the room.

The hooded figures were dressed in black robes with long, thick hoods concealing their identities. The only mark on the garments was the Seekers' sigil proudly displayed on their backs. At the head of the oval table was the only figure dressed differently. Wearing a red cloak, this elderly man was none other than Professor Claudio Calenstine.

On the table before him sat a small leather sack, which Calenstine slowly untied. He didn't utter a word to the people surrounding him;

instead, he slowly poured the contents of the bag out into his boney hands. Fine grains of powder pooled in his hands, and he rubbed it gently in his palms, feeling its coarseness against his skin. Underneath his hood, a hint of a smile was hidden from the group.

"Welcome, Seekers." Calenstine's voice echoed through the room despite the softness of his words. He tossed the powder into the flame on the altar, and the reaction caused a sudden and magnificent explosion of blue flames shooting as high as the top of the domed ceiling. "With the blue fire set, we can begin this secret meeting. I thank you all for your prompt visit. As you all may know, these are troubling times, and a discussion must be had."

"It must be serious, as it has been a very long time since we have met here in the chamber, sir," the familiar voice of Liv's father, Abram, spoke through the shadows of his hood.

"Indeed, a foul mix of evil is all but ready to create the perfect storm. Today we speak of a man who has been in my life for quite some time. A man who, until recently, has stayed off the grid, lost in the cracks of society. I made earlier attempts to keep track of this man, fully knowing the evil he was capable of, but I had minimal success. Now, he has made his presence known here in our very estate, within the very walls we call home. This man is named Professor Declan Aten, the founder and CEO of Aten Corporation. He is the very man who interrupted our Orientation with our old friend Dominick Winters. It was Aten Corp that funded Dominick's rogue monster hunting group, the MFPA., the Monsters and Fiends Protection Agency. It is my thought that Aten lured Dominick under his wing to learn more of our secrets."

"We've all heard the whispers of his name and his corporation." Gerald Krueger's voice now made its presence known. "Yet, you have kept your relationship with this man quite secretive. I know for many, at least in recent months, it has created some tension within the group. I, for one, do not like being kept in the shadows." The tension in his voice was evident.

"As always," Calenstine said flatly, "any information regarding the Seekers is based on a need-to-know basis. Up until now, the information referencing this man was no threat to the mansion or cause for alarm. So before you speak of such tensions, know that in the end, it is *I* who controls the flow of information."

"All I am saying is that, once that man broke into our estate, it worried many people. It was your duty *then* to hold this meeting, not three months later," Gerald added with a sharp tongue. "You have your little caretaker Patricia Ellingbee threaten to cast my children out of the Enlightenment because they dare speak what is on all of our minds. We hear the rumors about Aten and the Jakobs, and we see the truth."

"Silence your foolish tongue!" Abram barked across the table. "How dare you speak to the professor with such disrespect!"

"Abram, calm yourself," Calenstine interjected peacefully. "There is but a small bit of truth in what Gerald suggests. What he doesn't understand is the complexity of the matter at hand. I had to make sure I was doing the right thing before unveiling this information. I know now that we must move forward knowing what we are up against. Our society has called this place home for centuries; we have never been exposed to any outside threat. This man Declan Aten is more than just a nefarious man; he is a disease that aims to eat away everything that we have worked so hard to attain. As for the Jakobs," Calenstine paused momentarily before going on, "simply put, it's none of your business, so I will only ask once for the subject of their loyalty to be dropped. I do not need to explain how they were great Seekers. We are a family, and I will not let you speak ill of their name—not here, not now, and not ever. We must not lose sight of what is important: Declan Aten is a massive threat to everything we hold dear."

"Bah!" Gerald huffed.

"I have researched Aten Corp," another hooded figure said. This time it was Alistair's father, Benjamin Jenson. "They ran into some trouble with the U.S. government back in the forties. This was the only thing I was able to dig up about them, and it was a quick blurb. Supposedly, they had ties to Hitler and selling some sort of creatures of war to aid the Nazis!"

"The forties? We saw this man, and he was hardly a day over forty-five. You said he founded the Aten Corp, Professor? That can't be." Joe's voice now sounded.

"Everyone in this room knows that I have been able to defy the aging process. I grow old, yet I do not die. All one has to do is look through the records and do the math. I founded this estate back in 1802, and before that, I lived many lifetimes. It is a curse that runs through my veins."

"Yet, we still do not know how that is possible," said Gerald. "Another secret you keep from us."

"Nor will you ever know," Calenstine shot back. "No man will ever learn of that secret. If I am ever to find eternal rest, that secret will be buried with me. Do you know how many people I have loved and lost? How many of those loved ones' faces I have lost to memory? You do not want that burden weighing down your soul. No man does. If you knew my true age and the pain I have endured, then you would never speak of such things again."

"What does your age have to do with this Aten character?" Joe inquired.

"Declan Aten shares the same fate as I. He is ageless; we are cursed the same, to live a life with no end in sight."

"But he's only like, forty years old," Benjamin blurted out. "Why has he not aged?"

"This is the evil I speak of," Calenstine interjected. "I do not know how Declan Aten has reversed his age. I know when I last saw him a few hundred years ago, he was as wrinkled and as old as I. That's when I lost track of him. He went deep underground. It wasn't until about ten years ago that I got word of some high-frequency cryptid sightings amongst a batch of small islands near Costa Rica. That's when I sent Kimberly and Geoff Jakobs on an expedition to see if there truly were monsters lurking about."

"Their findings?" Margot now made her presence known.

"Indeed, three creatures were found. Creatures unheard of before, even from tales and legends... half-dead and deformed, as if they were some failed lab experiment."

94

"Experiments?" said Joe, dumbfounded.

"We began to hear rumors from the locals of a mysterious uncharted island nearby. They called it 'God's Isle' because they said evil men were creating monsters within the protection of the jungle."

"God's Isle," said another soft voice.

"Yes, we were never able to find its location, or if it even existed. We did, however, find a tag on one of the dead animals that had washed ashore. The tag had what we thought at the time was Aten's logo on it. We believed it was some sort of tracking device. I spoke with Kim and Geoff about the situation due to their heavy influence in the find."

"The traitors!" Gerald barked once again.

"Gerald!" Calenstine's voice cracked in anger. "Your disobedience will not be tolerated! Your ignorance on such matters has proven your blind hatred. Be gone from the chamber, and we shall speak in private about your insubordination!"

"You're a damned joke!" Gerald yelled back, slamming his hand down in anger. "You can't even keep us safe in the estate anymore. We've got beasts running around attacking children and killing our guests! A man died in our care; how soon you forget about Agent Roberts. How soon we forget the only reason Aten even knows where we live is because the professor invited Dominick back to our home to wipe up his mess!"

"Dominick already knew where the estate was hidden because he lived amongst us, remember?" Calenstine shot back with heated words. "We chose well before he ever stepped foot back onto our home, to give up our whereabouts. I was trying to persuade him to return to us... I was hoping to talk sense into one of our own."

"That's it!" Abram grabbed Gerald's arm with his mighty grip.

"Get your hands off me!" Gerald pulled away in defiance. "Touch me again, and all the Seekers in the world wouldn't be enough to pull me off of you!"

"Is that so?" Abram laughed.

"Wanna find out?" Gerald smiled back.

"Either you leave on your own accord, or I make you." Abram clenched his teeth, ready to strike.

"You know how I know Kim and Geoff were backstabbing

traitors?" Gerald untied his cloak and threw it on the large stone table. He was a stocky, middle-aged man with broad shoulders and thick arms. But even he didn't want to fight with Abram, despite his threatening words. "Because a month ago, I got a phone call from Professor Aten himself. He told me all sorts of information about us, and I'm talking top-secret intelligence. He said the Belmonte Estate was caving in on itself from inner turmoil. He said Calenstine was an old fool stuck on made-up *ancient* rules. He knew everything! He knew about the Demeter Station and the work on curing Alzheimer's! This came from Aten himself! He told me he had paid Kim large sums of money for the information. He offered my family a safe home if I would go work for him, and he promised me money and riches!"

"GET OUT!" Abram hit Gerald with all is might. His rock-like fist struck the man directly on the nose.

Gerald fell to his knees from the impact, his nose pouring blood.

"You'll see, you'll all see!" he yelled as he got up and stormed out of the chamber.

"Professor," Margot started, a sense of panic in her words, "are you okay?"

"Do not let those venomous words sway you. Gerald is lost; hopefully, I can help him find his way back to the light. I will speak with him privately about this matter. Anything Aten does or says, I promise you, it is evil. We have centered our society on bettering humanity and protecting the world from being misunderstood by prosecution. We seek out creatures to protect them from humans, and of course to protect humans from the wicked. We are a collective group dedicated to moving the human experience forward. Aten is a man who only cares for his own well-being."

"Professor," Abram shook his hand, which was now throbbing in pain, "not all of us are as easily persuaded, but I will stand behind you."

"Thank you, Abram," Calenstine said, letting out a loud sigh. "We may have a war on our hands. I need us to stand united against this darkness."

Chapter 10
A Day of Thanks

The days quickly turned to weeks, and the children realized how busy their young lives had truly become. Hunter and Elly were so swamped with homework and Enlightenment studies that they didn't even realize Thanksgiving was right around the corner. Hunter had already managed to fail his first test in Morty Latimer's Botany class when he couldn't tell the difference between a blood-sucking Romanian Blood Moon and a Western Lilly Drake, leaving him with seven stitches on his right arm from the attack. Elly, on the other hand, had passed with a perfect score.

"It's easy, Hunter," Elly joked at her brother's expense. "Romanian Blood Moons have teeth, and Western Lilly Drakes sparkle in the moonlight; how did you get those two mixed up?"

It wasn't much of a surprise for Hunter to learn that Elly was fairing quite well with her new studies, spending most of her free time alongside Liv and away from the boys, who she found quite irritating with their lack of studying. This was mainly due to Alistair and Hunter spending every waking moment searching for clues about the mysterious Solomon's ring. The only good thing about Hunter's new obsession was that he was able to write his first research paper for his Ancient Relics class on the subject, receiving the first A+ he had ever earned with a little help from Margot on the editing side.

It was a quiet and gloomy night on the eve of Thanksgiving. The air had grown chilly and a small light rain spattered on their bedroom window. Elly stretched and yawned, exhausted from studying, a handful of books laid out all around her on her bed. Trayer, their large green-haired companion, snored lazily at the foot of her bed, content as any dog could be. Hunter sat staring out the window, as he did most nights, not saying much at all. Elly never had the guts to ask Hunter what he dreamed about as he gazed out into the rainy night sky. She was afraid of his answer, knowing full well that it had something to do with their parents.

"Are you excited for tomorrow?" asked Elly while she was busy highlighting important quotes in her *Serious Series of Specters and Spirits* book.

"Why would I be excited?" answered Hunter dully.

"It's Thanksgiving tomorrow; we get the next three days off of school, and the professor is holding a giant festival in the main foyer for the entire estate! I'm super excited to see how they're going to decorate it. I hope they take down all those mounted cryptoid heads. They give me the creeps."

"I'd prefer our traditional Thanksgiving. You know Christmas is coming up too," Hunter replied.

"Yeah," said Elly, knowing full well where Hunter was going with that.

"First, Thanksgiving and then... Christmas without Mom and Dad." Hunter frowned. "Holidays suck now."

"At least we have Margot and Uncle Joe," Elly replied, closing her book and tossing it onto the floor. The weight of the book caused a loud thud that startled the slumbering Trayer, who jumped off the bed in a frenzy, running to the opposite side of the room with his tail tucked between his legs.

"Gosh, Trayer!" Elly laughed. "You're the biggest animal I know, and you're scared of everything."

"I know that we have Uncle Joe and Margot now," Hunter responded, moving slowly away from the window and towards their bedroom door. "They don't replace Mom and Dad though; no one can ever replace Mom and Dad."

"Where are you going this late?" Elly asked.

"I need to go out for a walk to clear my head," replied Hunter. His head hurt from thinking too much; he was filled with so many mixed emotions.

For a while, he had started feeling like a normal kid again because the concept of Solomon's Seal allowing him to speak with the ghosts of his parents had rejuvenated his spirits. He was laughing again and smiling so much more that even Patricia Ellingbee had noticed the difference in Hunter's temperament. He almost felt guilty about being happy again. Of course, he would never admit that to anyone. He knew he was allowed to be happy, but it just brought up an intense feeling of guilt. No matter how hard he tried to shake it, he couldn't.

Hunter decided to make his way down the long hallway that passed the numerous living quarters. He envisioned happy families spending time together and prepping their own Thanksgiving meals for tomorrow. The thought of all the families smiling and being happy made his stomach turn sour. He wanted nothing more than to eat turkey and stuffing with his parents and sit at their big dinner table passing around all the side dishes, his mom made the best sweet-potato casserole with melted marshmallow and all he could think about was the fact that he wouldn't get to have any with her. Tomorrow, all these families would go about their holiday like any other, happy as could be and never realizing how wonderful and perfect their lives were.

Hunter began to run down the hall, wanting more than ever to escape the "happiness" that each of the doors, at least in his mind, represented. He quickly got into the elevator and rode it down towards the main foyer, where the following day's big celebration would take place. The elevator hummed eerily until it finally hit the main floor. The metallic doors "dinged" as they slowly opened up to the large balcony where the two lavish staircases spiraled downward. Hunter immediately worked his way down the steps, fighting back tears of anger with every step he took.

There on the northern wall sat one of the strangest parts of the mansion. A large collection of mounted trophy heads. These weren't collections of regular game heads either; instead, there was a wide assortment of bizarre creatures that most men had never seen in the wild, and most men would never dare to see either. Suddenly, as

Hunter stared at the collection of trophy heads, he began to feel a little more at peace. The anger boiling inside him, causing him to grind his teeth had finally subsided.

At first, Hunter couldn't understand why he felt so at peace looking at the curious creatures staring back at him. He remembered the first day he walked into the estate, alongside Patricia Ellingbee, Margot, and his sister Elly. How he had stood and stared at the creatures in disbelief.

"Hunter?" A soft voice jolted him out of his deep thoughts.

It was Liv. Much to Hunter's surprise, she had come around the corner from one of the adjacent rooms in the foyer and walked up to him while he was lost in thought. Hunter didn't recognize her at first because instead of her traditional school uniform, she was wearing a large, baggy, blue sweatshirt with sleeves that hung past her slender hands and comfortable sweat pants.

"What are you doing staring at those things this late at night?" she whispered. Liv and Hunter both knew the caretakers didn't like the children wandering around the estate past their curfew.

"Err..." Hunter was never great with words when it came to speaking with Liv. On any normal day, he was extremely nervous just being in the same room with her. Tonight, adding on the simple fact that he felt like an emotional train wreck, he really was at a loss for words.

"You really like these scary things, don't you?" she added with a faint smile. "I hate them; they're so ugly. I'd prefer a pretty plant or flower any day."

"I sort of feel bad for them," answered Hunter as he extended his hand and petted the werewolf's head, despite its wild and evil eyes.

"Feel bad for them?" Liv's eyebrows rose in confusion. "They're monsters though. Look at that lizard; it looks like a man-eating dinosaur."

"I dunno... my mom always said looks can be deceiving." Hunter walked over to one of the large leather couches and fell onto it, almost in an act of defeat.

"You wander around the mansion late at night too?" She took a seat close to Hunter. "If my dad knew I snuck out, he'd ground me forever. It gets so lonely here without my mom. Sometimes I sneak out when I miss her a lot. I'm embarrassed you're seeing me in this. I snuck out of bed and didn't think I'd run into anybody."

"Oh..." Hunter wasn't sure how to respond. Did she care what she looked like in front of him? He wasn't sure what she meant by that, but it made his heart pound. "Ummm... I guess I do the same thing. I couldn't sleep tonight and kept thinking about not having my mom and dad here for Thanksgiving tomorrow." Hunter wasn't sure what he was saying, or why he felt inclined to say it. The minute he told her how he felt about his parents, he felt foolish, embarrassed even. He didn't want anyone to know how he felt. All he wanted to do was to bury the pain deep inside and never think about it again.

"I'm sorry... sometimes I forget you guys lost your parents. It was only a few months ago, huh?"

Hunter nodded but didn't respond.

"Elly and I spend all day studying together, and she never says a thing about it. They died in a plane crash, right?" Liv spoke softly, her words kind and genuine.

"Yeah... over the ocean. They never found the plane." Hunter tried with all his might to hold back the tears. "But..." He paused trying to compose himself. That's when he felt the warmth of the tears flood down his cheeks. He was immediately angry with himself. Crying in front of a girl? He wanted to stop, but he couldn't control them.

"But what?" Liv slowly put her hand into Hunter's and held it tight. Hunter felt the warmth of blood rush to his cheeks.

Suddenly a man's voice came from outside the window.

"Did you hear that?" Liv quickly shifted to her right, towards the voice.

"What?" Hunter hadn't heard anything.

"There was a man's voice from outside; it came from over here," Liv said, pointing. She stood up and darted towards one of the large double-paned windows. "Quick! Help me lift the window, but be quiet."

"Who would be out there talking this late?" Hunter whispered, wiping the tears from his cheeks.

"Let's find out."

They remained silent and listened.

"Did you make it safely? These woods can be dangerous," a raspy voiced whispered.

Two men were close to the main gate, which was quite a ways away, and Hunter and Liv couldn't make out who the figures were. The voices were low and hardly audible, but loud enough that the children could make out the conversation.

"I grew up here; I know what I'm doing," one of the men replied.

"Well, it's important that you stay hidden until the time's right because I'm on thin ice as it is," said the first man.

"Don't worry; I still have my friends here. Not everyone blindly follows the old fool."

"When we get inside, we go straight up into the living quarters until tomorrow. Understood?"

"I know the plan because I am the one who orchestrated this," said the mysterious man.

"Quick, we need to hide," Liv said, turning swiftly towards Hunter.

"Over there!" He pointed to one of the large couches. "We can hide underneath it; it's dark in here, and they won't be looking for us."

The kids scrambled on their hands and knees towards the closest couch and quickly ducked behind it. Side by side, they waited eagerly for the men to enter the dark foyer. Suddenly, Hunter felt Liv's hand once again slip into his own, the hand shaking in fear.

"We can't get caught!" Liv's whispered voice trembled.

"Shhh! It'll be okay," Hunter whispered back, holding her hand tight.

The two men made their way into the mansion, both covered in dark clothes, their faces concealed by black hoods.

"Never thought I'd have to sneak into a place I used to call home," the man said with a gruff voice.

"Well, in the eyes of the great professor, you chose the wrong side. Anyone who doesn't follow him gets exiled."

"Bah! He's an idiot. You will be paid handsomely for your aid in this matter." The gruff man replied.

"I can't wait to see the look on their faces tomorrow."

"Gerald," the other man said, "not here! We can talk more once we're in the clear."

The two men worked their way quietly up the spiral staircase. Liv and Hunter waited until they heard the elevator door open, and for the soft hum of the elevator going upstairs.

"'Gerald'?" Liv repeated as she and Hunter made their way out from their hiding spot.

"I've heard that name," Hunter added. "That's Corbin and Lunette's father, right? What's he up to?"

"We have to tell someone; my dad will know what to do." Liv turned towards the spiral stairs, but Hunter quickly grabbed her arm.

"Liv, we can't say anything. We both snuck out past curfew."

"Well, what do we do?" Liv frowned in confusion.

"Gerald has a couple of rotten kids, but he's been a Seeker forever. I'm sure he isn't up to anything too bad, right?"

"I dunno." Liv shook her head. "My dad came back super late at night a few days ago, and he was really angry. He kept talking about Gerald being a fool."

"I swear I recognize the other man's voice," Hunter said. "Did you catch his face at all?"

"No, sorry! It was too dark, and they had their hoods up."

"I think we should wait it out," Hunter suggested. "Plus, it's late, and we need to get back into our rooms before we're caught."

"My dad can sleep through anything," Liv said with a half-smile. "But you're right. We don't want to get caught out here."

"We can talk more at the morning festival. We can fill in Elly and Alistair and maybe come up with a game plan. C'mon, I'll walk you to your room."

Hunter escorted Liv back up to the living quarters and made sure she made it back into her room without waking her father. It was very late, and despite all the questions running through his mind, he was quite happy to get back into bed and catch a few hours of sleep before the big celebration the following morning. Even then, once he had snuck back into his cozy bed, his mind wouldn't let him sleep. At the very least, the thoughts of his parents were now replaced with the mysterious man that Gerald had snuck in. Who on *earth* could it be and why?

જી

Margot woke the children up bright and early the following morning. She was all fancied up for the holiday, dressed in an all-white strapless dress that sparkled divinely in the morning sunlight. Her hair was wrapped up tightly in a beautiful "up-do" with curls cascading down the back.

"You look like an angel!" Elly yawned deeply as she tossed off her bed sheets.

"Do we *have* to dress up?" Hunter said with a groggy tone, sounding many years older than he truly was. Already, he wished he could forgo the morning festival and sleep until the actual dinner later in the evening.

"Yes, this is a dress-up occasion; everyone will be adorned in their nicest suits and dresses. Heavens, Hunter!" Margot frowned a bit. "You look like you pulled an all-nighter. Are you feeling well? Look at those bags under your eyes!"

"Yeah… umm," Hunter replied, fumbling over how to respond. "I haven't been sleeping well lately"

"Oh, well… I see." Margot frowned. "I took it upon myself to ready your outfits for the festival. They're both in the bathroom. You two will look so cute!" Margot couldn't contain the excitement on her face.

"Great!" Elly jumped off the bed and darted towards the bathroom. "Me first!" she yelled, grabbing the bathroom door. "Can you help me with my hair, Margot?"

"Of course. I'd love to!" she replied.

Hunter waited for over a half-hour for his little sister and Margot to finally make their way out from the bathroom. He killed time by playing tug of war with Trayer, using a large thick rope they had gotten for him, he chewed through everything else! He thought about telling Margot about the mysterious man from the night before, but he decided against it. He was worried about the amount of trouble he would get into for sneaking out again. Whatever was going on, it didn't sit well with him. He tried to force the thought out of his mind, but it kept bugging him.

"Hunter, look!" Elly twirled out of the bathroom, like a ballerina, with a bright smile on her face. She wore a dress very similar to Margot's except Elly's ensemble was accompanied by a gorgeous purple cardigan. Her pretty, auburn hair was matched up perfectly with Margot's, including the cascading curls down the back.

"You look great, sis," Hunter said matter-of-factly, barely paying attention to her grand entrance. Instead, he focused more on the snarling Trayer, who was easily winning the tug of war. Hunter finally gave up, and the large Cusith pup ran happily to the corner of the room with the large rope.

"What Hunter meant to say was that you look like a *princess*," Margot corrected. "Sometimes boys don't get as excited as us ladies about these things." She winked.

"You're up, Hunter. Bathroom is all yours," Margot pointed to the door.

Hunter was quick, and made his way out of the bathroom, after a few short minutes, ready to go. He came out the bathroom wearing a black suit and dark maroon tie that hung loosely around his neck, along with a half frown across his boyish face.

"We never had to dress up in a suit for Thanksgiving with our parents," Hunter whined as he fumbled with his tie.

"Well, here at the Belmonte Estate, we tend to celebrate our holidays a bit more extravagantly. Professor Calenstine always goes overboard when it comes to any sort of event, especially those that center around food." Margot helped Hunter adjust his tie and added, "You look charming, Hunter. Very handsome."

"Is it going to be fun?" asked Elly, who was now pretending to be dancing with her Prince Charming in the mirror. "Do you think Sebastian will dance with me again? He's so handsome. You're so lucky to be marrying him."

"Perhaps he will." Margot blushed. "And yes, it will be an amazing time. I spent all morning in the kitchen with the cooks, and the amount of food being prepared is unbelievable. We're going to dine like royalty."

"Is everyone going to be there?" Hunter asked as he buttoned up his suit jacket.

"Yes, everyone at the estate will be there. Seekers, scientists, teachers, and caretakers alike. You know, before I swore an oath to help raise you children, I was the main receptionist in the foyer. Even though I worked with Professor Calenstine a lot, I had very few conversations with anyone in the Seekers Society. I always loved our holidays because it's one of the few times everyone gets together."

"So, Remy will be there!" said Elly with excitement. "We haven't seen him in a few days."

"Remy will indeed be there," Margot answered. "Now, come, we must finish getting ready."

❧

The children followed Margot to the elevator and all the way down to the main foyer, where Hunter and Liv had witnessed the strange man being snuck into the estate earlier that morning. Once the cool steel elevator doors chimed opened, Hunter stood in awe at the sight before his eyes.

Last night the foyer had just been the everyday foyer the kids were accustomed to seeing. Somehow overnight, the room had been transformed from the very gothic-inspired decor into a brilliant showcase of Thanksgiving splendor. The room was illuminated by extra lighting that glistened marvelously off the fancy crystalline dinnerware and plates.

The foyer had had its normal décor removed and placed in

storage. It had been replaced with numerous buffet tables adorned with a wide arrangement of delicious-smelling breakfast foods. High above the children's heads, which was normally dark and uninspiring, hung a marvelous chandelier that sparkled brightly from all the new lighting in the room. Below them was the almost deafening noise of hundreds of people chattering, laughing, and enjoying the glorious cuisine. Hunter was shocked to see the sea of people filling up the large foyer. He remembered the Orientation meal, but there weren't nearly as many people there during that event.

"There are so many people..." said Elly as if she was reading Hunter's mind.

"You haven't seen the entire estate together at once. We are a very large family here. It takes many hands to keep everything functioning properly: scientists, doctors, cooks, caretakers, builders, and of course, the backbone of the estate, the Seekers," Margot explained.

"Hey," Hunter frowned, pointing to the trophy wall, "where did they put all the mounted monster heads?"

"Oh, that's far too macabre for a Thanksgiving feast." Uncle Joe's voice surprised the children from behind.

"Uncle Joe!" Both the children ran over to their uncle. He was dressed up in a nice grey suit with a dark purple tie. He sat looking very uncomfortable in his wheelchair.

"How do you like being back in your apartment?" asked Hunter.

"It's not too bad. I even dressed myself today," Joe joked as he grabbed his young nephew in a playful headlock and ruffled his already unkempt hair. "Definitely a better view than out that dreary hospital window."

"You look very handsome," Margot said as she fixed Joe's tie who, much like Hunter, couldn't quite get it to lie perfectly. "You boys can never seem to get these ties straight, can you?"

"I suppose not," Joe said, fighting back a smile. He didn't say it out loud, but he couldn't believe how beautiful Margot looked. He tried not to stare, but that proved to be much harder than he imagined "You kids look great! Did you thank Margot for helping you get ready?"

"Of course!" Elly replied. "She did my hair. It looks really pretty, doesn't it?"

"It makes you look just like a princess'," Joe added. "Jump on my lap, and let's go for a ride."

Elly was happy to see her uncle joking around again, and she quickly climbed on his lap.

"How are we gonna get down the stairs in your wheelchair?"

"With my help." The deep voice of Abram Winters, Liv's father and Alistair's uncle, caught the children's attention as he and Liv exited the elevator. Immediately Hunter turned red in the face as the ever-beautiful Liv walked up to stand beside her tall muscular father. Liv's hair was curled, and she wore a long yellow dress that seemed to catch the attention of everyone in the room.

"Liv, my dear!" Margot eyes lit up with excitement. "That dress is so beautiful!"

"Thank you." Liv was more than a little uncomfortable with all the sudden attention.

"Honestly, you look so grown up!" added Margot.

"You look very pretty too." Liv smiled at Elly.

"I will take you down step by step." Abram took Joe's wheelchair in his strong grip.

"Thank you, Abram," Joe said as they began their trip down. "These stairs aren't the easiest to get around with this lovely wheelchair. Hang on tight, Elly!"

"We need to make the estate a bit more wheelchair friendly," replied Abram. "Elly, your uncle here is quite the hero; you should be very proud of him."

"We are proud; he saved us from that beast," Elly answered back.

"I know a lot of men, and not many of them could muster up that amount of bravery," Abram said with a sense of pride in his voice.

"Thanks, Abram, it means a lot. I want to see our kids safe," said Joe.

"Well..." Abram led the group down slowly, step by step, until they hit the main floor of the foyer, "here we go. I hope you all enjoy the festivities today." Abram shook Joe's hand with a firm grip.

"What a grip!" Joe shook the pain out of his hand with the hint of a smile.

Hunter and Elly quickly got lost in the sea of people all talking and laughing while filling their bellies with the wonderful food.

"Liv," Elly grabbed her friend's hand, "don't lose us."

"Look, over there. It's Alistair and his dad, Mr. Jenson." Hunter pointed over toward a large table of people.

"Hey, kids." Benjamin Jenson smiled in-between shoveling large forkfuls of blueberry pancakes into his mouth. "Food's excellent, grab a plate or three."

"Ben!" Joe rolled up behind the kids, happy to see his old friend. "It's been a couple of weeks since I saw you."

"Joe, the hero of Belmonte!" Ben stood up quickly, spilling his glass of milk in the excitement. "Bring it in for the real thing," he boasted loud enough for the entire room to hear, giving his old friend a big hug. "I'm sorry I haven't been up to see you more. The professor had me out in the field the last two weeks. Just got back in last night; even missed Alistair's first week of classes."

"I heard. Patricia filled me in. Up north, right? Looking for a potential goat man?"

"A goat man?" Hunter couldn't believe what he'd heard.

"Yeah, sightings of a half-man, half-goat creature on the outskirts of town," Ben explained.

"I'm guessing everything came up false?" asked Joe.

"Well… the fear up there is real. Residents claim that when it shows up, it brings death and bad omens. To be honest, I'm kind of glad I didn't run into it because I'm not sure what I would have done. One of the weirder cases I've been on based on the description of the cryptid alone."

"You remember that time the professor had us chasing that Mothman creature around?" Joe laughed.

"Gotta love what we do, right?" Ben chuckled loudly.

"Kids, why don't you run along and make friends. Leave the grown-ups alone to reminisce." Joe rolled his wheelchair up next to Ben's seat.

"Okay," Alistair said with a nod.

The kids quickly made their way over to one of the buffet tables.

"I'm sooo hungry." Hunter gabbed a large breakfast plate and started dishing up heaped piles of hash browns and smoked sausages.

"We have so much to catch up on." Liv sounded much more serious.

"What are you talking about?" Alistair asked with a mouthful of bacon, not even waiting to get to their seats to eat.

"We snuck out last night," Liv whispered.

"You *what*?" Alistair almost spit out his bacon.

"Shhh! Keep it down!" Liv scolded.

"You guys snuck out last night and didn't invite me?"

"We didn't do it together, but we ran into each other," Hunter replied, topping off his plate with a generous amount of maple syrup.

"Let's grab our food and go find a quiet place to eat; then we can fill you guys in," said Liv.

Hunter, Elly, Alistair, and Liv made their way towards the back of the foyer, where it was much quieter. Unfortunately, there stood Corbin and Lunette with wicked little grins on their faces. It appeared that the twins had spotted them first and were waiting for them to take a seat.

"Well, if it isn't the Jakobs and their bratty little friends. You know, I asked my dad about your parents being traitors, and he confirmed it. Your family deserved what they got!" Corbin laughed wickedly. There was hatred in his eyes—a deep and evil hatred.

"Leave us alone! You two are complete jerks!" His words stung Elly, and her eyes welled up in anger.

"We're getting really sick of you two!" Alistair dropped his plate loudly on the table, causing a scene around them.

"Go ahead and say that louder for everyone to hear!" Hunter's hands shook so much from the anger coursing through his blood that his pancakes fell off his plate and onto the floor.

"You're lucky all these adults are around," Lunette mocked.

"Seems to me like we're always lucky," Hunter shot back. "We're not going anywhere, are you?"

"Ahem!" Remy's voice broke the tension. He stepped between Hunter and Corbin with his large frame and giant smile, all the while holding two heaping plates of food. "You guys messin' with my friends, again?" Remy raised an eyebrow, almost as if he was mocking the twins.

"If you think I am afraid of a fat kid like you," Corbin leaned in and whispered into Remington's ear, "then you gotta be a hell of a lot dumber than all the kids say."

"Is that so?" Remy carefully put down his two plates of food making sure not to spill any of the delicious breakfast, and then cracked his knuckles loudly. "Now, I don't need to worry 'bout getting' expelled or losin' my spot in that fancy trainin' class. So, if I get my knuckles bloody over stickin' up fer my friends, so be it. If you want to get froggy fresh, then I think you should stop with all the trash talkin' and get jumpin'."

"Hmmph," Corbin snorted under his breath as he walked away in defeat.

"One of these days," Lunette snapped back at the group, "you'll get what's coming to you!"

"Sorry 'bout that, fellas," Remy said, turning back to the group with a friendly smile. "Those two don't seem to get it."

"I'm starting to think they're nothing but talk." Hunter sat down at the table. He stared at his food and suddenly realized he'd lost his appetite. *Idiot kids!* he thought to himself.

"Remy, you're our hero," Elly added, taking a seat next to him. "I'm so glad you found us with so many people around and all."

"It's no problem, little lady. My pops always taught me to stick up for my friends and family."

"That entire family is no good!" Liv shook her head in frustration. "I knew I should have told my dad about what we saw."

"Wait! What? What did you two see?" asked Alistair.

"That's what we wanted to tell you guys about," Liv said softly.

"Last night, I snuck out and ran into Liv down here in the foyer," Hunter added.

"Wait! Why did you guys sneak out anyway?" Alistair interrupted.

"Well, that's a little complicated," answered Hunter. Liv gave no further explanation.

"Okay, whatever! So, what's the big secret?" Elly asked, feeling more than a little impatient.

"Well, we were down here, and I found Hunter over by where the mounted heads were displayed. We heard some voices from outside."

"We ran to the window, and outside there were two men talking. One of them was sneaking the other inside and keeping him hidden in his room until sometime today," Hunter continued.

"Weird..." Alistair was deep in thought.

"Weirder than that, the one man called the other 'Gerald,' so we know it was Corbin and Lunette's good-for-nothing dad!" Liv blurted out.

"That entire family is up to no good," Hunter finished.

"Who in the heck would Mr. Krueger be sneaking into the estate and why?" Elly said before finishing off her glass of orange juice.

"They were talking bad about Professor Calenstine too!" said Liv.

"Why are we waiting? We need to tell an adult. Liv," Elly gave her a questionable look, "why didn't you tell your dad?"

"Elly," Hunter argued with a serious edge to his voice, "did you miss the part about us sneaking out? We can't get into trouble. This isn't like our old middle school; things are different now."

"But..." Elly tried to interject but not before Alistair silenced her.

"They're right; we can't go getting them into trouble. Even if Professor Calenstine goes light on their punishment, Liv's dad will ground her for life."

"Guys," Remy swallowed a mouthful of scrambled eggs, "let me take the heat on this one. I can tell one of your parents I was out sneaking around and saw those two men. It's okay, like I said, as I don't have nearly as much to worry about. I'm a construction worker's kid; no one cares about 'lil ole me."

"No," Elly said forcefully. "That's not fair to you. Every time we get into trouble, we can't expect you to get us out of it."

"Elly's right," Liv added. "Thanks, but no thanks."

"Then what do we do?" Alistair added. "Has anyone even seen Mr. Krueger around this breakfast feast yet?"

"We keep our eyes peeled," Hunter whispered. "We make rounds and meet up here every fifteen minutes. The moment one of you finds where Mr. Krueger is, we start following him."

"Not alone! We're going to search as groups," Elly clarified. "We meet back here and stick together once he's found."

"Deal," replied Hunter.

The group settled on the plan and spent the rest of the morning in hot pursuit of Mr. Krueger. Unfortunately for the group, their efforts were in vain. Even if Mr. Krueger had been present at the morning festival, the chances of the kids stumbling onto his presence was pretty slim. They gave up after a few hours and began to spend more time enjoying the Thanksgiving event. Once the breakfast portion of the festival subsided, the large buffet tables were taken away, and a live band set up at the heart of the foyer. The band was a sort of a "who's who" of the estate, with Jonathon Gates on the drums, Professor Hobbes on guitar, and, surprisingly to the children, Professor Pike showcasing her vocal talents as the lead singer.

As the afternoon grew into evening, the foyer was ever-changing. Caretakers and cooks worked effortlessly to move the dining and buffet tables out of the foyer and replace them with fun, carnival-like games and a slew of poker tables. The whole thing reminded Hunter of a mix between a carnival and a casino.

As much as Hunter didn't want to admit it, the Thanksgiving festival was turning out to be much more fun than he could have ever imagined. Even better, he got to spend every minute of it with his friends, and for the first time in a long time, he was having a genuinely good time.

Hunter and Alistair took turns trying to win stuffed animals for the girls but failed miserably at every attempt. Remy, on the other hand, seemed to have Lady Luck on his side, easily winning both Liv and Elly their pick of prizes. Of course, Remy had made the majority of his winnings at the "Test of Strength" machine, where he used a giant wooden hammer to hit a platform that measured his strength. Every chance he got to play, he'd max it out and set the bell off, signaling to the entire estate that he had won. Hunter and Alistair respectably couldn't get it past the half way mark.

"It ain't 'bout strength as much as it's 'bout finesse," Remy laughed, handing Elly the giant stuffed dragon he just won.

"Yeah, right," Hunter whispered to Alistair with a slight chuckle.

After his winnings, Remy parted ways with the group to meet back up with his father, who unlike the rest of the estate, chose to stay back at home and not celebrate.

"Why do you have to go back so soon?" asked Elly.

"Yeah, we haven't even gotten to the turkey yet!"

"My pops doesn't feel welcome here, I guess," Remy explained. "He stayed back at the living quarters making us our own Thanksgiving dinner. I felt sorta bad leavin' him earlier; I don't wanna miss having dinner with him, too."

"Oh," Elly responded. "Well then, we'll see you soon!"

It grew late in the evening as the caretakers began breaking down the games and card tables, getting ready to prep for the actual dinner fest. However, before the main course was served, the elevator doors suddenly opened and two men came out onto the balcony.

"Attention, my brothers and sisters of the Belmonte Estate!" Gerald Krueger yelled at the top of his lungs, halting everyone in their steps. "Before the main course and before our beloved Professor Calenstine joins with his annual Thanksgiving speech, I wanted to share with you what I am thankful for."

Immediately, everyone at the festival stopped what they were doing, and whispers spread across the large crowd. Hunter wasn't sure what was about to happen, but he knew nothing good was going to come of it.

"I am sure you are wondering who my hooded friend next to me is." Gerald smiled as he spoke. He could sense the fear and confusion in the crowd below him. "This man next to me is who I am thankful for this year. This man next to me was the first one to follow his dreams and not live beneath the shadow of our beloved professor.

Please, without further ado, allow me to introduce an old friend…"

The man pulled back his hood revealing a grotesque scar that ran down his face. It was Dominick Winters, Abraham's cousin and exiled Seeker, who had turned from the Belmonte Estate and gone into business for himself. He had created the Monsters and Fiend Protection Agency under the umbrella of Aten Corp as a financial backer.

"Good morning, friends and family!" He grinned bitterly as he spoke. "Oh, how excited you all will be to hear what I have to say."

Chapter 11
A Jealous Past

Twenty years before.
Belmonte Manor

"What's your problem? a young teenage boy yelled. His anger was evident by the large vein pulsating on his forehead. He stood up from a large table covered in thick and probably very "wordy" books. A few bystanders moseying around the library paused at the scene. A few gave the boy dirty looks, after all, libraries are meant to be places of peace and quiet.

The young man was accompanied by another, who was equally aggravated at the situation but was doing all he could to remain calm and stay seated at the table. This man was in his mid-twenties with broad shoulders and jet-black hair that was slicked back into a ponytail. Despite his ability to remain calm, he clenched his fists tightly underneath the table as he spoke. "You're not the Dominick I grew up with; I don't know who you are, but you're not him," The young Abram Winters replied, being as quiet as possible but making sure the anger in his tone was evident.

"Screw you, Abram!" Dominick was slenderer than his older cousin, and a few inches taller. He slammed his fist down on the desk with such force that the books and papers that sat atop of it jumped in place. Those few around them gasped at the sudden act of violence.

"You were the 'chosen' one; you're following in our family footsteps, and getting everything you wanted. You and that jackass Ben, you all got everything. I got nothing, and why? Because of my age. How is that fair?" Dominick's voice was growing uncontrollably louder. He didn't care where they were, and nobody was going to silence him, not anymore.

"You're being childish! It's the rules that the two eldest in the bloodline are chosen." Abram shook his head in disbelief. How could his younger cousin be so immature? "Now sit down, shut up, and stop making a scene before we get kicked out... or worse, get detention."

"No, you shut up for once!" In a fit of rage, Dominick picked up one of the thick books and tossed it violently against the wall. Now the random bystanders were fleeing from the scene. "Screw the rules! While you spend your mornings learning everything about the Enlightenment, I sit at home going to boring high school. You got all the praise and all the knowledge. I got a high school diploma!"

"What do you want from me?" Abram stood up from the table and got face to face with his cousin. Their noses almost touching, Abram stared him down, eye to eye.

"Isn't it obvious? I want to be a Seeker!" Dominick yelled back, unwavering from his larger cousin's intimidating presence.

"Attention!" The electronic voice of Plato echoed through the library halls. The floor beneath the two men vibrated with every step Plato took towards them.

"Great," Dominick said, dropping back into his chair in frustration.

"There is no hostile activity or practice of lurid language permitted within the vicinity of the library quarters." Plato looked down at the boys, his massive metal frame hovering over them. They felt as if the large automaton was judging them.

"Master Abram, it is very unlike you to be participating in such activities. Is everything okay?"

"-Yeah, I'm fine, Plato." Abram stared angrily at his younger cousin as he spoke. "I'm sorry we caused a scene."

"Yeah, Plato," Dominick interjected. "My hot-blooded cousin here is sorry he acted like an immature idiot in your library."

"Master Dominick, I am checking your user identification," Plato replied, calculating information within his processor. "The estate library has restricted limitations for all personnel, and you lack the proper clearance. You may use the library within the Friedrich Building of Higher Intelligence for your studies. If you wish to request clearance into the Belmonte Archive, you must have Professor Calenstine approve your user settings within the estate's mainframe directory."

"See!" Dominick threw up his arms in protest. "I don't even have 'permission' to study with you!" Dominick stood up and stormed out of the library, cursing under his breath.

"Dominick!" Abram yelled, trying to catch up. "Wait, we're not done here!"

Abram went to run after Dominick but felt a stern grip grab his arm forcefully. He turned and saw his other younger cousin, Benjamin Jensen, alongside his good friend Joe, both having witnessed the events. Ben stood there with a frown on his face, holding his cousin's arm and not quite sure what to say. Abram didn't realize how many people had been in the library to witness the argument. There behind the group stood a few dozen people staring awkwardly at them.

"Listen, cuz," Ben finally interjected. "We heard everything. This isn't your fault, and nothing you can say or do will make him feel better. Rules are rules. You were the oldest on that side of the family, as was I on my side."

"He's right," Joe added, a bit hesitant to speak and more than a little intimidated by the older Abram. Everyone knew Abram was the oldest in the Enlightenment group by more than a few years. A lot of the younger kids in the Enlightenment thought of Abram as an older brother who protected them and kept them out of trouble; everyone looked up to him. "This enlightenment thing isn't perfect. It happens once in a generation, and not everyone gets in. Just look at our age difference, I was twelve when we started, and you were seventeen. It's unfortunate, but..." Joe tried to explain.

"Listen," Abram said as he pulled his arm forcefully from Ben's grasp. "I appreciate your concerns, both of you. He's my family though. He's a Winters, not a Jenson—or a Jakobs for that matter. He deserves to be a Seeker; it runs in all of our blood." Abram shook his head in frustration.

Abram left Joe and Ben behind and quickly made his way over to the elevator. He rode it back up to the main foyer where he found Dominick in a heated exchange with the very young-looking Patricia Ellingbee.

"You're not listening to me!" Dominick yelled, his voice echoing off the foyer's tall walls. "I want to speak with him now!"

"Dominick, stop it!" Abram shouted down to them as he rushed down the spiral staircase to catch up.

"This is between Professor Calenstine and me so butt out, Abram."

"Dominick, under no circumstances, will demands and bullying get you anywhere, here at the estate," Patricia stated, her lips pursed tightly together. "I suggest you calm down and speak to me when you are ready to behave like an adult."

"Look," Dominick took a deep breath, his anger diminishing and quickly being replaced by tears of frustration. "This is important; I am sorry, but I feel like I'm going crazy."

"What do you think you're going to accomplish talking to the professor anyway?" Abram interjected.

"I just want my voice heard."

"What is this ruckus about anyway, and why are you so upset?" Patricia asked.

"He's upset because he's not in the Enlightenment. All of a sudden, he's making a big deal about everything."

"I'm being prevented from ever being a true Seeker. It's in my bloodline too," Dominick explained. "I'm sick of never being noticed."

"This generation's Enlightenment has less than one year to go. You're much too late anyway," Patricia explained. "Also, you know how the bloodline works."

"Enough with the bloodline crap!" Dominick caught himself before going too far into a rage. "I can wait until the next Enlightenment."

"Impossible, as it only occurs once every generation; you'll be far too old."

"I don't care as long as I know I have something to look forward to."

"Dominick," Patricia let out a deep sigh, "you and Abram follow me down to the Ocelot Room; I will see if the professor is available to see you."

Patricia led them back through the elevator, through the library, and into the hidden staircase that spiraled deep underground and into the state-of-the-art giant computer chamber known as the Ocelot Room.

Patricia took a seat at one of the many computer desks in the large over chamber. It was outfitted with giant computer screens for walls showing different aspects of the estate's conditions. There were a few technicians working inside of the room, all offering Patricia friendly smiles and some quizzical looks as to why she had brought students into this very secretive area of the estate.

"What is this place?" Abram was stunned at the level of technology before him.

"Pay us no mind; even if I were to explain it, it would confuse you even more." Patricia took a seat at her computer desk. On the smooth slick black desktop, she began typing, to both the boys' surprise, as the actual desk itself was a giant touchscreen keyboard. She entered her password and opened up a program on her desktop. Suddenly, the old but vibrant face of Professor Calenstine popped onto the window screen.

"Patricia, to what do I owe the pleasure?" Calenstine said through the computer. "Oh, I see you have some guests."

"Sorry to bother you, sir." Patricia did not return the smile.

"No worries," Calenstine replied. "You look troubled."

"I have the young Dominick Winters here, and he wishes to speak to you—privately."

"Dominick?" Calenstine repeated.

"Yes, sir. I believe it is important."

"Okay then," Calenstine said, nodding. "Please escort him down; I have some free time." Calenstine reached forward and clicked something outside of the screen. Suddenly, the signal was lost and the screen went black.

"Well, Abram, please remain here. I will escort your cousin down to see the professor."

Patricia led the way through the thick aisle between the computers and machines that made up the Ocelot Room. Dominick followed quickly behind her.

Abram sat in the bizarre large room, afraid to touch anything outside of Patricia's desk. His uneasiness wasn't settled in the least by the constant eyeing of the Ocelot workers, who whispered to each other about Abram's presence. There was no need for any of them to tell Abram that he wasn't welcome, as it was quite evident. Sitting amongst the sea of machines and computers, Abram couldn't help but feel that the room was actually alive, as if the Ocelot Room had some sort of sentient being hidden somewhere amongst the wires, mainframes, and databases.

An hour passed before Patricia and Dominick finally made their way back to the Ocelot Room. Sick and tired of Abram's wandering eyes, one of the workers had opened up a simple version of solitaire on Patricia's desktop to keep Abram's eyes from drifting too much. Abram pretended to play. He hated solitaire, but he wasn't keen on getting kicked out of the room before his cousin came back up.

"Abram," Patricia said, as she and Dominick walked up beside him. "If you and Dominick could please return to your quarters. Thank you."

"Yes, ma'am." Abram stood up quickly from her desk. It was evident by the sour look on Dominick's face that things hadn't gone well. "Thank you for your help today." Abram shook Patricia's hand. "C'mon, Dominick."

The two young men made their way out of the Ocelot Room and up the long winding staircase that opened up into the secret passage that led to the library.

"Didn't go very well?" asked Abram.

"No," Dominick replied bluntly.

"Well, what did he say? What did his office look like?" asked

Abram.

"He told me that I could work under you when you graduate the Enlightenment and are assigned your own team to help you."

"Well, that's great! I'd love to have you."

"No," Dominick replied simply. "I should have my own group. You're no better than me just because you're a few years older. It's not fair."

"Dominick..." Abram's mouth pursed with frustration, and he grabbed his younger cousin by the arm to halt his stride.

"Don't!" Dominick pulled away in anger. "Nothing you say will change the way I feel. I *will* be a Seeker, and I *will* have my own team. Screw you, Abram! Screw you and the Enlightenment!" Dominick stormed off up the stairs, leaving Abram behind.

Chapter 12
Dominick's Revenge

Gerald stood proudly next to the now unhooded figure that he had snuck into the estate early in the morning hours. There in front of the entire estate, and during one of the largest festivals of the year, he stood side by side with a man who had turned his back on the estate. This man was none other than Abram's younger cousin, founder of the Monsters and Fiend Protection Agency (MFPA), and the first member of the estate to join up with Aten Corp.

"That's Dominick!" Hunter was shocked. He and his friends knew Dominick all too well, as they had in fact saved Dominick from the Beast of Bladenboro only a few months before, but no one else knew that. Dominick weaved a much different tale, proclaiming that he and he alone had been able to capture the beast and save the children at the same time.

"I'd recognize the scar on his face anywhere," Elly said with an obvious tone of disdain towards the man.

"Good morning, friends and family!" Dominick grinned bitterly as he spoke. "Oh, how excited you all will be to hear what I have to say." He paused for a moment, taking in the gasps and whispers from the crowd below him.

"Dominick!" Abram yelled loudly from below. In a fit of rage, he knocked over the table he sat at, spilling the food and drink all over the place. "You had your chance to make amends with us; you are unwelcomed here! How dare you show your face!" Abram drew his pistol and aimed it at his younger cousin. This caused even more of a commotion, and the children screamed at the sight of the firearm.

"Abram!" Patricia yelled. "Put that away! There are children present!"

Abram's eyes burned in anger, but he quickly holstered his weapon.

"Just like my older cousin to let his anger get the best of him. You'll never change, will you?" Dominick mocked.

"What do you want?" Patricia yelled from below. "You've made your scene, so get on with it and leave us."

"You have some explaining to do, Gerald!" Abram cracked his knuckles, a bad habit in times of distress.

"Oh, do I now?" Gerald was now mocking Abram. "I believe that I will let Dominick do all the explaining for me."

"I come bearing no threats to my former brothers and sisters," Dominick explained. "I come with another offer in the name of Aten Corp—an offer Gerald was smart enough to take. An offer to leave these stagnate stone walls of the Belmonte Estate, where outdated traditions and superstition outweighs common sense. To join one of the largest and most innovated companies in the world, where you are free to do your research and where you are handsomely rewarded for your hard work. Where you will live a better and more meaningful life on the brink of the scientific discovery! Come with Gerald and I and join Aten Corp."

"This is why you were never to be a Seeker!" Abram yelled once again. "We are not about the material world. We are not about making the world a better place for us. We're about making the world a better place for everyone. You've never cared about anything other than yourself!"

"I am about making the world a better place for others *and* for myself. Is that so selfish? Is offering you all the same opportunity to pursue your scientific interests, and offering you a luxurious paycheck for your hard work, so evil?"

"Aten is evil!" Elly now yelled, sick of hearing Dominick bashing her new home.

"Brainwashing our young," Dominick said, laughing loudly. "If it wasn't for my MFPA, that young girl and her friends would be dead under your fearless leader's reign. Simply put, living here in the estate is not safe anymore. In less than one year, the estate has been broken into, and somehow your professor managed to lose a cryptid in your own home. Which by the way, I was able to capture singlehandedly when I saved those bratty kids. He called me in to clean up his mess; he didn't even bother to ask his precious Seekers. Instead, his foolish old bones got one of my best agents killed in action. Another death on your bloody hands!"

"That is unfair!" Abram was shaking with anger.

"Unfair?" Dominick's eyes went from cool and collected to wild anger, a deep-seated rage.

"The professor was hoping to win you back and to give you a second chance, Dominick, but instead you sold us out," Patricia replied.

"Shut up!" Dominick screamed.

"Dominick, calm down! We want to win people over," Gerald whispered.

"I've lost friends in these damned walls. I've even lost my family to these damn walls. Abram, tell them! Tell them you killed them, that you killed them both! Tell them the truth... That you're a murderer!"

"Stop, Dominick!" Abram's voice cracked, his eyes now watering up uncontrollably.

"Dad?" Liv looked over to her father.

Abram was built like a mountain, always so strong and brave, and she had never seen her father even let out a whimper, let alone shed a single tear.

"Murderer?" Liv repeated.

"Liv," Patricia grabbed her trembling hand, "your father is no murderer; those are words of a confused and angry man," she whispered.

"You let her die in my arms. You put the society before our own children! Before your own family! You've lost your wife, and you killed my little girl!"

"Excuse me?" The comforting voice of Professor Calenstine chimed throughout the entire estate's public announcement system.

"Everyone please remain calm. I would like to welcome our uninvited guest, Dominick Winters, to our wonderful Thanksgiving festivity. It is unfortunate that this seems to be a reoccurring theme in our estate."

"Professor?" Dominick shook his head in disbelief. "Won't even show yourself, hiding behind your fancy gadgetry?"

"You will have to excuse me, but precautionary measures are all it is. Perhaps this helps?" High on the wall opposite where Dominick stood, a computer image of Calenstine suddenly appeared. His old wrinkly face smiled brightly for the entire estate to see.

"Hiding behind your technology as always," Gerald cursed.

"Gerald," Calenstine said calmly, "I will take this act of defiance as your resignation from the Seekers?"

"I have found a new home with Aten," Gerald said, smiling brightly. "He's given my family a giant house, a luxurious paycheck, and he's giving me my freedom. Not to mention, Aten gave me an opportunity to pursue my interests in cryptozoology with no restrictions. Aten won't show favoritism towards other children and threaten to expel mine for telling the truth about traitors and turncoats!"

"The only traitor in this room is you!" Abram once again made his presence known, unable to control his anger.

"Slippery slopes often cause men like you to fall from uncomfortable heights," Calenstine mused as he took a long puff from his cob pipe, blowing a thick cloud of smoke out from his nostrils.

"What's that supposed to mean?" asked Gerald. "Is that a threat?"

"Dominick," the professor ignored Gerald, turning his attention back to Dominick, "you have stated your opinion and have said your piece. Now, I must ask you to leave. Go back to your new home and never return here. If you do, you will find my people not so friendly to your cause. It is only because of your history with us that I am offering this amount of respect. You have until tomorrow night for you and Gerald to be gone from our home. Don't forget, I already forbade you from returning once. There better not be a third time; I hope for your own well-being that you understand this."

"Sounds like empty threats to me," Dominick said with a smirk. "You have all heard what I have to say. Come with us to the wealthy Aten Corp or stay here with this old fool, living in fear for the next major screw-up that will put your lives at risk. What's next, a Sasquatch running loose in the kitchen or a banshee in Crooked Lake?"

"Enough, Dominick!" Calenstine's cool demeanor quickly soured. "This is the last time! Retreat back to Gerald's room, and tomorrow you can leave of your own accord, or keep rambling on and you will be forced out of our estate right this minute!"

"Even now, as I sit here and try to recruit his people from beneath him, your fearless leader allows me to stay the night?" Dominick smiled. "I shall retreat back to my quarters. Anyone who wishes to contact me about my proposed business plan, please feel free. I am sure we can work something out." Dominick simply nodded his head to the large mass of people below him and turned back towards the elevator with his new friend Gerald Krueger.

"Dominick," Calenstine cleared his throat a little as he spoke, "I will allow you a one-night stay because, despite how you have wronged us, you are still family, and we take care of our own. As for your recruitment efforts, any one of my people who even thinks of turning their backs on our estate is no longer welcome here as well. There is no room for even the smallest seedling of doubt."

"So quick to toss more people out of your lovely castle, huh?" Dominick half smiled.

"No, on the contrary." Calenstine returned a sly grin. "I highly doubt anyone will be contacting you. We are people of morals and respect; two things I fear you lost years ago to a blind, misguided hatred."

"Well," Dominick paused before entering the elevator doors, "We'll see about that...."

Dominick and Gerald entered the elevator and left the large sea of people murmuring and whispering below.

Hunter was at a loss for words. It all made sense now—Gerald sneaking in Dominick to disrupt the big festival. It wasn't the first time Dominick had tried to turn the estate against the professor, and he had succeeded with the Krueger family.

"My people," Calenstine's digital video feed was still 'live' high above the foyer floor, "please excuse my annual appearance this Thanksgiving. I am sure you understand that with the current situation, I have matters to attend to. Do your best to enjoy what's left of the festivities. I apologize for the inconvenience." Calenstine spoke with a much more somber tone now that Dominick had retreated and he could let his guard down. With those last few words, the signal was cut from the foyer and an eerie silence took over.

"I'm going to kill him!" Abram stormed off, making his way through the crowd of people.

"Abram, wait!" Patricia quickly followed.

"Wow! Uncle Abram's vein looked like it was about to explode." Alistair slumped into a nearby chair.

"Are you okay, Liv?" Elly took her friend's hand. Liv looked petrified; the streaks of dried tears were still evident on her now reddish cheeks.

"Did you hear what he said about my dad?" said Liv, still perplexed by the accusation.

"Yeah, but Ms. Ellingbee said it wasn't like that," Hunter added.

"But what did he mean?" Liv's eyes were red, and they burned when she blinked.

"Children," Joe wheeled his way through the thick gathering of people and over to the kids. "Are you all right?"

"Uncle Joe," Elly asked. "What's going on?"

"Nothing but a bunch of grown-up politics," Joe explained. "Forget about this, as it's not for kids to think about."

"Why did he say that about my dad?" Liv's expression hadn't changed. If Joe hadn't known any better, he would have thought she'd seen a ghost. "He called my dad a murderer...."

"It's lies! Your father is a great man," Joe said with a very serious voice. "Liv, you understand that, right?"

Liv hung her head low, avoiding eye contact and lost in her own thoughts.

"Liv," Joe held her head up with his warm, gentle hands, forcing her to look into his eyes. "Tell me you understand. Your dad is many things, a great Seeker, loving father, and a wonderful friend, but he is in no way a murderer. Dominick is misguided and lost in his own anger."

"Okay," Liv muttered.

"What are we supposed to do now?" Elly took a seat next to Alistair. Even if the kids couldn't comprehend the complexity of the situation, they knew it was serious. The air in the foyer had grown thick with tension. They felt the burden as much as everyone else.

"It's early, but I think we're going to call it a night. Too much of a frenzy has been caused to enjoy what's left of this now disastrous Thanksgiving. Sad, it started out promising."

"Kids!" Margot's voice echoed through the large sea of people. "Kids, are you guys all right?" She finally broke through the crowd and came running up to Hunter and Elly like a mother who had lost her children in a supermarket.

"Yeah, nothing happened except for a bunch of adults arguing," Hunter explained.

"Yes, dear." Sebastian had followed not too far behind her, although he didn't look worried about the children in the least. In fact, the smug look on his face implied he was more annoyed with Margot's reaction than anything else. "How could they be anything more than fine when nothing happened? Grown men had a verbal dispute; you are simply overreacting."

"Sebastian!" Margot gave him the vilest of looks. "Never tell me I am overreacting when it comes to these kids, not ever again!"

"Ridiculous," Sebastian said, shaking his head in disbelief. "We shall talk about this later." He turned from the group, cursing under his breath, and quickly vanished into the crowded foyer.

"I told you he was a jerk!" Hunter whispered to Elly, who looked as shocked as Margot over the rude comments.

"Margot, could you please help me out? I want to stay here and diffuse this situation, so could you take the kids to their rooms for the night?"

"Of course. Perhaps the four of them would like to have a slumber party with Trayer in Hunter and Elly's room?" Margot asked the group.

"Yeah, I don't wanna be stuck in my room alone for the rest of the night," replied Alistair.

"Liv, what about you," asked Margot.

"Sure..." Liv replied softly, "whatever."

Chapter 13
A New Lead

Margot led the four children to their rooms. Alistair and Liv packed up an overnight bag, including everything one would need for a successful slumber party. They made their way back into Hunter and Elly's room, where the large Cusith pup was eagerly awaiting his friends.

The moment Hunter and Elly opened the door, the mighty pup jumped up and onto Elly, licking her face in a rapid frenzy of excitement. The mighty dog's tail was wagging so fast and uncontrollably that its hind end was wobbling.

"Trayer, I missed you!" Elly giggled as she scratched the pup behind his large floppy ears. There wasn't much that Trayer's loving companionship couldn't mend in Elly's mind. On the nights when she missed her parents the most, she snuggled up to Trayer, and he made her feel safe. He was the best dog in the world.

"Children, make yourselves comfortable and try to have fun. We'll be up here sporadically to check on everyone. I know we ate a lot before the festival ended prematurely, but if you all get hungry again we can bring up some food. We did make a huge turkey dinner; we wouldn't want it to go to waste."

"Okay," the kids said in unison.

"Now, I know I don't have to say this, but please behave yourselves, children." Margot smiled kindly as she kissed Hunter and Elly on the forehead before exiting the room and leaving the kids to themselves.

"What a crazy day." Alistair dropped his overnight bag onto

Hunter's bed and began to rummage through it, looking for something.

"Well, at least we know who was sneaking in last night." Elly jumped up onto her comfy bed. Trayer quickly followed suit and curled up next to her, laying his large head in her lap.

"I can't believe Gerald is a traitor after those idiot twins, Lunette and Corbin, made such a fuss about your parents and the lies about them." Alistair shook his head in disbelief.

"Liv?" Elly looked over at her friend, who had taken a seat at their small dining table next to the large window overlooking the front courtyard of the estate.

"Yes?" she replied simply, never breaking her gaze from the window. Her mind was lost in the dark, grey clouds that stretched across the sky.

"Are you doing okay?"

"Yes," said Liv somberly. "I just…."

"Look," Hunter spoke up, surprising even himself, as he was normally a bit shy when it came to Liv, "you can't let what that jerk said get to you. I understand that it's hard, Elly does too. When we heard Corbin say our parents were traitors, it made us angry, sad… and a bunch of other things too."

"Hunter's right," Elly added. "People sometimes say things just to be mean."

"Thanks to you, Alistair, and Remy, we realized that. Most of the time, they're not even true, or maybe just bits and pieces of the truth."

"Yeah, I know…" Liv turned away from the window, wiping away a single tear.

"We knew our parents weren't traitors, and you know your dad is not a murderer," Hunter explained sympathetically.

"Yeah, that's crazy. Uncle Abram wouldn't hurt a fly. Unless it was a monster cryptid fly with, like, two heads or something," Alistair joked, trying to lighten the mood.

It worked and a small smile grew on Liv's face.

"The boys are right," Elly interjected. "You know your dad better than anyone. Dominick is crazy and we know he lies. He lied about what happened in the underground lake and lied about Hunter saving his life."

"Okay, you're right. I get it," Liv said, nodding. "I mean... I'm still confused, but you're right. It caught me off guard I guess, those words stung."

"Seems like there are a lot of secrets in this place," Hunter added. "I feel like every day something comes up and adds to all the confusion."

"Yeah, like Solomon's Seal," Alistair noted, finally finding what he was rummaging in his bag for and pulled out a large dusty book. "I was looking through my dad's collection and found this old thing. It's a book on ancient relics; there's an entire chapter on King Solomon and a ring."

"Really?" Hunter ran over to his friend with excitement. "What does it say?"

"It's a bit confusing. A lot of dates, talks about Israel, Judah, prophets... all sorts of stuff, and lots about religion."

"I wish you boys would stop with the Solomon's Seal thing," Elly protested.

"Forget her," Hunter said, annoyed. "So, what's it all mean?"

"Well," Alistair was running his finger across the browned page looking for certain passages, "it basically says that despite popular belief, there were actually two different King Solomons. One was this historical figure, and the other showed up centuries later as a magician and exorcist. It states in the book that this second figure is not spoken about in modern historical texts." Alistair continued to paraphrase, trying to soak in all the text. "It has some fringe theories on the second coming of the Solomon figure, maybe one of the first incidents of reincarnation! Hotly disputed, most reputable scientists and historians won't even humor the concept, as there is no scientific proof that reincarnation is a viable thing. Basically, it's saying that we know that after the first King Solomon died, he showed back up in ancient texts centuries later as the same person, but supposedly with magic powers."

"What's reincarnation?" Hunter asked.

"I wasn't sure either," Alistair smiled, "so I asked my dad. He said it was when someone dies and comes back to life in a different form or body. Like… if I die tomorrow, I could be reincarnated into a caterpillar or something."

"Well, it's understandable why our scientists think its rubbish," said Hunter. "Sounds like a fairy tale or something. Plus, I hope when I die, I don't come back as a bug!"

"Wait, what? There's two King Solomons?" Elly was starting to get intrigued, so she pulled up a chair with her Seekers Journal open, pen ready to jot down notes.

"It seems that way. I mean, there were centuries between the two, so it was maybe two different ones. Or he's like the professor and was a million years old, never died the first time and went into hiding maybe?" Alistair was musing aloud.

"Maybe, if he is like the professor, weirder things have happened," Liv added.

"Well…" Hunter was in deep thought, "to be honest, I'll believe anything. After what we've seen the last three months, who knows what's real or fake anymore?"

"So, it says that this second version of King Solomon was surrounded by mysticism." Alistair flipped the pages quickly. "Right, it says right here. 'Many mystical and magical items are said to be related to the powers of the late King Solomon, including the often-sought-after Solomon's Seal, a ring that is said to have granted the king the ability to not only speak to the animal kingdom but also to speak with and even control spirits and demons.' There's a bunch of others too, such as Solomon's crown, a bunch of ancient elixirs he brewed, and things like that."

"Right, we learned about the ring in class." Elly was now bored with the book.

"Yes, but look here." Alistair laid out the book and pointed to a section where someone had written something with blue ink.

"I can't make it out; what's it say?"

"It's my dad's handwriting," Alistair said proudly. "It says 'Found, real, too powerful, must hide.'"

"They *did* find it, and it's *real!*" Hunter's eyes grew wide with excitement. "I knew it!"

"Well, you will never find it," Elly said bluntly. "I'm sure the professor hid it far away."

"Anyway," Liv added, a bit uncomfortable with where the conversation was going, "your dad said it was too powerful. No one should be playing around with anything like that. If they hid it, then it should stay hidden."

Alistair began to listen to the girls reasoning. "I think the girls are right."

"Are you serious?" Hunter felt betrayed by his friend. "You're supposed to be on *my* side."

"Well…" Alistair seemed a bit worried, "I've heard some bad stories about messing with spirits and ghosts. I know the ring says it can be used to speak to the dead, but it also mentions demons. We want nothing to do with demons."

"Fine!" Hunter flipped the dusty book shut in anger. "I'll do it alone. It's a risk I'm willing to take. So, I *will* do it alone."

"I mean, you don't even know where to begin looking," Alistair said, feeling terrible about not helping his friend out.

"I'll figure it out," Hunter said hotly.

"Hunter," Elly shot back, "you can't get mad at us for not wanting to help you break the rules and get into trouble."

"Or worse, hurt yourself," Liv added.

"Fine, I said I'd do it alone. I'm not mad at anyone. Just leave me alone; I have to study for algebra." Hunter grabbed his book bag from the foot of his bed.

"Hunter? Doing homework on a holiday?" Elly joked. "We must've really gotten him angry."

***

A few hours passed before Margot made her way back up to the children's living quarters with a dining cart filled with all the Thanksgiving staples: roasted turkey, garlic mashed potatoes with creamy gravy, sausage stuffing, cranberries, mouth-watering green bean casserole, deviled eggs, and veggie and fruit platters. The children hadn't realized how hungry they had become until the moment Margot opened the door and pushed the large cart into the room. Immediately their stomachs began to rumble from the sweet aroma that filled their noses.

"Food!" Alistair yelled in excitement.

"Alistair, you just ate a giant breakfast." Elly laughed, a bit put off by his excitement.

"That was like six hours ago," he exclaimed, running over to the food cart, practically drooling. "I'm still a growing boy, right, Margot?"

Margot couldn't help but chuckle. "I'd wager you have some growing yet to do, so please, eat up."

"You don't have to tell me twice!" Alistair grabbed a plate and began dishing up food.

Margot looked over at Hunter, who sat by himself with a book in his lap. "Hunter, working so hard on homework that you're not going to eat?"

"I'm not hungry, thanks," he said, hoping to hide the bitterness in his voice.

"Well, I'll leave you a plate in case you change your mind later, if that's okay?"

"Sure," Hunter replied, not looking up from his book.

"He's angry with us," Elly said, scooping up a heaping pile of mashed potatoes.

"Shut up, Elly! That's not funny!" Hunter yelled, his face red with anger.

"Hunter, what are you mad about?" Margot asked.

"Nothing, honest..." Hunter answered.

"We got into a fight about our parents," Elly explained, feeling uncomfortable about mentioning her parents but not wanting to get Hunter in any more trouble.

"Oh, I see..." Margot frowned a bit. "It's important that the memory of your parents strengthens you. Whatever you fought about,

I'm sure your parents wouldn't want you two to fight because of them."

"Right," Hunter said, hoping to end the conversation as quickly as it started.

"Well, please enjoy the food. You have the extended weekend before classes pick back up, but don't forget to keep up on your studies. Your uncle has told me time and time again that school is hard enough, but the extra Enlightenment courses make it extremely hard."

"We'll make sure we're all caught up, promise," said Liv as she set her plate down on the table next to the window. "Margot, may I ask you a question privately?"

"Sure, let's head out to the hallway," Margot replied, opening the door for Liv.

Outside in the long hallway, which seemed to stretch as far as the eye could see in both directions, Liv nervously played with her hands.

"You seem distracted; what's on your mind? Is this about Hunter and Elly?"

"No, actually I wanted to know..." Liv found it hard to even verbalize the question, "about my dad, and what my uncle said."

"Oh." Margot let out a loud sigh.

"What's that mean?" Liv's hands were shaking.

"I haven't been here at the estate for that long, but I do know some things. It's best to ask your father though; I'm not sure it's my place."

"He called him a murderer." Liv again began to tear up.

"Okay, I can see you're hurt about this and confused I'm sure. But, honey," Margot held up Liv's chin and wiped away her tears, "you love your father, right? He is a brave man and loves you and this place. By no means is he a murderer."

"Then why..." Liv again paused before she could finish.

"Because there was an accident in which some people were hurt really badly and some died."

"What happened?" asked Liv.

"I don't know the details. No one is really willing to talk about it, but I think it's safe to say that your Uncle Dominick holds himself responsible. His fiancée at the time... well, I should stop there. It's not for me to say. But I promise you, your father loves Dominick, despite his anger. He blames himself even though we all know it was an accident."

"He never told me."

"Well, Liv," Margot opened the door once again, "you should eat before your food goes cold."

సౌ

While the group feasted on their amazing Thanksgiving dinner, Hunter chose to sit back and continue to study up on his algebra skills. He was more than frustrated with his little sister's lack of enthusiasm for getting a chance to speak with their parents one last time. Despite what everyone had told them, he had a lot of questions. Why did they hide their lives from him, why did the Kruegers think they were traitors, and more importantly, are they okay? The thought of his parents' souls living on somewhere made him happy, but he wasn't too sure if he believed in the concept.

A few hours passed, the smooth grey clouds faded into the dark night sky, only coming into view as they passed across the bright half-moon that lit up the night sky. Elly and Liv had both fallen asleep on Elly's bed with Trayer's large body stretched out in between them, taking up the vast majority of the bed. The sight was comical as it looked like one toss or slight turn by either of the girls could easily have them falling off onto the floor. Alistair sat at the foot of Hunter's bed wrapped up in a sleeping bag reading a couple of his favorite comic books while Hunter laid in his bed staring at the ceiling, lost in thought. After their dinner, it had been a fairly quiet evening. All of that was about to change, however. Suddenly, at a quarter past midnight, a small knock came from their bedroom door and a small white envelope was pushed under the doorframe and slid into the room.

"What was that?" Hunter shot up from bed, a bit startled.

"I dunno... it was a knock, but it's so late; who could it be?"

Alistair looked over and saw the envelope.

"Is that a letter?" Hunter jumped out of bed and picked it up.

"Look out the peephole," said Alistair, who had now joined Hunter at the door.

Hunter peered through the small hole, unable to see anything but the dimmed hallway and the wall beyond their door.

"No one out there," he answered.

"Let me look outside," Alistair unlocked the door and poked his head out into the hallway. There was no one, nothing but an eerie silence. "Empty."

"Let's open it up." Hunter ripped the envelope across the top with his finger. There was a small note within. He unfolded it and read it aloud.

Hunter and Elly,

It is important to know that the Belmonte Estate has very thin walls. News travels very fast. We have learned of your interest in finding Solomon's Seal. You may have already learned that it is indeed here within the very walls we call home. It is also very much real. Due to your interest in the ring, we are willing to provide you with the location, on one condition. You must promise that one of you will wear the ring and no one else. If you find the bravery in your heart, seek out Crooked Lake, where the ring lies under the lake's cross. Be careful on your journey, as the forest is forbidden for a reason. You will find a map on the back of this parchment. Use it wisely.

You're friends,
The Order of Shadows
P.S. No one must know of this letter.

"What on Earth?" Alistair looked dumbfounded as Hunter finished reading the letter.

"The Order of Shadows?" repeated Hunter as he flipped the letter over and began looking at the map drawn out on the back.

"They sound shady; I don't know if we should trust them," said Alistair.

"Are you kidding me?' Hunter shook his head. "They told us where the ring, Solomon's Seal, is hidden. See, they highlighted where the lake is. Looks like it's a few hours hike."

"You're not really thinking about going, are you?" Alistair said in disbelief because he couldn't believe Hunter was thinking of going out right this minute.

But Hunter was already tying up his hiking books and tossing some supplies into his book bag.

"What are you doing?" asked Alistair.

"What's it look like? I'm packing up some stuff and heading out into the woods to find the lake. If we leave now, we can be back before sunrise."

"Are you serious? The forest is dangerous." Alistair frowned.

"You already said you weren't going to help me. So, don't worry about it. I'm going alone. You need to keep it between us, okay? Don't wake up the girls and tell them."

"I can't do that," replied Alistair bluntly.

"Are you serious?" Hunter's frustration grew. "It's not like it's the first time I've snuck out into the forest. Remember the submerged lake and the Beast of Bladenboro? I have to do this."

"I meant I can't let you go alone," Alistair grabbed his sneakers and a flashlight from the desk. "Make sure you grab another light."

"Alistair…" Hunter stopped packing, "thank you."

"That's what friends are for, right?" Alistair slung his backpack over his shoulder and unbolted the bedroom door.

"I can't believe they took off the outside locks on our rooms," Alistair said, laughing. "With how often we've snuck out, you'd think they'd lock us up and throw away the key."

The two boys chuckled quietly, making sure not to wake the girls up or disturb Trayer from his deep sleep. They slowly closed the door and made their way down the long hallway towards the elevator. Neither one would admit it, but the fear of the dangerous forest was heavy on their minds.

Chapter 14
Crooked Lake

Hunter pushed the large, thick window open and held it for Alistair to crawl out. Alistair fell hard to the soft wet earth below, crushing some shrubs beneath him. He let out a faint cry as he hit the ground.

"You okay?" Hunter whispered.

"The drop is farther than it looks; luckily this thorn bush broke my fall," Alistair replied, picking small thorns out of his arms and legs. "C'mon, your turn!"

"Okay." Hunter used his shoulder to prop the heavy window frame open. He took a deep breath and dropped from the windowsill. It was about a six-foot drop, so he fell and hit the earth but used his momentum to roll forward.

"Nice moves," Alistair joked. "Where did you learn that tuck and roll? Was there a ninja Enlightenment class I missed out on?"

"Yeah, right," Hunter laughed. "Hope the noise didn't wake anyone up," said Hunter, turning on his flashlight.

"I think we're okay; the foyer isn't even patrolled at night." Alistair clicked his on as well.

"Hello? Who's there?" a familiar voice came from around the corner of the building.

"Who could that be? Quick! Off with the lights!" Alistair said, flicking his back off.

"Over here!" Hunter darted towards a large shrub, where he and Alistair hid as the footsteps grew closer.

"Hello?" asked a voice from around the corner. "Anyone out there?"

"Isn't that Mr. Burbank?" Hunter whispered.

Luther Burbank, the botanist the children had met earlier in the year in the botanical garden flashed his light near where the boys were hiding. He was wearing a long coat and winter hat to keep him warm in the cold fall climate. Over his shoulder hung a hunting rifle.

"We appear to be clear—over," Luther said into a small radio.

"Copy. Must've been an animal. Stay alert. We are to maintain a constant presence," replied a gruff voice over the radio.

"Too cold to be out here all night." Luther blew his warm breath onto his hands to keep them warm. He wandered back around the corner of the mansion.

"What are they patrolling for?" Alistair whispered.

"Probably because Dominick snuck in, and who knows what else he's been up to," answered Hunter.

"What's the map say?" Alistair turned his flashlight back on and lit up the letter for the boys to see.

"Looks like we need to go around the estate, then head north," replied Hunter.

"Nowhere near the submerged lake we found in the cave..."

"Nope. C'mon, let's get a move on. We'll walk close to the edge of the forest so we can duck into the trees in case we hear anyone coming."

Hunter and Alistair made their way out from the estate's buildings and walked near the edge of the dense forest. High above in the sky, the clouds had parted and the bright half-moon lit the sky amongst a backdrop of a million stars. It was going to be a long walk to find Crooked Lake, but at least the scenery was going to be beautiful. The estate grounds were large, and it took the boys over an hour just to walk around the grounds in their entirety. There, far beyond the estate's comforting walls, they found a small game trail that led them deep into the thick canopy of the forest, blocking out all the light the moon had given them.

"I hate this place," Alistair whined as he held back a low-hanging, thick branch, stopping it from smacking him in the face.

"We've got some ways to go still, so let's try and keep positive," replied Hunter. "We'll follow this trail for a while, and then we should hit a fork in the path, where we turn to the right."

The children continued on, fighting the thicket of plant life and forestry that scraped and cut them as they went deeper and deeper into the forest. It wasn't an easy hike into the dark and unknown world, but the thought of speaking to his parents one more time pushed Hunter forward. He would give anything for this chance, no matter how much his legs burned or the scrapes and cuts stung. He swallowed the pain and pushed onward.

"Weird," Alistair finally said, breaking the silence. "I haven't heard one animal noise, not even a hoot of an owl."

"The silence is pretty creepy," Hunter replied. He had been too lost in his own thoughts to notice until now.

"Need a break?" Alistair said between deep breaths.

"Sure, my shins are killing me," Hunter replied, not wanting to push his friend too hard. He took a seat next to Alistair on the damp log. He pulled a water bottle from his pack and guzzled down a few gulps before sharing with his friend.

"It's so cold... should've dressed warmer," Alistair stated, demonstrating with a visible puff of air.

"We're about halfway; not too much farther until the fork in the road," explained Hunter, laying out the map on his lap and studying it.

"So, I've been meaning to ask, did you and Liv sneak out together the other night?" asked Alistair after finishing up the last of the water bottle.

"Um... wait, what?" Hunter stumbled over his reply, a little shocked at the sudden question.

"When you guys saw Mr. Krueger sneaking in our uncle," explained Alistair.

"No, we ran into each other," said Hunter. "Honestly, I snuck out because I was having a hard time... you know... thinking about stuff too much. She was already down in the foyer when I got there."

"Really?" Alistair seemed surprised. "That's not like her; she's always such a goody two shoes. I thought maybe you guys snuck out… you know… because she flirts with you all the time."

"She does what?" Hunter seemed shocked at the notion, and a bit embarrassed as well. He hadn't ever noticed any sort of flirting. In fact, he was so nervous around her the majority of the time that he always felt foolish.

"Yeah, she's always talking about you, and she acts different around you," Alistair explained as he pulled a granola bar from his backpack, unwrapped it halfway, and took a bite. "Gross, almonds!" Alistair tossed the snack into the thick woods.

"So… you're telling me that she likes me? Like, 'likes' me?" Hunter swallowed hard. Somehow, even out in the middle of the forbidden forest, his nervousness over the beautiful Liv had overtaken him.

"Well, I dunno, but it seems that way to me at least." Alistair stood back up from the log and brushed off his butt, which was now damp and dirty from the log. "Let's go! We gotta get back before sun up."

"Um, yeah… right, okay let's go."

Hunter led the way, flashlight in hand and his head now wrapped around the concept of Liv having a crush on him. He was surprised how happy it made him feel inside, how the dull pain and sadness that normally lay dormant inside of him seemed to be swept away, at least momentarily. It didn't take long, though, for reality to set back in. It wouldn't matter if Liv liked him or not if he and Alistair never made it out of the forest alive to find out.

Despite the bitterness and chill of the night air, the boys were sweating beneath their clothes from the very intense hike through the foliage. After another hour or so, they finally came to the fork in the road. The game trail broke into two sections. A rickety old wooden sign had been nailed to a large oak tree that sat in the middle of the fork in the road. It pointed to the right with the words "Crooked Lake" written in white spray paint.

"We go right, correct?" asked Alistair, pointing to the sign.

"Yep," replied Hunter, triple-checking his map.

"Looks like there was another sign under it, see? Look. It's been broken in half though, it says 'Foot Alley' pointing to the left."

"Foot Alley?" Hunter laughed. "That doesn't sound like a fun place."

"Sounds like a smelly place; let's stick to the lake," Alistair said, snickering. Suddenly, a small pebble hit him in the right eye. "Ouch! What the heck was that?"

"What?" said Hunter, a few yards in front of him.

"Did you throw this rock at me?" Alistair picked up the small pebble and threw it, playfully, back at Hunter.

"Hey, watch it! I didn't throw a rock. Why would I...?" Suddenly, another rock came flying at them and hit the trees directly behind the boys as the ducked.

"Somebody followed us!" Hunter's heart began to race. If they were caught, they would surely be kicked out of the Enlightenment. Maybe even kicked out of the estate, which was the last thing Hunter wanted for him and his little sister.

"This isn't good," said Alistair.

Suddenly, a low and guttural howl came from a few yards in front of them, hidden within the thick forest.

"Oh my God. That sounded like an animal." Alistair felt sweat bead up on his brow.

"No, animals don't throw stones... right?" said Hunter.

Alistair bent over, picked up the rock, and tossed it gently towards the noise. Nothing. No noise or movement.

"Maybe it left?" Alistair hoped beyond all hope as visions of being mauled and eaten alive by some wicked monster ran through his head.

"Let's go and not wait around to find out."

"Yeah. The quicker we're out of the woods, the better." Alistair began walking much faster along the game trail.

They moved on, trying to ignore the ongoing sound of something large following them through the dense portion of the forest. Every once in a while, they heard a twig snap or the small huffing noise of something breathing. They did their best to swallow their fear because they were close now, less than an hour away from the lake Hunter thought. However, before they could get much farther, something strange happened.

"Oh God!" Hunter suddenly scrunched up his nose as a wicked and very potent smell struck his nostrils, and he almost lost his lunch.

"What on is that smell?" Alistair began to gag a bit. "It's overpowering!"

"Is it a skunk?" Hunter used his T-shirt to cover his nose, but the strong smell was too much, and it did little to help curb the stench.

"No way. Skunks are bad, but this is terrible. It's like rotten eggs mixed with death," Alistair was able to mutter before he fell to his knees and vomited from the smell.

"No, don't!" Hunter, having an already weak stomach from the vile aroma, joined his friend on the opposite side of the trail, tossing up his last meal into a bush. Suddenly, they heard a large and menacing growl in front of them.

"What was that?" Hunter looked up, wiping his mouth clean, and shined his flashlight onto a giant creature standing upright directly where they were heading. Its eyes glowed a bright red, and its large teeth were exposed as it snarled. The creature stood easily eight feet tall and was covered with red fur from head to foot. It let out a loud howl and began beating its chest with its mighty hands.

"Is… is… that Bigfoot?" Alistair wanted to curl into a ball and cry. He had never seen anything so frightening in his life with the exception of the Beast of Bladenboro. His legs trembled uncontrollably, and his hands shook.

The large creature stared down at the young boys, its mouth was watering, as if it couldn't wait to sink its teeth into a fresh meal. Suddenly, a large stone flew out from the foliage once again, but this time, instead of hitting the boys, the rock hit the menacing creature smack dab on the nose.

The thing snarled angrily, shaking off the attack. It stopped momentarily, turning its gaze from Hunter and Alistair and holding its chin up high into the air, sniffing. It made a menacing, low-pitched growl and, without warning, bounded quickly towards them.

"Run!" Hunter yelled.

Before the boys could make a run for it, another large creature broke from the foliage and tackled the large smelly ape hitting its side, preventing the children from being mauled.

"What happened?" Alistair shined his light on the two creatures, who were fighting viciously, gnawing and scratching each other with their long nails.

"It's another Bigfoot!" Hunter yelled, not believing what he was seeing. This one was a bit shorter than the first, with a stockier build as well. The colorations of the two beasts were completely different; the one who was tossing rocks had dark brown hair with grey streaks running through it.

"We need to get out of here and quick!" Hunter ran past the two beasts. "Don't look back!"

The two boys ran like they had never run before. They paid no mind to the twigs and branches scraping up their shins; the only thing on their minds was getting as far away from the two struggling beasts as possible.

They lost track of time, with no clue how far they had run, but suddenly Hunter and Alistair broke through the thick canopy of the forest and into a large clearing. From there, it opened up into a large and beautiful lake where the comforting light of the half-lit moon sparkled off its glass-like surface.

"We… made… it…" Hunter gasped, his lungs burning from a lack of oxygen. He fell to his knees where the grass from the woods began to give way to the sandy beach.

"This lake…" Alistair was attempting to catch his breath as well, "is… huge!"

Alistair was right; the boys couldn't even see the other side of it. It looked to them like it stretched for miles. It was a serene and beautiful sight for the children to behold.

"Quick, before those things catch up! We need to look for an 'X'," said Hunter, who was scoping out the long beach front with his flashlight.

"You know, I think that second Bigfoot was trying to save us," Alistair said, not venturing too far away from Hunter as they searched for the clue.

"Yeah, maybe," Hunter replied, still a bit shaken up from the attack. "Let's find this 'X' and get back; I don't want to run into those things again."

"Right," Alistair answered back. "I'm just saying it was tossing rocks at me earlier; it could've attacked before then, but it didn't! It only showed itself when we were in danger."

After about ten minutes of walking the shoreline of the large pristine lake, Hunter sat on a large rock, defeated and frustrated, and let out a loud sigh.

"This is stupid; maybe the letter was a lie," Hunter whined, kicking the sand beneath his feet in frustration.

"Well, I'm guessing it isn't going to be easy to find. I mean it *is* Solomon Seal after all," Alistair replied, not allowing himself to give up so easily. "Let me climb up this tree and see if I can get a better look."

Alistair wiped his hands on his jeans and grabbed a low-hanging branch. He hoisted himself up, using his legs to wrap around the thick branch and steady himself. Hunter was impressed with Alistair's ability to climb up the large tree with such ease. Alistair didn't look like a kid that had any athletic abilities, and although he'd prefer to be in front of a computer than out on a baseball field, he did love hiking and exploring the outdoors. He had always wanted to be like Jonathon Gates, going out on expeditions around the world and traversing bizarre and dangerous landscapes, and it was one of the things he and his father did a few times a year. They'd go camping in Yellowstone or some off-the-grid wilderness area. He loved it.

"Here's a good view," Alistair yelled down to his friend.

"What do you see?" Hunter called back.

"You're sitting on it!" Alistair laughed, looking down a few dozen feet at Hunter sitting on a large X-shaped rock.

"What?" Hunter got up, and sure enough, he was sitting on a giant 'X'. Unfortunately, the rock was huge; it was easily large enough for both the children to sit on, and they had no idea how deep the rock was submerged into the ground.

"Try lifting it!" Alistair began carefully coming down from the large oak tree.

"Yeah, right!" Hunter found two places on the rock for his fingers and tried with all his might to lift it, but it was impossible. "It must weigh a million pounds!"

"Let me help." Alistair jumped down from the lowest tree branch, and together the two boys used all of their strength to attempt to pull the large stone from the earth, but it didn't move an inch.

"Jeez!" Hunter's arms burned. "One problem after another."

"We gotta find a way to dig this thing up," said Alistair. Suddenly, a small pebble hit him in the back of the head. He stared at Hunter with eyes wide in terror. "Oh God, did something throw a rock at me?"

"Um... yes..." Hunter's heart raced again.

Suddenly, a slouching creature broke from the forest; its hulking frame bent over as it breathed heavily. The creature held its right arm as it moved into the moonlight. The boys quickly realized it was the second creature, it dark brown hair with streaks of grey covering its body, and its eyes glowed green in the darkness of the night. The kids could see the beast's face better now in the moonlight. It had a large, sloping forehead and a flat nose that was very humanlike. The creature didn't pounce or growl; instead, it slowly and very cautiously made its way closer to the children.

"W-what does it want?" Hunter asked nervously.

"I think its hurt." Alistair felt the fear leave him, and he took a cautious step forward, causing the creature to stop suddenly in mid-stride, almost ready to dart back into the forest. "Hey, it's okay," Alistair said softly.

The creature let out a small whine and tilted its head to the side as if it was trying to understand him.

"What are you doing? You're crazy!" Hunter whispered.

"I saw this once on *Myth Hunters* when they were trying to track down a Sasquatch," Alistair whispered back. He took a deep breath and let out small, low-pitched noise, sort of like a roaring noise with a welcoming tone. The creature stopped again, bobbed its head, and replied back with a similar guttural noise.

"I think he's nice." Alistair put his hand out, now only a few feet from the towering creature.

"This one doesn't smell," Hunter whispered back.

"Hi! I'm Alistair, and this is my friend Hunter." He kept his hand outstretched towards the animal. It slowly approached and sniffed Alistair's hand gently as if not wanting to scare him away either. Alistair could see the creature's arm was hurt from the earlier struggle; it looked like it was dislocated at its shoulder.

"Hunter, he's hurt," Alistair said, frowning. He noticed a wrapper in the hand of the creature's good arm. "There's something in his hand."

"What is it?" Hunter got up and slowly made his way up to the creature, not making any sudden movements.

"It's the granola bar wrapper I tossed into the woods earlier," Alistair chucked nervously. "He must have eaten the rest of it and followed us to see if we'd drop anything else."

"Are you kidding me? This thing likes granola bars?"

"Do you like?" Alistair pointed to the wrapper in the creature's hand.

The large animal let out a snort, tossing the wrapper towards the boys. Suddenly, it fell onto its butt, the weight from his body kicking up the sand around him. He sat with his good hand out as if waiting for something.

"Let me see." Alistair slipped his book bag from his shoulder and dug around until he found another granola bar with almonds. "Here you go." He unwrapped the bar and placed it in the creature's large hand. Alistair was amazed by the sheer size of the creature's palm, and he couldn't help but remember that the other creature was even bigger than this one.

The creature quickly devoured the granola bar with excitement. It stood up and made its way to the giant stone the boys were trying to unearth. The mighty creature tapped the rock with its good hand and made another grunting noise.

"What's it doing?" asked Hunter.

"I think it wants to help us," Alistair said, walking over to the creature once again. "See, I knew it. He saved us from the disgusting smelling one."

"Remind me to never come back out into these woods again," said Hunter.

"Can you help?" Alistair joined the creature by the stone and began trying to unearth the boulder. The creature gently pushed Alistair away. With its good hand and mighty strength, the creature let out a loud grunt as it lifted half the boulder up and out of the earth. Then the creature, holding up one-half of the boulder, slid its body underneath it, using its shoulders and good arm to completely lift the giant stone out of the earth.

"Holy crap!" Hunter gasped in awe at the creature's strength. "He lifted that giant rock with one arm!"

Then the creature tossed the large rock into the lake with ease, causing a large splash that sent water high into the air.

"You're amazing!" Alistair smiled as he dug out the last two granola bars from his bag and gave them to the creature. "Hey, Hunter, I think he smiled at me."

"I don't know what to say." Hunter said simply.

"I think we made a new friend. Could you imagine taking Trayer and this guy out for walks?"

"Umm, I don't think we can take this thing back with us; there is no way he can be a pet," Hunter replied.

"Yeah I know, but he's hurt. We can't leave him out here like this because that other one may attack him again."

"I dunno... maybe we can figure something out back at the estate," answered Hunter. "First let's find..."

"Found it!" Alistair blurted out, cutting Hunter off. He dug up a small metal case about the size of a jewelry box.

"Already? That was easy."

Hunter peered over his friend's shoulder and stared in awe at the intricate box. It sparkled in the moonlight, almost eerily. There were weird markings written all over it; the boys didn't recognize the language, but it must have been ancient, the box itself looked like something from biblical times.

"Look!" Hunter pointed to a part of the design of the box that looked as if it were an etching of a spirit coming out of a stick figure's hand. "It must be Solomon's Seal. You wear it, and you can speak to the dead."

"I dunno..." Alistair got chills looking at the creepy design.

"Let me see it." Hunter took the box from his friend and slowly opened it. There, nestled within the box, was a thin, dark, tarnished ring. "Should I put it on, here?" asked Hunter.

"No," Alistair said bluntly. "I understand you're excited, but let's wait in case something bad happens. Back home, we have hundreds of people to help if you get hurt. Out here, there's no one but me, and we're so far away from anything, I don't know what I could do if something bad happened."

"Okay, we'll wait until tomorrow." Hunter closed the clasp on the box and put it in his backpack.

"Can we head back now? It's been a long night," Alistair said with a hint of sarcasm.

"Yeah, it's a lot later then we thought."

"We gotta go now; it was nice meeting you." Alistair walked up to the creature with a smile. "I wish we could fix your arm."

"C'mon, we're losing time," said Hunter. "Thanks for the help." He felt weird talking to a giant ape-like creature, but Alistair was right, it was definitely a friendly animal.

The boys made their way back, and it was a long journey. They already felt the pain of exhaustion from their journey getting to the lake, and the return trip was even worse. However, to their surprise, their new friend followed them home, walking a few yards behind them, this time on the trail and not hiding in the thickness of the foliage. Alistair and Hunter welcomed their new friend's presence; they weren't nearly as frightened of the mysteries that the forest may hold with such a large companion to protect them.

It took over two full hours of non-stop hiking before the children made it back to the estate.

"Hunter, wait!" Alistair said before breaking through the last section of the thick forest and onto the estate's grounds.

"Okay, make it quick because the sun's about to come up."

"Listen," Alistair walked over to the animal, who was still holding its arm in pain, "I want you to come back here tomorrow night, and I will bring you more food, okay?" Alistair smiled and pointed to the ground. "Tomorrow, here," he said slowly. "When its nighttime." he pointed up to the moon. "Do you understand?"

The creature snorted playfully.

"That's our home." Alistair now pointed through a break in the tree line where the giant estate could be seen.

The animal cocked its head as if it was trying to understand Alistair. It snorted again, and with its good hand tapped Alistair on the shoulder. Then without warning, the creature darted off on the game trail, quickly disappearing into the forest once again.

"Do you think he'll come back tomorrow night?" Alistair asked with a frown.

"If he does, maybe we can get him some help to fix his arm," Hunter replied.

"Yeah, maybe."

"C'mon, we need to sneak back in."

Chapter 15
Demons

Hunter and Alistair had found it surprisingly difficult to sneak back into the estate than it was getting out. This was mainly due to the fact they hadn't gotten back nearly as early as they would have liked. The sun was already rising, and many of the estate's caretakers had already awoken and begun their daily routines. Luckily for the boys, they had gotten pretty good at sneaking around the mansion unseen and were able to get back up into Hunter and Elly's room without any further incident. They hadn't even disturbed the girls, who were sleeping peacefully in Elly's bed with Trayer snoring loudly between them.

"I can't believe we made it back without getting caught...or killed!" Alistair swung his backpack from his shoulder and onto the floor. He kicked his shoes off and immediately cozied up in his sleeping bag, letting out an exhausted yawn. "I'm going to sleep this entire day away; thank God for the holiday weekend."

"I can't believe we actually got the ring," Hunter whispered back. He too slipped into bed, feeling the weight of the day's activity. He held the metal box in his hand, staring at the intricate designs.

"Let's sleep on it before you go putting that ring on." Alistair's eyes grew heavy, and before he knew it, he was out-snoring Trayer.

Hunter, despite his body telling him he was exhausted and he needed sleep, couldn't even think of closing his eyes. There in his hands was the answer to all his questions. All he had to do was slip the ring onto his finger, and he'd get to see his parents again. He felt his eyes begin to water at the very thought of seeing his mother's beautiful face one more time and hearing his dad's voice saying he loved him. Hunter knew he couldn't wait. It was all or nothing; he hadn't risked his life out in the woods to wait a few days to see if it was all worth it.

Hunter slipped out of bed and pulled up a chair at the dining table near the bedroom window. The morning sun crept into the room, warming his hands as he played with the box nervously.

"Well, I hope this works," Hunter muttered to himself.

He flipped the metal container open, and there the tarnished ring sat, waiting to be placed upon his finger. Hunter carefully picked the ring up and let it lay in his palm. Upon closer inspection, he saw that the ring had the same ancient text etched into its band as on the box. Slowly, he slipped the ring onto his ring finger, expecting something to happen. Yet, there was nothing, no weird sense of power and no energy rushing through his body.

"It doesn't work," Hunter muttered in defeat. He felt his stomach sink as the dull pain of sadness took over. He stood up with his head hanging low and made his way back to his bed.

Suddenly, his ring finger exploded with pain. Hunter gasped, but the pain was so great that no sound could escape from his lips. He fell onto his knees with his left hand gripping his wrist and holding it high into the air. He looked on in horror as the ring burned the flesh beneath it. The sick smell of his own flesh burning hit his nose, and it took everything in his power not to pass out.

Hunter wanted to cry out for help. There, only a few feet away, his friends slept peacefully. If he could just muster the strength to scream... but he couldn't. He was completely at the will of the intense pain. Tears now flowed freely down his cheeks, and to his utter horror, something strange was happening. Hunter watched as the ring continued to burn his flesh, and as it did so, something started oozing out from the strange foreign words that were etched onto the ring itself. It wasn't a physical substance; rather, it was like a thick black cloud that seeped out slowly from the ring.

The pain was all Hunter could focus on. He didn't even realize that, now, hovering above his head was a giant mass of black smog.

The burning began to subside just enough for Hunter to pry the ring off his finger and toss it onto the floor. He fell down on his back from the pain. From there, he stared up at the smoke, which to his horror seemed to form into a human-like figure with a long slender body and a head with faint glowing red eyes that seemed to peer right into his soul.

Suddenly, the shadow creature shot out of the room and under the bedroom door, leaving behind a slight residue of black mist in its wake.

Hunter crawled over to the ring, which now lay dormant on the floor, and with his last ounce of energy, he slipped it back into his pocket before falling unconscious.

∽

Elly awoke with Trayer's enormous head resting peacefully on her lap. She glanced at the clock and saw it was nearly ten a.m. which was the latest she had slept in since moving to the estate. She peered over Trayer's hulking body to see Liv peacefully asleep and decided she wouldn't wake her friends. Instead, she would head over to the cafeteria by herself and catch a late breakfast. It was, after all, a holiday weekend, and she didn't want to be the rude one who woke up all her friends.

Elly slowly slipped out of bed, trying not to stir Trayer, and tiptoed over to her dresser, keeping her eyes on any sudden movement Trayer might make. She knew more than anyone else that if Trayer heard her trying to sneak out to breakfast, he would immediately jump out of bed and cause one heck of a ruckus. Trayer was always the most hyper in the early mornings; he would surely awaken the entire group. Step by step, she tiptoed carefully and thoughtfully. She heard the floorboard creak, but Trayer didn't move. She slowly continued forward, but suddenly, where the floor should have been was something large, warm, and soft. Since she couldn't see where she was stepping, she lost her footing and toppled over, falling on her butt, hard.

At the unexpected noise, Trayer's head shot up. He quickly jumped out of bed and ran over to Elly, his tail wagging a mile a minute and slamming into everything, making more than enough noise to wake up a large army.

What did I trip on? Elly wondered. She looked over to see her older brother sleeping awkwardly in the middle of their room with no blanket or pillows.

"What happened?" Alistair arose from his sleeping bag, rubbing his eyes so he could see better.

"Are you okay?" Liv jumped out of bed and ran over to Elly.

"What's with Hunter?" Alistair said, slipping on his glasses.

"I dunno. I tripped over him," replied Elly, a bit baffled herself.

"Hunter?" Elly nudged her brother. "Hunter, wake up!"

"Is he hurt?" Liv kneeled down and felt Hunter's head; he was burning up. "He's sick! We should get help."

"I'm going." Alistair quickly threw on his shoes and darted for the door.

"Let's get him a pillow and a blanket." Liv grabbed both off of Hunter's bed.

"Do you think he was sleepwalking?" asked Elly. She lifted her brother's head while Liv gently placed the pillow underneath him.

"I have no idea; I didn't hear anything last night," Liv answered.

"He's very pale and... gross! Sweaty too." Elly frowned.

"He's in here," Alistair's voice came from the hallway. He came back with Margot and Patricia, who ran directly over to Hunter.

"What happened?" Margot felt Hunter's forehead.

"We don't know," Liv answered.

"I woke up and tripped over him when I got up," replied Elly.

"Margot," Patricia grabbed Hunter from under his shoulders, "grab his feet and let's get him onto the bed."

"He's just sick, right? Flu or something?" asked Alistair, trying to stay out of the way. He took a seat at the table, and that's when he saw the open metal box. "He didn't..." he muttered aloud.

"What was that?" Margot asked as she placed the large pillow under Hunter's head.

"Err... nothing, I just... I've never seen someone so sick before." Alistair quickly grabbed the metal case that once housed the ring and slipped it into his pocket.

"We need Dr. Wong." Patricia grabbed her large orange purse and began rummaging through it. She pulled out her cell phone and quickly flipped it open. "Hello? Dr. Wong? We need you here...."

"Kids," Margot gathered up the children and escorted them out into the hallway. "Listen, Hunter is sick, and if he is contagious, we don't want you kids to stick around here. We don't want an entire school of children out with the flu, now do we?"

"Is he going to be okay?" asked Elly, growing a little more worried by the serious looks on the adults' faces.

"Of course! He's burning up with a fever, but we'll get him better. Everyone gets sick," Margot replied with a calming smile. "He's in good hands, so rest assured."

"What should we do?" asked Alistair.

"Go grab some breakfast in the cafeteria before they stop serving," answered Margot.

"Um... okay then..." said Elly, who wasn't all that keen on leaving her brother's side.

"We'll come down and get you once we figure out what's wrong." Margot hugged the kids before ushering them out of the room and closing the door behind her.

"I didn't even get to change." Elly frowned as she stood outside the main hallway in her pajamas.

"Alistair?" Liv gave her younger cousin a very cold stare.

"Uh... yeah? What?" Her tone immediately made him feel uncomfortable. "Why are you looking at me like that?"

"You muttered something, and then I saw you put something into your pocket." Liv pointed to the obvious bulge in Alistair's right pants pocket.

"That's nothing! C'mon, let's get down to breakfast before they stop serving. It's almost eleven."

"Alistair!" Elly yelled in anger. "That's my brother, and he's sick. What are you two guys hiding?"

"I can't tell you," Alistair said simply. "Hunter will hate me."

"You have to tell us," Liv demanded. "Are you that thick?"

"Shhhh!" Alistair nodded towards the opposite hallway where Dr. Wong was making her way towards them, her lab coat fluttering behind her.

"Children, good to see you all healthy," she said with a friendly smile. She stopped to speak with them before entering into the room.

"Good morning, Dr. Wong," Alistair replied.

"I hear Hunter is feeling a tad under the weather," said Dr. Wong as she took out a small notepad and a pen before jotting down some notes. "I got here as quick as I could. Luckily, I was making my way down to the foyer when I received the call. So, tell me what happened."

"We woke up and he was passed out on the floor," answered Elly. "I tripped over him."

"He was extremely hot, too," Liv added. "Margot said he has a fever."

"Does your brother have a history of sleepwalking?" Dr. Wong made no eye contact with the children, too busy jotting things down in her notepad.

"Not that I know of," Elly replied honestly.

"Elly, do you know if your brother has any allergies?" Dr. Wong asked.

"Nope, sorry."

"Okay." Dr. Wong finished scribbling in her notepad and said, "Thank you children, I won't take up any more of your time. Let's get your friend back up and running again, shall we?" Dr. Wong turned and entered the bedroom.

"Talk!" Elly barked at Alistair the moment the door closed behind the doctor.

"Okay... okay," replied Alistair. "Not here though. We need to find somewhere quiet to talk."

The group made their way up to the cafeteria and settled down at an open table, each with a plate of breakfast food. The girls had a few slices of fresh fruit and a glass of juice, while Alistair had a towering stack of buttermilk pancakes drowning in maple syrup.

"I'm starved." Alistair plopped a giant forkful of pancake in his mouth, syrup dribbling down his chin.

Elly gave her friend a disgusted look. "Don't inhale it," she said, passing him a napkin. "The point of eating is to get the food in your mouth."

"Why are you so hungry anyway?" asked Liv, who cut a small slice of cantaloupe and ate it gingerly. "You're acting like you ran a marathon last night."

"Err... well..." Alistair was caught off guard. "That's sorta what I wanted to talk to you about."

"What do you mean?" Elly dropped her fork on the table; she wasn't very good at hiding her anger. "What did you boys do this time? Is this why Hunter's sick?"

"I think so." Alistair took a large drink of milk to wash down his latest bite of pancakes.

"Okay, spill it!" Liv now joined Elly in protest.

"Well, okay. So, late last night after you fell asleep, a strange letter was slipped into the room. Hunter opened it, and it was from these people who called themselves the Order of Shadows. They basically told Hunter where the ring was located deep in the forest by Crooked Lake."

"Order of Shadows?" Liv frowned. "Never heard of them."

"Crooked Lake?" Elly shook her head. "That's like a two-hour hike from the estate! You guys didn't...."

"I tried to talk Hunter out of it, but he insisted, saying he was going to go alone." Alistair put down his fork, sensing the anger from the girls. "What? What was I supposed to do?"

"Wake us up for starters!" Liv scolded.

"Or go and tell an adult so they could've stopped him," added Elly.

"Yeah, right," Alistair snorted. "He's my best friend, and he would have hated me if I ratted on him. I did the next best thing; I went with him. You know, to make sure he was okay."

"So, why is he sick?" asked Liv.

"Well, we were out all night. It was cold… I dunno… must've just got to him."

"Wait, so what happened? Did you find it? Is that what you pocketed in the room?" asked Liv.

"This was out on the table so I snagged it before Margot saw it." Alistair pulled the metal box with the bizarre designs on it from his pants pocket.

"This is the ring?" Elly popped the box open, but it was empty. "Was it empty last night?"

"No," Alistair admitted. "He must have it on him. He said he was going to wait to put it on though, to make sure he was somewhere safe and protected to test it out."

"Knowing Hunter, he did it when everyone was asleep. He's such an idiot sometimes," Elly said as she snapped the metal case shut.

"That's a bit harsh, isn't it?" Alistair interjected, a little offended.

"No, it isn't!" Elly shot back. "What sort of fool just puts on a ring that's supposed to have some crazy, weird powers? That's probably why he's sick, because it probably didn't work. Maybe it was cursed or something." Elly shook her head.

"That's true," Liv added. "We need to tell someone."

"No!" Alistair was now the one getting angry. "We'll wait it out and see. If he's sick, then fine. For all we know, he just has a flu bug because we were out in the freezing cold all night, and he hasn't slept in forever."

"Fine," Elly said, pushing her plate towards the center of the table. "Tomorrow, if he isn't feeling better, I'm telling Margot right away."

"Deal." Alistair smiled. "I promise everything will be fine; I doubt he even tried it on. He probably just has it in his pocket or something."

"What a mess…" Liv stated with a shake of her head.

"Don't be so upset, and finish your breakfast." Alistair had now returned to enjoying his lukewarm, soggy pancakes.

"Liv," Elly ignored Alistair, "I was thinking last night, and I think I know who released the Beast of Bladenboro."

"Who?" Alistair asked, inserting himself back into the

conversation.

"It makes sense..." Elly paid no mind to Alistair, "...if it was Mr. Krueger."

"Mr. Kruger?" Liv's eyebrow rose in curiosity. "I didn't think about that, but after yesterday's fiasco, he seems to have a motive."

"I dunno... I don't think he's our guy." Alistair forked up his last bite of pancakes and swirled it around his plate, making sure he soaked up every last drop of the delicious maple syrup.

"Excuse me?" Elly seemed offended. "How do you figure that? He snuck Dominick in; he seems to hate us and the professor."

"Well, he has the motive," Alistair explained, "but I don't think he had the means to do it. This was an inside job and the person who did this knows a lot about computers, networking, and more importantly, about hacking. I don't think he's that computer smart."

"Maybe..." Liv pulled her hair back into a tight ponytail, something she did when she felt a bit frustrated. "Seems like there are a lot of questions, and we have no answers."

"Like, who are these Order of Shadows people? What do they want with Hunter?" asked Alistair.

"I want to read that letter," Elly added.

"Hunter still has it. Hey!" Alistair pointed towards Dr. Lannin, who was in line at the hot griddle section of the morning's buffet. "That's our Legendary Creatures professor!"

"Yeah, so?" said Liv, unimpressed with his sudden arrival. As much as she enjoyed being an all-A student, she didn't necessarily want to acquire extra credit points during a holiday weekend.

"C'mon, we need his help!" Alistair quickly got up from the table.

"With what?" Elly looked at Liv with an odd expression on her face.

"About the Bigfoot!" Alistair darted off towards the teacher without further explanation.

"Wait, did he just say Bigfoot?" Liv got up quickly and followed suit, grabbing Elly's hand to slow her down.

Alistair was a bit nervous approaching his professor outside of school hours, especially during breakfast. Dr. Lannin was scooping up some of the scrambled eggs and sausages to put on top of the three chocolate-chip pancakes on his plate. He carefully grabbed a ladle filled with extra thick maple syrup and poured it all over his plate.

"Dr. Lannin," the portly lunch lady said, smiling brightly. "How in heavens do you eat such terrible foods without gaining any weight?"

"Magical wonders of a high metabolism rate." Dr. Lannin returned the smile. He turned from the large buffet line and began making his way towards an empty table.

Alistair paused for a moment before proceeding. He needed to make sure he had thought up a feasible lie as to how he had found the Bigfoot. He knew if anyone could help him, it was Dr. Lannin.

"What are you talking about, Bigfoot?" Liv asked as her and Elly caught up with Alistair.

"Yeah, we ran into two of them last night. One of them got hurt protecting us from the other. I need to get him help," explained Alistair.

"You seriously ran into two different Bigfoots? Err... Bigfeets? Hmmm...." Elly faltered.

"Yes, like I said, one of them was friendly and got hurt saving us. So, I need to return the favor." Alistair was tired of explaining his predicament, so he made his move.

"Excuse me, Dr. Lannin?" Alistair approached.

"Umm, yes?" Dr. Lannin cleared his throat as if he were caught off guard, dabbing a large white napkin to his face. "Oh, Mr. Jenson, is it? Excuse me, I'm still learning my new students' names. I see you have Ms. Winters and Ms. Jakobs along with you as well."

"Yeah, well, they're sort of just following me around for some reason," Alistair joked.

"Well, sorry, but I have no extra credit at the moment." Dr. Lannin paused for a moment, taking a sip of his orange juice.

"No, actually I need your help," replied Alistair.

"Help?" Dr. Lannin repeated. "Well then, let's schedule something after next week's session; we can go over your notes. It's the holiday after all, and I would think you kids should enjoy it. It's never a good idea to let your schooling take over your life."

"Oh, trust us, Dr.," Liv hid her smile, "that is *not* a problem for Alistair."

"Cram it, Liv!" Alistair shot his cousin a dirty look.

"Well, whatever it is, I'm sure it can wait until next week." Dr. Lannin stood up and nodded politely to the group before grabbing his buffet tray and tossing it into the nearest trash receptacle without even finishing.

"Doctor, please wait. It's important…" Alistair begged.

"I am a busy man, Mr. Jenson…" The professor let out a semi-frustrated sigh, "but it seems important enough. You have two minutes before I need to be at the Demeter Station, so you better use them wisely."

"Bigfoot," Alistair blurted out.

"Bigfoot?" Dr. Lannin seemed confused.

"In class you said we had them living outside in the forest, right?"

"Well, yes, but no need to worry about them. They aren't able to harm anyone, at least not within the safety of the estate."

"One of them got hurt; he's got a broken arm or something."

"Why would you say such a thing?" Dr. Lannin looked a bit angry at what he considered to be a blatant lie.

"Because it's true," Alistair shot back quickly. "I didn't know who else to go to, but it needs help."

"How would you even know such a thing?" asked Dr. Lannin, still unimpressed with Alistair's story.

"Last night, I was out near the forest. I heard some noises in the nearby brush, so I tossed out a granola bar, and a giant ape-looking thing walking on two feet came out and ate it. Its arm was deformed looking, like it was broken."

"You must be mistaken, as none of the animals we've let roam free can come anywhere near the estate. They have microchips in them to keep them in certain areas."

"It's true. I swear it!" Alistair pleaded. "I promise you that it will be back tonight."

"Hmmm…." Dr. Lannin sighed, "I suppose you girls witnessed

this creature as well?"

"No," Elly replied. "But we believe Alistair because he wouldn't tell a lie, Doctor."

"It could really be hurt, and don't you think it's at least worth the time to check?" Liv added.

"Okay then," Dr. Lannin said with a smile. "Meet me by the statue of Monte, out back, at ten o'clock tonight. We'll check it out."

"Thank you, Dr. Lannin!" Alistair shook the man's hand excitedly.

"Don't be late!" Dr. Lannin nodded to the group and made his way out of the cafeteria.

"Thanks for backing me up, guys," said Alistair.

"Yeah, well… you owe us," Elly told him.

"Looky what we got here!" mocked a familiar voice from behind the kids.

Alistair recognized the voice immediately, and his stomach sank at the sound. Behind them stood the Krueger twins, who had just made their way into the cafeteria.

"Don't worry, they can't do anything in here, too many adults," whispered Elly.

"Where's that little traitor Hunter?" Lunette mocked in her brattiest of voices.

"Yeah," Corbin said as walked right up and got in Alistair's face. "Maybe he finally wised up and took a dive off the top of this cruddy old mansion. Save us all from ever looking at his traitor face again."

"Ha-ha!" Elly was now the one mocking the two older twins. "Real funny. How is it we're traitors when you and your parents are the ones going to work for Aten, anyway? You're betraying *us*."

"Yeah, and what are you still doing here anyway?" Liv replied.

"You're traitors because your parents were selling secrets to Aten. Not that we care about this place, but it's the principal. Aint that right, bro?" Lunette spit at Elly's feet.

"Our father said that old man Calenstine betrayed us." Corbin stared into Alistair's eyes, unflinching. "So, instead of sitting around here being mistreated, we'll go where we will be treated like royalty. Anyone who stays behind in this mess of a mansion is a fool."

"Yeah, you're all just lucky we'll be leaving this hellhole before we ever get a chance to beat the traitor out of your blood." Lunette cracked her knuckles.

"Excuse me, children?" Patricia Ellingbee's voice shot through the cafeteria, and suddenly, Corbin's and Lunette's faces changed.

"Looks like you two best be going." Alistair smiled back at Corbin's menacing glare

"Lunette? Corbin?" Patricia stepped between the two groups. "Shouldn't you kids be packing up? If I remember correctly, your family has chosen to leave us."

"Our ride doesn't arrive until noon," Corbin said bitterly.

"Well, I know that Professor Calenstine allotted your family the time to comfortably move out, but being up here and harassing my students was not a part of that option, so return to your rooms," Patricia said in a very serious tone.

"We'll meet again," said Corbin, grinning bitterly as he and his sister turned away.

"Children," Patricia pulled a few chairs out for them to take a seat, "it is for the best that their family leaves our beloved estate. They no longer share the same perspective of the world with us. Self-righteous, arrogant, and misguided is what they are. Luckily, you won't have to deal with their lies and being bullied by them anymore."

"I'm thankful for that because I really don't like them," replied Alistair.

"How's Hunter?" asked Liv.

"He is much better. Dr. Wong has him on some fluids and he woke up long enough to tell us he's feeling better."

"Can we see him?" asked Alistair.

"Maybe later tonight, he needs his rest."

"What was wrong with him?" asked Elly.

"We're not quite sure. Maybe the flu. Dr. Wong says he may need a few days of bed rest to get his strength up. He told us he hasn't slept much lately."

Liv glared at Alistair reprimanding him in silence.

"I want you kids to head up to Alistair's room. I gave Benjamin a fresh change of clothes for you, Elly. You kids can enjoy the rest of your Thanksgiving break. Hopefully, Dominick and Gerald will leave with no real commotion. We've had enough of that recently, haven't we?" Patricia winked.

With that said, Patricia left the children behind to sort through all that had happened. So many questions littered their heads, and they had come no closer to figuring out who let the Beast of Bladenboro out. Liv wanted to know what her Uncle Dominick meant by calling her father a murderer. Elly was determined to learn more about Professor Calenstine, and Hunter... well, Hunter was scared to death over whatever it was he had let loose in the estate.

Chapter 16
Bernie the Bigfoot

The rest of the afternoon went by with little excitement. Alistair, Liv, and Elly spent the day trying to brainstorm the many mysteries that haunted the group and unfortunately, there were many. While the other kids in the estate spent their day enjoying seconds from their amazing Thanksgiving meals or hanging out in the rec rooms, Alistair and the girls found themselves, once again, nose-deep in a myriad of large, thick books. Elly and Liv found it peaceful; they enjoyed spending their time learning about the wonders of the estate. Alistair was normally more into tinkering with a computer or getting into some sort of mischief with Hunter. Yet, there he was on his Thanksgiving break reading book after book about the legendary Bigfoot, and he was enjoying it!

"It's no wonder so many people don't believe in Bigfoot," Alistair muttered aloud to the girls.

"What's that?" asked Liv, who was too involved inscribing notes for Professor Hobbes' Spirits and Demonology class to pay attention to anything else.

"Bigfoot," Alistair answered. "I'm reading this book, 'Fact or Fiction: The Legend of Bigfoot,' and it follows a timeline of all the known Bigfoot sightings and photos around the world. They look so fake! There is maybe a dozen or so that look real."

"You're really into this Bigfoot thing, aren't you?" asked Elly, who took a moment's rest from reading. She rubbed her burning eyes before letting out a small yawn. No one ever said research wasn't a tiring job.

"Like I said, one of them saved our lives," Alistair answered.

"One of them also tried eating you," replied Liv, unimpressed.

It was about nine in the evening before Margot met up with the children to inform them that Hunter was finally awake and feeling much better. They quickly packed up their books and supplies and hurried back to his room, eager to find out more about what had happened.

"He was pretty sick there for a while," Margot said as she led the children through the many halls of the estate. "We finally broke his temperature a few hours ago. He should hopefully be ready and back on his feet in a few days. He just needs to get his strength back up. I think he'll even be ready for classes come Monday."

"I'm sure he's excited about that!" Liv said with a chuckle.

"Here we go." Margot opened Hunter and Elly's room. "You children can spend some time with him before lights out. However, Elly, we've made arrangements for you to sleepover with Liv at Mr. Winters' place tonight, so Hunter has some quiet time to sleep."

"Thanks, Margot." Elly gave her a big hug.

"You kids behave, okay? You can head back to your rooms when you're done." Margot closed the door.

"Hunter," Alistair wasted no time running over to his friend, "are you okay? What happened?"

Hunter forced a small smile. The minute Elly set eyes on her older brother she could tell he still wasn't feeling well. He was pale and extremely weak with large dark blue bags under his eyes. Trayer knew this as well, and the large pup hadn't left the side of his bed the entire time, not even to go for his daily walk with Margot. His bladder must have been near to bursting.

"Not sure what happened..." replied Hunter.

"We woke up and you were lying on the floor like you'd passed out," said Elly a bit forcefully. She suspected her brother was speaking in half-truths.

"What did you do?" Alistair pulled the metal box out of his pocket and flipped it open, showing Hunter that is was now empty.

"Right..." Hunter slowly reached into his own pocket and pulled out the ring to show the group.

"Hunter!" Elly began to use her scolding voice. "How stupid are you boys? Sneaking out to get that thing!"

"Save it," replied Hunter before continuing with his story. "I decided I couldn't wait until later to test it. So, after everyone fell asleep, I put the ring on. I didn't think it was working, but then all of a sudden, it burned so bad I couldn't even yell."

"It burned?" Alistair repeated.

"Look at my finger." Hunter showed the group the extremely swollen and burned finger.

"Hunter, that looks really bad," replied Liv. "Did you show Margot and Ms. Ellingbee?"

"No way!" Hunter shot back quickly. "They would have asked too many questions."

"So, what happened next?" Alistair interrupted.

"Well, all of a sudden, this black cloud came oozing out of the ring, and it formed above my head. Once the cloud had finished oozing out, the pain stopped, and I was able to get the blasted thing off my finger."

"A black cloud?" asked Liv.

"Yeah, and it was alive; it had red eyes. It shot out of the room, under the door. It didn't look friendly, either."

"That sounds really bad." Liv quickly unzipped her backpack and grabbed her notes from earlier; she frantically turned to a page. "I just read about something similar while I was studying for our Spirits and Demonology class. Some demons and spectral forces can be contained or 'trapped' into everyday items, by one who is an adept in the arts of alchemy."

"Are you saying Hunter let a demon out into the mansion?" Alistair's mouth dropped open.

"I dunno... maybe..." replied Liv, who was still frantically thumbing through her notes.

"Wait, what's alchemy?" Elly wasn't as quick to believe in this whole demon talk thing.

"Well, I didn't get that far, but they used King Solomon as an example of a master alchemist," Liv explained.

"Listen, I'm sure there's some other explanation. Ghosts, demons, spooks, whatever you want to call them, are not real." Elly shook her head in disbelief.

"Right," said Alistair. "Just like the Bigfoot out in the forest is just a fairy tale or the Beast of Bladenboro was just an imaginary creature! We already know that the point of the Seekers is to study the unknown. Ghosts seem a perfect fit, right?"

"He makes a good point, Elly," said Liv.

"I'll believe it when I see it, until then..." Elly shrugged her shoulders.

"Look at the time!" Alistair pushed up his sleeve to check his watch; it was a quarter to ten. "We got to go!"

"What?" asked Hunter, who didn't want to be left alone so soon. "Where are you guys going?"

"I got Dr. Lannin to come out with me tonight to see if that Bigfoot comes back to meet me," answered Alistair. "I'm hoping he can help fix its bad arm."

"You really think that thing understood you when you asked him to meet you back there?" asked Hunter.

"I do! I really think it understood me."

"Well, okay then. Good luck," said Hunter, who said his goodbyes to his friends as they all exited the room, leaving him once alone once again.

Hunter took his wallet out of his back pocket, opened it, and pulled from its tri-fold the folded up picture of his parents that Margot had given him when he first arrived at the estate. It was the picture where Hunter was sitting between his parents, holding his little sister for the first time. Whenever Hunter felt alone, this was his saving grace. It made him remember the good days, the normal days, the days before monsters seemed to lurk around every corner, before magical rings almost burned his finger off, and before he and Elly were orphans.

It reminded him what it was like to have a real family.

❧

The group had bundled up for the late-night walk to the back of the estate where the towering statue of Professor Calenstine's dog, Monte, stood towering high into the night sky. There, awaiting the young group, was Dr. Lannin carrying a large leather briefcase with him. He too was dressed for the occasion, with a thick goose-down winter jacket and a scarf to cover his neck.

"Children, proper timing as expected," the Dr. Lannin waved them over towards the statue, which he was leaning against.

"Hello, Dr. Lannin," said Elly with a smile.

"So, if I understand correctly, Alistair, you're the only one to have met this supposed Bigfoot, correct?"

"Yes, sir, just me," answered Alistair.

"And where was this exactly?" asked the doctor calmly.

"Right over there, near the tree line."

"And why were you out so late at night playing around the treacherous forbidden forest?"

"Err…" Alistair hadn't thought the lie out that well, so he got bit tongue-tied. He looked over at the girls to help him out.

"I suppose that doesn't matter," Dr. Lannin answered his own question. "I will say that even close to the estate, these woods are not meant for children. I would advise you to stay away from them."

"Yes, sir." Alistair nodded.

"Now this creature had an injured arm?" asked the Dr. Lannin. "What did it look like? Do you recall anything noteworthy?"

"Yes, it was huge. It had sort of a flat face, big nose…" Alistair was trying to remember every detail.

"What color?" the doctor interrupted.

"It had dark brown fur with shades of grey running through it; it looked sort of old."

"Hmmm…." Dr. Lannin stroked his chin, pondering something. "Okay then, I would like you to approach the forest and see if you can draw it out once again. We'll remain a few dozen yards behind you so as not to startle the creature. If there is any trouble, I will be right there."

"Okay," said Alistair, tightening up his jacket. He pulled another granola bar from his pocket. "He loves these things," he said, smiling.

Alistair slowly made his way towards the forest with the group following behind, but not too close. Once Alistair got fairly close to where the large lawn met with the thicket of the forest, Dr. Lannin held out his arm for the girls to stay back.

Alistair made his way towards the forest, whistling and calling out for the Bigfoot.

"C'mere, boy!" he whispered as loud as he could.

"Dr. Lannin, do you honestly think there's actually a Bigfoot out there wanting to eat Alistair's granola bar?" Elly asked, hiding a snicker as she watched Alistair calling out for his furry friend.

"Well, I'll be damned." Dr. Lannin unlocked his leather briefcase and pulled out a pair of funny-looking binoculars. "You kids smell that?"

"No, I don't smell anything," answered Liv, a bit confused.

"There are many different types of Bigfoots in the world: sasquatch, abominable snowmen, and Skunk Apes..." Dr. Lannin was playing with some features of the binoculars. "And each one has a unique smell; the Northern American Bigfoot smells like fresh cucumbers. Do you smell it now?"

"Yeah, I do," answered Elly.

"There, look!" Dr. Lannin handed the binoculars to the children, which turned out, to Elly's surprise, to be night-vision goggles. "Do you see it in the brush? Its eyes illuminate perfectly with the night vision."

"Holy crap!" Elly's mouth dropped open.

"Can I see?" asked Liv.

There in the awkward green vision from the goggles, Liv saw a massive ape-like creature sitting in the brush, holding its arm awkwardly. She watched as Alistair turned his head towards the creature and opened the wrapper of the granola bar. Liv could hear Alistair talking to the creature, who slowly made its way nearer to her cousin.

"Look, he's completely out of the brush now," Dr. Lannin whispered. "Brave chap, as I've never seen a Bigfoot react towards a human like this."

"He *is* hurt," Liv said with a frown.

"Yes, he is." Dr. Lannin opened up his briefcase again and began assembling a rifle with a large scope.

"No, what are you going to do?" asked Elly.

"It won't live with that injury. It will suffer unless we do something," Dr. Lannin replied calmly.

"You're going to kill it?" Liv's eyes widened with horror.

"Heavens, no!" Dr. Lannin looked dumbstruck by the accusation. "I can't walk up to a Bigfoot and expect it to let me operate on its arm, now can I?"

"Oh, I suppose not," Liv corrected herself.

"This will put it to sleep just long enough for me to at least check it out. See if there's something I can do for it now."

Dr. Lannin took a deep breath and held it in. Through the scope, he watched as Alistair sat next to the towering creature as it ate the granola bar. He was amazed and at a loss for words at the sight. Dr. Lannin had studied these creatures at the estate for years, but he had never seen any of the Bigfoot family react like this with any human. In fact, it was quite the opposite. They were evasive, nocturnal creatures even with the dozen or so that were known to live in these woods, therefore, finding one was near impossible. This is why they had been able to escape any sort of recognition as a real animal in modern science. He lined up the shot perfectly and aimed at the creature's neck…

⌘

"I knew you'd show up, buddy." Alistair couldn't hide the smile on his face if he wanted to. The creature was enormous next to him, but it looked very friendly. Abruptly, Alistair heard a gunshot from where the girls and Dr. Lannin were. The dart whizzed just above his head and struck the creature directly in the neck. Immediately, the creature fell over onto its side, snoring loudly.

"What happened?" Alistair screamed in anger.

"Calm down," Dr. Lannin said, swinging the rifle across his shoulder. He relocked his case and made his way towards them with the girls by his side.

"Did you kill him?" Alistair's eyes began to well up with tears.

"The thing is snoring louder than a lazy elephant; of course, I didn't kill him." Dr. Lannin chuckled as he knelt down by the creature's enormous head.

"What happened then?" Alistair asked, trying to compose himself.

"Just gave old Bernie here a nice nap while I check him out." Dr. Lannin held open the creature's eyelids and flashed a light into its enormous brown eyes. "He'll be asleep for a while."

"'Bernie'?" Liv asked.

"Yes, this here is Bernie. We captured him in Canada about ten years ago and brought him here to live in the forest away from those crazy Bigfoot hunters. You can thank your Uncle Alistair. Mr. Winters' group brought him back."

"Really?" Alistair was a bit shocked.

"Now, see this?" Dr. Lannin was looking at the injured arm. "Looks like his shoulder got popped out of socket! That's an easy fix; we just have to pop it back in."

"That thing's arm probably weights more than me; how are we going to 'pop' it back into place?" Elly looked a bit alarmed.

"I'm more worried about this here." Dr. Lannin turned the creature over onto its side, revealing that a large gash had been taken out of its arm. "Looks like he got into a skirmish with something big."

"Like another Bigfoot?" Alistair hinted.

"Maybe a Skunk Ape or Sasquatch; they tend to be territorial," replied Dr. Lannin.

"Skunk Ape? What's that?" asked Alistair, who already knew by the name that this was probably what he and Hunter had smelled just before Bernie had saved them.

"It's a much larger breed than this guy here. Skunk Ape's smell terrible, like rotten eggs and rotten flesh mixed together. They're very violent carnivores and scavengers; they'll eat and attack anything that's meat. Bernie here is more of a vegetarian. Bigfoot will eat some meat, but mostly nuts and fruits. They tend to fish a lot in streams and lakes too."

"So, maybe a Skunk Ape attacked it," Alistair suggested.

"Maybe, but the chances of them crossing paths would be very rare. Skunk Apes like a swampy area to call home. Bernie here can live in hot or cold climates, but he doesn't favor the wetlands."

"How could a Skunk Ape live around here when it's almost winter, and there's nothing like a swamp out there right now," asked Elly.

"I told you, kids, that these woods have a touch of magic to them." Dr. Lannin unzipped his backpack and took out numerous first-aid supplies. "To be honest, it has more to do with science than magic. We have certain control over parts of the forest, just like we maintain control of the atmosphere in the Demeter Station for the plants. Deep in the woods is an open bio dome with a swamp-like atmosphere. We can regulate the warmth of the climate and the waters of the swamp from inside the Ocelot Room all year. This is where the Skunk Ape will spend the majority of its time."

"Wow, this place is just crazy!" Liv shook her head in disbelief.

"We can fix him up," Dr. Lannin said as he took out some cotton swabs and soaked them in disinfectant. He then began cleaning out his wound. "This is what I was worried about...."

"What's that?" asked Alistair.

"You'll have to forgive me, Alistair, for not believing you when you said you found a Bigfoot this close to the estate. You see, the creatures we capture and let loose in the woods are all monitored through microchips. That's not to say every animal is, as I said, because these woods are magical, and we haven't cataloged every creature that calls these woods home. But as it goes for the Squatchy creatures, we were pretty sure we'd tagged them all. This one got his microchip damaged in the struggle."

"How does the microchip prevent them from coming near the estate?" asked Liv, who was still awed by the size of the beast.

"Simple enough. It sends nonlethal electrical shocks if they veer too close to the perimeter. They aren't permitted to come any closer than a mile from the estate. This method has worked for years." Dr. Lannin wrapped up the freshly cleaned wound. "I can't fix his microchip at the moment, but his wound will heal now. Now, for this arm."

"How are we going to fix that?"

"Well..." Dr. Lannin once again stroked his chin as he thought. "We need him lying flat first; let's all push him onto his back."

The group used all their strength to turn the giant hairy animal onto its back. Elly and Liv were both a bit worried about the creature waking up and attacking them in a pain induced rage, but Dr. Lannin assured them that Bernie would be asleep for hours. The creature never stirred; in fact, the moment Bernie was turned onto his back, he began snoring loudly.

"Setting a dislocated shoulder is not that tough to do," explained Dr. Lannin. "Help me bend his elbow inwards towards his chest at a ninety-degree angle. Yes... perfect, okay now..." Dr. Lannin carefully held onto Bernie's arm. "Now we have to slowly, but steadily rotate his arm and shoulder outward. Yes! Just like that. Alistair, you make a fist here at his arm, and I want you to hold him by the wrist and push his arm towards his body. Good, that's very good. Just a little farther..."

Suddenly, Alistair and the girls felt Bernie's shoulder pop back into place. The beast let out a small murmur in his sleep.

"Wonderful, children!" Dr. Lannin smiled and brushed off his hands.

"That was it?" Alistair asked, feeling a sense of accomplishment.

"That's it! He'll be in some pain when he wakes up, but he won't remember a thing. It's best we leave him here. I'll return tomorrow to see if he shows back up again so we can re-chip him."

"Can I come too?" asked Alistair.

"I suppose so; it's a very simple procedure. We may not need to put him under if you can keep him preoccupied. It's just a small shot into his forearm."

"Are you sure about that, Alistair? Dr. Lannin, is it safe?" asked Liv.

"Well, yes. It appears Bernie here enjoys Alistair's company. Plus, I'd like to study this behavior; never in the history of cryptozoology have I heard of a Bigfoot befriending a human—let alone a child."

With Bernie bandaged up and his shoulder relocated, Dr. Lannin returned the children to the estate for the night.

Chapter 17
Sleepover

Elly met up with Mr. Winters and Liv back at their quarters. Hunter was given the room to himself to rest after his incident with the "unexplained" illness. Alistair returned to his living quarters with his father, Benjamin. Elly was excited for a girls' night; she used to have sleepovers with her friends from dance class back at home. Her mom would rent a couple of movies, bake fresh cookies, and Elly would stay up late with her friends watching their favorite musicals. Those were some of Elly's favorite memories. It was those memories that made Elly face the reality of her parents' deaths, so she chose to forget them. She didn't like thinking about or remembering anything about her old life. When her parents died and she was moved to the estate, she knew those days were over. It was nice to think she could have a normal night with a friend, even if they would probably spend the entire night talking about monsters and ghosts.

"Are you girls going to be okay, out here in the living room, for the night? Will the sleeping bags be enough to keep you warm?" Mr. Winters asked. He had just come out of the kitchen with a fresh bowl of popcorn and a couple of glasses of freshly squeezed orange juice.

"Yes, we're fine, Dad. Thanks," Liv said with a bit of a hostile tone.

"Liv, dear, is something wrong? You've been acting weird since yesterday."

"I'm fine! I just want to hang out with Elly."

"Okay, well…" Mr. Winters frowned. He loved his daughter more than the world itself, and it wasn't like her to act so distant. "Your Uncle Benjamin and I have some work to do, so I'll be out until later."

"Okay," Liv replied.

"Just pick up the phone and page Ms. Ellingbee or call Margot's room with any concerns."

"Thanks, Mr. Winters." Elly smiled at him, trying to break off the uncomfortable situation.

Abram smiled back and closed and locked the door, leaving the young girls alone.

"What was that all about?" asked Elly.

"Ever since Uncle Dominick said what he did... I dunno, but it's hard to look my dad in the eyes without knowing what he meant."

"Why don't you just ask him?"

"Ask my dad if he murdered someone?" Liv frowned, almost insulted by the advice.

"Well, if you don't ask, how will you ever know?"

"Let's just change the subject; we need to figure out what Hunter let loose."

೧

"You look upset," Benjamin Jenson noted his friend's long face. Benjamin had known Abram Winters for a very long time, and he wasn't a man who showcased his emotions.

"Ever since Dominick snuck in and gave his little speech, my daughter looks at me differently."

"He said some harsh words," Benjamin added. "You don't think she believes his lies, do you? We know the truth, Abram."

"She doesn't... At least I don't *think* she does. I never told her about the accident. It's something I would much rather forget."

"Abram, it wasn't your fault. Dominick should have listened; if anyone is to blame, it's him."

"That's enough," Abram cut his friend off.

"Listen..." Benjamin grabbed Abram's arm, "we all knew the risks when we took the oath. The ones we recruited onto our teams knew the risks involved."

"Shhh!" Abram turned quickly, peering down the dimly lit hall.

"What's wrong?" asked Benjamin.

"The air just got thick." Abram slowly peered around the hall, but nothing seemed out of the ordinary.

"Yeah, I feel it too. It's getting cold," Benjamin noted, seeing his breath as he spoke.

"This isn't good... this should not be happening here." Abram frowned. Suddenly, a loud bang came from behind them, startling the two men.

"What the hell?" Benjamin jumped.

"Does your team do a lot of paranormal investigations in the spiritual field?" Abram whispered.

"A few, not many." Benjamin began to sweat. "I recognize the symptoms though."

"Yes, something paranormal is going on. But, why here? The estate should be safe."

The air grew thicker, almost dense. It was hard for Benjamin to breath; he began to get a heavy feeling in his chest.

"What's wrong? You're breathing funny." Abram grabbed Benjamin by his face. "Look at me!"

"I feel like..." Benjamin found it hard to speak, "like something... is pushing down on my chest... hard to...."

Abram sat Benjamin down, trying to get his friend comfortable.

"I need you to focus on your breathing," Abram said calmly.

Abram took his friend's hand and began monitoring his pulse—it was racing. Suddenly, Abram felt an ice cold chill run down his back. He looked up, and to his horror, he saw it. From the ceiling spewed a thick cloud of blackness slowly formed into a funnel that centered around Benjamin's head.

"Oh God..." Abram cursed. "It can't be...."

"What is... happening?" Benjamin eyes were now glazed over.

"Wait here. I'll be right back!" Abram stood up and ran back to his room. Within a minute, Abram barged into the room.

"Dad!" Liv jumped from the sudden entrance.

"Stay here!" Abram yelled as he ran into his bedroom.

"What's going on?" Liv stood up quickly, following her father into his room. There she saw him entering his combination into a large, thick, metal locker.

"I told you to stay put!" Abram barked. "This is serious."

Abram spun the combination lock to its final number and quickly threw open the locker's heavy door. From inside, he grabbed a large, shiny, square box.

"Batteries—damn it! Does it need batteries?" Abram fiddled with something on the bottom. "Kids, cover your ears, now!" Abram waited for the kids to cover their ears and then grabbed what appeared to be very large earmuffs before hitting a button on the bottom of the metal box. An earsplitting noise dropped both Elly and Liv to their knees, and Abram quickly turned off the device.

"Sorry, I had to test it," said Abram, but Liv could barely hear him from the ringing in her ears.

"Stay put!" he yelled one more time, using his hand to signal to them not to move.

Abram darted out of the room and into the hallway with the box, and with the earmuffs still on his head. There he met back up with Benjamin, who was now convulsing on the floor. His skin was pale white, and his eyes were glossed over.

The thick cloud had almost completely disappeared from where it formed, and there was just a little bit left funneling its way into Benjamin's body. Abram hit the button one more time, and the earsplitting noise took over the hallway. Suddenly, the black smoke cloud began to break up from its funnel form. Now Benjamin's body began convulsing even worse as the black smoke came slowly oozing out of every orifice of his body. It was a grotesque sight as his ears, eyes, nose, and mouth were spewing forth the foreign black mass until, finally, the last of it exited his body.

Abram grabbed the box and turned a knob that made the deafening noise even louder. With that, the black mass exploded into nothingness. Abram turned the box off and ran to his friend, throwing off the earmuffs.

"Ben! Can you hear me? Benjamin?"

But Ben didn't respond. He let out a small moan, but immediately passed out. Abram grabbed his cell phone from his pocket and dialed.

"Patricia! I need a medical team down here now! We just had an attempted possession!"

Chapter 18
A Turn for the Worse

Hunter had a restless night; he tossed and turned, moving in and out of sleep. When he did find rest, he dreamed of the dark mass that escaped from the ring, its red eyes staring at him in his dreams. He felt so stupid for not waiting for his friends to be awake before he put the ring on. If he had, perhaps they could have gotten it off him before that "thing" escaped. Hunter finally fell asleep in the early-morning hours, but only after the comforting morning light crept through his bedroom window. Unfortunately, he was awoken after only a couple of hours to an emergency announcement that chimed loudly through the entire estate.

"Attention," Patricia's voice rang through Hunter's room. "The estate is currently on a level-six lockdown. All members of the estate are to be housed in their apartments until farther notice due to safety concerns. Please refrain from leaving unless an escort is sent for you. We will keep you updated of the current situation as more news becomes available. Thank you for your understanding."

There was only one other time the estate had gone on lockdown, and that was when the Beast of Bladenboro had been released. He knew it was because of the black smoke that he had let loose. What else could it be? What had he done?

It wasn't until much later that Uncle Joe and Margot entered the room with Elly. It was pretty evident by the look on their faces that something awful had happened. Margot appeared to be paler than usual and definitely not herself. Uncle Joe was the opposite; he seemed more focused than ever.

"Hunter, how are you feeling?" Margot took a seat next to Hunter and felt for his temperature.

"I'm fine, but what's going on?"

"Something happened last night," Uncle Joe said, wheeling his way over to Trayer, who was lying at the end of the bed. He scratched the giant Cusith's ear.

"There was an attack in the estate last night," Margot explained with a hint of fear in her voice that she tried her best to hide.

"An attack?" Hunter looked over at his sister, who stood nervously by her bed looking down at the floor.

"Yes, something attacked Alistair's father last night," Margot answered.

"What?" Hunter's jaw dropped.

"He's in the infirmary, as we speak with Alistair, Liv, and Mr. Winters," answered Joe. "We just came from there."

"Is he okay? What attacked him?"

"He'll be okay. The attack took a lot out of him. He awoke momentarily but wasn't very coherent," Margot told them.

"We're not sure what we're dealing with yet," Joe added, his voice about as serious as it could be. "We can't say much, since everything is hush-hush, but luckily, Abram was there." Joe changed the tone of his voice for what he was about to say. "It's very important that you kids adhere to the rules of this lockdown. Do you understand? No sneaking out and no getting into trouble."

Hunter nodded; he was at a loss for words.

"I mean it! You cannot go anywhere without parental guidance," Joe stressed again.

"Classes are canceled for the next few days until we figure some things out." Margot bent over and kissed Hunter on the forehead.

"You kids hang out here for the rest of the morning. We'll send someone up with food. Maybe we can talk Ms. Ellingbee into allowing you to meet up with Alistair and Liv later. They could use some friends. There's talk of using the library or the foyer as a safe house so that people aren't holed up in their rooms the entire time." Joe wheeled himself over to give his nephew a hug. "Don't worry.

We'll be around to make sure nothing happens."

Margot and Joe said their goodbyes and left Hunter and Elly alone in their room. The air seemed thicker that afternoon; the children could feel the tension in the estate, like a heavy cloud of despair was hovering over their home.

Elly took a seat on her bed. Trayer, acting as if he hadn't seen Elly in years, quickly jumped up next to her and buried his enormous head in her lap.

"You really did it this time, Hunter," Elly said coldly. Her words were sharp and laced with anger.

"What do you mean?" asked Hunter.

"That thing that attacked Alistair's dad, it must've been that black cloud you let loose."

Hunter ignored his sister's words and jumped off his bed, grabbing a thick book from the dining table. He was frustrated with Elly. He couldn't put into words why he had done what he did, but he felt betrayed that she didn't understand. Of all the people in the world, the one person who shared his pain and anguish was his little sister. He had done it for his parents; he had done it to speak to them one last time. Why didn't she get that?

Hunter opened the thick book and began turning pages, looking for something.

"What are you doing?" Elly was annoyed by Hunter's lack of seriousness on the matter.

"When was the last time you heard of a cloud attacking anyone?" Hunter asked plainly, hiding his true frustrations with his sister. "We don't know if that was what attacked him. But if it was, I think we need to find out more about it before we go talking to anyone."

"Are you serious?" Elly was baffled. How could her brother be so daft? She was the younger sibling, and she was tired of trying to keep her brother out of trouble.

"Look," Hunter said sternly, "I was up late last night, reading. I've read every book in the last month I could find on ghosts and spirits. Alistair's dad will be fine; they said Abram scared the thing away. Who knows what it was, but until they tell us, I say we find out for ourselves."

"And how are *we* supposed to do that?" Elly said, slightly mocking her brother now.

"I think I know what we're up against. If it was that black cloud thing, then there are ways we can communicate with it. Maybe Liv was right; I think it was a possessed object like she said. When I put it on, I must have broken the seal or whatever and let it loose. We need to set up an investigation and see if it will talk to us."

"An investigation?" Elly staggered, sitting down abruptly. "If it *was* that thing that attacked Alistair's dad, do you really think it will want to talk to us? It will probably just hurt us."

"Maybe, maybe not. I just read the Spiritual Anomalies class's entire textbook. There are tools and machines we can use to set up a ghost hunt, track it down, and get answers!"

"What about capturing it? Does the book talk about that?" asked Elly.

"Well, not exactly, but maybe we can see if we can help it and figure out what it wants."

"Help it? It attacked your best friend's dad!" Elly shook her head in disbelief.

"*If* that was what attacked him," Hunter corrected again. "Anyway, this thing, spirit or ghost, could just need help moving on. The book says most spirits don't even realize that they're spirits and just need understanding. We have to at least try."

"I don't know…" Elly didn't like the idea in the least.

"Let me talk to Alistair and Liv to see what they think. If they want me to go to the adults right away, I will."

Elly and Hunter didn't talk much for the rest of the afternoon, even when Margot brought them their lunches. Elly chose to eat her food on her bed, away from Hunter. He didn't seem to mind; he was too busy reading his collection of books and skimming through his notes about spirits and demonology. It was well into the evening before Patricia knocked on the children's door.

"Children," Patricia cracked the door open and stuck her head into the room with a friendly smile. "Liv and Alistair are down in the library. Would you like to join them? We're working around the clock to keep the library under surveillance, so it should be safe."

"Yes!" Hunter quickly packed up his books, threw his rather heavy book bag across his shoulder, and quickly joined Patricia at the door.

"Elly? Would you like to come too?" Patricia asked.

"Yeah, I guess," Elly said, a bit less enthusiastically.

"Wonderful, I will escort you down," Patricia held the door open for the kids.

☙

Alistair and Liv sat at a large oak table at the heart of the library. Hunter and Elly had never seen the library packed with so many children; it was like wandering around a giant maze of noisy kids trying to get to their friends. There were numerous parents and adults as well, keeping an eye out for anything bizarre or paranormal. Hunter noticed that all the adults had funny-looking machines in their hands. The devices were about the size of long, skinny cell phones. They walked around holding the devices out in front of them and waving them around slowly. It appeared as if they were monitoring something in the air.

"Hey, guys! Over here!" Liv smiled as she saw the two break through a crowd of kids playing hacky sack in one of the wider aisles. She heard Ms. Ellingbee scold the children about the library being a place to study and read, not a playground.

"Never seen the library so noisy; Plato must be blowing a gasket," said Elly, a bit put off with the scene.

"There they are!" Patricia saw Liv waving over the large group of kids in front of her. "Yes, dear, it's quite loud in here at the moment. We thought the library would be an easier location to keep all the children together and monitored for safety. Plus, there are plenty of options in case you kids get bored; we have an extensive library."

"Trust me," Hunter smirked, "Elly has probably read them all by now."

"Don't be silly." Patricia didn't even crack a small smile at the joke. "Anyway, you looked to be pretty deep into your studies, Hunter. I'm proud to see you taking the Enlightenment seriously."

"Well…" Hunter felt a bit embarrassed.

"It's not what you think, Ms. Ellingbee." Elly rolled her eyes, but before she could explain, the group made their way up to Liv and Alistair at the large table.

"Hey, guys!" Hunter cut his little sister off.

"Hey," Alistair replied. His hands were folded on the desk with his head lying on them. He didn't move when the two approached. He sat lethargically, staring off into the corner.

"How is your dad doing?" Elly didn't really know how to ask the question.

Alistair didn't answer.

"Uncle Ben is doing much better," Liv replied, looking at her younger cousin with a worried expression. "He actually awoke not that long ago and started answering some questions. They even had Professor Calenstine in talking with him."

"The professor? Must be serious," said Elly.

"We've been down here for hours," Alistair finally said. "They won't even let us back up to see my dad."

"That's because he has awoken, is fine, and everything is stable," answered Patricia with a worried look on her face. "I promise, dear, that there is nothing to worry about. However, until we figure out what happened to him, we want to keep the rumors from spreading."

"Right." Alistair wasn't impressed with her answer.

"Patricia," the friendly voice of Professor Pike chimed over the chatter of children.

"Linda, how are you? Everyone holding up okay, down here?" Patricia asked.

"Yes, dear, no EMF spikes and no sudden or drastic temperature changes. All is quiet."

"Those are EMF detectors?" Hunter's eyes widened with intrigue.

"Correct, my young one," Professor Pike said, beaming. "Someone has been reading ahead in Professor Hobbes' class, I see."

"What does that do?" Alistair propped his head up. "I was wondering what everyone was carrying around with them."

"Well, these little devices measure electromagnetic fields in the surrounding—"

"Linda," Patricia interrupted abrasively, "let's not discuss such matters in front of the kids. We wouldn't want to worry them."

"Oh, of course. Sorry, dear," Professor Pike's cheeks reddened with embarrassment over her sudden lapse of judgment.

"Linda, let's leave the children and get back to our duties. Is Professor Hobbes down here as well? I have some more questions for him."

"Yes, I believe I saw him near the back," Professor Pike answered as she and Patricia disappeared into the large group of people moseying about the library.

"Alistair, I am sorry." Hunter took a seat across from his friend. He knew deep down that it was his fault Alistair's dad had been attacked.

"What're you sorry about?" Alistair's eyebrow wrinkled in confusion.

"Well… because of what happened! Elly is right; it was probably that thing that I let loose when I put that blasted ring on."

"I'm not mad at you, Hunter," Alistair said, finally picking his head up from the table.

"You're not?" Hunter immediately felt better.

"You're not?" Elly repeated.

"No," Alistair said bluntly. "Hunter didn't let that thing loose on purpose. I know why he did what he did. I'm mad that Patricia and the rest of the estate won't let us help or even let me talk to my dad. We know more about what's going on than they do."

"Hunter doesn't want to tell them the truth." Elly gave her older brother another dirty look.

"I already tried," Alistair said with a huff. "They wouldn't give me the time of day. They rushed Liv and me down here with the others. They're so worried about people finding out what they don't even know. They won't listen."

"Well, if I try talking to my uncle, I'm sure he would listen," Elly suggested.

"Elly!" a familiar voice broke through the background noise of the busy library. It was Remy, the children's anti-bullying friend. Remy squeezed his way through a large group of children blocking the aisle.

"Remy!" Elly smiled.

"Looky here," Remy walked up next to Hunter and Alistair and put his large arms around the two boys in a friendly manner. "The whole gang's together," he said, smiling brightly. "Surprised they let us regular students into the fancy, super-secret library. Normally, we don't get out of the Friedrich Building."

"It's been a few days." Liv returned the smile, quickly standing up. She and Elly both gave Remy a big hug.

"Somethin's amuck, aye?" Remy did his best to hide the fact he felt a bit embarrassed getting hugs from two cute girls.

"You could say that." Alistair rolled his eyes, unable to hide his frustration with the adults.

"Good news 'bout those Krueger turds," Remy laughed. "Looks like that professor of yours flushed the whole family out, aye?"

"Yeah," Hunter answered. "Except they're the least of our worries now."

"Lemme guess, somethin' about that spook that's been seen around the estate?"

"What?" Alistair's jaw dropped. "How did you know?"

"A bunch of the kids at my school been talkin' 'bout seein' some shadow people." Remy looked a bit put off by the kid's sudden response. "I'm sure it ain't nothin' though. I've heard so many weird stories about this place, nothin' surprises me anymore. If you listen to the regular school kids like me, you'd think all sorts of crazy things."

"Shadow people?" Liv repeated aloud.

"Yeah, they're a type of spirit." Remy was a bit shocked that Liv, a student in the Enlightenment classes, didn't know what a shadow person was. "Umm, basically they're these dark figures you see out the corner of your eye. Ya know? You see 'em' when you ain't expectin' to. When you turn to look at 'em though, they disappear."

"Wow, how did you know that?" Hunter was impressed. He had

read numerous books and articles on the concept of shadow people; it was a very popular theory in the spiritual realm of the fringe sciences. There was even an entire chapter dedicated to this phenomenon in one of their schoolbooks.

"Oh, I used to watch a lot of those ghost-huntin' reality television shows before we moved out here," Remy chuckled. "I know a bit about ghost huntin' and always wanted to make my own paranormal group when I get older. Sneak into old rundown asylums and penitentiaries! Sounds like fun, right?" Remy's smile stretched across his face.

"Do you know what the devices the adults are holding are?" Alistair asked.

"Sure do," Remy said. "Was wondering why they all had 'em; that's how I guessed this was about all the ghost stories I was hearing. They're called EMF detectors. They scan the room with 'em to see if they spike anywhere. A spike signals potential spiritual energy."

"But what's EMF stand for?" asked Elly, who felt a bit put out that so many people knew more about spiritual anomalies than she did. She prided herself on being the one in the group who knew the most, and up until this very moment, she put off the entire class of paranormal anomalies as a joke.

"Electromagnetic Fields," Hunter responded, feeling pretty good about himself, being able to answer his sister's question for once. "Not sure what exactly it is, but I know the things detect spikes of it in the air, like Remy said, and when it spikes higher, it means there may be a spirit nearby. A green light means normal, but the darker red the light gets, the higher the EMF."

"Exactly, so somethin' is going on; the adults must think the stories are true then?" asked Remy.

"Well…" Hunter nervously rubbed his finger where the scar from the ring was. He went on to explain everything to Remy, about the secret letter from the Order of Shadows, the map that was with it, and how it supposedly told him where to find the ring known as Solomon's Seal. He swore him to secrecy about the thick dark cloud that had oozed out from the ring once he put it on, and how it flew away out of sight under the door. And how it was probably what had attacked Alistair's dad.

"That's insane!" Remy couldn't believe what he had just heard. "I mean, we know there are secretive things going on and that we're not s'posed to stick our noses in the estate's business, but wow!"

"Exactly," Elly said, a bit forthright. "We're not supposed to go sticking our nose in the estate's business either. We're supposed to go to school, study, and pass our first year in the Enlightenment. Somehow, it seems we're always getting into trouble!"

"Either way," Remy finally took a seat next to the group, "what's with this Order of Shadows, and it sounds like they tricked you."

"Maybe they really thought it was the ring, or maybe the ring didn't do what everyone thought it did. Maybe the Seal was to keep something in and not out," Liv suggested. "We just don't know."

"So, we're gonna catch it, right?" Remy cracked his knuckles, excited at the concept of a spirit roaming free.

"Well…" Hunter looked over at Alistair, hoping for his approval, "I promised Elly I'd talk to you first. She wants us to tell the adults about the ring and the letter."

"Yeah," Liv butted in as if there was no other option.

"Hear me out." Hunter frowned from the interruption. "We can look for this thing. There is equipment that can help us track it down, maybe even communicate with it. I read the entire Spiritual Anomalies textbook. It's all about this ghost-hunting stuff Remy was talking about."

"Maybe we can find out what it wants," replied Alistair.

"Maybe," Hunter added.

"Guys, we should really talk to my dad or your uncle." Liv was definitely siding with Elly.

"I already tried," Alistair said, slamming his fist down angrily. He immediately felt embarrassed by his sudden outburst. "Sorry, I was going to tell them everything, but they wouldn't listen. They kicked me out of the infirmary. I say we deal with it."

"No way!" Elly shook her head in disbelief. She stood up angrily and started walking towards Professor Pike, calling her name loudly.

"What's she doing?" asked Hunter, baffled by his sister's reaction.

Elly abruptly shoved her big brother out of the way as she went to go fetch Professor Pike.

"Professor Pike!" Elly yelled for a second time, finally getting her attention from across the library.

"Elly, don't!" Hunter sped up to catch his sister, the group not far behind him. "What are you doing?"

"Professor Pike, I need to talk to you about this ghost," said Elly, but before she could finish her sentence, she was abruptly cut off by Professor Pike.

"Elly, I will not have you spreading rumors and scaring the other students with this nonsensical ghost talk!" Professor Pike scolded in a hushed voice, waving her boney finger in Elly's face.

"But w-we know about..." Elly tried to stammer out an explanation but to no avail.

"Enough! I will not hear another word. If you utter the word 'ghost,' 'spirit,' or anything similar, you will find yourself in detention for a week!"

"*Listen* to me! Hunter found this letter..." Elly tried once again to explain, but Professor Pike's face boiled red with anger, and she cut Elly off once again.

"Detention for a week. As soon as classes are resumed, missy, you will report to me. Now, not another word!"

"What?" Elly was furious, and her hands shook in anger and confusion.

"Elly, come with me." Liv grabbed her friend's hand and quickly ushered her back to their table. "Just stop talking and walk away!"

"Can you believe she did that to me? I was only trying to help!" Elly shot back, tears building in her eyes.

"I told you," said Alistair. "We're in this by ourselves. They won't listen."

Chapter 19
A Paranormal Investigation

It took a week before the estate decided it was safe once again to drop the lockdown from level six to level three. What that meant for Hunter, Elly, and the other students was that they were still confined to their rooms outside of regularly scheduled daily activities, but they were free to go to their classes, attend meals, and even spend some time outside of the estate for some extracurricular activities with parent or guardian approval. Alistair made good use of his time, spending it with Dr. Lannin and his new friend, Bernie the Bigfoot, in the late evenings.

Despite the more relaxed lockdown state, there was still a strict curfew adopted along with a twenty-four-hour surveillance team that monitored the entire estate. There were still whispers of people seeing what were referred to as "shadow people" around the estate, but nothing more than just hearsay. Benjamin was out of the infirmary after a few days and was back to normal. However, he was determined to figure out what had attacked him. With Professor Calenstine's approval, he, Abram Winters, and Joe banded together to lead the investigation and take control of the lockdown.

Hunter enjoyed the week off from classes and Enlightenment studies, but he too was determined. He went back and reread every book and article he had on spiritual anomalies.

"Guys, I think I know what we may be dealing with," said Hunter.

"What ya got?" asked Remy, who to the kids' surprise brought a wealth of ghost-hunting knowledge to the group.

"Wraiths are spirits of tormented souls. 'It is thought...'" Hunter began reading from a new book he had found deep in the back of the library called *Phantoms and Spooks: A complete directory of the Undead.* "'...that when a mortal lives a poisonous life, subjected to evil and wickedness, that all his pain and suffering, all his anger and hatred may in fact take a form of its own once the body of the subject expires. Once the death occurs, two spirits are born from one mortal: one of his soul and the other of his emotion.'"

"I don't get it," Liv said. "Two spirits from one person?"

"It says here," Hunter began to summarize, "that the human soul is more powerful than we could ever imagine. Under certain stress, the spirit can be split into two or more separate entities." Hunter paused for a moment. "Next to that line in the book, it looks like someone wrote a note, it reads: 'Think of someone suffering from mental illness, split personalities, etc. The mind and soul are connected, when troubled it can fracture.'"

"Okay," said Elly. "So basically, when someone dies, and they lived a horrible life or died tragically, their soul can split into a wraith?"

"Looks like it but wait, there's more," answered Hunter before continuing to read. "'Wraiths are entities born from an intense emotional battle. This can be from either end of the human condition. Because wraiths are born from intense feelings, one must surmise that any sort of feeling that is intense enough can alter the type of wraith that may be fractured and split from the host's soul. This means anger, sadness, despair, love, and happiness could all potentially create the needed ingredients for a wraith being born. Wraiths are pure emotional energy and will take the form of mist or smoke depending on the emotion they stem from. Most scholars agree that the more severe the case, the darker the wraiths appearance. Wraiths are born from the darkness. Cherubs, on the other hand, are born from the light.'"

"Cherub? Isn't that a type of angel?" Liv asked.

"I don't know, but there are more notes on the side of the page that go on to explain it," answered Hunter. "It basically says people who are evil or subjected to evil are the breeding ground for wraiths. It says to think of those pure of heart: martyrs for the better of mankind and heroes who sacrifice their own well-being for others, these are the symptoms for a cherub to be born."

"This is deep stuff," added Alistair.

"It says there are certain circumstances that must be met for this to happen. Whether it's evil or pure, the host must die in a quick manner. A slow death releases the human soul or energy slowly and naturally, allowing a safe passage. A quick and sudden death creates an explosion of the energy of the soul and may cause the soul and the intense emotion to break apart."

"I am not sure if we are up to dealing with this thing," said Elly, as the group seemed to be feeling a bit overwhelmed with everything they had heard.

"That doesn't sound good; the darker the mist means what type of wraith or cherub we're dealing with, correct?" asked Alistair. "You said the thing was a thick, black ooze."

"Yeah, but it also says the wraiths aren't always born from evil men but from tortured souls. Maybe this one is despair or fear? We don't know for sure, but don't you think that if we can help it find some answers, we should?"

"Do you know about this stuff, Remy?" asked Elly, who caught the look of fear on Remy's face.

"Naw," he said softly. "I mean, like I said, I watch the reality television shows, but they don't get into the deep stuff. Pretty freaky, aye?"

"Just a little," Elly laughed nervously.

"Well, we need a plan. I don't think it will hurt for us to go on with our investigation. It's been almost a week, so maybe it left the estate all together. I read somewhere that ghosts and spirits are usually attached to locations," explained Hunter.

"So, first things first, we need to get the right equipment," Remy stated, being practical.

"Right, I can get an EMF detector; after I knew what they were, I saw that my dad had like ten of them in his closet with the rest of his gear," said Alistair.

"We'll need flashlights too and digital recorders," said Hunter.

"Like a voice recorder?" asked Liv.

"Yeah, so we can collect EVP or Electronic Voice Phenomenon." Hunter whipped out his pen and began jotting down a list of things the group would need.

"Yeah, Liv," Remy explained, "you ask the spirit questions. Sometimes you can't hear 'em with your ears, but when you play the recording back with the volume up super high, sometimes there are hidden voices. They call it an EVP for short."

"I know, my dad has a bunch of those," said Liv. "He won't notice if one disappears for a night."

"Excellent!" Hunter jotted down Liv's name next to 'EVP recorder' in his notes.

"Now, we just have to figure out where to set up the investigation," said Alistair.

"I still don't think this is a good idea." Elly didn't like the idea of anything that had been said.

"Elly, no one will be upset if you don't come," Liv said, smiling and trying to give Elly an out if she wanted it.

"Are you really going through with it?" asked Elly.

"Yeah, I want to be a part of the investigation. It sounds kind of fun."

"Fun?" Elly couldn't believe her ears.

"Where have the kids been seeing the shadow people, Remy?" asked Hunter.

"Everywhere, really. I think it's more important for us to do it in a place where we don't have to worry about any adults findin' us. Maybe in one of your rooms, like a sleepover. If it's in the estate, and we can get its attention, it may come to us," answered Remy.

"Okay, I think it's settled. Let's try and get approval for a little sleepover," said Hunter with excitement.

With the plan set in motion and the children doing their best to obtain the supplies they needed to make the investigation a success, the hardest part was the waiting. It was impossible to ask for the sleepover until the estate ended the level six lockdown. Luckily, Margot and Joe thought it would do the children good to have a few friends over to stay the night on a weekend in the near future. As long as they were patient enough, it would happen as soon as everything going on with the attack was over. They even approved Remy as long as his father didn't mind. It took a lot of begging and pleading from Remy, but after a couple of days of constant harassment, his father broke down and gave him the okay.

"Just be careful hangin' out with those kids from the estate. Those Seeker families are into some weird stuff," said Remy's father. "Why don't you make friends with the kids from the Friedrich School? Normal kids, ya know?"

But Remy didn't like those kids, and those kids didn't care for him either. Remy's dad knew it had been a hard adjustment for his son due to moving away from his old school and into this weird place. He was happy to see his son make some new friends, so he decided to go against his gut feeling and let his son be a kid for once.

ॐ

The first week went by slowly, especially for Elly, who got to spend five straight days in detention with Professor Pike, who quickly became her least favorite teacher because she had reprimanded her and given her her first detention, ever. What Elly didn't know was that Professor Pike was just following orders; no one was to speak of or discuss the recent ghost sightings in the estate. The laundry list of things Professor Pike made Elly do during her time in detention was long. A formal letter of apology was written by Elly to Professor Pike for being disobedient to an instructor, one that Elly made certain her friends knew was filled with blatant lies because she wasn't in the wrong for trying to talk to her teacher. Elly also washed down every chalkboard in the Francis Drake Building of Enlightenment, dusted out every chalk eraser, swept all the hallways, and was even forced to help Professor Pike feed her disgusting pet vampyre, Natalia.

"Careful now, she's a vampyre, and she will bite!" Professor Pike chuckled from across the room.

Despite the estate's efforts to keep the rumors of the ghastly ghoul to a minimum, both schools were running wild with tales of shadowy images. Everyone seemed to have some sort of story in what was happening, the majority of which were lies and tall tales. Luckily, the students didn't seem too steeped in fear over all the stories running rampant. Hunter knew that if they actually saw the entity in the form of thick black ooze, they would probably be telling a different story.

Two weeks slipped by, and the blanket of winter fell upon the Belmonte grounds. A fresh layer of snow covered the courtyard for the first time that season. News slowly turned away from the ghost sightings and towards the quickly approaching Christmas season. The estate had already begun preparations by decorating the inside with all sorts of flashing lights and Christmas trees decorated with ornaments and fake snow. The girls fell in love with the foyer, which had the majority of the decorations.

With no new sightings and whispers of the ghost, finally, starting to die down, Patricia was given the order from Professor Calenstine to release the level three lockdown. Luckily for the children, once the lockdown was lifted, they were given the okay to have their sleepover.

Hunter wasted no time preparing for the investigation. He made copies of the list, highlighting what everyone was in charge of getting and passed it out to the group.

Saturday finally came, and Hunter and the group had their room set up with sleeping bags sprawled out all over the floor. Alistair and Liv had already shown up, and the group was waiting for Margot to bring Remy up. Joe was with the kids, helping them get everything in order for the night.

"Well, I think that's the last sleeping bag." Joe looked tired. He had large bags under his eyes, and he had let his beard grow out quite a bit. The kids didn't know it, but ever since the attack on Alistair's dad, their uncle, for the first time since his accident, was actually helping out as a Seeker. The problem didn't stem from the attack itself, but rather from how useless Joe felt at being unable to help in the ways he wanted. He cursed his wheelchair every night. He did his best to hide it, but those close to him knew he was letting his demons get the better of him. Margot especially, who had on more than one occasion tried to intervene, was only pushed aside.

"I think you're right," Hunter said after counting the sleeping bags.

"You kids are going to behave tonight, right? No funny business!"

"Of course not, Mr. Jakobs," Alistair said as he crawled into his sleeping bag. "It's comfy, and we'll be fine."

"Well, good! Don't forget we'll be here first thing in the morning to bring up breakfast. So, don't stay up too late."

"Okay!" said the group.

"Hey, guys!" Remy popped his head through the bedroom door with a bright smile.

"We made it," Margot said as she walked in behind Remy.

"Remy, we got your sleeping bag all rolled out for you." Joe pointed to the largest bag on the floor. "I was just telling the kids: no getting into trouble." Joe's voice was stern, yet friendly.

"Children." Sebastian popped into the room unexpectedly. "A slumber party? How that brings me back to my youth,"

"Sebastian, I thought I asked you to wait for me at the apartment," Margot said.

"And miss a chance to see the beautiful Eliza and Olivia's adoring smile?" Sebastian bowed towards the young girls.

Elly blushed.

"Joe, I'm sorry; I didn't see you there." Sebastian smirked as if his intention was to say that he couldn't see Joe because he was stuck in a wheelchair.

"Quite all right, Sebastian."

"Oh, but I am a proud gentleman and such disrespect does not live up to my chivalry. Please, forgive me. How are you?"

"I'm fine," Joe said, turning away from Sebastian and doing all he could to bite his tongue.

"Hunter, young sir, it's always a pleasure." Sebastian extended his hand to shake Hunter's hand.

Hunter felt weird; Sebastian had never shown much interest in befriending him before. He obliged and shook the man's hand. Sebastian smiled, but he held Hunter's hand slightly longer than expected. It was obvious to Hunter that Sebastian had noticed the burn mark.

Hunter quickly pulled his hand away, afraid he may say something to his uncle. Sebastian didn't, instead giving Hunter a confused look.

"Children, I am sure your uncle has already made mention of this." Sebastian spun around back towards his fiancée's side, taking her arm into his. "There have been some bizarre occurrences in the estate as of late, so please be mindful of your manners."

"Yes, Sebastian. I covered that already," Joe replied.

"Honey, why don't you meet me at the apartment? The professor gave us the okay to stay in tonight. I'll catch up with you in a few minutes."

Sebastian kissed Margot's hand and smiled at the group one last time before exiting the children's room.

Joe smiled, nodded his head, and wheeled his way out of the door with Margot behind him.

"Do we start now?" asked Liv, a bit excited.

"I can't believe you're okay with this." Elly was used to having Liv on her side and backing her up whenever the boys decided to do something dumb.

"Well, I wasn't at first, but you have to admit, it's a little exciting."

"I guess..." Elly frowned, taking a seat on her bed next to the slumbering, and very loudly snoring, Trayer.

"First thing, we gotta set up all the equipment." Remy cracked his knuckles, ready to get to work.

"Right, I was able to get my dad to lend me his camcorder and it has night vision. I can link it directly to my laptop." Alistair grabbed a large black computer bag and began pulling out equipment.

"You really are a computer geek, aren't you?" Elly chuckled, impressed by Alistair's knowledge of technology.

"Only if you mean that in a nice way," Alistair replied, knowing Elly meant no harm with her words. "It's not that hard actually;

there's just a bit of wiring involved. I'll take control of the camera for the investigation, recording everything we do." Alistair peered into the camera and slowly panned around the room, recording his friends. "Can someone hit the light? We can test it."

Hunter nodded, hitting the lights. Suddenly, the children found themselves surrounded in darkness with only a hint of moonlight creeping in through the window.

"We'll need to close the curtains so there's no light at all," Remy said as he cautiously made his way over to block out the moonlight.

"Perfect." Alistair flipped a little switch on the camcorder, changing it to night vision. Suddenly, the image capture screen on the device went from pitch black to a greyscale screen, picking up everyone in the room perfectly. "It's working; we can turn on the lights again and finish preparing."

"What else do we have to do?" asked Liv.

"First, we have to wait until the witching hour," answered Remy, who was checking all their flashlights, making sure they all had fresh batteries.

"Witching hour?" Elly jumped off her bed to help Remy with the preparations.

"Yeah, we got some time. The witching hour is at three in the morning. It's supposedly the best time of night to catch any ghostly apparitions."

"He's right," Hunter added testing out the EMF detector Liv had brought with her. "In all the books I read about investigating the paranormal, they always talk about the witching hour. So, I say we start up around two a.m., and work through the witching hour."

"I agree." Remy smiled brightly. "Thank you, guys, so much for letting me be a part of this. I have all the DVD collections of the reality shows back at home."

"To be honest," Elly shined her flashlight in Remy's eyes, "I think you know more about this stuff than we do."

The team had a few hours to wait until the timing was right to conduct the investigation. They prepped their equipment and worked out their plan. Alistair would be in control of the night-vision camera,

Hunter would take charge of the EMF detector, and Elly had a thermal recorder that Alistair had somehow managed to sneak out of his dad's equipment locker.

"So, what's this do? Looks just like a regular camera," Elly wasn't impressed at first.

"That is a thermal recorder. It picks up heat signatures." Hunter's eyes widened when Alistair said Elly could control one of his dad's other recorders. "How did you get that?"

"Easy, my dad has a bunch of stuff in his locker for paranormal investigations. He won't notice it being gone for a day."

"Okay, what do I look for?" asked Elly as she flipped the camera on. The screen in front of her showed bright colors of reds and oranges.

"Its color-coded for heat. See how we're brighter and you can see the outlines of our bodies? It's like heat vision. Sometimes spirits let off their own heat. You can't see heat with the naked eye, but this device can. You can actually see outlines of spirits with it!" Hunter was peering over his little sister's shoulder at the screen.

Elly found the machine very interesting, and she finally began warming up to the whole idea of the investigation.

Liv was in charge of the digital recorder and would be conducting the EVP session to hopefully capture any disembodied voices.

"What's a 'disembodied voice' again?" Liv was testing out the recorder.

"Sometimes when a spirit speaks, we can't pick up on what they're saying. But you can capture them on a digital recorder when you play them really loudly. It's a way to communicate," Hunter explained.

"Hunter, I'm impressed with how much you've learned about this," Liv smiled.

Hunter quickly turned away, afraid of going red in the face.

The night grew late, but the kids' patience finally paid off.

"Let's hit the lights!" said Remy.

"Okay, guys, we're going live. Everyone ready their flashlights, and get your equipment ready."

"Hunter, you're in charge of the group, so we'll follow your lead," Alistair said, turning on his night-vision camera.

"Everyone ready?" asked Hunter, standing with his finger on the light switch.

The group nodded with a mixture of excitement and trepidation. Hunter flicked the switch, and once again the friends found themselves in pitch blackness. Hunter turned his flashlight on and pointed it at his face. "Let's do this!"

Chapter 20
Terror has Arrived

"I am going to start with a quick read of the room with my EMF detector. We need to establish a baseline." Hunter walked slowly around the room with the small electronic device. "It's a steady green light."

"So, what that means," Remy began to explain to the group, "is that the room has nothing leaking EMF."

"Leaking EMF?" asked Elly, who slowly panned around the room with her heat-vision camera.

"Yeah, naturally some electronics will 'bleed out' electromagnetic fields. So if Hunter waved that device in front of a TV or a power outlet, it may spike. That wouldn't be a ghost, but a natural occurrence," answered Remy. "That also means if we do see a spike into the red, something is causing an EMF fluctuation, which *could* be a spirit."

"You learned all this from watching TV, huh?" Elly had no idea what she had been missing out on. "They ever catch anything on these shows you watch?"

"Oh, yeah," Remy said, unable to hide the excitement in his voice. "Alistair and I talk about it all the time. He likes the *Myth Hunters* series, which is a lot like my ghost series. They definitely catch stuff— voices, shadowy figures, and sometimes they even get scratches on them."

"Yeah, they don't usually catch anything on *Myth Hunters*, but I have seen a few of the paranormal investigation shows too. It's pretty creepy… so is looking through this night vision mode," joked Alistair.

"Seeing anything yet?" asked Liv, who was feeling more and more creeped out by the minute.

"No," answered Alistair softly. "Pretty quiet in here."

"Let's start with an EVP session," said Hunter. "Is it recording?"

"One second..." Liv began playing with the digital recorder. It made a loud beep to signal it was now recording live. "It is now."

"All right, let's start. Everyone feel free to ask questions. Speak slowly and clearly, and wait a few seconds between questions. Let's set the recorder in the middle of the floor, and I'll place my EMF detector next to it. Maybe it will spike if we get any responses."

"Good call," replied Remy. "Alistair and Elly, make sure you focus all 'round the room. Just pan slowly so you don't miss anything."

"Got it," said Elly.

Alistair nodded.

"Hello," Hunter said slowly to the room, feeling a little silly speaking to no one. "My name is Hunter, and these are my friends. We are wondering if there is anyone here with us tonight."

The room remained silent.

"We've heard rumors there is a shadowy figure lurkin' around the estate. Is that you?" Remy spoke up. They heard nothing. In fact, Hunter felt that it was an eerie silence.

The room was still, and the EMF detector remained green, sensing no electromagnetic interference anywhere.

"We want to know if there are any spirits in this room with us," asked Liv. "If there is, can you show us a sign that you are here? Can you make a noise?"

Suddenly, a loud thud came from behind Liv, which made her gasp loudly.

"Sorry... I just hit my elbow on the table. Ouch!" said Alistair with a grimace on his face.

"Seriously?" Liv whispered back angrily. "You scared the crap out of me!"

"Shhh!" Remy put his finger up to his lips to signal for the group to quiet down. "If you make a bump, just call it out so that if we hear it on the recorder, we know it was accounted for."

The group sat in the gloomy room for a long time talking into the darkness with nothing to show for it. None of their questions were answered. No disembodied voices were recorded, no heat signatures, no night-vision success; the room was quiet, and for the most part, fairly peaceful. It grew late into the morning hours, closing in on three a.m. when Elly had finally had enough.

"Guys," Elly yawned loudly, "I'm starting to think we're wasting our time with this stuff. Let's just call it a night and go to bed."

"I think Elly is right; if there is a ghost in the estate that attacked Uncle Ben, it's not in this room."

"Wait, that makes sense though," said Hunter. "I saw it leave this room, and it didn't show up here ever again. It attacked in the hallway and has been seen randomly throughout the estate, and even in the school buildings."

"Hunter, have you read about spirits being attached to items? In the TV shows, they sometimes use anchor items." Remy had just had a brilliant idea.

"Anchor items?" asked Liv, fighting back one of her own yawns.

"Some spirits are attached to items," said Remy, thinking out loud. "Hunter, do you still have the ring that you put on when this thing escaped?"

"Yeah, I keep it on me at all times," Hunter answered.

"Let's use it, see if it attracts it to us," Remy said, getting more and more excited by his plan.

"You sure about this?" asked Alistair.

"Yeah, this could work," answered Remy.

"A while back, I put this ring on my finger." Hunter pulled out the ring and placed it onto the floor in between the digital recorder and EMF detector floor. "Do you remember that? Do you remember when I put this ring on? Something weird happened after that. Was that you? Were you the black cloud?"

More silence.

"We want to know. Are you an evil spirit? Or do you need help? Can we help you?"

Remy started to say something else, but Elly suddenly gasped.

"What is it?" whispered Hunter.

"When you took the ring out..." Elly stammered for a second.

"Yeah?" asked Alistair. "Go on...."

"Well... this thing picks up heat, right? The ring was cold when you took it out of your pocket. You placed it down on the floor. Once Remy started speaking, the ring turned bright red... Like really, really red!"

"Let me see." Remy walked slowly over to the ring on the floor and went to pick it up. "OUCH!"

"What happened?" Liv jumped.

Trayer also shot up from the bed, worried about the sudden commotion.

"It's burnin' hot! I can't even pick it up!" Remy looked over to Alistair, who was recording the whole thing. Alistair had never seen Remy scared, not even squaring off with Corbin and Lunette. He was always so confident and strong. "Okay... well.... Things are finally startin' to heat up."

"Look!" Hunter pointed down to the EMF detector. The device was going off like crazy from dark green to bright red.

"It's goin' crazy with spikes!" Remy jumped back and away from the items in the middle of the floor.

"Okay, guys, I'm starting to get a bit freaked out..." Liv said, her hands beginning to tremble.

"It's okay, we're all here together," Hunter said, doing his best to stop his own voice from trembling.

BANG! BANG!

Suddenly, two consecutive loud thumps came from the other side of the room. It was as if someone was hitting the wall with their fist. Trayer quickly jumped off the bed and growled. Normally, the mighty canine would go crazy barking at such a noise, but this time the large Cusith yelped and darted underneath Elly's bed. Trayer was far too large to fit, so instead of hiding beneath the bed, the bed lay on top of him at an awkward angle.

"What the hell was that?" Remy turned quickly towards the noise and swallowed hard. He had seen this happen many times on the TV shows, but he wasn't prepared for the amount of fear and tension running through his body.

"Even Trayer is scared!" Elly's heart began to race.

"I don't see anything." Alistair zoomed in towards the sound, hoping to catch something on the night vision.

"Me neither," added Elly, who was shaking so badly that it was hard to keep the thermal detector steady.

"We all heard it though..." Liv answered. "Something is here...."

"If that's you, tell us what you want. Can we help you?" Hunter spoke slowly and a bit more methodically.

"The air is getting really thick in here... Do you guys feel that?" said Liv, who was now feeling extremely warm. She took a seat by the window and cracked it open for some fresh air.

"Just stay calm, everyone. Don't let this psyche you out..." Hunter told the group, doing his best to heed his own advice.

"The ring is losing its heat," Elly said as she watched the ring turn from bright red back down to a cool blue.

"The EMF went to solid green again too," added Alistair, hiding a breath of relief from the group.

"Did it leave?" asked Remy, holding out his hands in the air as if he were feeling for something.

"What are you doing?" asked Alistair, recording him.

"They say if a spirit is around, you can feel cold spots. I don't feel anything though."

"That was crazy." Liv laughed nervously.

"Still not a believer, Elly?" Remy winked playfully at her.

"Guys," Alistair's voice cracked.

"What?"

"Remy... don't move," Alistair added, zooming in on him with his night-vision camera.

"What's going on?" Hunter ran over to Alistair and peeked over his shoulder. His eyes immediately grew big at the sight on the camera.

"What's wrong?" asked Remy.

"Someone turn your flashlight on above Remy's head!" Hunter

ordered.

Liv fumbled in her pocket but quickly got out her flashlight and turned it on. She flashed it just above Remy's head, where a large thick cloud of blackness began to form.

"Oh God!" Elly shrieked.

"What?" Remy turned around quickly and looked above him to see the black cloud directly in front of his face. No one else could peer as deeply into the black abyss as Remy, and what he saw terrified him. There in the black cloud he saw red eyes; the evil and hatred they held froze him with terror. Before he realized what was happening, the black cloud reached out with a thin funnel from its base and shot down into his mouth and down his throat.

"Remy!" Liv yelled. Tears of terror stained her cheeks.

Remy stood there in the middle of the room convulsing from the black cloud entering his young body. He was helpless as his body seized up. The pain was intense, and his eyes felt like they were going to explode out of their sockets, a sight that made Liv sick to her stomach. She fell to her knees and gave into the sickness.

"Run! Get help!" yelled Hunter.

"Okay..." Alistair dropped his camera on the floor and ran towards the bedroom door.

"I'm coming, Remy!" Hunter ran to his friend's aid. He reached out to pull his friend away from the black cloud's grip, but he couldn't budge him. Suddenly, Hunter felt the scar on his finger burning up again, and he too fell to his knees. The pain was overpowering.

Alistair grabbed the door handle to open it, but suddenly the door slammed back shut.

"What in the hell?" Alistair cursed as he saw that Remy's large hand had forced the door closed.

Alistair turned around quickly to see the most terrifying sight he had ever seen. He was so in shock at the sight that he could barely hear Elly screaming from across the room.

Remy now stood in front of Alistair, face to face, his eyes vacant and black. His face was motionless, but his eyes moved involuntary in all directions, each eye looking in different directions. His mouth was half open, but neither jaw nor tongue moved despite speaking some weird language in an unfamiliar, eerie voice. He was pale white and covered in sweat.

"R-Remy? Is that you?" Alistair muttered.

The thing that was now Remy didn't respond. Instead, it grabbed Alistair by the throat, and with some sort of inhuman power, the thing lifted Alistair up and off the ground with one hand. Its grip was so tight around Alistair's neck that he found himself passing out.

"Children?" Margot's voice yelled from behind the door. "Open up! Unlock the door!"

"Heeeelp!" Elly yelled as loud as she could with a mixture of cries and screams.

Suddenly the door was bashed in by Sebastian, who had forced the door open with his shoulder.

"Oh my lord!" Margot shrieked as she saw Remy's vacant eyes and terrifying, motionless face.

Sebastian tackled Remy, loosening the grip around Alistair's throat. Remy, now on his back, tossed Sebastian aside easily and jumped up off the floor and onto the ceiling.

"Oh God!" Margot ran over to Alistair and away from this creature that somehow defied logic and sat sprawled out on the ceiling, staring down at the group.

Sebastian stood up from where he had fallen and stared at the thing that was once Remy.

"Get out! Leave!" Sebastian grabbed a lamp from the counter and tossed it at the thing. The lamp exploded as it hit the ceiling near Remy. The thing crawled like a spider, very awkwardly and very hastily on the ceiling, making its escape as it smashed through the children's bedroom window and outside.

"Margot, get the kids out of here. Now!" Sebastian yelled.

Margot picked up Alistair, who had just woken up and was coughing violently as he gasped for breath. Elly grabbed Liv and got her to her feet. With Remy's retreat through the window, the pain in Hunter's hand subsided and the group made their escape out into the hallway.

Sebastian stood alone in the room and slowly approached the broken window with a look of eerie calmness about him. He pulled out his cell phone and double-checked that he was still alone. He grinned as he speed-dialed a phone number.

"It worked," Sebastian whispered into the cell. "Unfortunately, it did not find either of the Jakobs as its host, but it did find one of their friends… Yes, I know… Very good, sir. I told you allowing me to be the head of the Order of Shadows would suit your interests… Thank you, sir… Go ahead and tell Gerald all is well and I will continue with our plan… Yes, sir… Have no worries, Professor Aten, I will continue to recruit for the cause… I did bring you Gerald, did I not? Yes sir… thank you." Sebastian flipped his cell phone closed and couldn't hide his evil smile.

Sebastian looked down at the broken glass, and beneath the rubble he found the letter he and Gerald had written Hunter under the pseudo name of the Order of Shadows. Sebastian brushed the shards of glass and debris off of the letter. He pulled a small lighter from his pocket and lit it.

"It's just a matter of time…" He let the burning letter slip from his hands and out the window, where it quickly burned away disappearing into the darkness.

"What happened?" Joe and Abram burst into the kids' bedroom.

"Ah, I daresay something terrible." Sebastian quickly turned around with a perfectly fake look of distress across his face.

"I wrestled the boy to the ground. He was then somehow able to attach himself to the ceiling."

"What? That's impossible!" Abram ran towards the window to investigate.

"Whatever the thing was broke through the window and escaped. I did everything I could to save the children," replied Sebastian.

"There's nothing out here." Abram turned away from the broken window and looked towards his colleagues. "How did this happen? I thought you said it wasn't an evil wraith. You said it was born from fear, not evil!" Abram yelled at Benjamin.

"I felt the thing, it attacked me! It was fear—I swear it."

"The kids must have done something to alter the fear; they must've scared it into lashing out like it did," Joe added, shaking his head.

"For Christ's sake!" Abram slammed his hand down on the table. "Get our kids; we need to investigate this."

Chapter 21
When All Hell Breaks Loose

"Tell us exactly what happened," Patricia said with urgency as she stood across a large table from the children. They were in a room they had never seen before; small with no windows, it sort of looked like one of those interrogation rooms from the crime shows Hunter's dad would watch on Wednesday nights. The group had been rushed from their room and escorted to the fourth floor of the estate, where the children hadn't spent much time before.

Patricia was not a happy camper either. She was tense, and she nervously played with her hands as she paced back and forth across the room. With her were the children's parents and guardians—Abram, Benjamin, Margot, and Joe.

Patricia had been awoken from a deep sleep in the early hours of the morning by a frantic phone call from Margot. She had had a hard time understanding Margot's frantic tone, something about the children getting into some serious trouble, and something about a young student from the Friedrich School running off into the night. She had hurried out of bed, tossed on the first outfit she could find in her closet and rushed to their aid.

"No half-truths, children; we need to know exactly what happened. Do you understand?"

The kids were tired, scared, and shaken up. Hunter sat in the middle of the group, his hands hidden under the table, visibly shaking, worse than Patricia's. He couldn't get the horrific look on Remy's face out of his head.

"Hunter should explain," said Elly, speaking up after no one else would.

"Hunter?" Joe asked. "You need to tell us. This is serious; someone got hurt tonight."

"Okay…" Hunter replied somberly. He took a moment to collect his words. "Well… we were doing a ghost hunt…."

"A ghost hunt?" Abram stopped himself from yelling and did his best to remain calm after Patricia shot him a dirty look. He knew that look all too well; it was her way of telling him to keep his cool.

"Why would you kids do a ghost hunt? How would you even know how to do one?" Margot shook her head in confusion.

"Well, for the last few months…" Hunter began to explain, he tried to choose his words carefully.

"Hunter has been studying for months, reading every book in the library about ghosts and spirits. He read the entire spiritual anomalies book too," Elly explained, not so much ratting her brother out but trying to explain that it wasn't hard to learn how to do one if someone really wanted to find out.

"And Remy knew a lot about it as well." Liv's eyes stung from her dried tears. "He knew almost as much as Hunter."

"Why such an interest in ghost hunting?" asked Benjamin, doing his best to remain calm as well. He didn't want the children to see them frantic; he knew that would only add to their fear. "Is this because of my attack? Why would you guys put yourselves in danger?"

"That was just a part of the reason," Alistair added. "I tried telling you guys about everything when you first got hurt, but instead of letting me explain, I got told not to 'spread rumors'," he explained.

"You tried telling us *what*?" Patricia frowned, stopping mid-pace. She was the one who was insistent on keeping the children from telling stories.

"We found a letter," said Alistair.

"A letter?" Joe repeated, looking over at his young nephew.

"Yeah, slipped under my bedroom door," replied Hunter.

He and Alistair did their best to explain to the adults about the night they snuck out into the forest, about the letter signed by the mysterious Order of Shadows, how it told them where they could find Solomon's Seal and how it would help Hunter speak to his parents one last time, to find out if they were really double agents. Hunter explained about the rumors the Krueger twins were spreading, how he was confused and missed his parents so much. How he would have done anything to say goodbye, one last time. Hunter admitted that Elly didn't want anything to do with it, and that it was his fault. He explained how he dragged Alistair out with him, and how Liv was just caught in the middle of everything. He then went on to explain to them about the ring they found buried underneath the large rock near Crooked Lake, and how he put it on later that night. He showed them the scar on his finger, and handed the ring over to Ms. Ellingbee.

"Hunter..." Joe felt the tears rise. He knew his nephew was struggling with the death of his parents, but he had had no idea how bad it was. He had been too busy mourning the loss of his legs to pay much attention. When he saw the terrible burn on his nephew's finger, Joe immediately left the room. He said nothing; he just rolled his wheelchair away from the group and left.

"Margot, please follow Joe and make sure he's okay," Patricia said with a frown.

"We're so sorry... We never thought..." Hunter couldn't speak anymore; he just didn't have the words. "Everyone hates me now."

"No one hates you, dear," Patricia said, waving off the notion.

"First things first." Abram took a seat across from Hunter. "Do you have this letter? I've never heard of this 'Order of Shadows'."

"No, I left it on the table in my room where Remy broke through the window."

"Hmmm..." Abram scratched his chin.

"What's wrong, Abram?" asked Patricia.

"Well, I checked that area out. The glass had shattered; it was all over the table, no letter though. Are you sure it was there?"

"I think so... I mean, I guess. I don't remember," answered Hunter, who wiped away the tears before they could roll down his cheeks. He was embarrassed enough; he didn't want any of his friends to see him crying, despite the fact that Liv and Elly's cheeks were soaked with tears.

"This ring you handed over," Benjamin said after inspecting it. "Obviously this group tricked you. This is not Solomon's Seal; the only person who knows where that ring is would be Professor Calenstine. Someone misled you into thinking this ring would grant you the power to speak to the dead, but instead, it released the dead."

"Do you recognize it?" asked Patricia.

"It's not from our collection, I know that much. How could this ring have gotten buried out by Crooked Lake?" Benjamin stopped for a second, choosing his words carefully. "Someone must've planted it. They knew they could use Hunter's emotions about his parents to get him to dig it up. They knew he'd wear it, and they knew it would release this spirit."

"I'm guessing this is no regular spirit we're dealing with?" Patricia frowned.

"No, we knew that when we first ran into it in the hallway. We spent weeks trying to find it, but after we got no spikes anywhere, we figured it had moved on," Abram answered.

"I don't understand." Margot looked the ring over. "What does a ring have to do with the ghost?"

"The ring acted as a seal to confine the spirit. Think of it as a magical prison. Someone powerful with ancient arts trapped it inside the ring itself. We see this quite a lot from ancient times," Ben explained.

"Yes, alchemists from the old world had the ability to manipulate items such as this to trap demons and evil entities," Abram added as Ben handed him the ring. "These markings are definitely the work of an alchemist. It's where the genie in the bottle myth comes from, except, replace the wish-granting genie with old-world monsters."

"Probably a wraith or a demon; either one, we're in trouble," Ben noted as he pulled a chair out and took a seat across from his son.

"Children, you were tricked. Some evil people fed off your pain." Abram squeezed the ring in his palm with anger.

"What do we do now?" asked Alistair. "It possessed our friend

Remy. We need to find him!"

"It was so scary," Liv added. "His face was lifeless, and his eyes were looking everywhere like a chameleon... He was climbing on the ceiling... He wasn't human anymore...."

"First things first, we need to find the boy," interjected Abram. "I'll start search parties. We start in an hour, and we'll go around the clock until he's found. Time is of the essence." Abram turned to take a step and almost ran into Albert Montgomery who was standing just inside the door. His eyes were flooded with tears. He had just heard Liv's description of his son.

"What did you freaks do to my kid? Where did he go?" he yelled, outraged. Emotions had taken over, and his fists were clenched tightly as he punched the metal door as hard as he could and leaving a large dent.

"Mr. Montgomery, please come with me." Patricia quickly turned to intercept Remy's grieving father. "Please, I will fill you in on everything.

"Ben, contact the professor for me; we need him to meet up with the children." Patricia turned back towards the group as she quickly hurried Remy's father out of the room.

"Kids," Ben looked over at the exhausted and fearful group, "I know you're tired and frightened, but we need to go see the professor, now!"

Chapter 22
The Evil Among Us

Benjamin wasted no time taking the children to the professor's subterranean office. He led the children through the grandiose library and unlocked the hidden passageway that opened into the technological and awe-inspiring Ocelot Room. There, the children were once again greeted by their gigantic robotic friend, Plato, who manned the station alone.

"Delighted Statement: Children, to what do I owe the pleasure?" Plato's monotone robotic voice broke the silence of the large room.

"Sorry, Plato, no time for formalities," Ben replied in a rush. "Will you please release the energy field so we can take the lift down to the professor's office?"

In the northern most section of the Ocelot Room was a large doorway protected by a potentially deadly electrical current, or rather, a state-of-the-art force field.

This force field separated the main computer room from a single, small hallway that opened up to the elevator that led to Professor Calenstine's enclave. As far as the children knew, only Plato had the proper authority to release the force field to allow admittance into the lift. Despite the many men who worked with Plato in the Ocelot Room at any given time, it was Plato who was the chief operator of system logistics as well as the head librarian. Plato volunteered his time as the librarian.

"Observation: Children, you look troubled. Master Benjamin, is all well? Formulating diagnostics... Checking estate's backlog of activity over the span of 24 hours... searching... Window breached within the young master's dormitory at approximately three forty-six in the a.m. Interested Cue: Are you children all right?"

"Plato," Benjamin spoke in a serious tone, "I'm sure the professor will update the records once we're done speaking to him. Forgive me, but you can be updated then. Right now, time is of the essence, please... your code." Benjamin stood patiently at the force field. It buzzed loudly in his ear.

"Apologetic Response: Yes, sir, right away." The large robot walked over to the PIN pad and entered its key to release the force field.

"I promise you'll be caught up with everything that has happened, old friend." Benjamin moved the children forward down the long hallway and towards the lift. Thank you."

The children hadn't said much during the long walk, nor had Ben, although he tried the best he could to settle the children down a bit and reassure them. "Don't worry, guys. Everything will be okay. We have people out looking for Remy, and trust me the professor will know what to do."

Of course, none of the children believed him when he said everything was going to be okay. They saw the terror hidden in his eyes and the look of despair on his face. Hunter couldn't remember the last time "everything was okay." The last six months of his life had been one disaster after another. He didn't even know what "okay" was anymore. He had lost his parents; his uncle had been attacked by a monster and left crippled from the waist down, and the kids at his new school were saying his parents were traitors. Hunter knew this was going to end badly for his friend Remy, and this time, it was completely his fault.

Ben hit the button to call for the lift, and the large metal doors slowly opened, allowing the group to enter. The air in the small elevator was thick and filled with tension. It was a long ride down into the estate's sublevels before the door finally chimed open once again.

The elevator doors unveiled a long hallway filled with all sorts of mysterious décor. The walls stretched out farther than the children's eyes could see. As Benjamin led the children down the corridor, Alistair and Liv couldn't help but notice all the strange and wonderful things displayed on the walls. The hallway itself was quite dim, but a small floodlight illuminated each fascinating item on display.

There were ancient paintings, old photographs of newspaper clippings dealing with a myriad of cryptids throughout history, some dating back to the mid-1700s, and framed letters written to Professor Calenstine from dozens of American presidents. Alistair and Liv did their best to soak up their strange surroundings, and normally they would have been very intrigued with the wonderful and mysterious sights their eyes beheld. However, considering their current emotional state, they simply moved on.

The group made their way closer to the end of the hallway, where it opened up into a large, oval study. There at the far end of the large room was a huge, half-circle mahogany desk. Behind it, deep into his work, was Professor Calenstine. The fresh smell of tobacco caught in the children's noses as the professor flipped through a large and ancient-looking textbook while blowing smoke through his nose. A long cob pipe was in his left hand. As he worked, he hummed a peculiar tune that Elly knew he had shared with her mother. She remembered when she had first met the professor that he had been humming the same melody. It immediately brought back memories of her mother.

Behind the ever-busy professor hung a giant, flat-screen monitor that covered the entire back wall. Hunter remembered being in awe of its size and how it had live feeds from all sorts of places in the world, including live feeds from around the estate. Now it was showing multiple news outlets on mute.

"Professor," Ben said, clearing his throat nervously. "Patricia told you we were coming?"

"Ah, well hello, Ben!" The professor lifted his eyes from his large, weatherworn book. He took one more puff from his pipe before speaking again. "Children..." He nodded to them with a smile spread across his wrinkly old face.

It was here, within his own personal enclave, that the professor spent the majority of his days, happily working on any number of ancient secrets and worldly mysteries. Everything he needed was at his disposal, and thus for the last decade, he had allowed Patricia Ellingbee to run everything above ground, only intervening when necessary. The professor sat comfortably in his wheelchair with his equally old best friend, the adorable lapdog Monte, snoring loudly on his lap.

"Yes, Ms. Ellingbee did notify me that you were on your way with the children." Calenstine's bushy left eyebrow rose in curiosity. "Interesting as it is, I dare say, I need to take a break from this little book of mine. I have been up for two nights reading it, crucial evidence of an alternate reality." The professor closed the large textbook but not before marking his spot with a piece of paper; the cover read 'The Journal of Bennett Kingsely.' "Judging by the sour look on everyone's faces, I do say something transpired last night?"

"Well..." Ben took a deep breath and, without sparing any details, told the professor the entire story.

"We must find Remington." The professor's friendly smile faded as he let the bad news sink in.

"Children..." he sighed softly, lifting his tired face from his palms, "I must apologize. Never in the history of our beloved society have we dealt with so many tragedies."

"It's my fault," Hunter blurted out. He held his head low, staring down at the marble flooring. He hadn't made eye contact with anyone since Remy's disappearance. He had even avoided his friends' gazes.

"Yes, I suppose that is partially true," the professor stated with a frown. He wasn't keen on seeing the pain on the children's faces, especially on Hunter's, who seemed to bear the most weight. "However, the blame cannot be solely put on your shoulders, my young friend. This group... this 'Order of Shadows', they fed off your pain and your childish innocence. If only you had brought the letter to us the moment you received it."

"I'm sorry, I just... I thought my parents..." Hunter couldn't hold back the tears.

"Hunter..." Elly too felt the warmth of her tears hit her cheeks, yet she didn't know what to say to make her brother feel better. She had been avidly against seeking out the ring, but deep down, she knew why Hunter wanted so desperately to speak to their parents again.

"Hunter, it is very important to understand," the professor's voice became very serious, "that you are as much a victim as anyone else in this matter. The true evil stems from this Order of Shadows... this inner-sect that is operating among us. They manipulated and preyed on you."

"We have been trying to think of anyone who could have written it," Ben now added as he began pacing around the room nervously. "They received it right after Gerald Krueger and his family left; perhaps he found a way to deliver it."

"Well, he does seem to fit the bill because, after all, he had just been exiled from the estate," replied the professor. "But I fear this group is bigger than just one man; I am afraid the Aten Corp has gotten their filthy fingers on some of our own and persuaded them to go against our cause."

"What can we do to help?" asked Alistair.

"Nothing. You kids have done enough," Ben blurted out a bit forcefully.

"We are all to blame." Liv looked over at Hunter, attempting to reassure him. There were so many emotions in the air: fear, sadness, despair... "We all wanted to do the investigation; it wasn't just you." She reached out with her shaky hand and held Hunter's.

"Children, Benjamin is right. Please leave it to us," replied the professor. "This is nothing for children to deal with. We're not dealing with a regular spirit here."

"We're dealing with a wraith," Alistair added. "We figured that out."

"Hmmm...." Calenstine couldn't help a faint smile. "You children have done your homework, I see. But this is not your average, angered wraith. Hunter, this ring Benjamin spoke of, may I see it?"

Hunter handed the ring over.

"Your finger," Calenstine noted. "The ring burned you..." He inspected the ring carefully.

"Do you recognize the ring?" Ben asked.

"I am familiar with this artifact... yes." Calenstine's lips pursed in fear.

"What is it? None of us had a clue," replied Ben.

"This is troublesome," the professor said, short on his words, trying to mask his fear. "I believe we are dealing with the entity known as 'Moloch'."

"'Moloch'? Where have I heard that name before?" Ben mused aloud, deep in thought as he continued his rhythmic pacing.

"Moloch comes from the first race of humans, who we refer to as the Ancients. Moloch is thought to be the first wraith born from evil. Ancient texts suggest he was an evil king who took it upon himself to sacrifice children in his name. He was one of the first truly evil people born into the world. His spiritual form, his wraith, is nothing short of wicked and malevolent. It is no wonder he took after a young boy's body."

"We're talking about *that* Moloch?" Ben gasped. "From the Ancients? Before Plato's time?"

"Correct. This wraith has spent millennia terrorizing and torturing human souls who he has come across. It has haunted this realm longer than our current race could ever fathom. That is until the legendary King Solomon hunted it down and was able to trap him within this very ring." Calenstine placed the ring on the desk for all to see.

"So, it was trapped in that ring for thousands of years?" Ben was in awe.

"What is troublesome is that I have dedicated many years of my life to finding this very ring and placing it somewhere safe so that it would never fall into the hands of the wrong person. This is the fabled 'Daupnir Ring'."

"Looks like we were too late in finding it," added Ben.

"I fear that Aten Corp found it first, but how did it end up near Crooked Lake?" Calenstine mused aloud, displaying a troubled and wrinkled forehead.

"We need to find out who this Order of Shadows are and we need to exile them from our home. This is all their doing."

"Benjamin, please escort these children back to their rooms and have them stay together under parental guidance until further notice. If the spirit has an attachment to any of these children, they need to be safeguarded. Understood?"

"Yes, sir," replied Ben.

"I need time to think and formulate an action plan. Until then, I want you to keep a team searching for the young Remington. We need to find him quickly. If we can incapacitate him physically, the wraith will be trapped in his body. We can then try and exorcise the spirit from his body."

"That sounds dangerous..." Liv frowned.

"Luckily, we have your father, Abram. He's well versed in the paranormal field. That's how he saved me," Ben added.

"Ben, please take the children and wait at the elevator. I would like to have a word with Hunter, alone. He will meet up with you in a few moments."

"Yes, sir," Ben said, nodding. "C'mon, guys, let's head back."

Hunter was a little worried about what the professor had to say to him. He was sure he was in more trouble than Calenstine had alluded to earlier. Perhaps he just wanted to save him some embarrassment in front of his friends.

"Hunter, it is important you do not internalize your role in this terrible tragedy. Yes, your actions led to this event, but you did not act alone. There were parties involved pushing your hand. It is important to take some responsibility for your actions, to grow and learn from your mistakes, but find some solace in the fact that you were a puppet being dangled by a string. I want to share with you a story, one that only a few other people in this world have ever heard. I must ask for your word, a promise that you must keep. You must promise not to share this secret I am going to tell you with anyone else. Can you promise me that?"

"Okay," Hunter answered a bit baffled. "I promise."

"Good then..." Calenstine sat back in his wheelchair, struck a match, and took another long puff from his pipe. "I want to tell you about how I came to be so old, and how I happened to play a very pivotal role in helping create the man you know as the figure head of Aten Corporation. Just like you, I unwillingly released this evil into our world. Unfortunately, in my case, I acted of my own selfish accord and had no outside sources influencing my decision; nor was I a young man like you so I should have known better."

Hunter was still at a loss for words.

"Tell me, Hunter, have you ever heard of the Fountain of Youth?"

Chapter 23
The Fountain

1785
The Everglades

"Sir, I... cannot go much farther..." Bartleby wiped the persistent sweat from his brow. He swallowed hard and pushed to keep up. He winced in pain with every step he took through the dense, swampy marsh, doing his best to watch out for snakes as they waded through a small patch of brush. He knew all too well that cottonmouths and diamondbacks were as deadly as the alligators. Venomous creatures and gators aside, the most formidable opponent was the blazing hot sun. Bartleby treaded lightly, doing his best to keep up. His sickly young face was hidden beneath a month-long growth of beard.

Bartleby thought they were ready for the two-week journey deep into the marshy climate, but when two weeks became a third and then a fourth he knew they were in a lot of trouble. Expeditions take a lot of planning and rationing, but they had been out of food for two weeks and hunting and fishing off the land were their only means of survival. Water was also an issue; they had started catching rainwater to keep hydrated, and as a last resort, they had been straining and boiling the dirty swamp water to purify it.

Bartleby had begged to turn back for the entire third week, but Calenstine wouldn't listen. He knew it didn't matter now, even if they turned back today, because Bartleby was sure they would succumb to the terrain. It was at least a three-week journey back to the last town. They had pushed their limits, traveled too far for too long off their course, and worst of all, he had hidden a deadly secret from the captain!

"There is no going back, son." A very young Claudio Calenstine stopped in his tracks and turned swiftly around to pass a metal flask filled with water to his last remaining partner. "Drink, but know it's our last few drops until the next rain or until we can properly set up a fire." Calenstine was in his early forties; grey had already taken over his hair and the majority of his beard. Despite the greyness of his face, Calenstine was in great shape and appeared to be in perfect health despite the long journey.

Calenstine didn't pay any mind to Bartleby's condition; instead, he was studying the sky as he handed the flask over. He then took a seat on a large fallen tree and took a scruffy little dog from his backpack. "Monte, I know you hate traveling in the backpack, but I assure you it is the safest way." He scratched the pup's ears playfully. "Once we break through this marsh, I will let you out to run around. I don't want you becoming a tasty treat for a gator." Calenstine kept his beloved dog on his lap while he took a journal from his pack and began writing.

"We will rest here for a bit, so find some shade and don't overheat." Calenstine nodded, pointing to a decently shaded area underneath a large cypress tree.

"We've been out in this damn swamp for too long; we lost our entire expedition to this place." Bartleby drank the last bit of water before finding the shade. "Four good people, dead, Claudio, I don't want to die out here alone! I... miss my family." He winced in pain, holding his arm.

"You won't, son," Claudio responded bluntly, not looking up from his journal. "More than likely, I will die alongside of you," Calenstine joked, but Bartleby found nothing funny about the comment.

"That gator... it ripped Clifton in half! We just weren't ready for this land; we don't know as much as we thought we did, and it's obvious we didn't come prepared for this crazy journey you set us on."

"Silence!" Claudio snapped, obviously agitated with his

comrade's remarks. He too felt the ominous effect of the daunting swamp and knew of the losses his team had endured in it. Of the five-team expedition, only he and Bartleby remained. One had been lost to a twenty-foot gator, violently snatched up as they waded across the swamp. The bloodcurdling screams still haunted Calenstine's dreams! Then there was Jeffrey, lost to heatstroke and fever. Worst of all was their third companion; no one knew what happened to Tanner, who just up and disappeared in the middle of the night. Claudio knew the voyage deep into these deadly swamps would come at a cost, but he could have never of known just how costly it would *truly* be. He did his best to not think about the losses and to keep his mind focused on the journey and their surroundings. He just kept on going as if nothing had happened.

"You knew the risk when you joined up," Claudio stated bluntly, as if he was trying to convince himself that the deaths weren't his to bear. He pushed them forward because he knew they were close to finding it, and he needed to find it! This was what he was born to do. There was no way he could turn around and go back empty-handed.

"We knew the risks of a two-week journey, not a month." Bartleby coughed hard. "So, now, I would argue that we didn't know the complete risks of this journey. If we followed the plan, all five of us would be at home with our families now."

"Yes, but you also knew the reward," Calenstine shot back. "I told you all before we left town that the possibilities of us never coming back were high. I know we suffered great losses, but...."

"You didn't tell us we'd be out here for damn near a month. We didn't bring enough provisions. We needed to turn back weeks ago when we were all still alive and well," Bartleby argued vehemently.

"Once we find what I need, I promise you all the riches in the world. Your family will be provided for, forever. We move forward for the ones we love, to go back as heroes, and to provide a lifetime of gold and riches." Claudio stood back up and pointed across the swampy marsh. "We have to wade through it. Be careful though. I don't want another death by gator on my conscience."

"Claud..." Bartleby stammered with his words, "I just... I

don't...."

"Out with it!" Calenstine turned back to see the worried look on his young partner's face. He saw now that he was paler than normal with deep black bags under his eyes. Calenstine knew the man didn't look well, but he had been so caught up with the expedition that he hadn't taken the time to even bother with Bartleby's well-being. He just kept pushing him on, pushing his team forward, and pushing to find his goal—to find the fountain.

"I am... not sure how much farther my body will take me..." Bartleby chuckled nervously. "I'm sick because something got me. Not sure what... It was two days ago...."

"Two days ago, what?" Calenstine picked up the scruffy Monte and placed him back in the backpack, tying it shut with just enough space to allow Monte's head to stick out. He walked over to Bartleby to check on him.

"I woke up with this on my arm." Bartleby rolled up his sleeve and exposed a gruesome infection. The skin was swollen and split down the middle with blisters and ulcers oozing yellow puss, everywhere! The wound looked deadly.

"Why didn't you say something earlier?" Claudio shook his head in disbelief.

"The first day it just itched, so I didn't think much of it. Then the..." Bartleby coughed hard once again, and he could feel his body burning up, "...the wound grew bigger andmore painful. It was already too late...."

"I have a few meds left and I want you to take them. I need you strong. We'll cross this marsh, and find a place to set up camp. We won't push forward until you regain some strength."

"What was it?" Bartleby asked. "What bit me?"

"Looks like a brown recluse spider. Small little buggers get into your clothing." Calenstine pulled out his large knife from a holster on his belt, cut a piece of his long sleeve off and used it to dress the wound. "It's not good."

"I don't want the meds" Bartleby said, waving off the pills. "What if you get sick too or bitten; one of us must stay alive to make it back and tell our families… to tell my wife and child I love them." A single tear rolled down Bartleby's face.

"I won't get sick," Calenstine said plainly. "Now take the pill! The quicker we cross the swamp, the quicker we set up our camp. I can hunt before it's late; we need some food in our systems. We need some fresh water as well. We need rainfall, or a fire to cleanse the swamp waters."

Claudio aided Bartleby through the swampy wetlands. The brush quickly turned to waist-high, murky waters filled with rotten leaves floating on top. There was little to no visibility in the water, and Calenstine knew all too well the dangers that could be lurking with every step. With one arm, he helped keep Bartleby upright and moving, and with his free hand, he extended a large thick branch out in front of him as a walking stick in hopes it would catch the attention of any predators before his foot did, better a gator take a snap at the branch than his own leg.

Luckily, the two men broke through the swamp and into a small clearing without complications. Wet, exhausted, and with little morale left, Calenstine found a small place to rest. He laid Bartleby under a large cypress tree and made his way out to find food.

Bartleby was in and out of consciousness, doing his best to keep his wits about him. Calenstine knew the fever was setting in, and he needed to be very careful over the next twenty-four hours if Bartleby was to live through this ordeal. The best bet was amputation of the arm, but even with all of Calenstine's knowledge, the act of amputating an arm in the unforgiving swamp with no real medical aid meant only death.

Calenstine was gone for no more than an hour, hunting, before he returned to the small clearing where he had left Bartleby. Calenstine carried with him three large canteens of swamp water and a large turtle he had managed to hunt down not too far from their soon-to-be camp. He was able to start a fire with the help of the flint he kept secured to a chain around his neck. Calenstine knew he could purify the swamp water as long as he boiled it for an hour over the fire making it safe for consumption. He also managed to set up a decent supper of fire-roasted turtle straight from the shell. Calenstine was excited with the catch, knowing it was the best the two men had eaten for the last few days. With little time for setting up camp or any real hunting, the two men had been living off of live frogs and small minnows they caught by hand in the tiny ponds they came across. They ate them raw, alive and wiggling, which had been gross at first, but Calenstine knew, when that insatiable pain of hunger struck, a man coul eat just about anything to stay alive.

Normally, Calenstine would crack and clean the turtle from the shell, but it was much easier to let it sit on the fire as a whole while he managed to work out a safe sleeping area for the two of them. It would take at least an hour before the turtle's shell became brittle, which would signify that the meat was cooked enough to eat. It would provide them with enough vitamins and protein to keep their strength up.

He used this hour to prep their sleeping arrangements for the night. It was growing late in the evening, and he knew they were too close to the water to sleep on the ground. That was how they had lost Margaret during the end of the second week of their expedition. They had made camp about twenty yards out from a wide riverbed. A twenty-foot, monster alligator snagged her out of her sleeping bag and dragged her into the swamp. Calenstine would not repeat the same mistake; he'd already lost far too many people on this expedition. The team hadn't known it, but they had made their journey during the alligator mating season, which was by far the deadliest time because male gators were extremely territorial and aggressive during the mating season.

Calenstine knew Bartleby couldn't go farther by foot until he regained some strength and his fever broke. So, as their meal cooked, Calenstine searched around for thick, sturdy branches and, using twine he had brought along with him on the journey, he was able to construct two beds about four feet off the ground. He was able to find a couple of sets of cypress trees with low-hanging, thick branches to construct the bedding. He tied the branches together with the twine, making sure they were strong and sturdy to ensure the branches and larger sticks could hold their weight. He then gathered up thick leaves from a native cabbage palm to use as bedding. He knew it wasn't going to be the most comfortable sleeping arrangement, but they would be safe for the night.

The sun had set and been replaced with a bright yellow moon that sat high in the starry night sky. Calenstine only had a few doses of medicinal herbs left, and after he was able to get Bartleby to eat some food, he handed him two more pills in hopes that come morning, at the very least, Bartleby's fever would break.

"I think we have enough doses of the meds to get you to kick this fever. However, I am not sure what to do about the wound." Calenstine inspected the area; the infection was spreading quickly. It had almost doubled in size, and the poison was eating away at the flesh on the man's arm—it was a grotesque sight.

"Look..." Bartleby managed to mutter as he slowly lifted his good arm and pointed behind Calenstine through a small clearing in the cypress trees.

Calenstine turned his head, and as soon as he saw it, his heart jumped in his chest! It was a cloud of thick black smoke that broke onto the skyline not too far away from them.

"Another camp?" Bartleby asked.

"Quiet," Calenstine whispered, not turning his head from the sight. "Take these pills and get some sleep." He helped Bartleby up onto the small sleeping platform he had made. "No gators will get you up here."

"Just the... spiders, right?" Bartleby somehow managed a chuckle. Gators were the least of his worries now. A damn spider was going to be his downfall; he just knew it.

Calenstine crawled up and lay in his own bed of sticks and cabbage palms. He stared for hours at the smoke. *Who would have traveled so deep into the swamps?* He knew he had to reach them as soon as possible. He prayed they hadn't endured as many hardships as his group. Perhaps they even had medical supplies and maybe Bartleby *could* be saved! But this was unchartered territory, and they were deep in the wilderness.

It was a sleepless night. Bartleby's constant, painful moans kept Calenstine awake, as did the ever-persistent curiosity about the other camp. At least Monte was doing well; the young, scruffy pup lay curled up in a ball on Calenstine's lap, throughout the night. Calenstine made sure to share some of his turtle meat and water with his furry friend. When the sun rose, Calenstine didn't hesitate.

Despite the lack of a good night's rest, he felt much better after the full meal from the night before. He hopped down from his small lodging and made his way over to Bartleby, who was now pale and very clammy. The bags under his eyes were even darker now. Calenstine was surprised because he had thought for sure that the medicine would have at least broken the fever.

"Come now, we need to investigate the camp. They might have medicine for you," Calenstine said, nudging his friend.

"Urrng…" Bartleby let out a small whimper. "Where… where am I?"

"Time is wasting; we must push on." Calenstine handed him the water canister and two more pills. "I'm doubling your dose, but after these two, we're out of medicine. We need to see if this other camp has something, anything, to aid your body in fighting off this infection."

"Okay… okay…" Bartleby, with the aid of Calenstine once again, took a step down from the raised platform. He was much weaker than the day before, barely able to hold up his own weight and almost completely relying on Calenstine for support.

"Leave me… just… leave… me… here…" Bartleby said through a raspy cough.

"Nonsense, we won't speak of such things. I'm judging it's only a half-hour walk from here to where the smoke was rising. We can do this." Calenstine helped his young friend towards where they saw the smoke. Luckily for the men, the wet swampy landscape began to dry up, and instead of waist-high, murky waters, they were pushing through a thicket of tall grass and solid ground.

The cypress trees, which needed the water from the wetlands to survive, were dwindling, and replacing them were solid trunks of oak and pine. The change of the landscape meant different dangers for the two men, and Calenstine knew to look out for the dangerous Florida panther and the always-dangerous black bears that no doubt called these woods home.

Luckily, the two men didn't stumble upon either, and after a tiring journey, Calenstine and Bartleby finally broke through into a small clearing. Calenstine was exhausted and quickly found a comfortable spot below an enormous oak tree and laid Bartleby down.

As soon as they had broken into the clearing, Calenstine knew it was the camp. There were two tents set up around the remnants of a fire, where the ambers still burned a dull orange. However, the camp seemed deserted.

"Bartleby," Calenstine used a cloth to wipe away the sweat from his friend's brow, "rest here and let me search the camp for supplies. Let the medicine work. Hopefully, whoever camped here will be back soon. Until then, I'll look around and see if there's anything we can use to help you. I'm sure we can barter for whatever we take later."

"Claud..." Bartleby choked over his words. "It's you... there's... two... of...."

"What? Bartleby? Hello?" Calenstine slapped his young companion lightly on the check to keep him conscious. "You're hallucinating... stay with me!"

"It's you..." Bartleby pointed behind Calenstine.

"You're delirious." Calenstine shook his head; he knew this was a significant turn for the worse. That's when he heard a twig snap behind him.

Calenstine turned quickly, his right hand ready to pull out his flint-locked pistol if needed. There, to his utter amazement, walked a groggy, middle-aged man whose appearance struck horror in Calenstine's heart.

"H-help... m-me..." the man stammered out in a low, weak voice before falling to his knees and down to the earth.

It wasn't the sight of the man's health that struck the fear of death into Calenstine, however. There, lying before him was a man who looked identical to himself as if he had a long-lost twin...

Chapter 24
The Fight

Joe had left the small room in a moment of weakness. He had wheeled himself away from the children, who needed him. He had left his own niece and nephew alone in an interrogation room, scared and frightened. He knew all they needed was his support, for him to hold them and say everything was going to be okay. When he heard his nephew try and explain to grown-ups how much emotional pain he was suffering and how much he had been struggling with the deaths of his parents, it just broke his heart. He couldn't handle seeing the looks on their faces. He had failed as an uncle and as a guardian.

"Joe, what was that about?" Margot chased after him down the hallway. "You can't leave them like that." She ran to catch up, grabbing Joe's wheelchair and spinning it around, forcing him to face her. "Why are you running away?"

"Running?" Joe mocked the concept. "I can't even do that!" he blurted out. He wasn't angry, no, but Joe could hardly speak. He was sobbing uncontrollably.

"Joe," Margot lifted his head, forcing him to look her into her eyes, "we're all scared! What's wrong?"

"I… I can't…" Joe took a deep breath, trying to compose himself. "I'm failing as their guardian! Did you see the pain and sadness in Hunter when he talked about my sister and Geoff?"

"Of course, I did! I see it in Elly's eyes too, but she just hides it better. Which is scary in its own right. Joe," Margot said in a serious tone, "they just lost their parents. They're going to be hurting and confused for a long time! That's why they need us."

"Us?" Joe shook his head as if that concept was a cruel joke. "I'm broken and I need as much help as they do! How can I raise them? I can't even take care of myself. I'm stuck in this god-forsaken wheelchair!"

"I know you have your own demons, but that's why I'm here, to help you beat this chair and to help raise those kids! I know you love those kids more than you hate that wheelchair."

"You?" Joe shook his head again. "Listen, you've been amazing, and those kids couldn't ask for anyone better. But, let's face facts, you have your own life to live. I don't even know why you agreed to be their guardian with me."

"What?" Margot's concerned look turned to confusion and a little anger.

"What are you going to do when you marry Sebastian? Have two families? Raise two sets of kids? Listen, it's just... you have your own life. Why mix it up in ours?"

"Are you serious?" Margot felt a different type of tears coming on, not from sadness but from anger! "How can you say that?"

"Because you have your own life!" Joe started to yell. "Your life is not with me, it's not with the kids—it's with Sebastian! You know that!" Joe wheeled himself away from her. "You won't be happy with this mess we call our lives."

"You have the audacity to say that to me?" Margot found herself yelling as uncontrollable anger boiled in her blood. "I have dedicated everything to helping you, Hunter, and Elly! I love those kids so much that I gave up my spot in the estate to be their guardian. But you? You're so caught up with your own limitations that you fail to see your potential!"

"Potential? Yeah... right..." Joe shook his head.

"Yes, potential! Instead, you whine and complain about your wheelchair. You stay up all night drinking and yeah, don't think we don't know. You drown yourself in pity and complain about being stuck in that thing, but you hardly try at all with your rehab classes. Given up is what you've done!" Margot turned to walk away.

"Right." Joe hung his head low because he knew it was true! It hurt, but he knew.

"Oh, and by the way," Margot turned around one last time, "no matter what curveball life gives you, it never makes it right to be a jerk to the ones who care about you!" Margot stormed off down the hallway, leaving Joe alone to drown in his own thoughts.

Chapter 25
The Doppelganger

Hunter had hung on every word the professor had spoken. He couldn't believe the story he was being told. Although he wasn't quite sure why the professor had decided to share this tale with him, he wasn't about to ask why. He just wished he hadn't been sworn to secrecy! Elly, Liv, and Alistair would die to know what he had just learned! This was what Elly and Liv spent the majority of their free time researching.

"So, wait... you had a long-lost twin?" asked Hunter, mouth still agape from the sudden twist in the tale.

"I am afraid not, young one." Calenstine stroked his white beard with his boney fingers. "My mother bore no children before or after me. I am an only child."

"How then?" Hunter asked confused.

"Have you ever heard of a doppelganger?"

"A doppel-ranger?" asked Hunter, never having heard the word before.

"Ganger," corrected Calenstine with a small chuckle. "It is said that the universe holds many secrets, and one of which is the mysterious phenomenon known as the doppelganger. This is the belief that some people have an exact replica of themselves living out their own life far from your own. The tricky part, and what I didn't know back then, is that this doppelganger version of yourself is evil—your evil, non-blood related twin."

"An evil replica of yourself?" Hunter shook his head, trying to comprehend what he had just heard.

"I should have let him die there and let the fever take him over." Calenstine frowned before taking another puff from his pipe. "If only I had known...."

"Wait, so what happened? He was evil?"

"Well, sit back and relax. Let me finish the story...."

❧

Calenstine was baffled, with a million questions running rampant in his head. He couldn't understand it. How was it that in the middle of uncharted territory and in the middle of the everglades, he would stumble across another expedition with a man who looks identical to himself? Surely this was no mere coincidence, as Calenstine knew all too well that the universe just didn't act that way.

As Calenstine stared down at this unconscious man lying before him, he felt as if he was looking into some sort of trick mirror—a mirror that took a man's reflection and relayed to him what he would look like on his deathbed. Except there was no mirror, this was not a trick and this was definitely real life! This man was dying, and he needed Calenstine's help.

"You... have... a twin?" Bartleby mumbled his words. Somehow, he had mustered enough strength to crawl over towards the man passed out at Calenstine's feet.

"What?" The question shot Calenstine back into reality. "No... I was an only child."

"But..." Bartleby coughed, spitting up blood and phlegm, "he looks just... like... you...."

"No, he is not a blood relative of mine! I do not know who he is." Calenstine dropped to his knees and inspected the man's condition, checking his pupils and checking for a fever. He too was burning up, extremely pale and clammy.

"Have you been bitten? Can you hear me? A snake or spider?" Calenstine poured a small amount of water on the man's face to awaken him and checked him over for any puncture wounds.

"Uhhh..." the man moaned. "No bites... no stings..." he

whispered in a barely audible voice. The man struggled with his words. "I got... sick two nights ago... fever... vomiting..." Calenstine's twin pointed towards one of the tents. "Err... Aarielle got sick before... me... is... she? I haven't seen her."

"Jesus!" Calenstine darted over to the other tent in hopes of finding the woman in better shape than the sickly man. Calenstine hadn't thought to check for other survivors. He felt stupid. Of course, there was another person in the camp because there were two tents set up. He quickly entered one, and the sweet smell of death hit his nose. She had already passed away in the tent from the fever, probably a few nights prior. Calenstine frowned and covered her body with a blanket.

"It's too late," Calenstine said as he reemerged with a cloth over his nose and mouth.

"She... died...?" the man choked on his words. "Aarielle... damn it!"

"Do you have any medicine, or anything at all?" Calenstine spoke matter-of-factly, searching the man's pockets.

"No... My team... we all got sick... we were... the last to fall... ill... No more meds..." the man replied, his eyes glazed and staring off into space.

"Claud," Bartleby managed to sit himself upright, although it pretty much drained away all his energy to do so.

"Bartleby, stop moving. You need to rest and let the last dose do its job," Calenstine snapped. "You're going to die unless we—"

"Here..." Bartleby opened up his palm to reveal the medicine Calenstine had been feeding him for the last twenty-four hours.

"What the hell is this?" Calenstine felt the anger boil in his veins, throwing up his hands in disbelief. "You haven't been taking the meds No wonder you're not getting better!"

"I wasn't going to live..." Bartleby took deep, shallow breaths. "If... the fever broke... the poison... the wound... it would still spread... it would get me... kill me."

"You don't know that!" Calenstine felt his eyes watering up. "I can't lose another! You can't die out here!"

"What then... cut my arm off?" Bartleby coughed hard. "Amputate... the dead part out here? That would kill me... it would... end me too!"

"If I had to, yes!" Calenstine sighed heavily and calmed himself. "I can save you," he whispered.

"No, you can't. Please... give him the meds... maybe... you can... save one life... today... but we both know it won't be me." Bartleby smiled through all the pain and all the tragedy that was spiraling out of control. "Please... tell my family... I love them... tell my boy... tell him... I died saving someone else... I want... to be a hero."

Calenstine stood there with his friend's hand held in his own. He couldn't bear to speak, unable to muster up any sort of response. All he could do was nod tearfully with a sympathetic smile. He took the meds and turned towards the man on the ground.

"You're in luck! My companion may have just saved your life." Calenstine dragged the semiconscious man over to the base of an oak tree. "Take these, and in three hours, you'll take another dose. Until then, you rest." Calenstine tilted the man's head back and forced the meds down his throat. He couldn't help but stare at the man. It was eerie because he was the spitting image of himself! Everything about them was identical.

There was nothing left for Calenstine to do. So instead of waiting around, he opted to formulate a plan of action. He knew that if there was going to be any sort recovery for either of his companions, they would need food to regain their strength. So, off he went under the baking hot Florida sun to, once again, hunt. However, Calenstine quickly learned that it wasn't as much of a hunt as it was picking and gathering anything he could find. He gathered up anything that he knew was consumable and would provide some sort of sustenance and vitamins. He didn't have a bow or a rifle to drop any big game, and he had nothing to snatch up one of the many rabbits he came across. Instead, he broke open sections of rotted tree trunks and gathered up as many grubs and edible insects as he could. It wouldn't be the tastiest of meals, nothing like the small turtle he had come across the night before, but it would have to do. Monte didn't seem to mind; he had a love for the grubs and could sniff them out with ease.

After a few hours, Calenstine finally returned to the camp. The man who looked identical to him was unconscious, but he already seemed to be gaining some of his color back. Calenstine woke him briefly to give him his second dose of the meds. He then checked on Bartleby, who sat awkwardly hunched over by a nearby tree. Calenstine prayed he had just fallen unconscious as well. However, the poison and the fever had proved too much, and Bartleby had died while he was on his hunt.

"Damn it!" Calenstine sat down beside his friend, the tears flowing freely.

Calenstine's grief was uncontrollable. Everyone who had trusted him to lead them on this expedition had died because of his inability to listen to reason. He had felt bad about the others, but he knew that on any expedition causalities were always an unfortunate possibility. At least that's what he kept telling himself. He couldn't help but think of himself as a fool. Even after two other deaths and one of his own men disappearing in the middle of the night, he just couldn't swallow his pride and turn back. He was consumed by the possibility of finding it.

The afternoon was spent with Calenstine feeding off the insects he had gathered while saving enough for the sickly man when he awoke. He did his best to dig two shallow graves and bury the woman named Aarielle and his partner, Bartleby. Thankfully, they were far enough inland for Calenstine not to worry about gators attacking, and the tents would make for decent lodging for the night. Calenstine was exhausted and needed to rest himself unless he too wanted to fall ill.

He wasted no time in making a fire near the resting man with his trusty flint; it was set ablaze within minutes. He welcomed the smoke from the fire. At the very least it would keep the mosquitoes away. Calenstine took a seat alongside the sickly man for the rest of the evening, checking on his condition and making sure he was getting the doses of medicine that he needed to survive. At least Calenstine still had Monte, his dog, to keep his spirits up.

"Who are you?" the man asked after he finally awoke.

It was later in the evening, when the sun had found its resting place, and the stars once again called the sky their home. "Am... I... dreaming this?" He stared at Calenstine, whose face came to life in the dancing firelight.

"My name is Claudio Calenstine. My friend and I found your camp. You were delirious with fever," Calenstine replied with somber words.

"Friend?" the man coughed sharply.

"He didn't make it. He was bitten and the poison spread too fast. He gave you the last of our meds and saved your life because he wanted to die a hero. I hope you're worth it." Calenstine tossed a thick log onto the fire.

"You... you... look just like... me!" The man blinked his eyes in confusion. He was still weak and still sick.

"Well, let's not worry about that right now. Your fever just broke and you were nearly dead when I found you. Try and eat this, and here... I boiled some water so it's safe to drink." Calenstine handed over the canteen of water and a small pouch filled with grubs and insects.

"Bugs?" The man frowned as he placed a handful of the squirming white grubs into his mouth. He did his best to chew them up and swallow them down quickly. Each bite caused the grubs to explode into sour goo in his mouth, and it took everything the man had not to toss the meal back up.

"Beggars can't be choosers and they're ripe with vitamins. In truth they are one of the best sources of protein one can find out here. Do your best to keep them down. You need them to build up your strength. Chase them with the water if needed."

"I am feeling much better." The man peered around the campsite, trying to regain his composure. His eyes paused as they lit upon the two shallow graves.

"I had hoped I was dreaming." The man frowned.

"I'm afraid your partner passed a few days before we discovered you," Calenstine explained softly.

"I was getting sick, and she had already been hit hard with the fever. It took her so fast! When I awoke, I could barely move, so I couldn't check on her."

"I see." Calenstine returned the man's frown. "I have one more dose of meds for you. "Hopefully, tomorrow your strength will be back and we can figure some stuff out."

"After a good night's rest, I think I can be ready to travel." The man turned his eyes away from the graves. He forced a smile before saying, "Thank you, you saved my life."

"I didn't..." Calenstine stared into the fire with heavy thoughts, "Bartleby did."

"I see," the man replied.

"What brings you out here? This is an uncharted area—a no man's land," Calenstine asked.

"I'm an explorer," the man replied as he reached into his pocket and pulled out an old piece of folded-up parchment. He tossed it over to Calenstine. "I could ask you the same."

Calenstine didn't answer. He unfolded the parchment, and there was a map leading deep into the everglades. A large "X" marked a spot on the map with a handwritten note that read "The Fountain of Youth."

"What's your name, traveler?"

"Declan," the man responded in a raspy voice. He shifted uncomfortably, letting out a loud painful sigh. "Declan Aten," the man finished. "It's a pleasure to meet you, Claudio. I will assume by your expression that we're looking for the same thing?"

❧

"Wait a minute!" Hunter's eyes grew wide with amazement. "That man... your twin, was Aten?"

"I am afraid so." Calenstine forced a smiled, although that part of the tale left little to be happy about.

"B-but how is that possible? He's so much younger than you are! I remember what he looks like from when he interrupted the Orientation!"

"Yes, just another mystery! I do not know how he has been able to defy the fountain's powers."

"So, wait, what happened?" Hunter pushed on.

"Well, the universe works in mysterious ways, my young friend." Calenstine leaned back in his wheelchair and took a deep breath. "Somehow, my doppelganger, my evil twin, had started at the same exact time as me to set up and plan out the very same expedition. We both left on the same day about four weeks before to travel out into the deepest, darkest parts of the uncharted Florida Everglades. We were both following a potential lead that said within this area was where the mysterious Fountain of Youth could be found. Both our teams suffered severe losses, and in that small camp, we somehow managed to find one another. There I spent two days nursing him back to health, and we stayed up underneath the stars discussing the Fountain of Youth and the glory and riches we would have if we found it. We were very close, if his map was correct! It was only a day or two by foot. Once he was ready to set out again, we moved on.

"We hadn't a clue how close we had come. It only took four hours to hike there. I remember it like it was yesterday! We broke through a clearing, and there in the middle of nowhere stood a small spring. It was crystal clear, the water was just... words cannot describe how magical it looked! In the center of this tiny spring, no larger than five feet in diameter, was this ancient stone well. It had a language neither of us had seen written on it. But we knew we had found the Fountain of Youth."

"The Fountain of Youth?" Hunter repeated.

"That name is misleading," Calenstine said as he chuckled.

"What do you mean?" asked Hunter, not quite understanding the humor in the name.

"Well, let me ask you a question, and please answer honestly. Do I look youthful?" Calenstine smiled.

"Oh... no, I suppose not."

"Yes, Deckie and I thought the fountain would let us live forever and also keep us young. We were only half-right. Well, I should clarify, because somehow, he has managed to defy the aging process, but knowing him, it comes at a grave cost to others. It does let anyone who drinks from it live forever; however, it does not defy the aging process. Thus, my withered old body."

"You actually found it? In Florida?"

"Well, it wasn't Florida back then," Calenstine replied with a half-smile.

"So, is it still there?"

"Well, the story is not over. We had just found the Fountain of Youth. We were not sure what to do. It was so deep into the uncharted area that we weren't sure if we could ever get back here and find it again. The journey was just too dangerous. We made camp, and Deckie and I stayed up all night talking and trying to figure out a plan. We decided to sleep on it, and in the morning, we would make our decision. I remember I woke up because Monte was barking angrily. I noticed he wasn't in my tent, and then I heard him squeal, loudly, as if something had attacked him.

I grabbed my flintlock pistol and emerged from my tent. I saw him lying awkwardly in the small spring, whimpering. I ran over to him, but I saw no one. His leg had been broken, and he was bleeding internally. But as I watched him, I saw him changing and his leg was healing itself. The blood coming from his mouth stopped! Within minutes, he stood back up on all fours as if nothing had happened. That's when I heard Deckie laugh...."

ຎ

"It worked!" Aten smiled brightly. "It healed his leg!"

"What do you mean it worked?" Calenstine shot back, picking up his beloved Monte, who growled viciously at Aten. He slowly backed away from the spring and towards the campfire.

"Yes, of course, let me explain, my friend. From the beginning, shall we? You see, Aarielle was to be the test subject, and when she died, I needed a new one, so your little dog was perfect." Aten pulled from his belt a small pistol and pointed it at Calenstine. "Poor, Aarielle. She died before she was able live out her true purpose. She was the perfect companion, who followed my every word and was one-hundred-percent dedicated to the greater cause. She had a bit of a temper though, that girl. You know, she helped me kill off the rest of my team, one by one. She was a little too good at it! Of course, we waited until we got far enough that we didn't need them anymore." Aten aimed the gun steadily at Calenstine's chest. "I needed help traversing through this bloody swamp, but the end game was always to be the same: only myself and Aarielle were to walk out of this swamp with the goods."

"Wait... calm down..." Calenstine began to sweat, and his heart pounded in his chest. He had no idea who this man was because he seemed so different from the man he had nursed back to health. Calenstine knew he had been played for a fool and had fallen right into this man's trap. He was talking madness and was clearly insane!

"See, we weren't supposed to get sick... damn Mother Nature." Aten shook his head with a sly smile as if he was impressed with the turn of events. "She almost ruined everything by getting us sick with the fever. When Aarielle died, I thought all my plans had fallen apart. I thought I would die alone in these damned everglades. Even if I lived, I needed a replacement. Who would I find out in the middle of the uncharted swamps? Then I heard you rustling about my camp. I needed someone else to test the fountain, and the universe brought me you and that bastard dog of yours. At first, I thought I would trick you and shoot you so your wounded body would fall into the spring. But if the spring was real and its magical properties were true, then how would I get rid of you?"

"What are you talking about?" Calenstine frowned. "To test it, you were going to kill her and me?"

"Yes, but only if the fountain was a fake. I had planned to kill her later, back in the safety of our home. She knew she had to give her life, so her only wish was to go peacefully. Poison perhaps as she slept? We hadn't thought that far... Oh, come now, don't give me that look." Aten smirked at the look of disgust written all over Calenstine's face. "Aarielle was nothing more than a follower and she knew the plan. She had given herself to me and given her life to my cause. She knew that I was the only one who could come out of this expedition alive. Don't tell me you didn't have a plan. You must have had a subject. You can't be that foolish, can you? How were you to know how or if the fountain even worked?"

"I would have taken samples back and run tests," Calenstine answered matter-of-factly.

"Foolishness is why you will die here, and I will live on to reap all of the benefits." Aten shook his head, mocking Calenstine. "See, it was all planned. I would have shot Aarielle in the chest. She would position herself so that her body would fall into the spring. If she rose from it, I would know the spring was real and that it truly was the Fountain of Youth. I would bathe and drink from its waters, and together, we would carry back as much as possible. Right after we blew the hell out of the spring, of course! That's why I packed all the extra gunpowder sticks wrapped and rolled in sawdust. Highly explosive stuff." He motioned towards a large traveling bag that contained the ingredients.

"You're going to blow it up?"

"Yes, and I will have the only remaining samples. It's all about business, so don't take it personally."

"So, why didn't you shoot me when my back was turned, let me fall in, and be your test subject?" Calenstine clenched his fists in anger. "Why sit here and tell me all of this?"

"Because I don't want your wounds to heal," Aten answered with a grin. "Are you not following? That is why I stole your annoying little pet, broke its leg, and tossed it in. I had to see if it would heal. Then I would know once I drank from it if I would live forever. You see, the fountain is said to have two magical qualities: to bathe in it will heal all wounds, and to drink from it shall grant one, eternal life! Then again, I am sure you knew that already, right? After all, we both ventured out into the middle of nowhere searching for this little slice of heaven. You're not a piece of this puzzle, but just a random piece of collateral damage."

"So, what now? Why must you kill me? You know it works, so let me live! You said it yourself that you plan to blow the spring up.

Nothing will be left for me to find if I ever came back anyway."
Calenstine slowly moved his hand towards his side, where his
flintlock pistol was tucked into his belt.

"Are you that daft?" Aten frowned in disbelief of the statement.
"There can be no witnesses. I will leave this hellhole of a place as the
only living human to know of its magic." Aten smirked when he
pulled the trigger of his pistol. A loud earsplitting boom echoed
through the forest.

Calenstine felt the sudden pressure in his chest. He looked down
and saw a sea of red flowing from his wound. He expected pain, but,
strangely enough, he hardly felt much of anything except an intense
heat emanating from the left side of his chest. He then felt dizzy and
fell over, face first, into the dirt.

"Right through the heart." Aten holstered his pistol. "Pity really…
such a waste of life."

ↈ

Calenstine awoke with the terrible taste of blood in his mouth as his
beloved pet, Monte, licked his face until he regained consciousness.
He was groggy and confused, and he felt something sticky
underneath him. It was a warm pool of his own blood. He didn't
move, but once he had regained his composure, he saw the man who
had shot him hunched over the spring. Aten was filling up vials with
the spring's magical waters. It looked like he was trying to get as
many as he could physically travel with. After he had gathered as
much as he was able to carry, Aten walked away from the spring and
back towards the camp, where Calenstine lay supposedly dead.

"I must apologize," Aten said to Calenstine, who he thought was
dead. He kneeled over his body and looked one last time at
Calenstine's face, ignoring Monte's growls. "You must understand
that as a businessman, I cannot let anyone who knows of this little
miracle live. It must be *all* mine. A shame really, and very peculiar for
us to meet up here the way we did. I suppose it was fate! Because if
you were to think of the odds that you were to stumble upon a man

who looks identical to yourself, searching for the exact same things, and leaving the exact same date, I imagine it is nearly impossible. Such a pity that you had to die. I had so many questions for you."

Aten went through Calenstine's pockets and pulled out his canteen. He poured the water out and went back to the spring to fill it with every last bit of water he could.

Calenstine looked over and saw that the bag with the explosive ingredients had been emptied out. On a small tree stump next to it sat five large sticks of the rolled-up gunpowder mixed with sawdust and a long black wick sticking out of the middle of them. He watched as Aten finished filling the last canteen.

"Monte... old... pal... 'ankles'..." Calenstine muttered, spitting up blood.

Monte cocked his head for a moment after hearing the word. The dog quickly darted off towards Aten, whose back was still turned to them, tail wagging a mile a minute.

Aten had just stood up from filling the canteen, cursing the hot sun and wiping his brow, when he felt a sharp pain at his ankle.

"Damn it! What the hell?" Aten kicked at Monte, who had just sunk his teeth into the man's leg. "You little bastard!"

Aten pulled out his gun and took a shot that missed Monte by a few inches, sending up chunks of the earth into the air. Monte darted off into the forest. Aten cursed and followed with his weapon drawn.

Calenstine, with what little strength he had left, crawled his way towards the spring. It was only a few meters from where he lay, but it seemed like miles. Finally, his face hit the cold water, and he drank in giant mouthfuls of the refreshing spring water. He continued to crawl his way deeper into the spring, letting the water cover his body so that he was completely submerged. He felt a bizarre warmth overtaking his body, and then an extremely hot pain from within his chest. Despite the burning agony, he felt his strength coming back, and he was able to muster enough strength to stand back up.

There he stood, waist-deep in the spring, when just a few moments earlier, he had been nearing his last breath. Now he felt completely revitalized. Yet, the dull burning pain persisted as he quickly pulled off his bloodstained shirt and tossed it on the ground next to the spring. He looked down at his chest and saw the gaping wound from the bullet. To his surprise, it was no longer bleeding out, but he could tell something was moving around inside the wound. He watched in awe as the bullet that had lodged deep into his chest cavity was somehow being pushed from his body. Slowly the bullet came out of the open wound until it finally popped out and feel into his hand. Calenstine couldn't believe his eyes as he watched the gaping wound slowly close in on itself. His deadly wound completely healed, on its own!

There was no time to think about it despite the miracle that had just happened before his very eyes; Calenstine knew time was of the essence. It wouldn't be long before Aten returned. Calenstine ran over to the small tree trunk where Aten had laid out the sticks of explosives. He very carefully grabbed them and found a dry branch that he would catch on fire and use to light the long wicks of the explosives. Calenstine then returned to the middle of the spring to wait for Aten's return.

Suddenly, Monte came darting back out of the thicket of the trees, and Aten quickly followed. The moment he broke through the clearing, he stopped dead in his tracks.

"Impossible..." Aten's eyes grew wide. "You're dead; I shot you dead in the heart!"

"You were right about one thing," Calenstine took the burning stick and lit the wick from the explosives. "This fountain needs to be destroyed. It stirs up nothing but evil in a man's heart. We're both proof of that."

"This isn't over!" Aten's mouth pursed tightly. He peered over to his right and saw his bag with the dozen or so canteens he'd filled with water from the spring. He darted over towards them and quickly snagged up as many of the canteens as he could, quickly tossing them into the bag.

"Goodbye!" Calenstine dropped the explosives down the small well that fed into the heart of the spring. The explosion was enormous. The entire well and spring were blown to smithereens with chunks of dirt blown fifty feet into the air; dirt and sod rained down for over a mile.

Calenstine had run as far as he could before the explosion, but he got caught in the blast and flung high into the air. The momentum sent him crashing down into some nearby shrubs.

∽

"Wait a minute," Hunter frowned, "if Aten shot you in the heart, how would you have lived long enough to crawl into the fountain?"

"Yes, a fine question." Calenstine smiled. "Good attention to detail, my young friend. Have you ever heard of dextrocardia?"

"Err... no."

"A rarity and it means my heart is on the right side of my chest, not the left, like yours is," Calenstine said, pointing towards Hunter's heart.

"Wouldn't he have the same issue if he was your dopple... person...?"

"My doppelganger? I also thought about that and spent many years pondering that little question. I think it's safe to say that when it comes to Declan's and my own heart that they are nowhere close to being mirrored, neither physically nor mentally. A bit poetic, don't you think?" Calenstine chuckled slightly.

"So, then what happened? You blew up the spring. How did you survive?"

"Well, the force of the explosion sent me flying, no doubt about that. I can thank this beloved little pal of mine, Monte." Calenstine scratched the old dog behind its ears. "I awoke once again to him licking my face. I don't know how long I was out or how long it took Monte to sniff me out and wake me, but when I awoke, there was no sign of Aten. I had hoped the blast had killed him. However, I knew that we had both just consumed the spring's water, and we had both just bathed in it. I didn't have a scratch on me, despite the intensity of the blast. I knew it had to have been the healing effects of the spring. It was still inside our bodies, healing us."

"So... wait, you can't be hurt?"

"Well, that's not entirely true. The effects wear off once the body is done consuming the water or once the water dries off your skin. We were lucky because if the blast had happened an hour later, there may not have been enough water left in our systems to heal us. I was still soaked with the spring water when the blast occurred, so I think it healed me right away."

"That's incredible! So, if the power of the spring goes away once the water is gone, how is it that you're so old?"

"Because we drank from it. Same as little Monte here, who drank from it when Aten tossed him into the spring. Once consumed, it will heal all ailments at the time, but it also grants immortality."

"So, you *can't* die?" Hunter asked.

"Not by old age or disease. We're immune to most things. However, I am still prone to bodily harm, as is Aten, unless he still has vials of the spring stashed somewhere. I have been lucky enough to escape any physical tragedies, despite my adventurous youth."

"Wait, but Aten is so much younger looking," Hunter stated, trying to let the story settle in his brain.

"Yes, just another mystery I have not unraveled yet." Calenstine gave Monte his favorite bacon-flavored doggie treat. "Hunter, I told you this secret for a reason; do you know why?"

Hunter thought for a bit before answering, but he honestly wasn't sure why the professor had opened up to him at all. After all the events that had transpired that night, he knew there was sure to be some sort of lesson the professor wanted him to take away.

"I was younger then, still had much to learn about the world, and when I led that team deeper and farther into those swamps, my emotions and pride made my decisions. I was overcome with this obsession and crazy need to find the Fountain of Youth. I am telling you this because I too made the same mistakes you did when you didn't listen to your friends about putting the ring on. You didn't listen to your sister when she told you it wasn't worth pursuing, and you ignored Alistair's request that you wait to even attempt to put the ring on. You became obsessed to speak to your parents one last time, and it was because of this that you let darkness and evil manipulate your actions. Just like I let it out in those swamps. I told you this story because I wanted you to know that we all make mistakes, and sometimes those mistakes can weigh down your soul for an eternity. This won't be the last time you must face something like this, so please learn from it. Your friend is not entirely lost, yet. There is still time to save him. That's more than what I can say for Bartleby and my team."

"Do you think we'll find him soon?" Hunter asked, humbled by the story.

"I have hope… and so should you."

"I…" Hunter put his head down once again as the shame began to resurface, "I want to help as much as possible to find him."

"I know you do, my son," Calenstine had a proud smile on his wrinkly old face. "When you want something bad enough, sometimes you find help in unexpected places. Remember that and if you're pure, you will find the answers. I will allow you to catch up with your friends at the elevator now. Please, be safe."

"Yes, sir," Hunter replied, nodding. His soul was heavy, and a million different emotions swirled about his head. He hadn't felt so confused and lost since the day he had found out his parents were never coming home. However, he did feel that his spirits were lifted after the professor's story. He knew he had made some mistakes, but if he was pure with his intentions, he could right his wrongs, assuming he had the power to do so.

"Oh, Hunter," Calenstine shouted.

"Yes?"

"Did you know our ancestry can be traced back to the very first bloodline of the Seekers? You can thank Bartleby for that. I returned home fully intending to make good on the promise of finding his wife and kids and looking after them. When I found them, and delivered the terrible news," this time it was Calenstine who found his face being overshadowed with shame, "let's just say I did everything in my power to help raise and protect his family. Together with his wife, we trained his children to follow in his footsteps, and they were the first bloodline, outside of my own of course, that founded the Secret Seekers Society. Bartleby was one of your great-great-great grandfathers."

"Bartleby was my great-great-great grandfather?" Hunter didn't know too much of his family tree outside of his grandparents.

"Bartleby Jakobs was a great man. All of the men and women I lost on the journey, I found their families and offered the same deal. It was only Bartleby's family that took me up on the offer to raise his children and train them in the Secret Seekers Society. The others just thought I was a crazy old coot living in a dream world. Your grandmother knew there was more to this world, and she didn't want Bartleby's death to be in vain. You come from a long line of amazing and brave people who understand the way the world works. Your family puts the well-being of others first; they do what's right for the greater good! Never doubt yourself, and more importantly, never doubt your parents' allegiance to the society."

"You... you're talking about the thing about them being double agents?"

"There was no reason you should have ever heard of such nonsense. Those Kruegers have always been jealous of your family. It goes back for generations. However, Gerald and his children were cut from a different cloth, more self-centered, and a bit too focused on their own cause and not for the society. I waited, but I should have exiled Gerald from the Enlightenment when he was a kid due to the rotten little child he was, even back then. I had hoped that with the proper guidance and mentoring, he would grow out of his selfishness but it only got worse."

"What about my parents? What were you going to say?"

"They *were* double agents. That much is true."

"What?" Hunter's mouth dropped open. He couldn't believe it.

"They worked hard to gain Aten's trust, and it was your mother's idea. She would feed him information that I approved that was big enough to keep Aten's whistle wet, but not to give up too much information that could damage the estate. They did this for years, and after a while, they had gained enough trust that they were able to return the favor. They learned so much about Aten and his corporation that it was finally paying off. Right before they died, they were working on finding out the location of a mysterious island that was rumored to have been purchased by Aten for terrifying scientific research. They were on their way to a meeting with some of Aten Corps higher-ups when their plane crashed."

"They were going in as spies..." Hunter felt a tear roll down his cheek. He had cried so much that night that he hadn't thought it possible to cry anymore.

"Yes, they were spying on Aten Corp for us. They had given up the monster-hunting, the paranormal researching, and dedicated their time and their life to unraveling the evil nature of Aten Corp."

"They were heroes, weren't they?"

"You can share that part of the story with your sister. I want her to know the truth about your parents. You come from a long line of heroes, Hunter. I know you and your sister will follow in their footsteps."

Hunter nodded and felt a weight of pressure lifted from his chest. His parents weren't traitors—he knew it, but now he had the proof.

"Hunter," Calenstine cleared his throat, "remember that if your heart is pure, you may find help from unexpected sources."

Hunter wasn't sure how to take Calenstine's final words, but he had much to think about. He couldn't wait to tell Elly and his friends about the truth behind his parents, but even that was soured by the pain and fear of their lost friend Remy. Hunter knew they had to do something; he wasn't going to stop trying, especially after Calenstine had opened up to him.

Chapter 26
The Grimoire

When Hunter caught up with the group, he was greeted with a flurry of questions.

"What did he say?" Alistair ran up to him, wide-eyed and worried.

"What did he want?" Liv followed suit, still panicked from all of the commotion.

"Did the professor expel you?" Elly asked as she, of course, was worried about the worst possible scenario.

"It's okay, guys," Hunter said, his voice exhausted and muddled from the lack of sleep. "No, I wasn't expelled! I'll be in class with you guys next Monday in Professor Pike's intro class."

"I'm sure the professor just passed on some wisdom to Hunter," Ben said as he cracked a small smile. "The man has a way with words. Hunter, kids, we will find your friend, and he will be okay. Right now, it's time to go up to your rooms. It's been a long night, and you kids are running on no sleep, so let's head up."

The children had no qualms with being sent to their rooms. Hunter wanted nothing more than to go out with the adults and help search the estate and the surroundings woods, but he knew he was no good to anyone in his current state. Benjamin dropped the kids off at their room, where they met a familiar-looking man at their bedroom door.

"Hunter, Elly," Ben walked up to the man and shook his hand, "I think you've met Luther Burbank before. He's one of the primary caretakers and botanists that run the botanical garden."

"Luther!" Elly smiled. She spent much of her time outside of class helping Luther maintain the garden. She and Liv loved spending as much time there as possible, especially when it came to studying.

"Good afternoon, children. I hope you don't mind, but I volunteered to take first watch over your room."

"First watch?" Hunter asked.

"We have strict orders from the professor," Ben added. "Because you kids are on your own until living arrangements with your uncle and Margot are figured out, we need twenty-four-hour supervision for your safety. The professor thinks that thing may come back, and it might be connected to you kids because you were the ones that let it escape."

"Oh, great." Elly dropped her head in defeat. "We're never going to sleep because that thing is out to get us."

"We don't know that for sure," Luther said as he smiled and lifted Elly's chin up. "I'm sure the professor and Mr. Jenson here are just looking out for you kids." Luther pulled from his pocket a small yet vividly bright, fluorescent pink flower that seemed to sparkle, and he handed it over to Elly. "This is a Star Bright flower, and it's very rare; it's said to bring whoever holds it good luck. Maybe it will help you sleep."

"Thank you," Elly said as she tried to hide her frown.

"Kids, I'll be out here if you need anything at all. Just pop your head out and let me know what I can do."

The kids nodded and thanked their friend one last time before making their way into their bedroom, where they immediately snuggled underneath their warm covers.

Elly was happy to see that Trayer was back in their room waiting for them. However, he too was still quite spooked. Trayer jumped on Elly's bed and burrowed himself under the covers with her.

"Elly, before you fall asleep," Hunter said, sitting upright in his bed and staring out the bedroom window, which had been smashed and now replaced with thick plastic to cover it.

"Yeah, what is it?" Elly fought off a yawn.

"Mom and Dad weren't traitors. They were working with the

professor, trying to gain Aten's trust; they were spies on our side. That's what Calenstine was telling me. He also told me that we could still save Remy by following our hearts."

"I knew Mom and Dad weren't traitors," Elly said bluntly. "You didn't really think they were, did you?"

"I don't know. I think I just really wanted to speak to them one more time, because I miss them so much." Hunter once again fought back the tears. He felt so stupid sitting in that bed fighting off tears again.

"I miss them too," Elly said softly. "But... they're gone."

"I know... I know they are."

"What did he mean 'follow our hearts'?" Elly asked.

"Not sure—he just said if our hearts were pure, we would get the help we needed.

"Well, I think we start by sleeping." Elly felt her eyelids growing heavy; she was barely able to keep them open as she spoke to her brother.

"Goodnight, Elly," Hunter whispered as he lay down on his bed.

He reached and grabbed the wrinkled photo of his parents off of the nightstand—the one where he sat holding Elly for the first time; the very same photo Margot had given him when they first moved to the estate. He sat there for a while just staring at the photo, letting his mind wander off, and thinking of as many happy memories as he could about his parents.

"I'm so sorry," Hunter whispered to the photo. "I would do anything to fix this mess I got everyone into; I just want to find Remy... more than anything in the world."

Hunter soon fell asleep with the photo held tightly in his hands. He had strange dreams about Remy's disjointed, possessed body crawling around the ceiling and walls as his eerie, soulless eyes stared at him.

He woke suddenly, covered head to toe in sweat. Hunter felt a strange weight on his feet, and he sat up to inspect his bed. There, between his legs, sat a thick and ancient book that he recognized right away.

"Elly!" Hunter blurted out.

"Huh? W-what?" Elly rolled over, rubbed her eyes and yawned loudly.

"What, Hunter? I was sleeping."

"Look!" Hunter held up the book for his sister to see.

"So, you found a book. Good for you." She rolled back over, trying to ignore her brother.

"No, don't you recognize it? It's the sacred Grimoire! The one that we did the séance with when we became Seekers!"

"What?" Elly rolled back over and turned on the small lamp on the nightstand. Sure enough, she recognized it right away. "How did you get that? Did you sneak out again?" she scolded.

"How could I have snuck out when Luther is out there? I woke up and it was on my lap. Remember, the professor said it would come to us in our greatest time of need!"

"Okay, so what do we do now?" Elly rolled out of bed and took a seat next to her brother.

"I dunno... the pages are still empty." Hunter flipped through the book, but to his dismay, the yellow and aged papers were completely void of any written words.

"How do we use this?" Hunter said aloud. Suddenly, he felt the book turn warm where he touched it. He opened it to a random page and watched as the blank sheet started to bubble up with blots of boiling ink. Right before his eyes, he saw the book answering his questions.

"Wow! Are you seeing this?" Elly peered over her brother's shoulder. "What's it say?"

"'I come to those pure,'" Hunter read slowly as the words fizzled out and bubbled back up. "'...in times of dire needs,'" Hunter went on.

"It's so slow!" Elly whined.

"'To show the Seekers the way...'" Hunter waited patiently for that phrase to dissipate and for the next to bubble up. "'So, ask the right questions, and the path will be enlightened for all to see.'"

"Wait, so we just ask it stuff?" asked Elly.

"How can we save our friend Remy from being possessed?" Hunter asked quickly.

"'Turn to page 333,'" Hunter read aloud as the words appeared.

"Quick, turn to it!" said Elly impatiently.

"Okay, okay... calm down." Hunter thumbed through the book until he hit the right page. To his surprise, something fell out from the book's pages and onto his lap.

"What is this?" Hunter held up a strange-looking leaf.

"Did that fall out of the book?" asked Elly, who took the bizarre leaf, which appeared to be in the shape of a key. "Look, it's one of those Raskovnik plants that Liv was telling us about."

"The ones that are supposed to open any lock?" Hunter scratched his head in confusion.

"Except this one's a different color! Look, its stem is golden," Elly held the leaf up to the light, "and it's really thick."

"Okay, what do we do with the Raskovnik leaf?" Hunter asked the book.

"'High above the estate, where all the secrets lie,'" Hunter went on to read as the book began answering his questions. "'Bring your friends and seek out the seal; Solomon holds the key to the Daupnir Ring's power.'"

Suddenly, the book snapped shut forcefully.

"What the heck?" Hunter went to pick the book back up, but before he could grab it, the book began to hover.

"Um... is that book floating?" Elly swallowed hard, not knowing how to react.

The book started spinning in place extremely fast, and right in front of their eyes, they saw the book implode upon itself until there was nothing left. Gone. It had just disappeared.

"This is what the professor was talking about," Hunter pointed to the Raskovnik leaf Elly still held.

"What are you talking about?" Elly was still a little freaked out by the magical, floating, and disappearing book.

"He said if our hearts were pure, we would find a way to help our friend. He meant the Grimoire because he knew it would come to me with answers."

"What answers? That book wrote nothing but weird riddles," Elly stated.

"No, it's telling us to head up to the top floor and use this Raskovnik leaf to get into the locked door."

"We've never been past the third floor; we don't even know what's up there," said Elly, who shook her head. "No, we are not sneaking out. You've caused enough trouble! Every time you talk us into something, bad things happen."

"The book told us to!" Hunter argued. "The professor said to look for the answers; he basically told us to do this!"

"Hunter!" Elly jumped off his bed, doing her best to hide her anger.

"What?" Hunter protested.

"I am going back to bed. There is no way we're doing this!"

"You don't get it," Hunter said, shaking his head. "This time, it's not about me. This time it's about saving our friend. This is about Remy!"

"If this is about Remy, then we need to tell Uncle Joe and Margot about it and let the adults take care of it," Elly shot back.

"Okay." Hunter fell back into his bed, defeated. His sister was right, and he knew it. Every time he tried to go out and do something good, he always messed up, causing people to get hurt. It was time he learned his lesson and left it to the adults.

Hunter tried to fall back to sleep, but it was pointless. All he could think about was the book, and the strange Raskovnik leaf that was now sitting next to his family photo on the nightstand. Deep down, he knew he was supposed to do this and he knew the book was telling him that it was his chance to make things better! Yet his sister's words stung him, since he was always so fast to sneak out and get into trouble.

After a few restless hours, the children's bedroom door opened and Joe and Luther quietly came in.

"Hope we're not waking you," Joe said as he wheeled his chair into the room.

"Guys! My shift is up, but your uncle is going to hang out with you for the next shift." Luther nodded with a smile and made his exit.

"Uncle Joe?" Elly rolled out of bed and ran over to hug her uncle. "We're so sorry about all this."

"It's okay. We understand there was more to all of this than just you kids playing with spirits." Joe picked Elly up and sat her on his lap.

"You're getting too big for this," Uncle Joe said, forcing a smile.

"Where's Margot?" Hunter asked as he too rolled off his bed, slipping the Raskovnik leaf into his pocket.

"Well," Joe froze for a second, "we sort of had an argument, so I'm not sure if we'll be seeing much of her."

"What do you mean?" Elly jumped off Joe's lap with a frown on her face.

"I'm sorry… it's just… She is really busy right now. You know… with her wedding coming up and all. She is just super busy, but I'm sure she will make time to come and visit you guys."

"What did you guys fight over? I hated it when Mom and Dad would fight," said Elly.

"Listen, it's just complicated. I don't want her so caught up in our lives that she forgets to live her own."

"What's that supposed to mean?" Hunter asked, not following his uncle's reasoning.

"What? She doesn't like us anymore?" asked Elly.

"No, she loves you guys! But listen, I just told her she needed to spend more time getting her life together. We got each other; we can do this without making her miss out on her own life."

The children fell silent.

"So, anyway…" Joe knew now, that it was far too late to remedy the fact that dropping that little bomb, about he and Margot's argument, was not the best parental decision. He was new to this too though, and he didn't want to lie to the children. "Next week, it's you're fourteenth birthday, Hunter! I came up here to talk to about it. Maybe we can make some plans and get our minds off all this nonsense."

"I can't think about my birthday with Remy out there," Hunter said bluntly.

"We will find him; we have the entire estate looking. We're taking shifts—"

"Just a few hours ago," Hunter interrupted his uncle, "I woke up with the Grimoire on my lap."

"What?" Joe's jaw dropped. "Hold on." Joe flipped open his cell phone and began dialing. "Ben," Joe said, fast. "Hey, I need you to get everyone together. Get Patricia and bring them to the children's room! NOW! Ok, thank you."

"Why did you call Alistair's dad?" asked Elly.

"We need to know what it said. As soon as they get here, I want you to tell us."

"Why is it such a big deal?" Elly interjected once again.

"The Grimoire... let's just say it only appears under very important circumstances," explained Joe. "Like I said, it only came to me once, and it changed my life forever."

"What's all the commotion?" Patricia Ellingbee entered along with Margot, Ben, and Abram.

"Luckily, we were all getting some food together when you called and were talking over everything that's happened," Ben explained.

"I came to relieve Luther and hang out with the kids, and Hunter just told me the Grimoire came to him a few hours ago," Joe explained.

"What?" Patricia seemed baffled.

"I told them to tell us once you all arrived."

"No!" Patricia blurted out, almost angrily. "Hunter must not tell us anything."

"What do you mean?" Joe asked.

"Yeah, don't we need to know?" added Ben.

"Wait, I don't even understand what's happening." Margot walked over to Elly and gave her a big hug. "Are you okay?" She brushed Elly's hair out of her face. "You look so tired."

"Uncle Joe said you guys got into a fight and you won't be seeing us anymore," Elly said, frowning.

"You said what?" Margot shot the most disgusted look over at Joe. "You told them that?"

"I... I..." Joe stuttered.

"You two can deal with that later." Abram waved off the argument. "Patricia's right! What the book said is between Hunter and the Grimoire. It's not to be shared with anyone unless the book allows it."

"So, you're saying we're not allowed to know what the book told Hunter?" Margot argued back. "That sounds stupid, not to mention that it could be dangerous."

"It's one of our Seeker guidelines. We do not question the sacred Grimoire. It guides us down the right path, but its knowledge should never be shared unless it allows you," Abram explained.

"You're telling me Professor Calenstine is okay with this?" Margot argued.

"I thought under the circumstances," Joe added, "the book would have wanted us to know."

"Professor Calenstine would have it no other way," Patricia answered. "Unless... Hunter, did the Grimoire tell you to share what it told you with *us*?"

"No," Hunter felt confused, "it just said to bring my friends along."

"Then your friends can know, but we cannot." Patricia frowned.

"You're serious?" Margot threw up her hands in anger. "It could have told Hunter to do something dangerous!"

"Perhaps," Abram said. "But our children are now Seekers; they have much to learn through the Enlightenment even though the rest of their lives might be filled with adversity. However, the Grimoire will guide them. It is in Hunter's hands now. Until then, we continue our search."

"I can't stand for this." Margot's hands shook.

"You took the oath," Patricia reminded her.

"I took an oath that Joe won't even honor," Margot once again yelled in Joe's direction.

"What is she talking about, Joe?" Patricia gave him the evil eye.

"It's personal," Joe replied, not wanting to get into the details in front of the entire group.

"Don't be an ignorant jerk, you have an amazing person helping you raise your niece and nephew."

"It's too late for that," Margot said as she hugged Hunter and Elly, a bit more forcefully than she normally would. She whispered into their ears and stormed out of the room.

"What did you say to that girl?" Ben poked his best friend in the shoulder.

"It's all messed up…" Joe shook his head.

"Children, as much as I find it hard to say this," Patricia said slowly and clearly, "we follow the Grimoire's words. Whatever the book said, Hunter, you have the professor's and my own blessing. Just please, be safe."

"Yes, ma'am," Hunter assured her with a nod.

"This is what being a Seeker is *all* about. We do what's right for the greater good. These trials and tribulations will make you the man you're destined to become, Hunter," Abram said with a small hint of pride. "You would make your parents proud being so brave."

"I have a feeling our kids are going to be a part of this too," Benjamin whispered to Abram.

"Yes, I know," Abram replied. "We must allow them to follow in our footsteps no matter how hard it may be."

"Hunter," Patricia spoke up, "we shall leave you be. Classes are back on tomorrow, and despite whatever the Grimoire said, you must still attend. Understood?"

"Yes, ma'am!" Hunter replied.

"And, Joe," Patricia turned to Joe with her head shaking in discontent, "whatever you did to mess up with Margot… you need to fix it. That woman is not just a part of your life, but she's a big part of these children's as well."

Chapter 27
Secrets in the Attic

Hunter and Elly rose from their beds early the next day and prepared themselves for school. Despite the tragedy that had happened two nights prior, Patricia had opted not to cancel classes. Instead, every teacher in both schools was to address the issue first thing, and to make sure every student knew there were school counselors available as needed. Remy's disappearance wasn't a secret; in fact, it was quite the opposite. The professor had wanted high awareness in case anyone ran into Remy anywhere. With his disappearance, the tension was pretty high at the estate, including both schools. People were just worried for both Remy's well-being and their own. Discomfort among people was at the highest it'd ever been. Two tragedies in less than a year—first the escape of the Beast of Bladenboro, and now, a student was missing.

Like every morning, Hunter and Elly met up with Alistair and Liv outside the estate's entrance and started towards the Francis Drake Building. The group didn't say much because they were all lost in their own heavy thoughts. Instead, the group attempted to mentally prepare themselves for their Enlightenment course with Professor Pike. Today, they were scheduled for a written quiz about the myths and facts of the vampyres, but with all the commotion over the weekend, none of the children had studied up on the difference between a Ukrainian "Upir" vampyre and the Philippines "Aswang" vampyre.

How were the children supposed to study when everything was still fresh in their minds, and the estate had still not found Remy? He was still out there with his body taken over by some evil entity, contorted and twisted so he hardly even looked human anymore. It was just too much for the kids to comprehend, and it still showed on their faces.

The walk, which was normally Hunter's favorite part of the school day, was awkward. So, Hunter decided there was no better time than now to clue in Liv and Alistair on what the Grimoire had said. And so with as much detail as possible, he described what happened the night before.

"Wait a minute…" Alistair stopped mid-stride, his mouth agape in awe at the story. "You're telling me that the Grimoire showed itself to you, and the adults wouldn't let you tell them what it said?"

"Can you believe that?" Elly interjected, a bit heated. "After all this, they said it's a part of the Seekers' creed to do what that dirty old book says, and that you're not supposed to share its secrets with anyone unless the book okays it. I think it's reckless! I swear that sometimes I feel like the only responsible person in this entire place — including the adults!" Elly was red in the face with anger. "I made Hunter tell them, and they didn't even want to listen!"

"So, you can't tell us either?" Liv asked, obviously quite curious.

"I can because the book told me to take my friends with me, so I would think it's safe to share," Hunter explained. "We're going to save Remy and make things right. We just need the right timing."

"How are we going to do that?" asked Alistair. "Make things right?"

"All I know is that the book told me to take you guys with me up to the top level of the estate, and we'd find Solomon's Seal there. It's real, and it said it holds the key to the Daupnir Ring." Hunter held out the ring that had burned his finger and released the evil wraith. "I think we have to trap the spirit back into the ring. Therefore, the legend must be true that Solomon's Seal must have some way of controlling or talking with spirits."

"So, we just head up to the top level of the estate? That shouldn't be hard," Alistair responded.

"I doubt something like the Solomon's Seal is going to just be lying around the seventh floor for us to pick up and grab." Liv frowned. "That ring just seems too powerful; I'm sure it's hidden and locked away from people who would want to steal it. Plus, everything above the cafeteria is always locked. We can't just go taking the elevator upstairs."

"That's why the book gave us this." Hunter handed Liv the Raskovnik leaf.

"This is…" Liv's eyes got wide with excitement.

"Yeah, it's a Raskovnik leaf," Hunter said proudly, knowing Liv was impressed.

"Yeah, but this is no regular Raskovnik leaf. We saw the plant with Luther, remember? None of those leaves had the golden stem, but this one does! Only the Raskovnik leaves with gold stems have the magical powers. I've read up on these." Liv held the small leaf in her palm.

"Yep," Hunter smiled.

"What do we do now? We can't wait. Remy is out there. We need to rescue him now."

"Heeeeeey! Hey… you kids!" the deep frantic voice of an older man yelled over the open field.

The children turned to see Remy's father, Mr. Montgomery, stumbling towards them, red-faced and frowning like a grumpy old man. He rushed his way over to the children, almost losing his balance multiple times. The children didn't know it, but he had been out in the field near the Francis Drake Building for hours, waiting for the kids to make their way to class. Mr. Montgomery wobbled as he tried unsuccessfully to run towards them with a bottle in his hand. His eyes were glassy and bloodshot, and the moment he approached them, an awful smell hit the children's noses. Mr. Montgomery had spent the last two nights drowning his sorrows in the bottom of a bottle. He was messy, scary drunk, slurring his words and very angry.

"What… what… hic… did you kids… do to my Remy…?" The man scowled bitterly as he spoke. His eyes, glossy and red as they were, were filled with anger and resentment. "You freeaaksss… you and your s-s-society… you… ruined… my life… our life."

"We didn't do anything to him." Hunter took a step backwards. "We tried to help...."

"Liar! He was with... *hic*... you..." The man stumbled to his knees and spilled the contents of the bottle out on to the damp, cold earth. He picked it up quickly, trying to save as much as liquor as he could.

Professor Pike heard the commotion and came running out from the Francis Drake Building with a look of disgust written across her face. She came out as if on a mission, speed-walking while waving her finger back and forth yelling at the top of her lungs, "Stop! Stop it at once!"

The man stopped dead in his tracks, looking up as Professor Pike raced towards him.

"Sir, how dare you threaten these children! Just look at you. You're drunk! Get out of here before I call security and have you escorted away from here. What would the professor think?" she scolded the grown man, who held his head low as she berated him.

Hunter had never been so fearful in his life; not so much because of the threatening words from Remy's drunk father, although he was quite creepy, but because he'd never seen Professor Pike so angry before. He never wanted to be on the other end of one of her lectures.

"Who do you think you are, acting in such a disgraceful way? And in front of children no less!" Professor Pike's hands shook in anger as she spoke.

"I am... I'm Remy's father! You... you people... you took my boy away..." Mr. Montgomery's rage turned to sorrow, and he tried to fight back tears.

"Heavens! You're the father of the boy who went missing?" Professor Pike's tone changed immediately from scolding to somewhat comforting.

"I just... I want my boy back... I want Remy home with me," Mr. Montgomery sobbed. He dropped down onto both his knees again, allowing his emotions to completely take control of his body.

The children had never seen such a heart-breaking image. They had met Remy's father a few times, and he always seemed like a strong and confident man. But now, he stood before them broken and shattered.

"Let me take that." Professor Pike took the bottle from his hand and poured it out, allowing the earth to soak up its contents. "Children," She turned and faced the kids with a very strict look, "get to class, and I will be in shortly. I want to get this man some help."

"Yes, Professor Pike." Alistair nodded as he grabbed Hunter by his arm and pulled him away from the scene.

"C'mon, Hunter," Elly begged as they made their way towards the Francis Drake Building.

"Just leave it to Professor Pike. She'll take care of him," Liv explained, noting Hunter's worried look. "There's nothing we can say or do to make him feel any better."

"Yes, there is," replied Hunter.

"What?" Elly was surprised with his answer.

"We don't wait any longer! We need to go now." Hunter took the Raskovnik leaf from his pocket. "This is all we need to get to the top floor. The quicker we save Remy, the quicker his dad stops worrying! Why should we wait until after class?"

"Because we can't skip class!" Elly frowned. "What if we get caught?"

"Seriously? Class is more important to you than finding Remy?" Hunter threw up his hands as if he just couldn't believe what he had just heard his sister say.

"The adults are searching for him everywhere. It's not like everyone is doing nothing," Elly said, defending her words. "We're just kids! I don't care what that book said; the adults should handle this. We could just make it worse! One of us could get hurt, or worse!"

"The book said this is how we would save him," Hunter argued. "The adults obviously think the book is important, so who are we to argue?"

"I think Hunter is right," Liv added. "I couldn't sleep the last two nights. There is no way I would be able to pay attention to anything, especially the quiz about the different versions of vampyres. Remy is out there somewhere, and it's all of our faults. If the book says we can save him, then I believe we can."

"Thank you." Hunter looked at Liv with a smile. He wasn't quite sure what else to say to her, but he needed to hear that and know his friends had his back.

"Then it's agreed, we head to the top floor and find the 'real' Solomon's Seal." Alistair nodded, getting a bit excited. "We're going to bring our friend back!"

"Anyway," Liv looked at Elly with a comforting smile, "what are they going to do? Expel us for trying to do what's right?"

"Yeah, I suppose that wouldn't make sense," Elly replied. "We just have to be smart about this."

"Aren't we always?" Hunter smiled.

"Sorry, Professor Pike," Alistair turned back towards his teacher, who was trying to console Mr. Montgomery, "but we'll be missing class today."

"Wait, what?" Professor Pike furled her brow. "What are you kids talking about? Hey… come back here!"

But the children didn't listen. Instead, they turned around and made their way towards the estate. The adults had had no luck in finding Remy, and it had been over two days since he had disappeared. But with the magical Grimoire aiding them, Hunter felt invincible. They were off to find Solomon's Seal, save their friend, and restore their lives to something close to normal.

☙

"We need to keep close to the forest and work our way back to the estate, away from the main grounds," Alistair said, pointing towards the edge of the thick, daunting forest.

"I really hate that forest, why do we need to keep close to it?" Elly pursed her lips tight, because nothing good ever seemed to come from it.

"Alistair is right," Hunter stated, pushing the team towards the forest. "We're skipping classes and we don't want to get caught. I'd prefer to make it to the seventh floor, not get caught, and not end up in detention."

"Yeah, even if the Grimoire wants us to go to the seventh floor, that doesn't mean anyone other than a few of our parents know about it. We run into any of our professors or the grounds men, they're going to send us right back to school. Professor Pike will definitely give us detention for skipping," said Liv.

"Hey, guys. Wait!" Alistair swung his backpack off his shoulder. He unzipped it quickly as they finally approached the eerie forest's edge.

"What are you doing?" asked Elly.

"Here," Alistair took out a small remote radio, "I snagged these from my dad's locker. They're two-way radios. Elly, you should have this one, and I will keep the other, you know, just in case."

"Smart thinking!" Hunter gave him a high five. "Those will definitely come in handy."

"Yeah. Ever since we snuck out to Crooked Lake, I figured it's better to be safe than sorry. I have these binoculars that have night-vision too."

"Awesome, can I see?" asked Hunter.

"Boys, let's not waste any more time." Liv pointed towards the estate. "We have a friend to save."

Hunter and Alistair didn't need any more persuading. They packed up their goggles and radios and slowly made their way back towards the estate, away from any onlookers who may catch them ditching class. It was early Monday morning, and the main grounds were as busy as ever. This made sneaking back into the estate all the more difficult. Marching through the front door wasn't an option, so the group decided to follow the forest around to the south end of the mansion and enter through a small backdoor that normally remained locked all hours of the day. Luckily, the group had the Raskovnik leaf, and Hunter was eager to try it out.

The forest made sneaking around the outskirts of the estate a breeze, and it didn't take long for the children to see the side entrance in the distance, unguarded, like they had hoped.

"Good thing this door is never used. I dunno what we would've done if it was guarded," Alistair whispered.

A twig suddenly snapped from behind the group, and Hunter turned quickly, alarmed by the noise. "Did you hear that?" he whispered.

"Yeah, probably just a squirrel or something though." Alistair didn't seem fazed. "Don't worry."

"Sounded like a big squirrel." Liv had also been startled by the noise.

"Wait..." Alistair whispered. "What is that noise?" He had heard something other than a random twig.

"What? I don't hear anything." Elly paused for a moment, and then she heard it too.

"Is that breathing?" asked Hunter.

"Look!" Liv pointed high into the treetops. There, perched on a branch fairly deep into the thick forest were two dark red eyes staring down at them.

"What is that?" Alistair's eyes grew wide with curiosity.

"Give me the binoculars," Hunter whispered. "Slowly though."

Alistair gently unzipped his bag, making sure to make no sudden movements or noises. He carefully handed them over to Hunter.

"Let me see..." Hunter adjusted the binoculars, zooming in on the red eyes.

"What do you see?" Elly tugged on her brother's arm.

"Stop it!" Hunter whispered sharply, swiping his sister's arm off of his.

"Quiet, guys! C'mon!" Liv was nervous and swallowed hard.

"It's Remy!" Hunter dropped the binoculars onto the earth and darted off towards the dark red eyes without warning.

"What? Hunter, wait!" Alistair yelled as he picked up the binoculars. He looked over to the girls with a confused look on his face.

"Hunter!" Elly also yelled after her brother. "What are you doing?"

The sudden commotion caused the thing that used to be Remy to shriek loudly. The noise stopped Hunter dead in his tracks. It was a loud shrieking howl that sent the hairs on the back of his neck standing straight up. It didn't sound human at all—it was an evil, monstrous, noise. Remy jumped from tree to tree, escaping deeper into the forest. Hunter was amazed that Remy moved like an animal—so fast and agile.

"Hunter! Wait!! What are you doing?" Liv grabbed his hand tightly when she finally caught up with him. "You can't run off like that!" She breathed deeply, catching her breath.

"We can't let him escape," Hunter said with panic in his voice.

"What's going on?" Elly and Alistair came a few dozen yards into the forest.

"There's no time to waste; that was Remy!" Hunter pointed towards the treetops. "He's escaping deeper into the forest."

"We need the Seal first." Elly shook her head. "We can't do anything without it."

"What good will the ring do if we can't find him again?" Hunter argued back.

"I think Hunter's right," said Liv, doing her best to hide the fear in her voice. She wanted to be brave and to be strong. She just never realized how frightening it truly was to be heroic. "We need to split up; we have radios to keep in touch. Once we get the Seal from the estate, we can hopefully lead them to where Remy is hiding."

"It's the only option," Hunter added. "But we need to move fast because that thing is getting away."

"I'll go with you," Liv said, taking a step closer to Hunter.

"Are you sure?" Alistair was surprised because he knew how much Liv and Elly both hated the forest. "I can go with him."

"Yes, I'm sure! You two get back to the estate and get Solomon's seal. Alistair, toss me the radio. We'll be in touch." Liv swallowed hard because of the fear creeping up in her throat.

"Let's go," Hunter said, nodding to Liv. "Elly, we'll be safe, I promise. You'll need this." Hunter handed his sister the Raskovnik leaf.

"Okay."

Hunter and Liv quickly took off. They made haste, traversing deeper into the thicket of the forest and doing their best to keep up with Remy.

"Elly," Alistair turned around to her, "they'll be okay. I promise."

"I know," Elly said softly. "I just… this place… it's just too much for me! I don't know if I can handle all this misery all the time."

"Our friend needs our help," Alistair said as he held both of Elly's hands. "I know you're as brave as Hunter. So let's get that ring, then let's find Remy and save him."

"Okay." Elly smiled. "Let's do this."

☙

Elly and Alistair made their way to the side entrance of the estate. Elly held out the Raskovnik leaf and frowned.

"How do I use this thing?" asked Elly, staring at the mysterious leaf with the golden stem.

"Yeah, I guess these things don't come with instructions," Alistair said with a frown. "There's the keyhole… maybe try to put the leaf in it?"

But that idea didn't work. After all, it was a leaf, not a key. It just got balled up and squished as Elly tried to insert the leaf into the hole.

"This thing doesn't work." She frowned again, feeling frustration boiling up inside her.

"Let me try something." Alistair took the leaf and held it in the palm of his hand. He used it sort of like a glove and wrapped the base of the leaf around the door handle. His hand began to tingle, and suddenly he felt the door handle turn. The door unlocked and the side entrance was now open.

"It worked!" Elly's eyes grew wide with surprise.

"Awesome!"

Alistair entered the side door and into a small back room. To their dismay, the room was nothing more than a large storage shelter littered with lawn equipment and chemicals to kill weeds.

"Crap!" Alistair cursed. "A dead end."

"Not entirely." Elly pointed to a large vent high on the western wall of the storage room.

"The vent?" asked Alistair.

"Yeah, the vents must be huge if the Beast of Bladenboro was able to move around the estate so easily."

"I'm impressed." Alistair smiled. "I think you're finding your adventurous side."

"Excuse me? I have an adventurous side!" Elly was taken aback by Alistair's statement, even though he meant it playfully.

"Er... okay..." Alistair found a large sturdy crate that he pushed over towards the vent.

"What did you mean by that?" asked Elly bitterly.

"Nothing, I mean... nothing. C'mon, we need to shimmy up into this thing."

"Just because I don't go running into a forest in the middle of the night to look for treasure or think it sounds like fun to hold a séance in my bedroom, that doesn't mean I'm boring!" Elly argued as Alistair hoisted her up into the vent. "Yuck! It's super dusty in here."

"I didn't say you were boring," Alistair explained as he hoisted himself up into the vent behind Elly.

"Sounded like it to me," Elly snapped back.

"So, where are we going?" Alistair whispered, avoiding the conversation at hand.

"I guess we just follow this until we find another ventilation grate that we can get out through."

"Awesome," replied Alistair, coughing from the dust.

"Quiet. The sound echoes in here, and we don't want anyone to hear us; who knows where these vents lead."

They pushed on, deeper into the long ventilation system. They had spent ten minutes crawling through the dusty steel shafts before Elly finally saw light at the end of the tunnel. She hurried over to the opening and peered through the grate to see if it was clear.

"What do you see? Where does it open up to?" asked Alistair, sweating profusely in the confined area.

"Finally, some good luck," Elly said, smiling. "This is the vent right next to the stairway heading up to the elevator in the main lobby."

"You're kidding me? How easy is that? Is it clear?"

"Yep." Elly gently pushed the grate out, making sure it didn't make any noise when she dislodged it and slowly crawled out, dropping into the main foyer. There, in the middle of the room, sat two well-dressed men drinking coffee and chatting. She looked back at Alistair and signaled for him to keep quiet.

He nodded and slowly followed suit.

They tiptoed their way up the stairway that led to the balcony where the main elevator was housed. Elly hit the button to call for the elevator, and the two of them waited patiently for the doors to open. It chimed open and they swiftly entered, Alistair hitting the button to take them up to the top floor. The doors closed and off they went, riding the elevator to the top floor with no one any the wiser.

"Gross!" Elly said as she wiped the sweat from her brow. "Look how dirty we are from the vent."

"All in a day's work, right?" Alistair chuckled.

"What do you think is on the seventh floor?" Elly watched the elevator buttons light up as they passed each floor.

"Who knows? This place has so many secrets; it could be a doorway to another universe for all we know." Alistair wasn't joking for once, he had no idea what to expect.

The elevator door opened, and the children walked out into a small, square room, roughly about the size of a large walk-in closet. It was largely barren, but there was one small, cream-colored end table with a single lamp that turned on the moment they stepped out of the elevator door.

"Interesting..." Alistair stared at the only thing worth looking at, a door on the opposite side of the elevator. Except this was the strangest looking door he had ever seen and there were no hinges, no doorknob, or keyhole. It was just the threshold of where a door should be, but no way to open it.

"Great, a room with a lamp and a fake door." Elly shook her head in disbelief. "What's next? A stairwell with no stairs?"

"How do you open a door without a lock or handle?" Alistair looked all around the room for anything that might help them, such as a hidden switch or a keypad to enter a PIN into, but he found nothing worth noting. He was baffled.

"Look!" Elly pointed at the ceiling. "There's an entrance to the attic! Help me reach the string so we can pull it down."

"Good eyes."

Alistair put his arms around Elly's waist and hoisted her up just high enough so she could grab the rope.

"We had an attic like this in our old house. You pull down on the string and the stairs unfold." Elly pulled down the string and the latch opened. A small set of stairs unfolded before their eyes, and to their amazement, the stairs led to another door placed in the ceiling.

"A door in the ceiling? How weird *is* this place!" Elly wasn't surprised by the bizarre-looking door. It was pure metal and thick too. It was obviously meant to keep people out of the attic. It looked nearly impossible to break into.

"Well, it's a good thing the Grimoire gave us this Raskovnik leaf, because there is no way we could get into the attic with that door any other way," said Alistair, who took the stairs first. He placed the leaf back into his hand and reached up towards the door handle. Once again, his hand began to feel tingly, and he heard the lock mechanism in the door click. He went to open the door, but it was too heavy.

"It's... so heavy!" Alistair pushed with all his might but was only able to lift the door about halfway open.

"Let me help." Elly made her way up the small ladder, and with her help, the two were able to push the door open.

They climbed up through the opening and found themselves inside a pitch-black room. The air was thick and stale, and despite being able to see only a few feet in front of them, the children had the feeling they were standing inside of something enormous.

"Let me get my flashlight out of my backpack. I have a small one I carry with me all the time," Alistair said.

He flicked the little flashlight on to see that the attic was huge, so massive that they couldn't see where it started or ended. It appeared that the mysterious door opened up somewhere in the middle between where it started and ended. They realized they stood within a small circular clearing, and all around them were giant cabinet-like structures that went on for what looked like miles.

"This looks like the safety deposit room at my parents' old bank," said Elly as she and Alistair walked up to one of the rows to inspect it further. Sure enough, the cabinets were categorized in various sizes with locked and sealed deposit boxes.

"Yeah, look, each one is sealed up so it must be top-secret stuff stored up here!" Alistair flashed the light on the key hole on each cabinet door. "They're like safes and no one can get in them without the right key."

"This entire row looks to be about Atlantis." Alistair could hardly contain his excitement. Alistair had always been fascinated with the concept of Atlantis. It was something he and his father shared.

"I wonder what could possibly be inside these safes. Look, this one is huge!" Elly was a bit awestruck.

"This one says 'Atlantis: Plato's Keep,'" said Alistair.

"Our Plato? He's from the lost city of Atlantis?" Elly struggled with the thought.

"We need to go deeper. We have to find the one that contains anything about Solomon's Seal," Alistair suggested, trying his best to swallow his curiosity and focus on the problem at hand, which was saving their friend.

Alistair and Elly explored the room, moving up and down the makeshift hallways in between the numerous shelving units. It was overwhelming how large the attic was. They searched frantically for any sort of clue.

"Elly?" A voice crackled over the two-way radio. "Alistair? Elly? Are you there?"

They recognized Liv's voice.

"Liv? We can hear you. Is everything okay?" Elly spoke frantically into the radio.

"Yes, we followed Remy. We're hiding," Liv whispered over the radio.

"Tell her to speak up." Alistair continued to thumb through the safety deposit box labels.

"Where are you?" asked Elly.

"Followed him to..." But the radio reception was breaking up, and Liv's voice was cracking up bad. "...oods, Big area... about a... to the west... creepy... house... do... read... staying put...."

"Did she say 'creepy house'?" Alistair frowned.

"Liv, do you copy?" asked Elly, but the radio was silent. "Where did you say you were?"

"A creepy abandoned house," Liv's voice came over clearly now. "Hurry before he leaves."

"We haven't found the Seal yet, but we're close," Elly replied.

"Okay, we'll stay... Hunter, look out!" Liv's voice sounded panicked and she let out a blood-curdling scream.

"Liv!" Elly yelled back. "Liv, are you there? Answer me!"

"That didn't sound good..." Alistair froze upon hearing his cousin scream.

"We need to find the Seal, NOW!" said a frantic Elly.

"Look, I found something." Alistair continued down the row of boxes until he came across one labeled 'King Solomon.'

"That's it! Don't stare at it," said Elly. "Open it!"

Alistair held the Raskovnik leaf in his hand one more time and put it up against the small handle of the safety deposit box. It clicked open effortlessly, and there inside the large safe was a piece of folded cloth. Alistair grabbed it quickly and unfolded it.

"What is it? Is it the ring?" Elly asked.

"Look..." Alistair shined the flashlight onto the cloth. There it sat, Solomon's Seal, the ring that the Grimoire had told Hunter could save Remy's life.

"We actually found it." Elly smiled.

"We need to find Hunter and Liv right away!" Alistair folded the cloth back up and secured it in his book bag. "Try the radio again."

"Hunter? Do you read me? Liv? Does anyone copy?"

But there was silence.

"What do we do?" Elly's voice cracked.

"I think we need to find our parents and see if they know of a house out in the woods. Maybe they know where it is. It's our only chance!

Chapter 28
Captives

"It came this way…" Hunter gasped. His chest burned, but he knew they couldn't stop to rest. The thing that had taken over Remy's body was too fast and agile, and if they let up, they would surely lose track of him. "Through this thick brush over here, c'mon!" He waved Liv on, pushing aside the thick leaves and trying to keep pace with Remy.

"Slow down, I'm trying to keep up!" Liv was breathing hard too. The forest terrain was extremely difficult to travel through, even when following the game trails. Unfortunately for Hunter and Liv, the thing that was now Remy didn't follow any trails at all. Instead, the creature was traveling high above them, jumping and swinging from tree to tree and leading them through some of the thickest parts of the forest, which the children had to push through.

"Look, it's a small clearing." Hunter pushed back a thick leafy bush to scope the area out. He squatted down to keep in the cover of the foliage and watched Remy crawl up the side of the house and enter through one of the broken windows.

"What is that?" Liv gasped to catch her breath. The sight made her frown.

"It's… a house," replied Hunter, who was awestruck by the sight.

There, in the small clearing, out in the middle of the forest, sat a two-story, rundown house. It wasn't much of a house anymore since the forest had taken over much of what it used to be. Large vines had overcome the exterior walls; a giant tree branch had fallen at some point and crashed into the back, leaving the interior room exposed to the outside elements. The few windows were smashed out, and there was no longer any door—just an open threshold where it used to be.

"Why is there a house way out here?" Hunter wiped the sweat from his forehead. There was a cold winter chill in the air, but the rush of adrenaline was making him sweat.

"Who knows? Do you think Remy is using it to hide out?"

"If I was that thing, I would, so yeah, I think so!" answered Hunter. "Are you okay? I got cut up all over from the forest."

"Yeah, I did too, but I'm okay." Liv unclipped the radio Alistair had given them from her belt. "I'm going to try and get Elly or Alistair over the radio."

"Okay, just head down a bit so that your voice isn't carried over into the clearing. If Remy is in there, I don't want him to hear you. We need to be sneaky until the others get here."

"Okay, yeah," Liv whispered. She slowly crept back into the thicker foliage, making sure she didn't snap any loud twigs or make too much of a ruckus. She wasn't very fond of walking off alone into the darkness of the woods, but she knew Hunter had made a valid point. She walked a few yards away until Hunter's head was barely visible through the thicket of the trees.

"Elly?" Liv held down the button on the radio and spoke softly into the receiver.

"Liv? We can hear you. Is everything okay?" Elly's friendly voice crackled back over the radio.

"Yes, we followed Remy. We're hiding," Liv replied back.

"Where are you?" asked Elly.

"We followed him to a clearing, deep into the woods. It's a big area about forty minutes to the west... Found a creepy old house. Do you read me? We're staying put." She clicked the button and waited for Elly's response.

"Oli... do... opy?" Elly voice came over the radio, but it was broken up badly. "Wher... you say... were?"

Liv fiddled with the knobs on the radio, trying to find a better frequency. "We're at a creepy house. Hurry before he leaves."

"We haven't found the Seal yet, but we're close," Elly replied, her transmission much clearer now.

"Okay, we'll stay put..." Liv peered back to check on Hunter through the clearing. To her horror, she saw Remy stalking Hunter from behind one of the trees. Hunter! Look out!"

"Liv!" Elly yelled back over the radio. "Liv, are you there? Answer me."

But Liv didn't hear the calls. Instead, she ran frantically towards Hunter and watched in horror.

Hunter was startled by Liv's sudden, blood-curdling scream. He turned around quickly, his heart pounding so hard in his chest he thought it might explode. Before he could do anything else, he saw the dark glowing red eyes come from his right side. Hunter was knocked down on the ground when the thing that was once Remy had tackled him so hard that Hunter heard a loud cracking from his chest; then he immediately saw black. He hadn't been passed out for long, but once he regained his composure, the pain in his side was intense. It was hard to breathe; all he wanted to do was crawl away and try to escape, but Remy was still on top of him, clawing through his clothing as if the creature was looking for something.

"Remy..." Hunter winced in pain his voice barely audible.

Remy stopped what he was doing and stared with his dead, evil, red eyes back into Hunter's. Hunter saw Remy clench his fist and raise it to strike him. He tried to put his arms up in defense, but even that simple motion caused the pain in his side to explode in agony.

'Remy, STOP!" Liv broke through the clearing. She grabbed a large thick stick and waved it at their friend. "Get off of Hunter!" she threatened.

The creature cocked its head as Liv spoke, as if it were trying to understand her words.

"Remy, I know you're in there," Liv pleaded, gripping the large stick as hard as she could. "Please, fight this thing inside of you... I know how strong you are," Liv begged.

The red in Remy's eyes slowly faded, and he fell onto his knees, allowing Hunter to slowly crawl a safe distance away.

"Remy is that you?" Liv approached her friend with caution.

"Where... am I?" Remy's voice cracked. He was pale white, but his eyes no longer glowed an eerie red.

"Remy! It's you!" Liv ran towards him, her arms outstretched for a hug.

"No!" Remy tried to warn her, but he felt so weak and it was hard for him to speak at all. "It's a trick..." he muttered.

"It's okay; you beat it out of you!" Liv dropped her stick and radio to the ground and helped Remy back up to his feet.

"No... something... isn't right..." Remy whispered, but Liv didn't pay any attention because she was caught up in the excitement. They finally had their friend back! Things would finally go back to normal!

"We will get you back to the estate, back to your father and fix you up." Liv put his arm around her shoulder to aid him in standing up. "I'm so glad you're back."

Hunter watched Liv help Remy up. He couldn't stand and couldn't even get to his knees. The pain in his side was overwhelming. He thought Remy had broken one of his ribs since every breath he took felt like there was a knife stabbing into his right side. He just lay there, watching and praying Liv was right.

"I don't know how I'm going to get both you boys back by myself," Liv said as she helped Remy walk towards Hunter.

"He wants... the ring..." Remy mumbled.

"What?" Liv frowned. "What do you mean?"

"He is... telling me... he's still inside of me... he wants... the ring... or he will... he will kill us all!"

"Liv, RUN!" Hunter tried to talk, but speaking hurt worse than breathing. All he could muster was a small whimper.

"He's still in you!" Liv pushed Remy away and slowly stepped back. She knew she had dropped her large stick a few feet behind her and she hoped she could grab it and fend him off if needed.

"Yes... the ring..." Remy replied. "He wants to... destroy it...."

Suddenly, there was a strange look on Remy's face. His eye bulged out, his mouth went agape, and he let out a violent and pain racked scream that echoed through the forest. His body began to convulse once again as if he was in excruciating pain. It only lasted a few seconds, but when it was over, he stared back down towards Liv, his eyes once again glowing with a dark red haze. Eerily they blinked one at a time, and each eye looked in different directions. Remy wasn't human any longer; he was once again controlled by the wraith.

"Remy!" Liv screamed and darted towards the radio and the stick.

Remy dropped to all fours as his body contorted awkwardly like some sort of human-spider hybrid and jumped high above Liv's head.

"Liv... just run!" Hunter began to crawl towards his friend, but it was useless.

Liv bent over to grab the stick, but Remy came crashing down from above, directly in front of her. He grabbed her by the waist and hoisted her up onto his shoulder with ease.

Liv screamed loudly for the thing to let her go. She kicked and punched the creature, but it was so powerful that she didn't have a chance. The thing that was once Remy lifted her like she was weightless and carried her over to where Hunter was. The creature simply grabbed Hunter by his left ankle and began to drag him towards the house.

Hunter was powerless to fight him off.

"Liv..." Hunter looked up at her as he was being dragged on the cold hard earth. Her eyes were completely taken over with fear, which crushed Hunter! There was nothing he could do to save her. "I'm sorry..." he whispered.

Chapter 29
Time is of the Essence

Liv's blood-curdling scream was still fresh in Elly's mind. She felt like it had been playing on repeat in her head. She did her best to remain calm, but the fear made her sick to her stomach. Elly was afraid that she was going to vomit at any moment. She had never heard anyone sound so terrified in all her life, and it just so happened to be her best friend.

"Elly, are you going to be okay? Snap out of it!" Alistair snapped his fingers to wake Elly from her deep thought.

"Um… yeah… sorry…" she said softly, shaking her head to bring herself out of her nightmare.

"C'mon, we don't have much time! That sounded really bad!" Alistair grabbed Elly's hand and led her through the maze of hallways, using his flashlight to guide them through the rows and rows of safety deposit boxes. It didn't take them long to find the exit. Alistair swiftly lifted the heavy metal door and hurried Elly through it.

"We just need to find my dad or Uncle Abram…" Alistair winced as he spoke; holding up the metal door took all his strength. "They'll know what to do—promise."

The kids had no idea what had happened to Liv, or why she had screamed Hunter's name with such terror, although they had a good idea. They knew the forest offered more dangers than just the thing that had inhabited Remy's body. It could be any number of foul beasts or creatures that had caused her to scream.

"Let's hope that Skunk Ape Hunter and I ran into, didn't find 'em!" said Alistair as he hit the button to call the elevator.

"That's not helping the matter." Elly frowned.

"Err... sorry." Alistair led Elly into the elevator and hit the button to take them to the main foyer. They awkwardly stood in the small elevator, with the normally calming elevator music doing nothing to calm their nerves. It felt like the longest elevator ride they had ever taken. Alistair paced back and forth—as much as he could in an elevator, and Elly tried to focus on the music to force the echoes of Liv's scream out of her mind.

"Everything will be okay," Alistair assured her, breaking the silence. "We've got the ring now."

"I know," Elly responded quietly, doing her best to calm her anxiety.

The door chimed open and the two stepped out onto the balcony overlooking the foyer. There below them sat Margot and Sebastian in what appeared to be a very serious conversation. Margot's normally jovial appearance was gone, replaced with a very unsettling look.

"Margot!" Elly yelled at the top of her lungs. She wasted no time running down the stairs, oblivious to Margot's conversation with Sebastian.

"Elly? Alistair?" Margot stood up quickly. She was a bit surprised by their sudden appearance, but she quickly composed herself, wiping the few tears from her eyes and quickly pulling her hair back from her face. She cleared her throat before saying, "Umm, shouldn't you children be in school?"

"Eliza, dear, you look awfully bothered," Sebastian said as he also rose from the couch.

"Hunter and Liv are in trouble!" Alistair spoke franticly. "We need help! Have you seen my dad or uncle?"

"Children, let's calm ourselves down a bit, shall we? Sounds a bit to me like you're speaking nonsense." Sebastian smiled, hoping his charm would calm the children down a bit. "How about I brew us up some fancy tea? Do children like tea?" He looked to Margot for an answer.

"I need my dad or Uncle Abram, right now!" Alistair shot

J.J. Hickey

Sebastian a dirty look.

"Alistair, calm down." Margot knelt down before them and looked them in the eyes. She immediately knew something was wrong based on the fear she saw in their eyes. "All of your parents went out searching for Remy. I have no way of getting ahold of them. Can Sebastian and I help? What's the matter?"

"We skipped class, ran into Remy out in the forest, and Hunter and Liv chased after him!" Elly was speaking a mile a minute, barely allowing herself enough time to breath. "There was a scream over our radio. Liv sounded scared to death... something happened to them... Something awful!"

"Okay, let's calm down a minute." Margot stood up and looked a little frazzled, taking in all the information. "First things first... where did they run off to? Where *exactly* in the woods?"

"Liv said something about an old rundown house in the middle of the forest," Alistair answered.

"An old house?" asked Margot. "I know where that is!"

"We need to go there, now!" Alistair was panicking, already darting off towards the large front door.

"Children, children..." Sebastian said, frowning. It was evident by his composure that he was more than a little bothered by the children's intrusion. "Margot and I were in the midst of a serious conversation. It is a bit rude of you to barge in here telling tall tales, and trying to rush us off."

"What?" Elly couldn't believe what she had just heard Sebastian say. Her mouth fell open in disbelief.

"Sebastian, are you kidding me?" Margot turned to her fiancé, who sat back down on the couch with an arrogant look.

"Just because their friends went out wandering about the forest it doesn't mean we drop everything to go on some fool's errand," Sebastian said in a smug voice.

"Are you telling me you don't believe them?" Margot frowned. She was also put out by his response because anyone could tell by the children's frantic nature that their fear was real. They truly did need help.

291

"Who is to say their little friends aren't just playing a childish prank? They are just children after all. Have you kids ever heard of the little tale about the child who cried wolf?" Sebastian shook his head in disapproval.

"All it takes, Sebastian," Margot's voice suddenly changed, "is to look into their eyes to know they are not telling any tales!"

"We're not six-year-old kids; we know what that stupid story is about," Alistair argued back.

"Well then," Sebastian seemed a bit hesitant with his reply, "I mean… what would you have us do? Go run around that forest? We're not the Seekers. We are not skillful enough to go running about that forest alone. We must wait until their parents return. It's settled, then! Yes? That is the right thing to do."

"The right thing to do?" Margot threw up her hands in disgust. "We're going out in those woods, and we're going to bring back the children — safe and sound."

"Surely you cannot be serious, my love! The four of us, out there? I know nothing of ghosts and monsters; I am an archeologist for God's sake!" Sebastian protested.

"The children are in danger, Sebastian!" Margot grew red in the face. "Are you *serious* right now? You're going to sit there all smug on that couch while your fiancée and a couple of students go out by themselves?"

"Shouldn't we at least try and see if we can track down one of the parents or any of those Seeker characters?" Sebastian seemed baffled by Margot's objection. "They will know how to handle the situation."

"Sebastian, I know where the building is!" Margot turned from him. "I am going, and if you don't act like a man and help us save Hunter and Liv, I will never speak to you again! And you can consider the wedding off!" Margot's eyes burned with rage. "I have never met such an insecure and frightened so-called *man* in all of my life!"

"What do you mean by 'so-called man'?" Sebastian snapped back, taking offense at her choice of words.

"Forget it, I'll go by myself!" She sighed loudly, completely frustrated with her fiancé.

"Don't be ridiculous. Fine, I shall accompany you!" Sebastian shook his head in disbelief.

The group exited the estate with Sebastian in tow, despite the obvious cloud of tension that followed them. Sebastian, clearly frustrated with the sudden turn of events, did his best to mask his true feelings in favor of trying to patch things up with Margot. Margot ignored his every word.

"Sebastian, now is not the time or the place!" Margot scolded.

Alistair led the group as they made their way towards where Hunter and Liv had entered the forest. It was about a ten-minute hike from the estate's main entrance.

"This is where you saw him?" asked Margot, surveying the thick forest in front of her.

"Yeah, he was jumping from tree to tree," Elly explained.

"The kid was jumping from tree to tree?" Sebastian frowned. "Like a monkey or something?"

"Yeah. He's possessed by some sort of demon," Alistair replied bitterly. He was the first to enter the forest. "We need to move fast. They went off that way I think." He pointed towards the western skies.

"Yes, the house you spoke of is out in the western woods. It's been abandoned for... well, as long as I've ever known," explained Margot, now taking the lead. "Legend has it that before the estate was built, Professor Calenstine had a single house in the middle of a giant forest. That's where he lived while he saved up money and started constructing what we now know as the Belmonte Manor. He didn't have the heart to knock down the original home, so he allowed the forest to take it over. I don't know the last time anyone set foot in it, and not too many people even know it's out here."

"So, these woods..." Sebastian slowly followed the group, doing his best to not dirty up his steam-pressed khaki pants. "Rumor has it that they are filled with... well... monsters."

"Yeah," Alistair replied as if that was the stupidest comment he had ever heard. "Don't you live here at the estate? Everyone knows that."

"He doesn't live here," Margot corrected. "The professor outsources his talents when needed. He comes to spend time with me."

"Oh..." replied Alistair, not impressed with her answer.

"Great!" Sebastian shook his head in frustration. "Bloody trampling around a muddy forest in a pair of six-hundred-dollar loafers."

"Excuse me?" Margot shot Sebastian a dirty look.

"I'm just saying that I think we should have at least equipped ourselves with the proper gear," he whined bitterly. "Damn it! What is that I stepped in, bear droppings?" Sebastian lifted his loafer to see a smear of fecal matter mashed into it.

"If you're lucky." Alistair couldn't help but smile.

"Funny, is it?" Sebastian scrapped off his shoe on a nearby rock. "Now why would stepping in bear crap make me a lucky man?"

"Because it could have been Bigfoot crap," Alistair replied.

"Bigfoot?" Sebastian frowned.

"Enough!" Margot shot back. "You can buy new loafers, Sebastian," Margot scolded, already sick of the constant complaining.

Margot led the group on, pushing through the thick forest and not stopping for a moment's rest. She was on a mission; she had no idea how long Hunter and Liv had been out in these woods, but she didn't want them lost out here any longer.

The group had been going strong for about a half-hour before Margot turned to ask Sebastian a question. Surprisingly, he was nowhere to be seen!

"Sebastian?" Margot yelled out.

"Children, where did...?" Margot stopped in her tracks and surveyed the forest, looking for any sign of him.

"He was right behind me just a minute ago." Elly frowned. "I swear it because he was complaining about getting dirt on his khakis."

"Sebastian!" Margot yelled again, this time a little more fanatically.

"Where did he go?" asked Alistair.

"He must have gotten separated from us!" Margot cursed beneath her breath.

"Should we go look for him?" asked Elly.

"Let me try and call him; hopefully I can get a signal out here." Margot flipped open her cell phone and dialed.

"Will he be okay out there? He doesn't seem like the outdoorsy type," added Alistair.

"No... he is not," Margot said, frowning.

Chapter 30
Sebastian

"Bloody reception is terrible out here!" Sebastian cussed. He had waited until no one was looking before turning off the path that Margot, Elly, and Alistair were following. He needed to get far enough behind them to make an important phone call without causing suspicion. He wandered around the eerie forest for a bit, holding his cell phone up high above his head until he got a small signal.

"Finally!" He flipped open his phone and dialed. "C'mon answer..." He tapped his foot nervously on the ground until someone finally picked up on the other side. "Hello? Sir, this is Sebastian reporting in on Operation Moloch. Yes, it is in full effect. As I said before, it hasn't taken either of the Jakobs as its host, but it took one of their friends. Yes, sir, it has Hunter and the young Winters girl. The estate is in disarray! Yes, sir... What? Excuse me... you want me to... to... kill them? Sir, murdering them was never a part... I understand the importance... I just... No... I do not know the exact situation at hand. I am out in the forest tracking it down! They're just children. Possession and sabotage is one thing, but murder? My fiancée forced my hand to follow... Sir, I understand... I am sorry, sir, but you said there was no harm to be done to her—that was our deal! Yes, sir... yes, I understand." Sebastian clicked his phone shut, and in a fit of anger, he hurled it into the woods.

"Damn it!" Sebastian sighed heavily as he fell to his knees in a moment of panic. It felt like his entire world was crashing down on him. His heart raced in his chest, and he could barely swallow down the huge lump in his throat. One little phone call—a two-minute conversation—was all it took to change Sebastian's life. He had it all planned out, and everything was going perfectly! He would work for Aten Corp through the rest of the year. How could he have passed it up when he was paid a huge lump sum of money to be one of their moles inside the estate? It was simple: sabotage the estate and recruit their people to come work for Aten. No one was to ever know, and he could spend the money to create a new life for him and Margot by whisking her away to some beautiful island to live a life of pure bliss. He had done it for them—for their future! Now he had been given an ultimatum.

Aten's purpose had grown even more sinister, sabotage was no longer enough! Declan Aten wanted the Jakobs children and all their friend's dead. If Sebastian didn't find a way to make it happen, Professor Aten had made it clear that the ramifications would be deadly for him. His next intended target would be Sebastian's fiancée; he had threatened Margot's life.

Sebastian was a lot of things, but a murderer he was not!

"Oh God… what am I going to do?" Sebastian frowned as his hands shook uncontrollably.

He had no clue what his next move was, but he knew either way that he needed to catch up with Margot to make sure she was safe. He quickly realized he hadn't a clue where he had wandered. He didn't know where to go or how to get back to the group. The forest was disorienting, which only added to his panic. There was nothing he could see to remind him of where he had come from or where he should go.

"Damn it! All these trees look the same!" Sebastian cursed loudly. "Margot! Darling!" he yelled, but to no avail. "Wonderful… heaven help me."

As if heaven heard his plea, the familiar ring of his cell phone went off. He had tossed it out into the forest in his fit of anger. He ran towards the sound of the ringer and found it stuck inside of a large, thorny bush. Cuts and scrapes aside, he fished it out and quickly flipped the phone open.

"Hello? Margot, dear! Thank God! Yes, um... I'm okay! I don't know. I bent down for a second to rest, and when I looked back up, I had lost you. Where are you? No, I don't want to head back! Let me help... I won't get lost again. No, I don't have a compass on me! A rock with moss? Yes... let me see. Yes, I see one. Head the opposite way? But you can't be out there alone... I must protect you! Damn it... Okay... I love you, dear, please be safe."

Sebastian stared down at his cell phone as he flipped it shut. He felt helpless because he had just been told to commit cold, senseless murder. If he didn't, Margot would be the next victim of the Aten Corporation.

Chapter 31
Captives

Hunter sat in the corner of a rundown, windowless room; he could hardly manage the simple task of taking a breath. Every time he tried to inhale, a stabbing, unbearable pain throbbed through his side, but he tried his best to hide his discomfort from Liv. He wanted to stay strong for her, to tell her everything was going to be okay, and that they would somehow get out of this crazy mess they found themselves in, even if he wasn't sure he believed it himself.

Remy had dragged them into the house, tossed them onto the dusty floor of the room and locked them away. There they sat for what seemed like hours in the musty and damp quarters. It smelled of mold and mildew. The floor and walls were stained with water spots and the floorboards were swelling. Weeds and other plant life had found an unlikely home within, and small rays of light passed through parts of the walls where Mother Nature had chipped them away.

Liv sat next to the door weeping after she had spent the first half-hour pounding on it and screaming for help, but no one came. She had since given up and fallen to the floor, burying her tearful face in her hands.

"I'm sorry." Hunter grimaced in pain. He could barely move and was sure he had cracked a rib.

"What are we going to do?" Liv sniffled after she spoke.

"I… I… don't know," replied Hunter.

"He wants the ring, maybe we should just give it to him!" Liv stood up, doing her best to collect herself. She took a seat next to

Hunter on the opposite side of the room.

"Elly and Alistair should be coming soon. Hopefully, we can wait it out," replied Hunter through shallow breaths.

"You're hurt bad, aren't you?" Liv wiped the sweat off Hunter's face. She slid her cold sweaty hand into his and held it tightly.

"Hurts... to breathe... to talk," said Hunter.

"What do we do if he comes back?" Liv frowned. "I'm scared."

The words stung Hunter, causing angry thoughts to swirl in his head. He could feel her hand trembling as she held his tightly. All he wanted to do was protect his friendsH he had done so many stupid things to get them into this situation. Why couldn't he fix them?

Hunter and Liv's moment of silence was interrupted by the sound of the door slowly creaking open. Through the gloom in the room, the kids could see familiar dark red glowing eyes hovering on the threshold. The creature that once was Remy let out a beastly snarl that sounded nothing like a human.

"Riiiiing!" The voice emanating from Remy's mouth was nothing short of blood-curdling. The thing that was once Remy stepped into a small ray of light, showing its gruesomely pale face to the children. Its eyes moved independently from one another, each one darting across the room sporadically.

"We... don't... have it." Hunter attempted to sit himself up. He was ready for a fight and to do whatever he had to do to protect Liv and himself.

"Please, leave us alone. We just wanted our friend back!" Liv begged.

"Riiiiiiiiing!" the thing hissed once again. This time it snarled as well while its mouth hung open and drooled a thick, pasty substance.

"We don't have your ring!" Liv screamed.

The thing stared into Hunter's eyes with unspoken hatred. It moved slowly towards him as if it was hovering ever so slightly above the floor.

"Leave us alone!" Liv stood up between Remy and Hunter. "I won't let you hurt him anymore. We're not afraid of you!" she yelled.

Remy snarled at Liv and grinned the wickedest grin she'd ever seen. Swiftly, the creature backhanded Liv square across the face, smashing her nose! The sheer strength of the creature sent Liv flying into the far wall, and she crashed hard onto the floor. She didn't move afterwards.

"Liv!" Hunter shuddered, used all his strength, and did his best to ignore the ever-burning pain in his side. He crawled towards her. She had only landed a few feet away.

The creature looked on with a sickly smile.

"Riiiiiing!" it moaned again.

"Are you okay?" Hunter had crawled his way over to Liv and found blood pooling beneath her face. Her nose was broken, bent awkwardly to the right, and she was unconscious. He felt the cold clammy hands of the creature wrap around the back of his neck and hoist him effortlessly from the floor.

"Riiiing… nooow!" the creature demanded.

The thing slammed Hunter up against the wall, face first. The pressure on his head was intense, and he felt as if the creature was trying to push his head right through the old moldy wall! There was nothing but blinding white pain. He couldn't see a thing. He could, however, feel the sickly hot breath from the creature as it slowly leaned in to whisper in his ear.

"Giiive it… or she dieeessss!" it hissed.

"Okay!" Hunter tried his best to speak through the pain. He reached into his pocket where his fingers found the ring, and he wrapped them tightly around its steel framework.

"Hunter!" Alistair's voice echoed through the old weather-torn home. The creature must have locked them in a room upstairs because the voices were coming from below.

"Liv!" Margot's voice soon followed.

The thing immediately dropped Hunter and turned swiftly towards the noise. It snarled before jumping onto the wall above Hunter's head and crawling over to one of the small holes in the wall. There it viciously tore into the small opening, ripping and clawing through the wood until it made a hole big enough to escape through.

Hunter had fallen back to the floor, causing even more pain to shoot through his body.

Blasted ribs, he thought.

"We're... up... here..." Hunter tried to yell.

He heard the clamoring of footsteps from down below and muddled voices as they ran towards his voice. The door burst open and Margot, Alistair, and Elly entered in a panic.

"Hunter!" Elly ran over to her brother.

"Oh, God..." Margot's eyes fell upon the body of Liv, who was lying in a pool of blood.

"Liv!" Alistair had already run to her side and placed her head on his lap.

"Careful," Margot said as she joined him by her side. "She's breathing... but she's out of it."

"What happened?" asked Alistair, using the sleeve of his shirt to wipe away the blood from his cousin's mouth. "Her nose looks busted up."

"The thing... Remy... hit her," Hunter explained through the short puffs of breath.

"What about you?" Margot lifted Hunter's shirt and felt his side.

"Ouch!" Hunter screamed in pain. "It tackled me... can hardly move ever since...."

"Where did it go?" Alistair took off his backpack and rested Liv's head on it.

"Ripped that... hole... in the wall..." said Hunter.

"We missed it?" replied Elly.

"Let's not worry about that thing right now." Margot sat beside Liv, trying to wake her up.

"C'mon, Liv... I need you awake!" Margot gently slapped her cheek, trying to bring her around.

"Unngg..." Liv whimpered. "My nose..." she muttered as her eyes finally opened.

"Hello, hun! Welcome back to us," said Margot, pulling Liv's blonde hair out of her eyes.

"What happened?" asked Liv. She made a funny face as she swallowed hard; all she could taste was blood.

"The thing hit you pretty hard. Sorry, honey, but I think you have a broken nose." Margot said, sitting Liv upright.

"Liv, I'm so glad you guys are safe. We were so worried!" said Elly, rushing to her friend's side.

"So, potentially cracked ribs and a broken nose." Margot frowned.

"What do we do now?" asked Elly. "Remy snuck away again."

"I'm not too sure about that." Alistair's eyes grew wide as he pointed back towards the bedroom door they had just kicked in.

There, once again in the doorway were the glowing red eyes.

"It wants... this..." Hunter held out his hand, holding the Daupnir Ring.

The creature saw it and bounded towards Hunter.

"Riiiing!" it shrieked as it flew through the air, colliding with Hunter once again. The impact sent the ring flying into the air and crashing a few feet away from them onto the floor.

"Grab it!" screamed Elly.

"Got it!" hollered Alistair as he jumped across the room to snag it before Remy could see where it had fallen.

"Hunter!" Margot tackled Remy to the floor. She had no idea how powerful his possessed body was, and he easily tossed her off of him, causing her to fly through the air and crash into the wooden wall, splintering it where she hit.

"Hey, you!" Elly yelled, holding out Solomon's Seal. "Does this scare you?"

The thing that was once Remy paused immediately, staring at the ring. For the first time, the children saw fear in its evil red eyes.

"Quick... put it on!" Hunter said, spitting up blood.

"Stop it from escaping!" Alistair tackled Remy to the ground. "Help me hold it down!"

Liv ran over to help Alistair by grabbing Remy's arms and pinning the creature down.

"Now, Elly!" Liv yelled. "Put on the ring!"

Elly slid the ring onto her finger. At first, the ring was too big, and she thought it would easily slip off. To her utter dismay, the ring slipped past her knuckle and started to glow with an exuberant blue hue. She felt the ring shrink down to size to fit perfectly around her ring finger. Then the strangest thing happened. As if there was some sort of weird switch that turned on inside her body, everything in the room turned different colors. A blue translucent color seemed to spread out all over the room. She stared at Remy, who now emitted a dark red, pulsating energy that seemed to leak out from his body. Her friends had the same translucent blue color emanating from their essence as the ring did.

"Do it now!" Alistair yelled, trying to hold down the creature.

"Elly, your eyes!" Liv's mouth fell open. There, across the room, stood her best friend Elly, whose eyes were expelling a blue mist.

"Do what?" Elly shrugged. She didn't have a clue how to use the ring. She was baffled by the sudden change in her vision. From the corner of her eye, she saw a dark figure that had blue mist flowing from it, most notably from its feet.

"Holy crap!" Elly shrieked. "Who are you?"

"Who are you talking to?" Alistair yelled. "Quick, do something! It's getting away!"

The thing was tall and slender, and its face was hidden beneath a dark black robe. Only its clear blue eyes could be seen through the darkness.

"Dauknir! Signo! Effigia!" the tall slender entity said in a calm and peaceful voice.

"What?" Elly shook her head in confusion.

"Dauknir! Signo! Effigia!" This time the entity pointed towards Remy, who had just kicked Alistair off him.

"Dauknir…" Elly muttered aloud.

Remy stood up, snarled and grabbed the ring from Alistair's hand.

"Signo…" Elly said louder.

This time Remy's body tightened as if every muscle in his body was convulsing. The creature shrieked loudly and painfully, causing it to drop the Daupnir Ring back onto the ground. Alistair pushed it away from the creature's reach.

"Dooon't… pleeeeaasseeee!" the creature hissed.

"Effigia!" Elly yelled the word with all her might.

A sudden, ear-splitting explosion echoed through the room. It was so loud that the children couldn't help but cover their ears in pain and fall to their knees.

It was an awful sight. Remy's body rose two feet into the air, his head shot backwards, and his mouth opened as wide as it could. A black cloud was being expelled from his body, shooting out into the air above him.

Remy then fell to the ground, unconscious, and lay beside Alistair, who immediately pulled him away from the lingering dark mist.

All the children could see was the hovering black mist, spinning like a tornado in the room.

Elly, however, saw something entirely different. She was seeing the world through a different lens—a lens that Solomon's Ring seemed to empower within her. To her it was not just a swirling black tornado. She could easily see the outline of a monstrous image inside of it. The evil entity within the swirling black mist was outlined with a dark red color. Its body was shaped like a large man with hooved hands and feet. Its face was snouted like a pig, and was not at all human! It was pure evil, and the image frightened Elly, making her heart pound in her chest.

"Moloch," the blue entity said softly. "Child, you have no cause to fear this monstrosity anymore!" the entity added calmly.

"Who... are you?" asked Elly.

"I am the spiritual energy of King Solomon and you hold in your possession my ring," it replied. It hovered closer to Elly, allowing its hood to fall to his shoulders. There before her stood an ancient-looking man with long silver hair that seemed to glisten in the darkness. His long slender face smiled as he approached.

"With this ring, you have the power to govern this entity. This is why I bestowed such powers within it, to keep these wretched creatures from torturing and punishing mortals such as you. Seal him away by sending him back into the Daupnir Ring."

"How?" Elly asked.

"With your mind, just will it to happen and watch it be."

Elly looked at the snout-faced entity, and with her willpower she condemned it. She watched as the black mist and the creature within it slowly began to get sucked back into the ring. It screamed and snarled in anger as the ring seemed to suck up all of its mist until there was nothing left, nothing but the blue translucent figure of Solomon standing beside her.

"With this ring, you have opened your soul to the hereafter and to the realm of the eternal."

"I did what?" asked Elly, a bit fearful of his explanation.

"All will come, child, in due time." Solomon reached out his ghostly hand and held Elly's in his own. The blue color around her finger slowly fizzled out, as did the coloration of her vision. Solomon then disappeared, and Elly suddenly felt dizzy, falling to her knees.

"Elly, what happened?" Margot ran over to her, helping her back to her feet.

"Your eyes went all crazy like they were leaking out a blue mist!" replied Alistair.

"You... you didn't see him?" asked Elly.

"See who?" answered Liv. "We saw the black mist get sucked back into the ring and we saw you speaking in some weird language to someone who wasn't there!"

"King Solomon was standing beside me and told me what to say," explained Elly.

"We'll talk about this later!" Margot walked over to the Daupnir Ring.

"Do you think it's safe?" asked Liv.

"I hope so," Margot said as she bent down to pick the ring up. "All that trouble over this ring."

"Where am I?" Remy had finally woken up.

"Remy!" Liv ran to his side.

Remy was awake, but he looked ghastly ill. He had no color, his eyes were bloodshot, and he was running a high fever.

"Oh God..." Remy frowned. "My body feels like I was hit by a truck."

"Can you walk on your own?" asked Margot.

"No... sorry..." Remy barely had enough strength to speak, let alone carry his own weight.

"Elly and Liv, help Hunter to his feet. Alistair and I will carry Remy out. First things first, let's get out of this place," said Margot.

That was easier said than done. Remy was a big boy, and Margot and Alistair had a hard time carrying him through the old rundown house and onto the creaky porch. Luckily for the girls, Hunter was able to support most of his own weight. He just needed their assistance to relieve some of the pain.

"We have an issue," Margot said, breathing hard and trying to catch her breath. "It's a long way back home. I don't know how we're going to get everyone back, because we can't carry Remy all the way."

"I have an idea!" Alistair unzipped his backpack and pulled out a small whistle.

"What's that?" asked Liv.

"It's how I call Bernie. He always comes when I call for him!"

"Who?" asked Margot.

"Bernie—a friendly Bigfoot." Alistair blew the whistle as loud as he could.

"A what?" Margot asked.

"You'll see!" Alistair smiled.

It only took a few minutes before the large, bulky, ape-like creature burst through the forest canopy. There, before Margot's eyes, stood a towering hairy creature, who in her mind, seemed to be rather excited to have heard his friend's whistle.

"Bernie!" Alistair ran over to his friend. He grabbed a granola bar from his backpack, and the creature gently took it from him.

Bernie made quick work of the granola bar. He then sat down next to Alistair, and with his large rough finger, he poked Alistair's face gently.

"These are my friends," Alistair said as he pointed to the group.

Bernie stood up and slowly approached the group.

"What do we do?" whispered Margot, a bit nervous. She had never seen such a huge creature up close and personal.

"He's nice..." Hunter winced. "Be... yourself."

"Um... hello." Margot forced a smile as she extended her hand as if to shake.

The Bigfoot let out a small grunt and placed his giant finger into her hand.

"Oh… he knows how to shake?" Now her smiled turned genuine.

"Bernie," Alistair walked over to his friends, "we need your help,"

"Can he understand you?" asked Elly.

"Yeah, pretty much," said Alistair. "Hunter and Remy are hurt. Can you carry them and walk with us?"

Alistair gestured to the two injured boys. He then walked up to them and pretended to pick them up. "Like this," Alistair motioned.

Bernie snorted, walked over to Hunter and Remy and sniffed them. He let out a small whimper, as if he knew they were in pain.

"Good boy! Can you pick them up, gently?" asked Alistair.

The large creature carefully picked up Remy and held him like an infant, cradled against his chest. The creature then kneeled down and gave Hunter his back.

"I think he wants you to climb up on his back," said Alistair.

"Let me try…" Hunter pulled himself up onto the mighty creature with the aid of Liv and Margot.

"Hang on tight up there," said Margot.

"Okay, I think that should help, right?" Alistair smiled.

"Well, let's not waste any more time, it's still a decent walk back," Margot said.

It had been a long and tiring day. The children were beat up, sore, injured, and yet they still had to get back home before they could experience any sort of relief. The sun was setting, and soon they would be traveling through the thickness of the forest in pitch-blackness with nothing more than Alistair's flashlight to lead the way. Luckily for the group, one of their companions was one of the fiercest creatures in the forest, and they highly doubted any of the other dangerous creatures would dare pick a fight with a group traveling with a Bigfoot.

Knowing it would be a long journey on foot, the children readied themselves for the trip home.

Chapter 32
A Warm Welcome

"I am so sorry to bother you, sir," Patricia seemed distraught, "but Mr. Bell was insistent that I bring you to him immediately. He would not take no for an answer."

"It is quite all right, my dear friend." Professor Calenstine nodded with a kind smile. "Did he mention what was so important?"

"He wouldn't say," replied Patricia. "He came into my office covered in dirt and said he got lost out in the forest, but he wouldn't say what he was doing out there. Mr. Bell demanded to speak with you and said it was urgent."

"Okay, dear, send him in. No need to keep the gentleman waiting any longer," replied the professor.

"Of course," said Patricia, who stood up and excused herself. She made her way back towards the other end of the long hallway.

"Heavens, Monte," Calenstine scratched the old dog behind its ears, "I wonder what all the bother is about."

The professor waited patiently and poured himself a fresh cup of tea. He took a sip and frowned at the sight that walked in to stand before him. There stood what appeared to be a war-torn Sebastian Bell with a frown on his face.

"Professor…" Sebastian looked frantic. His clothes were tattered and dirty, which was very uncharacteristic of the Sebastian the professor knew. "I must speak with you—it's urgent."

"Well, young man, you have my attention." The professor took another long sip of his tea. "Please, go ahead."

Sebastian didn't know where to start; he started to open his mouth, but he found no words. He stammered, ran his fingers through his disheveled hair, and instead of saying anything, he fell into a chair and wept.

"Sebastian, it is obvious you are in need of some help," Calenstine said, leaning forward. "Please, take a deep breath and explain."

Sebastian did just that. He inhaled deeply, and before he knew it, he was opening his soul to the professor. He explained about how Aten had come to him and offered him wealth and riches to help sabotage the estate, how he had fallen in love with Margot and wanted the money to start a new life, how he had been asked to create a secret society within the Seekers Society to aid him, and how Gerald had been the first person he had convinced to help him in his mission. He went on to explain how they had founded the Order of Shadows, which they operated independently, how he had hacked into the computer program and was able to release the Beast of Bladenboro, and how Aten Corp had given him and Gerald the Daupnir Ring and were told to give it to the children. Finally, he told him how Declan Aten had told him that he was to murder the children if the wraith known as Moloch failed to do it. He told Professor Calenstine that if he didn't do as he was ordered Aten would find another way and add Margot to his hit list.

Sebastian told him everything through tears and with a feeling of disgrace. He laid it all out on the table. Finally, he told the professor about the children, how they had run out towards the abandoned house, about the forest, and lastly about Margot.

"Sebastian," Calenstine sat back in his chair and let out a long sigh, "how could you be so naive?"

"I know," he replied.

"How many others are there? How many people did you turn against us?" asked the professor.

"Once I got Gerald to join me, he took over the recruitment process. He operated independently, so I don't know for sure! He had more connections, so he did all of that. He did recruitment and I did the sabotaging."

"I see. How about you give me a guess?" Calenstine suggested, his words heavily laced with anger.

"A handful...."

"This is problematic." Calenstine frowned.

"What do I do?" Sebastian pleaded. "Can I make this right?"

"You are to say nothing to anyone," Calenstine stated sternly.

"What?" Sebastian was baffled by his words.

"Does Aten know you came to me?"

"No. He knows nothing."

"Then perhaps we can use this to our advantage," said Calenstine.

"What about Margot?"

"Yes, you jeopardized your own fiancée's life, as well as countless others—including your own."

"Shouldn't she know though?"

"It would scare her more than any good that would come from it. She will be safe here with us. It will be hard for Aten to attempt anything as long as she is here, even if there are a few moles within our walls."

"I feel like I need to... I need to come clean, but how can I look her in the face knowing that because of me, a very powerful man wants us dead?"

"No matter what, you cannot. This is not negotiable. You will stay here in the estate. You will not leave for your job and there will be no more trips outside of these walls. You will remain here, and if I were you, I would devote my time to making it up to her! I have always known the man you are Sebastian, and you have always been a bit brash, but you are a charming man. You let your ambition get the best of you, and for that, you are a fool. That is why you find yourself in this predicament. It's time you grew up," Calenstine scolded.

"I thought... I thought... you'd blacklist me like you did Gerald."

"No," Calenstine said bitterly. "As much as I would like to never see your traitorous face again, I think your connection with Aten may prove useful, at least for the time being."

"Professor!" Patricia screamed from down the hall.

"Let's hope this is good news because if anything happened to Margot and the children, we will be having a different discussion."

"Professor!" Patricia ran up to the large oak desk. She could barely catch her breath. "Joe and Ben just found Margot and the children. They have Remy with them and a Bigfoot!"

"Are they all right?" asked Calenstine.

"A little beaten up, but yes!"

"Get them to the infirmary, take good notes on what they say, and return to me," Calenstine told her with a nod.

"You don't want to see them yourself?" Patricia frowned.

"Unfortunately, Sebastian and I have some serious matters to discuss. I will get with them soon enough. For now, I leave it in your hands. Please see to their safety."

"Yes, of course, Professor." Patricia turned and made her way towards the exit.

"So," Calenstine looked deeply into Sebastian's eyes with a pure, intense hatred, "are you ready to make it up to us?"

"I will do anything... as long as Margot is safe!"

Chapter 33
A Birthday Goodbye

A week had passed since the events in the forest. Hunter had received good and bad news about his injuries. His ribs weren't broken, thankfully, but they were fractured, which meant the only thing they could do was wrap them up tightly and allow them time to heal. The wrapping did a decent job in easing the discomfort, but for the next few months, he was going to have to deal with the tenderness. Dr. Wong told him to take it easy, no sports or other physical activities. Basically, Hunter was allowed to read and do homework. He even had to make Alistair, Elly, and Liv promise not to make him laugh, as sad as that sounds, because it just hurt too much. Even the faintest chuckle shot pain through his body.

"I guess I can try and not be funny," said Alistair slyly, "but it's pretty hard for me not to be hilarious."

"Right," said Elly with a sly smile. "I'm not too sure Hunter will have a problem with that."

"Yeah," said Liv. "Just don't look me in the face because I know you'll want to laugh."

Liv had definitely broken her nose. When they rushed her to the infirmary, they were forced to reset it by hand, which was easily the most painful thing she had ever experienced. Even worse, in the following days, she developed two giant black eyes as well. Alistair joked and called her new look "raccoon-chic," which quickly turned against him.

"How do you even know what 'chic' even is?" joked Elly.

"Oh, you guys didn't know? Alistair steals Liv's teen-girl

magazines and reads up on all the fashion trends," said Hunter, holding back the painful laughter. He couldn't resist, and the pain was worth it.

"Yeah, sure!" Alistair smiled, a bit embarrassed. "I mean I've read a few of them, you know, because sometimes it gets boring in the bathroom. Good reading material."

"Oh geez," Elly chuckled.

Margot thought it was nice to see the children laughing once again. It took the kids a while, but knowing that their friend Remy was once again safe, they were able to settle back into their normal lives. Well, as normal as any Seeker's life could be anyway.

Saturday quickly rolled around and thanks to Margot, Hunter was treated to a magnificent birthday party. She stayed up all night with the help of Sebastian, who didn't complain once, and they decorated the game room on the third floor. Banners and balloons hung from the ceiling, all screaming "Happy fourteenth birthday!"

All of Hunter's friends were there, from both his Enlightenment classes and his regular studies. All except the one friend he really wanted to see — Remy.

"Sorry, Hunter," Margot said, frowning. "I invited Remy and his father, but I don't think they'll be coming."

Remy had spent the majority of the week recovering in the infirmary. He had been extremely sick from the possession, severely malnourished, in pain all over, and was struck with a high fever that wouldn't go away.

"I understand. His dad probably hates us anyway." said Hunter, picking at his food.

"Remy will always be our friend though," said Liv from across the table.

"Yeah, I really hope his dad gets over it soon," Alistair said with a mouthful of chocolate cake.

"Hunter, did you thank Margot for this amazing party?" Joe wheeled himself up to the group. There on his lap sat two presents.

"Yeah, I did," said Hunter. "It's pretty amazing!"

"Fourteen... where has the time gone?" Joe smiled as he playfully punched Hunter on the shoulder. "You'll be driving soon, and going out on dates with girls! Man, to be young again!"

"Yeah, right!" Hunter blushed. Of course his uncle would try and embarrass him in front of Liv.

"Margot, I'm sorry I wasn't able to help set this up." Joe said and averted his eyes from Margot's gaze. It was evident that she was still quite upset with him.

"It's okay. Sebastian was up all night with me helping," she said bluntly.

"Oh." Joe did his best to hide the surprise on his face.

"You got me two gifts?" Hunter's eyes got wide with excitement.

"Well, no... only one of these is yours." Joe handed the heavier of the two presents over to Hunter.

"Awesome! Thanks, Uncle Joe!" said Hunter.

"Finish up your plate and then go ahead and open it with your friends. I'm going to speak with Margot, in private, if that's okay with her." Joe looked at her for approval.

"I suppose..." Margot rolled her eyes.

Joe wheeled himself over to a quiet corner of the room.

Margot hesitantly followed. "What's this about?" she asked.

"I want you to have this." Joe handed Margot the second present.

"I don't want your gifts, Joe," Margot stated as she waved the gesture off.

"Just..." Joe frowned as he spoke. "Just open it, please."

Margot shook her head in disbelief, but she took the present and unwrapped it.

"A liquor bottle, Joe? Really? Why would you give me this?" Margot tossed the bottle into the trashcan next to her. She turned to storm off, angered by the thoughtless gift.

"You were right," Joe said, hoping to stop her. "That wasn't a gift to you; it was a promise to myself. I stayed up all night and poured out every bottle I had. That was the last one."

Margot did stop, but she kept her back to him.

"I'm a mess; I didn't think anyone knew. The words I said to you were unfair, and I wish I could take them back, but it was more than just that, more than just my insecurities with this chair. Margot, I want to be a better man! When I first met you...."

Margot turned now, her eyes meeting his.

"That doesn't matter—forget I said anything!" Joe shook his head, fumbling with what he was about to say. "Listen, I'm the luckiest man in the world because I have you to help me with these kids. You were right. I love them more than I hate this chair! Nothing I can say will make up for the pain I caused you with all that stupid stuff I said. So, instead, I *am* going to have the surgery and I *am* going to sober up, with Plato's help. He came to me a few weeks back and said he thinks he could fix me. That crazy old robot saw me struggling, so I don't know how anyone can say he doesn't have a human heart, as there has gotta be one somewhere in all that metal!"

"What do you mean? Plato is going to operate on you?" asked Margot, a bit baffled.

"He has some new treatment that he's been working on, without telling anyone, for months now. It's something out of this world and crazy, but he swears he can fix me."

"Joe, is that a smart idea?" asked Margot. Joe's eyes revealed that he was being genuine, and she felt her anger towards him fade.

"When have I ever claimed to be a smart guy?" Joe laughed. "I almost screwed up this amazing thing we have. If that doesn't define stupidity...."

"Joe..." Margot smiled, leaned in, and gave him a huge hug.

"I am so very sorry," he whispered into her ear. For the first time in months, sitting there and holding Margot in an embrace, Joe felt alive. He didn't want to let her go!

"You're forgiven." Margot wiped away a single tear behind Joe's back.

"Sebastian is a lucky man. I hope he can keep you happy," said Joe softly.

"If I didn't know any better," Margot pulled away slowly, looking into Joe's dark brown eyes, "I would think you're a bit jealous," she whispered back.

"Uncle Joe!" Hunter's excited voice broke the tension. "What the heck is this thing, a rock?" He lifted up a large, dense stone that was the size of his fist.

"You got your nephew a rock for his birthday?" Margot cracked half a smile.

"Not exactly." Joe turned his wheelchair and smiled brightly at his nephew. "Hunter, that is the rarest mineral in the world," Joe said as he took the stone from his nephew's hand. "It's called Orichalcum."

"Never heard of it!" said Alistair.

"I wouldn't expect you to have," replied Joe. "Before your friend Plato was our librarian, he was a miner in a very ancient civilization."

"Atlantis?" asked Elly as she stared in awe at the glistening black rock. It was the darkest black she had ever seen, but it seemed to sparkle in the light.

"Good guess," replied Joe. "Orichalcum was native only to the mines of Atlantis, and when the lost city was swallowed up by the ocean, Orichalcum disappeared from the world forever. That rock is more than rare. It is one of only two objects in this world that are proof of Atlantis' existence."

"One of two?" asked Hunter.

"Yes, the other is Plato himself!" Joe chuckled. "But that's a story for another day. I just want you to know that it took me a long time to convince Plato to give me the stone. I've always wanted it. It's more than just a mineral, Hunter. That rock is the hardest substance on earth, more so than a diamond. It represents our family because no matter what this world throws at us, we will stay strong. I promise you and Elly that I will always be here for you guys."

"Wow! Thanks, Uncle Joe!" Hunter took the rock back and stared at it in awe.

"So, how did you get Plato to give that rock up?" asked Margot, turning away from the children's table.

"I told him the only way I'd allow him to do the surgery was if I could give Hunter the Orichalcum as his birthday gift," said Joe. "That's all it took."

"That's pretty cool," said Alistair. "Can I see it?"

Hunter handed the heavy stone over to Alistair.

"Whoa! It's so heavy!"

"Hey, guys!" Liv smiled brightly. "Look who just came in!"

The children all turned to see Remy and his father walking through the double doors of the gaming room.

Remy immediately smiled when his eyes found the children at their table. He said something to his father, who didn't seem too happy with the fact that they had shown up, but he nodded.

"Guys!" Remy walked up to the group. "Happy birthday, Hunter!"

"Remy!" Liv and Elly both stood up and gave their towering friend a warm hug.

"Thanks, Remy! How're you feeling?" asked Hunter.

"Lost a little weight, but I'm feelin' good," Remy joked.

"What was it like? Being possessed and all?" asked Alistair.

"Alistair!" Liv scolded. "Don't ask him that!"

"No, it's okay," Remy chuckled. "I mean, I don't remember anything, to be honest, until I woke up in the infirmary. I have some pretty gnarly nightmares though."

"It's my fault," said Hunter. "I haven't been able to say I'm sorry."

"For what?" Remy shrugged off the apology. "I wanted to be a part of that ghost hunt. I was excited about it. It was no one's fault."

"So, what's going on? Do you wanna hang out for a bit?" asked Alistair, offering Remy a piece of cake that he had cut for himself.

"Sorry, I can't," Remy said, frowning. "My dad barely allowed me to come, I had to beg him."

"He's never going to let us hang out again, is he?" asked Elly.

"Worse… he's moving us," said Remy sadly.

"What?" said Liv.

"Yeah, I guess he took an offer with Aten Corp, so he's moving us somewhere to work construction on an island. All top secret he says— I dunno…."

"But Aten is evil!" said Alistair.

"Well, after all this, he thinks Professor Calenstine is the dangerous one. We're leaving as soon as I say goodbye."

"You're packed already?" Hunter frowned as he spoke.

"Yeah... I'm going to miss you guys. You were the first real friends I'd had since movin' here. Now, I gotta start all over again. He won't listen to reason. I told him I was to blame. He thinks I'm just coverin' up for you guys. The worst thing is that Corbin and Lunette will be there! I guess their dad talked him into going after he heard about what happened to me."

"Man, that sucks," said Hunter.

"Remington, come on, wrap it up," his dad yelled from across the room.

"Well, I guess this is it then." Remy gave the group one more giant hug before walking off.

The kids spent the rest of the party trying to keep their spirits up. They did their best to not think too much about Remy leaving, but they couldn't help but feel responsible.

The evening passed quickly, and the rest of their classmates went on their way. Just as Hunter thought the party was going to end, Ms. Ellingbee showed up alongside Professor Calenstine.

"Did we miss the festivities?" Patricia smiled.

"We're just wrapping up," answered Margot with a handful of dirty plates and dishes.

"Children," Professor Calenstine said, waving them over. "I am sorry I couldn't be here earlier, but I wanted to speak to you alone and away from the rest of the families."

"Uh-oh!" Alistair whispered to Hunter. "I think we're finally getting in trouble for sneaking out into the woods."

"Let me start out by saying that of all the generations of Seekers, your group of friends have, by far, found themselves in more trouble than any others—including that of your parents." Calenstine looked up at Abram, Joe, and Ben, who were across the room finishing up the last bit of cake.

"We're sorry," said Hunter, hanging his head down low. "We don't mean to."

"Sorry?" Calenstine questioned Hunter's choice of words. "Don't mistake my words. You may have found trouble, but I daresay you're not always going out looking for it. It seems to me that it tends to find you just as often. I know all of your lives have been changed drastically since entering the Enlightenment. For better or worse, it has planted the seed for the young men and women you will become. Over the course of this school year, you have all found yourselves in some very scary situations. I am proud to say that I think you have all acted with honor. When push came to shove, you all put your friends and loved ones first! How can I be upset with such valiant acts? Perhaps we made some wrong choices along the way, but through life's mistakes, we learn and grow."

"You're not upset with us?" asked Alistair.

"I am upset that you young children found yourselves in such situations, yes, but I believe those were beyond your control. Outside elements led you down some dire roads, and in the heat of the moment, you all proved why you will become amazing Seekers when you're older."

"Wow! Really?" asked Hunter with a smile that stretched from ear to ear.

"Now, I came to speak to you as a group," Calenstine said, changing the subject. "Events have transpired that will change one of your lives forever. It is very important that you are ready and willing to accept the responsibilities."

Hunter looked a little puzzled. He peered over at Alistair, who just shrugged.

"Elly, could you please step forward," Calenstine instructed.

"Yes, sir." Elly cautiously approached the professor.

"Can I see your right hand, the one with the ring on it?" Calenstine pointed to Solomon's Seal.

Elly extended her hand, which was shaking slightly from nerves.

"Elly, you were the brave soul who slipped this ring on and sealed the evil entity back into the Daupnir Ring, correct?

"Yes, sir, but I tried to get the ring off afterwards. I wanted to give it back to you—I swear!"

"It is no longer my ring, child. It now belongs to you. It has adhered itself to you forever. It will only come off that pretty little finger of yours when you've grown into an old woman and pass on.

Your soul is now connected with its powers."

"But I don't want powers!" Elly frowned.

"I am sorry, dear but you have no choice."

"But I don't even know how to use it," Elly stated, shaking her head.

"Nor can I share with you any wisdom on the matter. The last person I know to have worn the ring was King Solomon himself. But I assure you, in due time, you will learn of its power, much like you knew how to seal Moloch back into the ring. Ready yourself and please know that if you have any questions, my door is always open." Calenstine smiled.

"Thank you…" Elly wasn't sure how to reply.

"Children, I do not know what sorts of adventures may lie beyond the doors of tomorrow. However, there is never a dull day when it comes to the Enlightenment. Now heed some elderly advice and finish up this school year strong because next year, things will get a bit more exciting," Calenstine said and winked.

"Yes, sir. Thank you," said the group.

"Yes, children," Patricia beamed, "year two of the Enlightenment is full of surprises!"

"Now, Patricia," said the professor, "let's not go and tell them all the secrets."

With that said, the children helped clean up the mess from the party. Hunter was excited to move on to the next chapter of his life. There were only a few months of school left before their summer break, and then they would be right back in school. More importantly, they would be entering into the second year of the Enlightenment.

To be continued in:

Secret Seekers Society

WRATH OF THE WENDIGO

View other Black Rose Writing titles at <u>www.blackrosewriting.com/books</u> and use promo code **PRINT** to receive a **20% discount** when purchasing.